W9-AGL-993

SANDRA MIESEL

SHAMAN

Copyright © 1989 by Sandra Miesel

A shorter and substantially different version of this novel was published in 1982 as *Dreamrider*.

A Baen Books Original

Baen Publishing Enterprises
260 Fifth Avenue
New York, N.Y. 10001

ISBN: 0-671-69844-3

Cover art by Dennis Beauvais

First printing, October 1989

Distributed by
SIMON & SCHUSTER
1230 Avenue of the Americas
New York, N.Y. 10020

Printed in the United States of America

DREAM RIDER

The steps were treacherously narrow and steep. It was such a long way down if she stumbled.

Why was she here? Would the view from the top be worth it? The calves of her legs were beginning to quiver already. She brushed vainly at gnats. The sun was making her dizzy. It hadn't seemed so hot when she started. She should have waited for a cooler day.

The carved stone heads of the feathered serpent flanking the stairs shimmered in the heat. They were melting before her eyes, gaping jaws softening into a blunt muzzle, scales flowing into fur. The whole pyramid was stretching and flexing like a living thing.

The pitch of the steps rose ever steeper. She was crawling up them now on all fours, tearing fingernails as she clawed for purchase, yet the gap between her and the summit only widened.

A broad, bewhiskered head as big as a temple appeared on the platform above. The stairway was no longer stone but rippling hide. She lost her grip and skidded down into darkness. . . .

❋   ❋   ❋

Dedication:

To Jim who invited,
and
Gordy who inspired,
and
Dave who revived,
and
John who endured
the writing of this book.

Acknowledgments:

With grateful thanks for technical advice from Robert and Juanita Coulson, Dr. William Jackson, Sam Long, Summer Miller, Mike Resnick, and Leah Orr.

Lyrics from the song *Lute Lessons* by Mercedes Lackey is copyright 1985 Mercedes Lackey, Firebird Arts and Music, Inc., Box 453, El Cerrito, CA 94530. Used by permission of author and publisher.

"For an angel went down at a certain season into the pool and troubled the water; whosoever then first after the troubling of the water stepped in was made whole of whatever disease he had."

—John 5:4

I

The child stepped up to the rocking horse. She threw her right leg over its sleek maple body and pulled herself up on the contoured seat. She bent down to whisper in her mount's ear, her long black hair hanging down along its neck like a mane. She gripped its sides more tightly with her chubby calves and set it rocking. The rhythmic motion soothed her. She closed her eyes and pressed her fingers against the lids to make spots of brightness flash.

The rocking horse neighed. Living eyes appeared in its blank wooden head. It sprang from the rockers and clattered across the playroom on stiff legs that now numbered eight. The walls dissolved and the horse bore its rider over a prairie of clouds.

Suddenly, a chain of mountains pierced the quiltlike plain. The girl urged her steed forward but the higher they climbed, the higher the mountain barrier grew. They rose until the air grew too thin for her to breathe. The girl shivered in the searing cold. Tears of rage froze on her cheeks.

✳   ✳   ✳

She rubbed her sleepy eyes. The red warning light still glowed on the dashboard.

"E-LEC-TRI-CAL MAL-FUNC-TION," the alarm chimed.

Her headlights were perceptibly dimmer. Damn! She might not make it to Edwards to watch the test flight. But

1

according to her route display, she was only a few kilometers from Palmdale. She ought to be able to get that far on emergency power. She put the Nissan's controls back on manual and anxiously guided her car through the heavy traffic heading for the Air Force base.

She was practically coasting when she turned off at a 24-hour Exxon station. Its big digital calendar clock read: 0230 HOURS MONDAY 21 SEPTEMBER, 2009.

She swung into the parking area and rolled to a stop near a fenced-off Joshua tree. As she walked towards the service building, she could see a smiling CHiPs officer inside, drinking coffee with the attendant. Maybe the place was okay.

Her nose wrinkled at the sight of an old man smoking a cigar—a cigar of all things—while the kid he was riding with filled the tank of their Hyundai. How could anybody stand to—

The earth tremor caught them all by surprise. It shook the cigar free and slammed the car against the pumps. She skidded on slipped gas and collided with the kid in a tangle of hose as the world exploded.

❋   ❋   ❋

Ria Legarde awoke in a cold sweat. Two nightmares? She'd been expecting only one—the one she'd been having for years.

She couldn't remember a time when she didn't have The Dream—she inevitably thought of it in capital letters —of riding up to the mountains. In the beginning, she used to make it come by dozing astride her daycare center's rocking horse. Then a new teacher disapproved of her attachment to the toy. One day it was removed for repairs and never returned. The Dream kept returning at regular intervals for the next sixteen years.

No time to worry about that crazy second dream.

Ria lurched towards the bathroom, almost tripping on a heap of yesterday's clothes still lying on the floor. Once inside, she automatically snapped the lock to the adjoining apartment. Since her bathmate worked different hours, she had successfully avoided all contact with him in her three months of residence. Unless he complained about her aloofness to the House Committee, her treasured privacy was secure.

Showering failed to clear her head. She was getting one of those headaches again. A weather front must be coming through. Ria flicked on her video display to check the local forecast.

MONDAY 21 SEPTEMBER: RAIN ENDING BY AFTERNOON. PROJECTED ACCUMULATION, 1 CM. HIGH TODAY WILL BE 7° OVERNIGHT LOW –5° UNDER CLEARING SKIES. KILLING FROST TONIGHT WILL END THE GROWING SEASON IN THE CHAMBANA AREA.

By punching codes for private and University announcements, she discovered that a special mid-morning staff meeting—"sharing session" as the Director preferred to call it—was scheduled for her section of Information Services. Her headache ought to make that even more of an ordeal than usual.

News updates played while she dressed. Ria's interest in world affairs was minimal. Had anything happened since the year 1600? But the announcer's voice was company of sorts. Her own data base program would be storing anything of personal interest for later examination. The latest disaster unrolled while she was putting on her underwear.

"Yesterday's devastating earthquake in Sumatra is believed to have claimed . . ."

Ria was thankful to live so far inland, away from mountainous shores. Nothing like that to worry about here, nothing except the New Madrid fault. Wasn't any place on earth safe?

"At a Sydney news conference following the tragedy, North American Science Minister Jon Detmold again urged increased funding for seismic research. Detmold called for . . ."

But Ria was far more interested in squeezing into her uniform than in heeding a bureaucrat's call. She noticed a small rip in the jacket's left seam. She'd better remember to fuse it tonight before the whole side gave way.

Ria counted herself lucky to wear the University's coveted blue-and-orange livery, although its colors dulled her olive skin and pale gray eyes. The pantsuit model thickened her figure, too. She must have chosen the least flattering style among the options available. Back in the bathroom, she pinned up her long hair, creamed her hands, and dabbed the excess lotion on her cheeks. She grimaced at the straight-nosed, heavy-boned reflection in the mirror before her.

She'd settle for a square of food concentrate instead of a depressing breakfast in the cafeteria downstairs. But where was the canister? She found it hidden behind a box containing the microfilmed works of twentieth century mythologist Mircea Eliade. She stuffed the printout of his book *Rites and Symbols of Initiation* into her briefcase to read on lunch hour. Gripping the food cake in her teeth, she reached for her coat.

"Meanwhile on the North American scene, a tremor measuring five point zero on the Richter Scale struck Palmdale, Pacifica this morning at 0235 PDT causing minor injuries and property damage estimated at . . ."

Ria stopped short with one arm in her coat sleeve. That was the name of the town in her second nightmare. The video screen showed a tape of clean-up operations at a Restricted Status restaurant. The legend on its crumpled sign caught her eye: The Joshua Tree. A shot of the tree itself revealed the same stubby, shaggy branches she had seen in her dream, slashed by the very same lightning scar.

She ran for the Illibus even though there was time to spare.

Once on board, she tried to sort out the strangeness of the gas station dream. Private use of gasoline-powered cars wasn't unthinkable, just forbidden. But what was a CHiPs officer? And where'd those brand names come from? "Nissan" and "Hyundai" sounded Asian but "Exxon" wasn't a word in any language she'd heard of. She'd look into this more at work when she had a free moment.

The blue-and-orange commuter bus disgorged its load of University workers at the corner of Wright and Green where they mingled with streams of students. The wet, clean-scented wind struck Ria's face. She squinted through the raindrops at Laredo Taft's heroic bronze group *Alma Mater*.

There stood old Mama Psi as she had for nearly a

century, growing nobly greener with the years. She stretched out brawny arms towards her children, eager to crush them against the University of Illinois monogram blazoned on her bodice. Behind the Mater and oblivious to her maternal yearnings, proletarian Labor gripped the hand of olympian Learning.

Little meaningful learning or labor on campus these days, yet the University endured. It had outlived the old State of Illinois by almost a generation and its namesake Illini Indians by how many? Ten? She might as well look that up, too, when she got to work. The data might prove useful in case of imminent extermination.

Resolutely ignoring other pedestrians, Ria veered right to avoid construction barriers around the new student union. It would have to be an improvement over the former building, burnt down last March by a noncomp celebrating Federation Day.

Passing the Romanesque bulk of Altgeld Hall, she strode down the broad quadrangle, irrationally glad the western sidewalk was the quicker path to work. That way, she did not have to pass close by the gaping archway marking the entrance to Noyes or the toothy grillework covering Foley Center. Someone, anyone might be lurking out there on a gloomy morning like this. The crowd with its tramping, purposeful feet offered protective insulation. She shortened her strides to match those of the others.

Ria's eyes strayed to the huge locust trees lining the quad. They had grown noticeably bigger even in the few years since her parents started taking her to summer band concerts here. The wet grass was littered with their yellowed leaves and long brown seed pods. Tomorrow the groundskeepers would be out to sweep the area bare.

Ria hunched her shoulders against a sharp gust of wind and nearly tripped the woman behind her. Mumbling apologies, she turned left at the end of the quad toward the main door of Information Services. She went down the steps to the familiar round portal rather too fast and almost tripped on the rain-slicked marble.

Mother liked to say she could trip on a mote of dust. Of course, she hadn't been saying it—or anything—lately. The fresh scar reopened: the memory of a body hurtling from the roof of Sherman Hall. If Ria had reported her mother to PSI when the depression first set in, she might still be alive—in a manner of speaking.

After a quick detour to the locker room, Ria reached her office just before nine o'clock. Carey Efroymson and Ali Newton were already there conferring on the day's assignments.

Carey, a wiry young man only a few years her senior, always gave the impression of straining at an invisible leash. He tugged at his shaggy brown mustache and shifted weight from foot to foot while Ali briefed him. Although Ria never saw him after working hours, she assumed he twitched more away from their superior's soothing influence.

Ali's looks were as mild as her temperament. Her skin and hair were uniformly tan, the color of weak tea with cream. Few signs of middle age had yet marked her broad face or short, plump body.

Ria took indecent pleasure in the absence of Hannah Wix, the fourth member of their history research unit. Perhaps she would be late again and finally earn a reprimand from Ali. Small chance of that. Ali could no more judge another harshly than Ria could judge another generously.

"Morning, Ria." Ali greeted her while Carey made a quick nod in her direction. "Nasty weather, isn't it?"

"I think ice skates may be the footwear of choice by tonight," Ria replied.

"Repair Services promised to send someone over to look at your terminal today," said Ali. "Maybe it'll oblige us by malfunctioning while they're here. Meanwhile, could you proof and transmit this preliminary Lisbon Earthquake bibliography to Professor Clyde for me? He had me work over the weekend to finish it and expects to see it first thing this morning."

Ria's face clouded at the mention of Professor Gunnar Clyde.

"I know he's difficult," Ali remarked, "but we are responsible for serving him regardless."

"Well, I've never found him the least bit difficult." It was Hannah Wix. She had slipped into the room unnoticed by the others. "He's such a . . .distinguished scholar," she continued with a slight, reverential catch in her throaty voice.

"That's easy for you to say, Hannah. You've cleverly avoided working for him." But before Carey would relate any pertinent anecdotes, Hannah had glided away to her own console and was examining papers with admirable zeal.

Ria mentally awarded the point to the petite blonde. Her earlier headache was getting worse. She forced herself to pay attention to what Ali was saying.

"I do wish you'd mentioned the problem with your console as soon as you noticed it. Every bit of downtime hurts our productivity."

"I thought it was just static build-up. Nothing serious."

"Let me be the judge of that in the future, Ria. I've had many more years to learn the quirks and crochets of our system."

A gentle reproof was still a reproof. Ria felt like a child who'd been careless with an expensive plaything.

She walked over to her terminal and switched on the display. It failed to light up. Had the power cord worked loose? Ria got down on her hands and knees to look, an operation made awkward by her exceptional height. She fumbled at the floor plug. It seemed in order. She levered herself up to check the back of the chassis. No sooner had she touched the port than numbing current surged through her body before she had time to scream.

II

Ria awoke on a hard mattress under a blue and white coverlet. A giant otter was leaning over the bed.

She closed her eyes and held her breath for a count of three. When she opened her eyes, the otter was still there, a sleek russet-furred presence. Its huge brown eyes were level with her own and she could smell its warm, fishy breath. The otter patted her hand. Hand and paw were the same size.

The hand was not Ria's own.

The nails were flat and broken, the palm calloused. It was a young man's hand. Ria pulled it under the covers, frantically searching for breasts that were no longer there. She was too horrified to utter a sound. The otter began to call in a shrill but understandable voice: "She's here! Kara, she's here! Told you she'd come. Said it was certain this time." The otter's speech disintegrated into trilling chirrups. The creature bobbed up and down, jingling the silver bells on the harness it wore.

"Calm yourself, Lute. If you frighten her away, she may never return to us."

As the second speaker approached Ria, the otter retreated, still murmuring cheerily. The person it addressed as "Kara" was a short, stocky woman of great age and even greater dignity. She had moved out of the shadows and into a patch of sunlight at the foot of the bed so Ria could see her clearly.

Kara wore a kind of white woolen poncho adorned with silver ornaments, some shaped like stars, others like bones. This garment was fringed with strips of snakeskin and fur. A lacy metal cap rested on the thick white braids coiled around her head. In her right hand she held a wooden wand; in her left, a dinner plate-sized disk of stretched hide that Ria somehow recognized as a drum. A long white skirt and high boots completed the outfit.

But it was the woman herself, not her exotic garb, that held Ria's attention. Kara's dominant impression was squareness—in the shape of her face, the set of her jaw, the breadth of her unbowed shoulders. Although her skin was weathered and spotted with age, every feature was still crisply defined. Deep stillness shown in her dark blue eyes.

"By sunlight, starlight, firelight, be welcome here forever, Victoria Legarde." Kara raised her staff like a scepter in ritual greeting. "I am Kara ni Prizing, once Wise Woman of Chamba. This is my companion, Lute Twin Stars of the Rolling Shores."

The otter sprang forward and bowed with such exaggerated courtliness, Ria could not help but smile at it.

No, at *him*, she corrected herself. She struggled to sit up in bed but Lute hastily motioned her back down.

"Lie still, dear lady. You aren't used to Julo's body. Best to stay put while we talk."

"What's going on?" Ria asked. Her voice sounded as disconcertingly wrong as her hand had looked. "Who are you? How do you know who I am?"

"All in good time," replied Kara. "For the present, let us say that we know you very well and are eager to know you better. Tell us, Ria, do you want to see the other side of the mountains?"

"Which mountains?"

"The ones you keep trying to ride over in your Dream."

"How do you know about that?"

" 'Cause I made it for you myself, I did." Lute started to say more; Kara silenced him with a glance. He sat back on his haunches once more, gripping his harness straps with his stubby-fingered paws.

Ria sighed. "I guess I never really thought it was a

natural dream." Her bewilderment gave way to indignation. "What right have you to interfere with my mind?"

"Ask again when you've grown wiser, child." The old woman stayed serene. "I repeat: those towering mountains can be crossed. Do you wish to try?"

"What if I say no?"

"The choice is yours. But are you truly satisfied with your present life? Could it be changed for the better?"

"Or worse." Ria dreaded change. Her practiced caution was not about to desert her even under these preposterous circumstances. "Suppose, just suppose, I agree. What happens to me then?"

"You'll be given opportunities to learn and grow in ways few have ever known." Kara awaited her answer, impassive as a statue.

Knowledge? Ria did not know love. She cared nothing for wealth or power. But knowledge . . . She wavered towards consent.

"Please trust us," begged the otter, with unexpected earnestness.

Could she? Would she? It went against her instincts, yet she could not imagine this appealing creature causing her harm.

Ria hesitated, scarcely breathing. The room grew so still she could hear a cardinal singing for his mate somewhere beyond the open window.

"All right." Ria gulped. The words nearly choked her. "I'll try. I accept whatever it is you're offering. But when I get across those mountains, I expect a happy ending to my Dream."

"We can't promise you that," replied Kara. "The ending of your Dream is yours to shape, just as your life is." She traced an arc with her wand. "Remember us, Ria. Remember our home."

Ria's eyes obediently swept the small, neat room like a camera. She recorded its whitewashed walls bright with woven hangings, the rag rugs on its tile floors, the bands of carved birds flying across the wooden chest and bedstead, even the forsythia boughs in a tall black vase standing in one corner.

"Come back to us when you're ready, child."

Kara smiled. Lute hugged himself for joy. The scene dissolved into spiraling darkness. . . .

✳   ✳   ✳

Ria opened her eyes in an ordinary hospital room. Her own hands rested on her own bosom. The brown face peering into hers belonged not to a giant otter but to a slender Pakistani physician.

"Ah, you are back among us again. But one is expecting unconsciousness after an accident of that sort. I am Dr. Abdullah Zair. May I inquire how you are feeling?"

"I've felt better." Ria clutched the covers.

"You are most fortunate to be able to feel anything."

"What happened? You said there was an accident?"

"You suffered a moderate electrical shock at your place of work this morning." He tapped the chartboard he was carrying.

"I can remember checking one computer cable connection but nothing afterwards." Ria strained to recall more.

"You must have only touched the device. If you had been gripping it, you could have easily perished before anyone even noticed you were in distress. But I cannot understand how you escaped being burned." He shook his head. "Most strange."

"Stranger things than that have happened to me, Doctor." She turned her head away from him. "But I'm not going to question my luck—until some Safety Officer requires it."

Dr. Zair frowned. He finished his examination in silence, then said: "Your condition is satisfactory. If no contraindications develop, you can be discharged tomorrow morning. However, I am going to order another dose of muscle relaxant for you. This may make you drowsy. Attempt to sleep or at least rest quietly."

He stressed the last word as he scurried out.

Ria had not meant to react so tartly but the doctor had the bedside manner of an unctuous rat. She could almost picture a rat's whiskers sprouting beneath his sharp nose. What would he have said if she'd mentioned that she'd never suffered a serious burn in her life? Just as well not to attract special attention. That could be dangerous. She

ought to concentrate on pleasanter matters—like being
alive.

Although the prescribed medication did not put her to
sleep, it blunted the edge of her boredom and helped her
endure the Infirmary routine. That effect wore off by
dinner time.

Ali appeared during the evening visitors' hours, bringing Ria motherly solicitude and clean clothes to wear
home. Ria wished she had also thought to include a book.

In the absence of reading matter, she had time to reflect
on her curious dream about the old woman and the giant
otter. It was so much more vivid than her everyday reality. Yet if it were a drug reaction or a hallucination, why
hadn't additional medication produced a similar effect? Ria
was sure she'd never seen a costume like the old woman's,
even in a fantasy film, yet it looked tantalizingly familiar.
A man-sized intelligent otter was a novel concept, but, she
had to admit, a delightful one. She didn't think she could
have imagined the amiable creature all by herself.

Too much rest during the day made it difficult for Ria to
sleep that night. She poured herself a glass of water from
the supply left on her night table. The steel tray holding
the carafe glittered in the moonlight like a small, still
pond. Suddenly, the mirrored surface trembled as if stirred
by an unseen hand. Ria felt herself drawn down through
silvery waves into the depths of thoughts not hers. . . .

✻   ✻   ✻

How much longer was it going to take? Twelve hours—no,
eleven hours, forty-three minutes by her watch—on this
wretched beach with no release in sight. And if that thunderstorm brewing out at sea sweeps in, we may all be back
here tomorrow running through the farce all over again,
she thought numbly.

"Go down there and get the texture of the place," said
her editor. "Catch those colorful little details the wire
services will miss."

She'd gotten the texture all right—every gritty, sweaty,
prickly bit of it. Color was in short supply, though, unless
you counted the green of the palmetto swamps. The editor
seemed to think he was doing her a tremendous favor with

this assignment. Actually, she was only a last minute substitute, pressed into service after Ed had broken his ankle shooting baskets with his kids and Kim had picked up a case of food poisoning. Either of them would have loved being here.

Maybe she would have, too, under better conditions—less heat and more action. At the moment, she'd gladly trade her glory for a deep bath and a cool motel room.

But her paper had to send somebody. Local pride demanded it, what with the Mission Co-Commander being a hometown boy. She felt that her interview with Colonel Blackford's wife was a creditable piece of work, but she'd gotten it over the phone and sent it in by modem. The whole thing could have been handled from the comfort of her own office. Besides, the interview itself was no weightier than the ones she used to do with Depression-glass collectors or muzzle-loading riflemen before her recent promotion. This time last year she'd been quizzing hog breeders and expert quiltmakers at the Grant County Fair. Maybe that was the best analogy: a Mars shot was a county fair without the manure.

Once more she walked past the bleachers where the major media people had seats and work tables. Few of these were in use at the moment as their tenants surged aimlessly up and down the aisles or scattered across the beach.

She limped slightly. Earlier, the heel of her right sandal had broken off. The cuff of her good yellow slacks dragged in the dirty sand picking up cockleburrs. She wished she'd had the sense to have worn rugged clothes and a sun hat.

It was dark now—a small blessing—but no cooler. The air was thick enough to swim through. The skin on her face and arms stung from extravagant use of sunblock yet she knew she'd lost her battle with the Florida sun. An unwelcome crop of freckles was sure to appear in the morning. The insect repellent was still holding its own against the mosquitos and sand fleas but they'd doubtless find some breach in her defenses before the night was over.

As she passed the television networks' prefab headquarters,

she repressed an urge to play the hick tourist and stare through the windows at the famous commentators. The box of fried chicken she'd brought along for lunch was a distant, greasy memory. She'd tried one sodden horror of a sandwich from the canteen trailer and vowed not to repeat the experience. But a root beer ought to keep her from fainting.

She joined the slow-moving line for refreshments. Eventually, she secured her drink.

She turned back down the beach, away from the stands. Photographers had established their gear in a battle line across the entire press site. A battery of cameras on tripods stood poised to shoot the Great Event—on the off chance the Great Event managed to occur. She found her chosen vantage point in front of the camera lines and sat down in a patch of dead grass close to the water's edge.

She'd studied every item in her press kit four times. Her notebook and pocket recorder were filled with impressions. Hazy ones. The crash briefing she'd gotten at home hadn't prepared her for the reality of the Cape. It sure was a long way from Marion, Indiana.

She wished she'd been able to get a pre-launch press tour but those had all been filled before she arrived. There'd been nothing for her to do but wait since countdown had stopped at 1028 hours this morning.

Most people here seemed a lot more relaxed and knowledgeable. They were taking the hold with far better grace than she. Only a few meters away, a dozen or so people were laughing and chatting as they passed binoculars around or took turns looking through the eyepiece of an elaborate camera belonging to one of them. She tried not to eavesdrop on their conversations.

The preponderance of gray or balding heads suggested that these were old veterans of space reportage. Maybe they'd even covered the Apollo and Shuttle missions of a generation before. She wondered what papers they represented. They certainly were a jolly bunch. One elderly man with a pronounced cowlick in his shining white hair was sketching a dark and haughty middle-aged woman. Many of the others were drinking from cans carefully muffled in paper napkins. She was sure these didn't contain pop.

Perhaps she ought to go over and introduce herself. The longer she sat alone, the more their cheerfulness would irritate her. She watched a trio of tall old men on the edge of the cluster. The fine-boned one spoke directly into his bespectacled colleagues' ears. The rangy one grinned at the balding one with the crisp moustache. Then they all began to sing in low, wavering tones, keeping time by clashing their beverage cans together. She didn't know the tune, something about three kings riding to hell. So intently was she staring, she accidentally locked eyes with the one who'd suggested the song. He grinned and saluted her with a courtly wave. She turned away, blushing at her own rudeness.

Best to save long stares for the vehicle yonder. The orbiter stood only five kilometers away across a stretch of water. With its stubby wings and strap-on fuel tanks, it made a less romantic image than pictures of earlier rockets she'd seen. After all, it was only a ferry, a means of getting the astronauts up to their orbiting Marscraft. Yet it sparkled so brightly in the glare of interlaced spotlight beams and cast a splendid reflection on the inlet's surface.

She felt guilty for not responding to the wonder of the scene. A pair of ducks bobbing placidly on the still water mocked her turmoil. They did not care whether men flew to Mars or nested at home, so long as there was clean water for ducks to swim in. Plenty of birds around here—that big fellow she'd seen on the bus trip out to the Center must have been an eagle.

The loudspeaker blared: "Countdown resumed."

The message echoed and re-echoed in a babble of newscasters' voices on scores of personal TV sets all over the site. The crowd applauded wildly and swept down to the very edge of the beach, anxious to be as close to the coming event as possible. Photographers yelled at the invaders to leave their lines of sight clear and were good-naturedly obeyed.

Tension wound tighter as the last minutes of countdown unreeled. They were all longing for fulfillment "more than watchmen for the dawn," as her pastor would say.

Despite her weariness, she found herself captured by the surging current of anticipation. Her pulse quickened and her hands became very cold. She rose to a kneeling position, leaning forward to catch the moment of ignition.

The orbiter rose abruptly on waves of fiery cloud and rolled onto its proper path. The thunder of its passing kept ripping the sky apart even after it was lost to their sight.

A tag from Isaiah rose unbidden in her mind: "By the shores of the sea, the people who sat in the darkness have seen a great light. Upon them my salvation rests."

She was on her feet now, cheering as madly as everyone else.

The tide of celebrating people carried her towards the parking lot, into the path of the old man who'd smiled at her earlier. She threw her arms around him in a short, fierce hug. Then she turned to fight her way onto the bus with soaring heart.

"We're on our way," she murmured. "We're really on our way."

✻   ✻   ✻

III

By the time the hospital released Ria early Tuesday afternoon, the accident had dwindled in significance. As far as she was concerned, it had been nothing more serious than a slip on a loose rug.

The dreams were uppermost in her mind now. She chose to walk home rather than take a bus in order to be alone with her thoughts. Along the way she walled herself off from the crisp bright air, scuffing heedlessly through the heaps of gold and scarlet fallen leaves. Her inner eye was still fixed on the low, low skies of last night's dream, not on the clear vault overhead.

Arrival at her apartment snapped that reverie. A single day's absence had subtly altered her perspective: she felt as though she were a stranger entering the place for the first time.

How had she managed to tolerate such sterile quarters? And she couldn't even rearrange the flimsy plastic furniture—each piece fitted one spot and one spot only in the single room.

Well, at the very least she could get the place cleaner. She'd been doing the bare minimum necessary to pass housekeeping inspections. That wasn't good enough to suit her now. This one small aspect of her life was hers to control—and she meant to control it.

Three hours later, every surface in her apartment shone. Ria returned the cleaning tools to Supply and made herself a cup of tea. She sat down to drink it, automatically brushing the cockleburrs off the seat of her pants. She sprang up in keen alarm. Burrs? Why had she expected burrs on her clothes?

She stared at her hands, looking for pricks and scratches that were not there. She had become curiously ill at ease about her body since the accident. It, too, felt like a dwelling-place she had left for a while and found unfamiliar on return.

Her hands were strong and square as ever. The same white scar still ringed her left thumb. Yet . . . she could not entirely banish the images of two quite different pairs of hands flickering like ghosts above her own.

A good dose of reality would cure the delusion. Nobody had gone to Mars yet—wouldn't for another decade. Her tea grew cold while she tapped out queries on her computer. There was no record of an astronaut named Blackford, past or present.

So there. Her dream of the space shot was a mere fantasy, something her imagination had concocted out of old news tapes.

A sensible answer, but since when were dreams equipped with cockleburrs that pricked and cardboard sandwiches that assaulted the stomach? Ria remembered the sensory details of that launch as well as those from any other real experience. Nothing had faded on awakening.

No harm in making completely sure. She entered a request for pictures and descriptions of the Atlantic Space Center's press site in the late twentieth century. She washed the cup and teapot while the data came on line.

When Ria scrutinized the photographs and drawings her screen displayed, she found that they corresponded to her dream in every particular. A reporter in that era would have seen exactly the sights she had dreamed. Contemporary articles in obscure publications mentioned the same physical discomforts she'd felt there.

The coincidence defied explanation: she couldn't possibly have known any of this. A final question to the data bank revealed that a joint American-Soviet Mars program employing the Space Shuttle had once been contemplated for the 1990s, before worsening economic conditions had forced its cancellation.

The launch she'd witnessed was plausible, but it hadn't happened. Could her dream have been a vision of an alternate reality, one in which history had taken a different course?

She'd played the counterfactual game often enough herself in school. Did the old woman and the otter belong to another world of might-have-been? Did time itself have branches like some mighty tree?

She thought of the University orchard's apple trees that she'd climbed as a child. Did every gnarly branch stand for a path in time? Every blossom, fruit, and leaf a world? But why had she viewed those alternate worlds through eyes that were not her own?

It would be simpler to assume she was merely losing her mind. People did that every day. Some of them did it violently and went noncomp. The attractiveness of her delusions was ominous.

Ria stared out of her window until dusk had turned to darkness. Then she decided to eat in the apartment-complex cafeteria rather than cook for herself.

Tonight the cafeteria's resolute cheerfulness failed to depress her. It was no longer important enough to merit her attention. Other residents bustled about smiling carefully at one another, but she ate alone, locked in the dominion of her own mind. Not even the sight of Hannah surrounded by an adoring coterie stirred the usual resentment—let the whole choral dance corps drool over her if they wished. Ria's thoughts were of darkness and dreams.

Later, Ria wandered aimlessly around her tiny apartment trying to occupy herself until bedtime. There was nothing of interest on the campus stations. She couldn't think of any video tapes worth borrowing from the House collection. She considered calling up a reference work on space exploration but more facts about space were not at issue.

She made herself read a bit of Eliade's *Myth and Reality*. His study of initiation myths was still in her briefcase at work; she'd get it back in the morning.

Then she took a sinfully long shower, washed and dried her long hair, and climbed into bed.

"*O lente, lente, currite noctis equi*," she muttered. She wanted the stallions of the night to course slowly for reasons Doctor Faustus—or Ovid, for that matter—would have understood. The longer the night, the longer the dream. What would happen if she imagined those silvery waves again, if she tried to call for a dream?

Another dream came uncalled. . . .

✳   ✳   ✳

"No longer a bridge, but a raft. Sir."

That weary engineer was still trying to persuade General Sumner to call off the crossing.

If the man who built Grapevine Bridge feared to tread on it, well . . . he, Tom McCauley, wasn't rushing in to test it a minute sooner than ordered.

He could make out snatches of the debate from where he and a clutch of other junior officers stood waiting, twenty feet farther along the bluff. He and his fellows huddled together in silence, straining to follow the distant battle by the muffled roars and crashes filtering through the woods on the opposite bank. Their eyes drifted back and forth between their superiors and the flood-swollen Chickahominy River. Otherwise, they stayed still, for anytime a man shifted his feet, oozing red mud did its best to suck his boots off.

The dreary afternoon threatened more rain.

Now the engineer had to rehearse his arguments all over again as yet another commander—that had to be Meagher of the Irish Brigade—joined the circle around Bull Sumner.

"Since last night's thunderstorm, this trickle of a river has grown 300 yards wide"—The engineer spread his arms like the surging torrent—"spilling out into a mile of surrounding swamp."

The man's Regular smartness was fraying under stress as fast as the ropes holding his bridge together. While he was pointing toward gaps in the flooring, an uprooted tree thudded against the bobbing structure, nearly tearing the main span loose. More logs broke away from the corduroy approaches and floated free.

"An impossible passage, General, impossible."

Sumner scowled at the engineer and strode a few paces closer to the floodwaters. Tapping his battered hat against his knee, the white-maned commander glanced back towards the road where II Corps stood stacked up in the mire. The troops had been waiting there, ready to march, since an hour before the crossing order arrived from Headquarters.

A bugle sounded beyond the raging river.

Sumner slammed his hat back on his head.

"Impossible? Sir, I tell you I *can* cross. I am ordered."

Bull Sumner couldn't let the Old Man down. Neither would any man there.

Grapevine Bridge was a slippery nightmare, barely wide enough for a column of two's. It creaked and trembled at the river's fury, but miraculously, the sheer weight of the troops passing over it held the bridge in place.

The First Minnesota Volunteer Infantry took its turn. They marched on in good order, keeping their footing better than some of the units ahead of them. It must be all those nimble lumberjacks in their ranks.

None of his doing, surely. He was simply there to bring up the rear as Colonel Sully had directed him.

The tail of his column reached the approach. He flipped back the cape of his coat and shortened his grip on his mount's bridle.

"Easy, Columbia," he murmured, patting the bay mare's nose.

Columbia snorted as the flood hit her legs, but she held steady.

Uttering soothing noises, he led his mount forward, feeling out gaps lest either of them come to grief. He stifled a curse as cold water sloshed over his boot-tops.

Somebody in the New York regiment behind him went down noisily. Poor bastard. Poor bastards, all of them.

They made it to the central span, which still arched clear of the river. The mare stepped lightly over the damp logs but he kept his eyes locked on their footing, unwilling to notice how fast the water was rising.

More whispers of encouragement got Columbia through a second flooded stretch, wider and more treacherous than the first.

They were out of the sodden marsh, back on what passed for a road in Virginia. He remounted gladly as his regiment moved out in a column of four's.

They were starting to get close enough to hear the shellfire and the screaming.

Though their grumbles and jokes seemed to grow louder, the troops slogged ahead with maddening slowness—were they making as much as a mile an hour? Had they survived the perilous waters only to drown in mud? The damn muck was deep enough to drown a mule. God help the gunners today.

He brushed futilely at the clouds of mosquitos enveloping him. Columbia twitched and tossed her head.

The road meandered right and left through misty woods of pine, oak, and maple where trees were entangled with honeysuckle vines thick as cable and great bramble-patches of wild rose.

But the scent of the flowers could not mask the reek of sweating men in sodden uniforms, of lathered horses and wet leather.

And nothing could mask his own fear of the coming battle.

He'd been worried about his ability to measure up from the beginning, when he joined the regiment in St. Paul and was elected its major. Couldn't his comrades in arms see that he was a man better suited to the counting house than the camp?

The rigors of training and the excitement of this campaign up the Peninsula had shunted those worries aside. Now they were back, fiercer than ever, here on the brink of battle.

Every step brought judgment nearer.

They passed wounded Federal troops streaming back from the front—staggering, stumbling, holding their mutilated bodies together any way they could. A drummer boy who no longer had a right eye nearly blundered against his stirrup.

He gripped the reins harder, refusing to shudder. Refusing to meet the stare of that powder-blackened face.

The men of the First Minnesota surged forward, towards the rising smoke of battle. Ahead of them, volleys of musketfire crashed closer together. Rebel yells whooped louder. The woods were thinning out into farmland.

"Fix bayonets!"

The order raced down the column, answered by a clatter of metal.

He drew his saber like a man in a dream. *Pray for us sinners*. . . .

"Guide right—Double quick—Charge!"

They roared out onto the meadow in a line, wheeling behind the beleaguered Union position to catch the Rebs in a crossfire.

Screaming with the rest, he spurred Columbia into the whistling hail of Minié balls.

He could not see enemy faces through the smoke, only their muzzle-flashes pecking at his men, only the crashing flames of their cannon.

He waved his saber furiously.

His mare sped across a field of clover and roses, nimbly dodging tree stumps and fallen men. She gathered herself to jump a rail fence the infantry had yet to push down, rose in a smooth arc, and—

A Rebel shell caught Columbia in the chest, rolling her over on top of him, crushing him senseless against the shattered rails.

Lights and voices. . .

"Hey, Buck, we got us a live 'un. That's mostly hoss blood."

The stretcher-bearers were still blurs of mercy when pain drove him back into darkness.

His right arm hurt. Staring at his bandages, he blessed the pain, devoutly, rapturously savoring it from shoulder to elbow to fingertips.

It proved his arm was still attached to his body, not lost in a stack of severed limbs beside the barn that served as a field hospital, here at Savage's Station.

Breaks generally healed crooked, but a gimpy arm was better than none. He would still have his chance to fight.

Unless, of course, this victory proved to be the Big Thing that would end the war.

A battery of twelve-pounders continued firing inside his head. He closed his eyes against the early morning light and gingerly shifted his stiff left leg to a new position. That side of his body had taken a lot of shrapnel—the bits Columbia's body failed to block.

They would be burning what was left of her and the other dead animals sometime today, on pyres of railroad ties and fence rails.

A fly buzzed past his ear and tried to land on his face. He flinched away in disgust, knowing where it might have lighted last.

Damn the waste of it all.

But he was alive, sitting on a pile of straw under a peach tree where one of the walking wounded had propped him. He had hot coffee to drink and a cracker to gnaw.

Assuming he could keep it down, this close to the burial trench.

The row of corpses under a 'paulin was already starting to stink. Even while the sanitary detail shoveled, the ranks of the dead kept swelling, as more hospital patients moaned their last and more broken bodies were carried in from the field.

He watched a stretcher bearer cut brass buttons off the coat of a headless officer in gray. Meanwhile, another scavenger looted a plug of tobacco, scraped away the blood, and happily took a chaw.

The breeze bore faint sounds of Sunday morning church bells from the enemy capital ten miles distant.

And soon other sounds as well—martial music and marching feet.

All eyes were turning back to the Williamsburg Road. Any man who could leave his post—or move—was heading past the commandeered farm buildings, craning for a glimpse of the passing troops.

Fighting pain and dizziness, he struggled upright on his good leg. One of the grave-diggers lent him a shoulder to lean on. Together, they limped up a knoll that gave them a view of the road through a gap between the slave-cabins.

Proud banners waved past to the music of fife and drum. There was Sumner, bareheaded as usual, clutching his hat while his long white hair and beard streamed wildly about him.

But no one had eyes for Bull Sumner, nor for Big John Sedgwick riding beside him.

The Old Man himself was with them today. Every soldier here knew the price their Chief had paid to bring them to this hour.

Their leader was a gentleman born, silver-haired and splendid, well-mounted on a sleek gray horse. Acknowledging their cheers with smart salutes, the Commander and his party swept forward.

Mine eyes have seen the glory . . .

The strains of their *Battle Hymn* flowed down the line of march. Every living throat took it up.

Hale or wounded, the whole army's spirit was high as the morning sun. The wine of victory sang in their veins. The sword of lightning was theirs to wield. The truth that they served was marching to certain triumph.

Glory, glory hallelujah!

And the blue-clad legions of Robert E. Lee took Richmond by sundown.

❋ ❋ ❋

IV

The server deftly smothered the last of the flames and carried the platters of *saganaki* to the corner table where Ria and Carey sat. The spareness of the early evening crowd at Spiro's Restaurant permitted them the luxury of prompt attention.

"I wish they still let them flame it right in front of you," said Ria. She helped herself to a slice of the bubbling cheese. "But safety first, as always." She frowned at the candle-shaped electric lamp in the center of their table.

"It must've made a better show up close," said Carey.

"Sure did. They'd pour on the brandy mixture and *whoosh*! That's the only way to get it hot enough to suit me."

"I don't think I could stand this any hotter." Carey took his first cautious bite and winced. "Don't get me wrong, Ria, Spiro's is a great place." He ran appreciative fingers over the colorful paper mat beneath his dish. "And being treated to dinner here—"

"Makes it taste even better, doesn't it? Relax, Carey, or you won't last the evening. This is the least I can do for you after your first aid saved my life Monday." She raised her wineglass to toast him.

Carey ducked his head as if avoiding a blow. He scratched at a rash on his neck. "Everybody has to know resuscitation techniques. Ali or Hannah could have gotten you breathing again just as easily."

"But they didn't." She smiled down on her smaller companion.

The arrival of their salads spared Carey further embarrassment.

"Did you hear that Repair is still buzzing about your terminal, Ria? They came around while you were on break this afternoon. All the connections checked out. They insist there's no way that equipment could've shocked you." He rubbed his moustache. "The service rep was fairly whimpering at the prospect of all the extra forms she'll have to fill out trying to explain."

"So let them blame it on me and be done with it." She spit out an olive pit. "I've no objection to using the terminal if it's working properly again."

"You don't?" Carey looked up sharply.

Ria's boldness surprised her but she continued: "I refuse to be frightened by my own tools."

"Well, the service rep's frightened. She has to come up with an explanation or lose performance points. No allowance for mysteries. So she has this theory—" he leaned forward for a piece of bread—"that the accident was the work of a noncomp."

"That's absurd! Noncomps run amok. Everybody knows that. They haven't the wits or the patience to plant booby traps, much less traps that leave no trace afterwards."

"Maybe there's a new and devious breed of noncomps hatching, one that skulks in dark corners to plan mischief, that even . . . conspires." He glanced around the dim restaurant melodramatically and finished in a whisper: "Or maybe it would be to someone's advantage to say so."

"Another excuse to watch and pry. One of these days Security will have the whole world wired for monitoring. It doesn't bear thinking about. But look," she said, "here's our chicken."

Other tables filled, the noise level rose, the honest smells of garlic and cinnamon, lemon and olive thickened in the air. Their server pointedly kept returning to check their progress but Ria would not let her hurry their meal. Finally, over coffee and *baklava*, she casually raised her question.

"Carey, you're an American specialist. Tell me something. What would have happened if Robert E. Lee had fought for the Union in the Civil War, instead of going over to the Confederacy with his state? For instance," she added, "how would he have fared in the Peninsular Campaign? I don't know much about it, of course, except that it took place on the Virginia peninsula."

"Lee would have won it, of course. No question about that. Marched right up, taken Richmond in the spring of 1862, brought the war to a quick and merciful end."

"Surely that would have been all to the good?" Ria nibbled at her pastry.

"You'd think so, considering the huge numbers who died. But things are never that tidy. Suppose the rest of the South had refused to admit defeat after their capital had fallen? Suppose they waged dirty guerrilla war for a whole generation? Might have been worse than what actually happened." He took another sip of coffee. "Why do you ask? I didn't know you were interested in the American Civil War."

"Oh, I was just playing a sort of mental game, making a list of historical what-if's." The intentness of his stare was making her uncomfortable. "Haven't you ever wondered: what if Mohammed had died in his cradle? What if the Spanish Armada had conquered England?"

"There used to be a whole genre of speculative fiction based on premises like that. They called it 'alternate history,' " said Carey.

"You sound as if you've read some."

It was his turn to be defensive. "Anything wrong with a historian enjoying old-fashioned literature?" He began tearing at his paper napkin and rolling up the pieces.

"Nothing. We're authorized to like the past, aren't we?" replied Ria. "I must confess, the past looks better and better every day. Sometimes I think I must have been born in the wrong century."

"I know the feeling." Carey stopped shredding his napkin and managed a bitter grin.

Ria returned to her apartment feeling well pleased with the evening's work. Getting to know Carey better had more than repaid the evening's cost in money and alcohol allowance. He was a person now instead of the body at the next terminal. In time perhaps a friend? Though not a lover, surely. She chuckled at the thought. Making friends was so hard for her, she had long ago convinced herself that she really preferred being alone. Where did this sudden hunger for companionship come from?

In any event, she and Carey were now planning to see the new art exhibit at the Krannert Gallery on Saturday. Right now she was eager to follow up some of the suggestions he'd made on Civil War references. She threw her coat on the nearest chair and set to work on her computer.

A topic search yielded summaries of the Peninsular Campaign, a Union attempt to capture Richmond by marching overland after landing at Norfolk. By correlating events and proper names, she tentatively identified the action in her dream as the Battle of Fair Oaks, 31 May–1 June, 1862. She was certain she'd never heard of the event before. European history was her specialty, not American. Could her subconscious have invented so many vivid details without memories to draw on? But which parts were fact and which fancy?

She began checking the identities of all the officers mentioned. There was no Major Thomas McCauley in the First Minnesota Volunteer Infantry or in any other detachment present at that battle, although Union Army rolls did list a Private Thomas McCauley of Minnesota serving on the far Western frontier.

General Edwin "Bull" Sumner was real enough, however. Her screen even flashed a full-length portrait of that worthy gentleman looking untypically neat. She recognized him at once despite his stiff pose in the old engraving.

Sumner had indeed saved the day at Fair Oaks. One authority compared his crossing of the Chickahominy River to the fortunate arrival of Blücher at Waterloo. Without his bold decision—

There was a knock at the door. The unwelcome caller was Hannah.

"What can I do for you?" asked Ria.

"Aren't you going to invite me in?" Her sharp little chin tipped up.

"I'm sorry, but you've caught me at a bad moment."

"It's a matter of some importance." Hannah was not used to refusals.

"So is the work you're interrupting."

"As your representative on the House Committee, I could demand entrance. If I cared to exert my rightful authority . . ." She tried to peer into the apartment past Ria's body.

"You wouldn't do anything that direct." Ria became pleasantly aware of her own superior size. She lounged against the door frame and folded her arms.

"The purpose of the House Committee is to facilitate cooperative living among residents and thus enhance their proper mental, physical, and emotional functioning." Hannah recited the quotation in her mellowest tones.

"That's word for word from the Guidebook, isn't it? Are you here to charge me with some infraction of the rules?"

"You make me sound like a Security Officer." Hannah pouted.

Ria shrugged. She wanted to say "you have all the right instincts," but thought the better of it. Two women heading for the stairwell were now within earshot.

"It's just that people—several people—have remarked that you keep to yourself all the time." Her pale brows wrinkled with an approximation of concern.

"I don't have the time to mingle because I'm working so hard at being a productive unit of society."

A door slammed at the end of the corridor.

"Unmutual behavior is not permitted."

"Neither is laziness. I'm sure there's a point in this conversation somewhere, Hannah. Would you be so kind as to state it so I can get back to my desk? My keyboard's getting cold." Ria began tapping her fingers against her arm.

"You simply must make some gesture of mutuality."

"No doubt you've a specific one in mind."

"I'm going to offer you the chance to make a healthy show of community spirit." The hint of a smirk tainted her lips. "You could help me serve refreshments at tomorrow night's Gathering. We're going to have real cider from the Illini Orchard." Her voice fairly caressed the word *real*.

"I plan to be busy tomorrow night too." Ria didn't

bother to apologize or mention that she'd won three liters of the luxury beverage in that morning's House lottery.

"This refusal will go on your record. Every byte of data counts. If you face eviction some fine day, remember, the choice was yours."

Ria stood silent, not trusting herself to reply. The blonde woman retreated down the corridor bearing rejection with weary benevolence.

Ria closed and relocked the door behind her. If Hannah had just asked her to take her turn, she might have agreed. But no, she had to simper and wheedle. She probably didn't know any other tactics. The sheer pettiness of the thing! Why had she resisted? No sense risking a bad report over something so minor. Being seen in Carey's company ought to show enough sociability. The gossip-mongers might even be stupid enough to imagine it was something sexual.

Ria poured herself a glass of cider, but the cold, fragrant drink did nothing to soothe her temper. She grimaced at the smiling Indian on the jug's label. After her run-in with Hannah, she was too agitated to concentrate further on the Civil War and that puzzling dream.

A change of topic was in order, something quite irrelevant to her present situation—mythology perhaps. She located the copy of *Rites and Symbols of Initiation* that she meant to start last Monday. The stately cadences of Mircea Eliade's prose usually relaxed her.

But this time, the remedy failed. The restless, dreamless night that followed made her regret reading so far past her accustomed bedtime.

Next morning, Ria felt as dismal as the gray skies above, although the overnight weather change had not left her with the usual headache. Not for the first time she questioned the necessity of her physical presence at the Library. But home terminals like the one that came with her apartment were permitted only a limited degree of interface with the major nets that ran the world, and access time was rationed. One was never allowed to forget that computers served the good of society, not the convenience of the individual. Wanting to work—or even play—alone was a dangerously unmutual thought.

She had barely gotten settled at her desk when the bickering started. Hannah chose to interpret her gestures of conciliation as further attacks and Ali felt obliged to intervene. The supervisor's preference for peace over justice worked against Ria, but Carey was quicker to back her than before.

Back home, Ria tried to put it all out of her mind. She resolved to ignore any calls or knocks at the door and concentrate on unraveling her dreams. Best to get at it as quickly as possible before noisy partygoers clogged the hall.

She put the teakettle on the cook-surface while a frozen dinner heated and she started to set the table.

Rubbing a spot off the teaspoon, she fell into rapture. She stared at the utensil as if she had never seen one before. Her caressing fingers warmed the cool, shiny metal. She caught sight of her own face unsteadily reflected in the bowl of the spoon. As she rocked it back and forth, the image of the ceiling light above her danced like the sun on rippling water. . . .

❋   ❋   ❋

She drew her cloak about her rounded shoulders and leaned far out of the window. A damask banner fluttering from the sill shifted beneath the stiffness of her gloved fingers. She might yet rue this folly. By rights, a woman of her years and infirmity ought to be huddling by a roaring fire, not defying January's cold. Yet the glory of the day was worth the risk it carried. Afterwards she would pay and pay gladly in whatever coin should be required. Hailing the neighbors who watched from windows opposite her, she applauded the brave display of hangings they had made.

Two storeys below her, the silk-and-fur-clad merchant gentry of Cheapside awaited their new sovereign's coming behind railings draped with tapestries and other costly stuffs. The throng swirled against the barriers in clamorous waves. Men stamped their feet and women thrust their hands deep inside their sleeves to ward themselves from chill. Their breath made puffs of cloud in the air. Gems flashed in the afternoon sunlight and golden chains of office turned to rippling bands of flame.

Farther down the street, a platform had been erected for the staging of a tableau. The district sought to flatter His Grace's well-known taste for allegory by presenting a mighty tree, like unto a Jesse Tree, sprung from the loins of Father Time. In its branches sat children in stiff finery and gilt crowns portraying the King's royal ancestors, holding the arms proper to each. The young ones were grave as painted statues in a church, taking no notice of the musicians and the schoolboy orator gathered beneath them. She doubted that her old ears would be able to catch the songs and verses that would greet the monarch when he stopped at this station of the processional way.

A tumult of cheers and bells and trumpet blasts grew ever louder from the direction of Cornhill to the east. Cheapside's assembled worthies and lesser folk alike craned their necks to descry the King and his attendants proceeding to Westminster for tomorrow's coronation. But she, for her part, was content to wait in stillness. Age had given her patience in exchange for all the strengths it had taken away.

A shout went up as the heralds came into view. After them strode a troop of halberdiers splendid in crimson doublets worked front and back with the Tudor Rose and the monogram of Henricus Rex. Then came the King himself, clad entirely in cloth of gold, riding at the head of a thousand mounted gentlemen. Fresh rejoicing greeted each smile the pale-haired young ruler bestowed: he had his people's hearts as they had his. In him the kingdom's fortunes were renewed.

She counted herself well blessed to watch the royal cycle turn a third time. Long years before, in her childhood, she had seen this monarch's dour grandsire come to take the throne. Nigh two score years ago she had cheered his parents, old King Henry and his sainted Queen, the Spanish Katherine, as they fared to their own crowning on Midsummer's Day. With more vigor than she would have believed she yet possessed, she raised her ancient voice to cry: "God save and keep your Grace. . . ."

※　　※　　※

Ria came to herself just as the teakettle started to boil. She was slumped against the table, far wearier and hungrier than she had been only moments before.

No need to research this dream. The scene was obviously a Tudor coronation procession. No, not quite. What was the term she wanted? "Recognition Procession," that was it. The king would receive his crown the day afterwards. But *which* king? No son of Henry VIII and Katherine of Aragon had lived past infancy—in history as she knew it. Yet if a Henry IX had reigned on some other time track, English history would have branched off in an entirely different direction.

So what did sixteenth century England have to do with a Mars expedition or the Civil War or that old woman and the giant otter who'd called her by name? She could see no common feature in the dreams. Except . . . in each of them people were waiting for a dramatic event to transform their lives. Was she being told to await a comparable transformation of her own? Ria shuddered as if with cold.

Impossible! It was all impossible. Alternate universes didn't exist. Dreams only spoke to one's subconscious mind. It was insane to think otherwise. The madness she'd feared since childhood was sprouting, rooting, growing day by day. She stifled a scream.

The kettle whistled, indifferent to her anguish. She forced herself to rise and take it off the heat before the water all boiled away. The oven buzzed to signal that her dinner was ready.

V

"You've almost got it, Ria. A little to the right now."

"How's that, Carey?"

"Perfect."

Ria stepped back to admire her newly hung poster. The glossy back and white image depicted furrowed ridges thrusting out of misty lowlands. A single mountain faceted like a giant crystal soared beyond its fellows into the dark sky. The exhibition's title, "The Mountains of the Mind," was printed on the border.

"This one is called—" She bent down to check the label. "—*Strange Peaks Above the Clouds*." She turned to face her friend. "Which one are you going to put up first at your place?"

"*Dense Snow in the Tai Mountains*." He held up a wintry landscape. "It reminds me of home, back in Cascade. Thanks for talking me into splitting the cost of a portfolio."

"I'm the one who should be grateful. Attending that art show was your idea."

Carey scrutinized the remaining posters. He did not look up as Ria sat down beside him on the studio couch.

"The printing's not too bad for mass production," he remarked. "Not that they can do much more than suggest the luminosity of the originals in any event. I'll bet C.C. Wang's official rediscovery was decreed in the interest of ethnic balance. Some joke on the arts bureaucracy that he

39

happened to be a genius, the last of the traditional *wen-jen* scholar-painters. Most of their other twentieth century choices were better left unexhumed."

"You seem to follow these things rather closely." She cocked her head towards him.

"So?"

"Don't bristle at me, Carey," She clumsily patted his shoulder. "No accusation intended. It's just that you sounded so authoritative at the museum. All that technical talk about atmospheric effects, dry brush technique—way out of my line."

"Once upon a time I wanted to be an artist. I still play at calligraphy a little."

His rabbity face sagged. "Let's talk about something else."

He squared the posters, slipped them back into the package, and resealed it.

"Would you like some cider?"

Carey nodded. Ria got a glass for each of them and returned to her seat.

"Clever of you to fasten the poster to the coathooks, Carey. I'll see it there on the door every morning when I wake up." She traced the line of sight with a wave of her arm.

"It saves you a trip to the House Committee, too."

"I don't expect they'd give me permission to hang anything on the walls. Hannah would make sure of it—she's my floor rep." Ria studied her cider glass before drinking some. "She was snooping around here Thursday night but I wouldn't let her in."

"No, Hannah won't forget that. She has an exquisite sense of her own privileges."

"It's not that I had anything to hide. I simply made up my mind not to submit." Ria's mouth set in a hard line.

"That's more than I manage to do." Carey's slight body tensed at the very thought of their co-worker. A siren blared on the street outside the building.

"I didn't know you used to live in Cascade," said Ria gently. "Is it really as beautiful as it looks in pictures?"

Pride got the better of Carey. "You can't begin to imagine it: gulls crying over Puget Sound, walks through cedar

forests in the rain, snow gleaming on Mount Ranier. . . ."
His voice faded out. "I'm getting carried away." He combed
his fingers through his curly hair. "It comes of trying to
live on a child's memories."

"I was born and raised right here in Chambana. I've
never been near a mountain. I did see a steep hill in
Indianapolis once, but it didn't impress me."

Carey grimaced. "Seattle isn't Indianapolis."

"I'm not likely to get a chance to compare them."

"Me neither. Travel taxes keep rising faster than my
savings. I haven't been back to Seattle since my father was
transferred to St. Louis ten years ago. He's . . . I don't
usually tell people this, Ria." Carey scratched furiously at
the rash on his neck. "He's the First Assistant to the
regional Security Chief for Prairie Region. He's just three
jumps away from Tarleton herself."

Ria shivered and took a deep breath. "Couldn't he . . .
couldn't he help you get a job in Cascade?"

"Bend rules? My incorruptible father? He keeps a picture of Noreen Tarleton on his desk, none of his family.
That might be construed as sentimental." Carey drained
the last of his cider. "I bet you can't put a face to Tarleton's
name."

Ria shook her head. "So no way back to the mountains."

"None. I'll have to make do with the high-rise buildings
of Chambana instead."

Ria winced. "There are still the mountains of the mind."
She pointed at the poster. "In the long run, they may be
the only ones worth seeking."

After Carey left, Ria's anxiety crept back like fog. The
afternoon's outing to Krannert hadn't mended her mood
after all. She thought of calling Carey back and making
dinner plans, but that would only postpone the inevitable.

No matter how long she persuaded Carey to stay, she
would eventually be left alone to face herself.

What was wrong? She didn't used to mind being alone
before. She'd actually relished each respite from together-
ness. If she really wanted company, she could go down to
the lounge. So what good would it do to surround herself
with strangers? Much less pick up a man?

Ria shuddered at the thought of what she had never dared experience. Did she want companionship or solitude? Both? Neither?

She'd been decisive enough earlier when Carey was around; though who couldn't be more forceful than Carey?

The familiar pathways of her life were blurring and fading away before her eyes. Ever since the accident, she'd lost her bearings and was blundering in panic through regions unknown.

Ria turned to the simplest remedy she knew: no problem is so large that it can't be nibbled away.

She fixed herself a sandwich. Her appetite vanished after the first few bites, replaced by twinges of nausea. She wrapped up the sandwich and stored it in the refrigerator for tomorrow's lunch.

Then she tried to distract herself with a frenzy of housework. She scoured surfaces that were already clean. She laundered. She mended. She rearranged the contents of every drawer and shelf in the apartment. It was evening before she ran out of things to do.

A slight throbbing behind Ria's eyes signaled a coming change in the weather. Mercifully, the ache was nothing like the ones she used to feel. She began to leaf aimlessly through books, unable to concentrate on any of them.

She threw down a copy of *Cosmos and History* and started prowling her apartment with no idea what she was looking for, like a pregnant woman searching for an unknown exotic food. The fear of another hallucination kept her moving.

Too much quiet reverie might trigger another spell. She mustn't let her gaze linger too long on shining metal. There was some connection between that and dreaming.

But danger lurked everywhere once one started looking for it. Even a doorknob could be hazardous to her mental health. . . .

What if she collapsed in the bathroom, thrown into a trance by the sight of the faucets? She could wake up in a PSI ward.

Ria decided that the safest way to avoid one thing was to focus on another. She put a cassette of Mussorgsky in her tape player and settled down to stare out of her window into darkness.

Lights atop a new building going up on Lincoln Avenue marked the horizon. Ria considered taking a walk in that direction—*Pictures at an Exhibition* always made her think of walking.

But a storm had begun to gather. Trees bent. Pedestrians scurried on the street below. The lightning that flickered to the west was still too far away for the sound of thunder to reach her. The music shifted to *A Night on Bald Mountain*. She turned off the lights and watched the bright rumbling glory roll in.

At length, the thunderbolt-breeding edge of the storm passed, leaving insistent rain to pelt her window all night long. The white noise of it lulled her to sleep. . . .

❋ ❋ ❋

She was climbing a rope hand over hand and biting back screams to save her breath. Acrid chemical smoke raked her lungs and eyes. Her arms—unmistakably her own weak, heavy arms—were being pulled from the sockets by the strain. Her bleeding hands kept slipping on the cable. Every movement sent her sweaty hair flapping in tangles about her shoulders. Although she could see the flames erupting below, her refuge above remained shrouded in murk.

Ria knew she was caught in a dream. She struggled to awaken, but some will more powerful than hers kept whipping her forward.

She had no choice except to go on climbing up from hell.

❋ ❋ ❋

The nightmare faded with the dawn; the terror remained.

Waking or sleeping, her mind was at risk. There was no hiding place left.

Sunday proved to be the kind of well-scrubbed autumn day Ria would have reveled in under other circumstances. She walked for hours, all the way out to the University experimental farms.

It was familiar territory. She'd worked there four summers as a stablehand and loved it—animals accepted her better than people did. Despite a precocious taste for scholarship, she'd once considered horse training as a career. She might've done more than consider it if her mother hadn't been quite so eager to get her "out into the fresh air and away from all those books." She'd fled to the Library by way of rebellion.

Ria approached the pasture fence. Shading her eyes with one hand, she searched for familiar horses in the inner paddock. That red mare cantering on the fringe of the herd had to be Ember, her old favorite. She didn't recognize any of the others. No point in walking around to the barns—visitors were only admitted on official business.

She ached for the chance to ride again, or just to touch warm, living horseflesh. But even the lowest grade of public stables required an Access card for admission, a privilege she was in no position to earn.

Ria gripped the fence so hard that the wire hurt her hands. Straining to hear the sounds of their distant whinnies, she tried to be glad for the animals. A bit of crisp weather was enough to set them frolicking.

She considered buying a snack at a campustown food stand, but the first whiff of frying oil turned her stomach so thoroughly that she fled back to the street. She watched as Security Officers took a giggling woman into custody. It did little to restore her appetite.

When she returned home, she started to punch out Ali's telephone number, then replaced the receiver. Ali would be too curious about the cause of her gloom. Tomorrow was soon enough to face her prying eyes.

Ria thought of working out in the House gym—a drastic and distasteful remedy, but vigorous exercise was supposed to ease depression. A check of the House calendar eliminated that plan. The choral dance group was scheduled to practice tonight. She didn't care to encounter Hannah on hostile ground.

With curious shyness, she turned at last to Carey. She half-hoped her call would find him absent and thus spare her the necessity of admitting loneliness.

Carey answered on the first buzz.

"Ria?" he stammered. "Such a surprise. A pleasant surprise, of course."

He burbled on without giving her a chance to interrupt. "Look, I was just going through my files. If you don't already have something better to do, would you like to come over . . . and look at calligraphy?"

"Sounds interesting."

"I don't show this stuff to . . . just anybody."

"Be there in a minute."

Ria hung up smirking. She was certain that Carey didn't realize how much his invitation sounded like a proposition.

Another time Ria might have been able to give Carey the praise he so obviously craved. At the moment she was too drained to respond to his enthusiasm. She was still sweating from the long trek across the House and up three flights to his floor, as well as being so lightheaded from lack of food that she could scarcely sit up straight.

It disoriented her to be in an apartment that was the mirror-image of her own, with identical furnishings. The lights were starting to look like bright points while shadows swelled.

Was Carey going to show her every page he'd ever penned in this one sitting? If he didn't offer some refreshments soon, she'd have to ask for them.

Carey was burbling on about the latest medieval bookhand that he'd mastered. "Now look at those dynamic diagonals in *littera bastarda*. I pick up energy from the script itself when I'm doing it. Contrast that with the stiff verticality of *capitalis*—"

"Maybe you get energy from letters, Carey, but I require food. Tea would do no end of good for my dynamism right now."

Carey flushed and swept the stack of matted pages off the table. They slipped and scattered every–which–way at his touch. "Of course. This instant. How rude of me. Would you like some jam tarts to go with it?"

Ria nodded. She closed her eyes and imagined heavily sugared tea pouring like syrup.

Carey put a sheet of frozen pastries in the oven and set the kettle to boil. He made a clattery production out of assembling the tea things, managing to gash his left hand on a can opener. He excused himself to bandage the cut in the bathroom.

The oven timer buzzed. By reflex, Ria sprang up to turn it off. The sudden move was too much for her. She staggered towards the kitchenette, dizzily groping for support. She grabbed for the counter but touched the hot cooking surface instead.

Her recoil sent the tea tray flying and knocked over the kettle. Its contents spilled over her arm as she collapsed against the cabinet, gouging the side of her head on the drawer handles on the way down.

She came out of her faint as Carey was struggling to heave her upright.

"I'm sorry, Ria, I'm so sorry. Please try to get up—you're too heavy for me to lift." He tugged ineffectually at her arms.

"It's nothing. Don't pull at me like that. I can manage."

Ria sat up cautiously. There was something warm and sticky in her hair. She took Carey's hand and lurched to her feet.

"Good thing you didn't yell when you fell and trip the crisis monitor," Carey whispered.

"Give me some credit for discipline. At home, I had to fend off Conciliators every time my parents fought."

"Let me help you to the couch."

"No, get me a towel first—not a bath towel, paper ones will do fine. I don't want to bleed over everything." Ria crumpled a pad of paper toweling over her flowing wound before settling herself on the couch.

"It's food I need, not fussing. I went too long today without eating and it's caught up with me. Have you got some milk, juice, anything?"

Carey poured her a glass of milk, still apologizing.

"Stop that. I'm the one who made the mess." She winced at the pile of broken dishes beside the stove unit. "I don't remember how many pieces you'd set out. What'll the damage charges be?"

"You let me worry about that. I'll report the breakage to the House Committee as mine."

Ria frowned. "I like to take care of my own obligations."

"Make an exception this time. I don't get many chances to be noble. I don't want you stuck with a tour of punitive work."

"You're sure you want to handle it this way? It's awfully good of you." She turned the pad over to absorb more blood.

Carey quickly contrived an ice pack for Ria's head out of a plastic bag and cleaned up the broken dishes while she ate.

"Now will you let me look at your arm, Ria?"

"Trying to undress me, are you?" Ria chuckled. "I didn't think I was your type. There's nothing wrong with my arm."

"Why isn't there?" He was caught between a blush and a frown.

"I don't burn easily." She lowered her gaze.

"That water was almost boiling."

"Nowhere near that hot. Really." Ria still avoided his eyes.

Carey clicked his teeth together. "In any case, you can't go home soaked like that—with an ice pack, yet. People would talk."

"I don't need any more of that." Ria hunched her shoulders. "Do you expect me to stay here until I dry out? Is it a nefarious scheme to get a captive audience for a calligraphy lecture? You can't be that enamored of my company."

He stood frowning, hands on hips. "Ria, you are the hardest person to do a favor for. I was going to offer to take your clothes to the laundry for drying."

"Still trying to shuck me, eh?" The absurdity of it all set Ria giggling.

"You could cover yourself with a blanket. I'd offer to lend you my bathrobe but it'd be way too small."

Ria sighed. "All right. Bring a blanket."

As she wrapped it around herself, she showed him that her arm and shoulder were barely pink from the supposed scalding.

"Ria, I don't know how to say this, but there are too many odd things going on. You haven't looked or acted quite . . . normal since the accident. Make all the excuses you like, but I think there's something wrong. Are you afraid to find out what it is?"

"Yes." She nodded and drew the blanket closer about her.

"So afraid you don't even want to ask the Medivise about your symptoms?"

"At this point, any inquiries I make for medical data are likely to trip a monitor and get me a summons." She shivered.

"Then why don't you enter your questions on my ID number?"

Ria's eyes widened. "You mean that?"

"While I'm down in the laundry room, I expect you to use that computer any way you see fit." He wrote his ID on a slip of paper and placed it beside the unit.

"If we're going to be conspirators, we might as well seal the pact in blood."

"You mean that literally?" Carey blanched.

"Humor me." Her tone was light but her face was grim. She touched her oozing scalp and held out bloody fingers to touch Carey's bandaged hand.

Later, back in her apartment, Ria studied the printouts of medical advice she'd gotten at Carey's: she had either neurological damage from the electric shock or a budding psychosis.

Whether brain or mind were at fault, PSI would catch her in the end. How much time did she have before someone reported her?

It took Ria a long time to fall asleep that night.

❊   ❊   ❊

The climbing dream returned. The rope and the smoky fires were exactly the same as before. The pain was worse. She struggled even harder to wake herself with no more success than on the previous night.

Although her will was tethered, her reason ran free. She was convinced that she was actually dreaming, not hallucinating history, this time. This nightmare had an arbitrary quality quite unlike her earlier adventures. It made no pretense to reality. She was overweight and out of condition. She shouldn't be able to hold on to the ropes, muchless climb for what seemed hour after hour. Smoke that thick ought to kill her outright instead of tormenting her.

And since when did a dreamer analyze a dream in progress?

Nevertheless, she dreamed on.

※   ※   ※

When finally released to wakefulness, Ria started to gasp for breath as if actually starved for clean air. Her arms and back trembled with muscle tension. She slowed her breathing to a normal rate and willed her rigid body to relax.

At least she seemed to have kept her misery quiet so far. Whatever happened, she mustn't trigger the alarm or make the neighbors suspicious. That might raise questions for which she had no answers.

Riding to work Monday morning might have been an ordeal, but Carey chanced to take the same bus. He wasn't a morning person either. Although he was content to merely sit beside her without inflicting conversation, a narrowing of his eyes said he noticed that she'd arranged her hair to cover the scalp wound.

When they reached their office, they were surprised to find Hannah already there, chatting with Ali.

"Tell them your good news," said the supervisor, beaming like a daycare aide about to dispense crackers.

"I'm taking orders for dream tickets today," said Hannah. "Our session is scheduled for this Friday evening. What'll you have, Carey? Up, Down, or Out?"

"Up, I always chose Up. You ought to know that by now." He took a step backwards and suddenly discovered a spot on the hem of his tunic.

"And you, Ria? You weren't here the last time Library workers went." Ali looked up, awaiting Ria's decision.

"I'm not going." She folded her arms.

"And why not?" Ali rose to confront her.

"I'm . . . . allergic." Ria clasped her arms tighter to keep from shaking.

"That's impossible. Dream drugs are perfectly safe. Guaranteed safe. Health wouldn't certify them if they weren't."

"I'm not criticizing Federation safety policies, Ali," Ria said.

"Some people just aren't mature enough to avail themselves of the enriching experiences our society provides," murmured Hannah. "I always enjoy my sessions. They make me feel so close to my fellow workers."

"But I do have a medical problem," Ria protested. "It's in my record."

"Then perhaps you should consult a doctor again. We don't want you to miss any of the recreational privileges the rest of us share."

"Allergy treatments take a while." Carey broke in. "I know." He touched the eczema on his neck. "She couldn't be cured by Friday in any event." He beckoned to Ria. "If you come over to my desk, I'll brief you for your appointment with Professor Clyde this afternoon."

There were no further discussions of dream tickets in the office that morning, but Carey raised the issue again as he and Ria walked over to the history department in Stearns Hall.

"I never heard of anyone refusing a ticket before. I wish I had the guts to do the same myself."

"You mean you don't like going Up?" She stared down at the small man.

"I like it all right, but I hate myself for liking it. Almost as much as I hate the padded rooms at the Center and those flimsy paper costumes they give you to wear."

"Then why do you go?"

"It's easier to do what's expected, at least in public. Why are we walking on the right-hand side?" He gestured at the other pedestrians. "Because that's the way the traffic flows."

"No one's made me go back since I got sick my first time out."

"You really did get sick, then?" Carey stopped short.

"Yes." Her voice went flat.

"I thought you were making that up."

They resumed walking.

"I'll tell you about it someday," she said. *When the memory makes me less queasy*, she thought.

Would she ever trust Carey enough to describe what actually happened two years ago? She had fallen into a state of hysteria so violent, she'd had to be removed from the Center and de-toxed.

No lovely visions for *her* while Out. Her dream was of a magnificent black horse with all of its legs cut off. It screamed horribly and long as its life gushed away in red torrents. . . .

VI

Carey departed for his own appointment, leaving Ria at Professor Gunnar Clyde's door. She needn't have worried about being on time: the eminent scholar wasn't at home.

The minutes dragged by. Students thronged the corridor as classes changed. Ria considered sitting on the floor, but that would attract attention. She leaned against the wall and closed her eyes.

"So there you are."

The hearty bass voice brought her to instant attention. No wonder he was called "Boom-Boom" even to his face. Clyde unlocked his door, waved her inside with a curt "Back shortly," and was off again in a tornadic bustle. Despite his bulk, he moved surprisingly fast through the crowd.

Ria could now at least sit while waiting. The office was an utter jumble. Books bristling with slips of paper were stacked everywhere, including the floor. A mound of microfilm boxes nearly hid the reader on his desk. Computer printouts were taped on the walls between framed documents and testimonials. A silvered plaque identifying Clyde as a past president of the North American Historical Association hung directly behind his desk.

"You weren't waiting long." It was a statement, not a question.

Clyde rammed a stack of folders onto a handy shelf and strode behind his desk. "I have a splendid prospect to put before you, Legarde. As the newest staff member in historical research, you're ideally suited for my needs. You have the fewest standing assignments. You do right by me and I'll see you get performance points—maybe even a jump in grade for you—certainly will mean one for me."

"I'm sure the project'll live up to your expectations, Professor." Ria kept her hands neatly folded and her knees firmly together. "But may I ask what it is?"

"Remember that Lisbon Earthquake biblio Newton did for me?"

"Yes. I was looking at it right before my accident."

"What accident?" He raised one thick eyebrow.

"I was almost electrocuted by my computer. A problem—"

"So that's why I got my data late." He glared at her lack of consideration. "Well, that Lisbon study was just a dry run for my idea. I'm planning a new book, *Disasters and Destiny: The Impact of Tectonic Catastrophe on History*. I like that title. Gets me itching to start work, just thinking about it." He rubbed his pudgy palms together.

"You'll only be interested in earthquakes and volcanoes?"

"Well, if I tried to cover every kind of natural disaster, I'd never get done. Not going to spend years tied to one project. I have too many notions to explore. One category this time, but a panoramic overview. Breadth—I've always been in favor of breadth."

Ria thought he should speak up for girth, too. She didn't like the way he flapped his huge arms for emphasis.

"Take your Lisbon Earthquake, 1755," he continued. "Fifty thousand people dead, whole city smashed. Tidal wave. Fire. The shock was felt all over Europe—metaphorically, if not literally. Sir Kenneth Clark said it brought the Age of Reason to an end. I don't know but what he may have been right. So it started me thinking—I was buttering my breakfast bagel when the thought hit me—what about other quakes? What about tectonic catastrophes generally?" His jowls quivered. "How did the Romans feel about Pompeii or the Indonesians about Krakatoa? Let's revive the old controversy about the Thera eruption. Did the destruction of the Minoans start the myth of a lost Golden Age?"

"I don't think so, Professor," Ria managed to slip in, "the idea of a Lost Paradise is nearly universal. Eliade says—"

"That's as may be." He waved her objection aside. "If you want to argue, bring me the numbers. Bring me lots of cases. Pro and con. What about the rise of militarism in Japan after the Tokyo quake of 1923? Unrest in Latin America and Iran in the 1970s? Stress the majors: Tangshan, Reelfoot Lake."

Ria nodded at the mention of a familiar name. "I've heard of the Reelfoot Lake Disaster. It was the worst shaking this continent's ever had. Even made the Ohio River flow backwards. And the New Madrid Fault that caused it runs right through Prairie."

"I'm glad you're beginning to catch on. Now do you see the possibilities? A non-fiction bestseller. Maybe I'd get a TV documentary series. This could go Federation-wide." His swooping arms sent cassettes flying.

Ria scrambled to retrieve the boxes. Still on her knees, she asked, "Begging your pardon, Professor, but what's this got to do with me?"

"You're to write the research protocol, of course." He scowled. "If you can't draw conclusions any faster than that, maybe I should try someone else."

Ria returned to her seat. "I still don't understand why you want me to do it. My core specialty is medieval and Renaissance Europe. I can't think of any major disturbances—"

"Think harder."

She swallowed. "There was a big Antioch quake in Byzantine times. . . . More than one, actually."

"Aren't you ambitious, Legarde?" He leaned towards her, still scowling. "You don't sound like it. I just said a minute ago that I don't hold with narrow specialization. If you're a competent researcher in one period, you ought to be able to handle anything. You *are* competent? Newton assured me you were. I've worked with Newton for years and she's been right about most things. Fact is, I offered her the job first, but she wanted you to have it."

"She's always looking out for me." Ria sagged imperceptibly.

"*Disasters and Destiny* will be an education for you. I want you to really burrow in. Don't be content with print-outs and microfiche. Go over to the rare book room. Leaf through those sources yourself. Start with the ones you know: the *Monumenta*—"

"I don't think they have earthquakes or volcanoes in Germany."

"—and Muratori." He swept on unperturbed. "Find medieval Italian cases. There are twenty-four volumes of Muratori. I want you to have a look at them."

Yes, they're half-leather quartos badly in need of re-binding. Aloud, she said: "I know the set."

"It's not every library that has the originals, worm-eaten though these are. When I was in school . . ." He galloped off into an involved anecdote.

Ria's attention wandered from Clyde's bobbing jowls to the shiny plaque behind his head. She stared transfixed at its glittering silver surface. . . .

✴   ✴   ✴

It pleased him, here in barbarous Moscovy, to tread on bold crimson carpeting of English manufacture. With it beneath his feet, he could maintain his countenance fit-tingly composed, undaunted by the outlandish splendors of the Uspensky Sobor. Such a wasteful blaze of candles in a house of worship! "Away with them," Gloriana had once said of such tapers. "We see well enough."

The air was thick with incense and chanting. The som-ber, large-eyed idols the Moscovites styled *ikons* stared from gilt-touched walls and pillars and from the barrier that hid their inner *sanctum sanctorum*. These outraged him more than the papistical abominations he had been forced to witness on the Continent.

He freely granted that the young Tsar Ivan and his Tsarina cut imposing figures in their gemmy robes, for all that informants claimed that the old Tsar Ivan had been a scarecrow of a man who favored monkish attire.

Now the infant Tsarevitch was being borne in with commendable solemnity, escorted by those who were to stand as godparents to the heir. How did the Tsar's lack-wit brother contrive to keep his fair wife content? He could feel the radiance of the lady's beauty even at this remove.

He likewise marveled that the aged presiding churchman Dionysii could move under the weight of his gold-encrusted vestments. "Metropolitan" they styled him, but he was a prelate nonetheless and detestable like all his breed. His heart rejoiced that no issue begotten by him would be christened with such mingle-mangle and mummery. What end could be awaited from such a queer beginning? . . .

※　　※　　※

"Legarde, have you been paying attention? You should've been taking notes all the while. Now go think catastrophe."

Ria stumbled getting out of her chair and knocked over a pile of books. It took all her willpower to keep from running. How long had she been out? Had Clyde noticed? Would he report her? It probably wouldn't occur to his chaotic mind. But it was dangerous to make an ego like that feel slighted. He'd forgive her only if she fulfilled her assignment well.

No more trances came that day. She was not transported to sixteenth century Russia or anywhere else. But at night the same dream of deadly fire awaited. Night after night, for the rest of the week, it repeated—a desperate climb to a goal that constantly retreated. Night after night until dawn.

Ria's face grew steadily paler. Her appetite faded. A permanent tension just short of pain settled below her cheekbones. Her condition worsened in bad weather. Colors seemed to lose their vividness as though a filter lay before her eyes. Sparkles danced in the air every time she changed position abruptly. She could never quite get her breath.

Surely her co-workers would notice. . . . She couldn't plead insomnia much longer. Fearing even Carey's company, she refused his invitation to attend a concert by the Hudson Region's acclaimed orchestra.

She was glad Professor Clyde's order to inspect primary sources firsthand gave her an excuse to be out of the office. Her great show of zeal for Clyde's project permitted her to minimize contact with her colleagues. At least no more trances attacked her during working hours.

By Saturday, Ria was desperate enough to squander some money on cosmetics and experiment with ways to hide the ravages of stress. She was surprised at how much she liked the effect of makeup.

Saturday afternoon, Ria managed to take a sound and dreamless nap.

What would happen to her dream-cycle if she stayed up all night and slept during the daylight hours Sunday? She read and drank awesome quantities of tea to keep awake. She played music over earphones until her head ached. By dawn, she felt herself losing the struggle. She fell asleep sitting up. . . .

✳ ✳ ✳

The deck pitched wildly as another great wave smashed the ship. She nearly lost her footing on the icy mast ladder. Her body was as rimed with frozen spray as the metal rungs she clutched. There was more ice in the howling wind to sting her cheeks. The cold burned her lungs and froze her breath. Dampness seeped between mittens and cuffs and around the edge of her hood.

Step by treacherous step she climbed. She had to reach the crow's nest. She could see it through the sleet as a blur overhead. There was something she had to do there, if only she could remember what it was. The ship was depending on her. She was too exhausted to think. The heavy seas were churning her stomach sour. She was barely able to keep moving upwards. . . .

✳ ✳ ✳

The force shoving Ria along finally released her for a stretch of dreamless sleep. It was Sunday afternoon by the time she awakened. This time she was more indignant than desperate. First scorched and now frozen, but seasickness was too much! She glanced about the apartment to make sure the furnishings were not tilted at crazy angles.

She was equally indignant with herself for failing to break the dream spell. If only she could marshal enough willpower, she could banish these symptoms—she had almost called them visitations—permanently.

Life had given Ria an inexhaustible store of passive stubbornness. She hardened under compulsion. But she had always been too busy repelling outside influences to be able to harness her will in any positive direction.

Passive resistance wasn't enough anymore. She had to win back control of her own mind lest she be mastered by madness.

As her mother had been.

There was something exhilarating about anger in a society that forbade it. Righteous anger was healthy. The surge of adrenalin swept away her weariness. She needed that impetus to fight back—and fight back by herself. If she fell into the helpful hands of PSI, the mind she'd get back might not be her own.

Ria refused to let the apartment hold her today. She dressed, ate, and was off into the crisp afternoon. The cold didn't bother her. It only made her cheeks tingle pleasantly. She wanted to be moving, to see how briskly she could walk. There were few pedestrians out on campus. No need to match strides with slower folk. Down the broad sidewalks she sped, past the main quad, past the Library, past Krannert Gallery. She turned away from the Assembly Hall and into the old Mount Hope Cemetery on Florida Avenue.

No need for speed here. She wandered about trying to read inscriptions on the weathered limestone markers. Bronze stars, now corroded green, marked the graves of Civil War veterans. No one had been buried here for decades but the University still maintained it as an historic site. It was a favorite trysting spot for students in the warm months. Fortunately, no one else was around at the moment.

The long walk had tired her more than she realized. She

looked around for a place to sit. There were no benches so she sat on the exposed roots of an old oak tree. The tree had lost most of its branches to storm damage. Soon the arborists would be taking it down. Still, she was grateful for the support of what survived.

Ria leaned back against the trunk and took off her gloves to feel the ridgy bark. She tested its resilience with a fingernail. Contemplating the many subtle shades of gray it displayed, she spied a tiny insect tunneling through the layers. She picked up a fallen leaf and rubbed it until only the lacy skeleton, the essence of the leaf, remained. She discarded it on the grass. Something glittered where the leaf fell.

Ria flinched as if she'd seen a snake but refused to panic. Her new-found resolution wouldn't let her. She reached over and picked up the object. It was nothing but a service button. Somebody had been rewarded with this trinket for faithful employment—seven years' worth, by the seven stars that ringed the University monogram.

Instinct urged her to throw it away but she wanted to test herself against the peril that lay in shining metal. She stared into the glitter, daring it to do its worst. It did. . . .

❋   ❋   ❋

He swirled the urine flask and held it up to a candle for examination. The contents were dark, malodorous, and scanty. The humors were farther out of balance than yesterday, farther yesterday than the day before. He set the flask down to attend to the patient.

Only a feeble pulse beat in the bony wrist. Fever, not the normal heat of springtime, spread an ominous flush across that sallow, ancient face. The eyes flickered restlessly beneath their wrinkled lids. Was the crafty mind of the Doge busy with fresh webs of malice, even here on his deathbed?

Thanks be to Our Lady those eyes were closed. He never rid himself of the fancy that the Doge's blind gaze could penetrate his soul. Now if he were still able, let Ser

Dandalo attend to the state of his own soul. He would have much to answer for before the Judgment Seat of the Almighty. *"Cui multum datum est, multum quaeretur ab eo"*: to him much had been given, from him much would be required.

Were the priest delayed, the Doge might perish unshriven and unannointed, sending forth his spirit with all its stains intact. An evil thought: *absit, absit.* He would summon the chaplain as was his duty. The Council must be told— and also the Marquis. The Crusade would sail from Venice with one illustrious member the fewer. He beckoned a servant and drew the bedcurtains shut. . . .

✳   ✳   ✳

The stuffy Venetian bedchamber vanished. Ria was back in the familiar cemetery. Once again, the trance had lasted only a few moments—the bark had left no imprint on the back of her hand. The silver button still lay in her palm. She let it fall. So much for a show of bravado. Her teeth chattered as she walked home.

Ria didn't need books to sort out the event shown in this most recent dream. From her knowledge of medieval history, she concluded that it must have been the deathbed of Enrico Dandalo, Doge of Venice and vengeful mastermind behind the Fourth Crusade. His machinations—plus a lot of bad luck and worse judgment—had diverted the crusaders to sack Constantinople in 1204 instead of fighting Saracens.

But if he had died before the expedition left Venice, perhaps the tragedy would not have occurred.

She still couldn't see what this or any of the previous dreams had to do with her. Yet . . . she remained convinced there was a pattern and a remedy to these bizarre episodes, if only she could find it before she went mad.

Once home, Ria entered requests for data on sleep phenomena, shuddering at the cost of all this computer time. But if there was ever a necessary expense, this was it.

She got information on alpha waves, REM sleep, circa-

dian rhythms, psychology and neurophysiology of dreams,
even the effects of prolonged sleep deprivation. She spent
an anxious hour investigating whether dreams could be
artificially induced.

Was she the unwitting subject in some cruel experiment? PSI was powerful, not omnipotent. They just tried
to make people think they were all-powerful. If they could
induce dreams, then facts about dream control wouldn't
be so readily available—unless that was an especially devious cover? Lies within lies. . . .

If dream induction were possible, who else beside PSI
could do it? That mysterious old woman and her otter?
Why had she spoken of teaching Ria new things? What
was she supposed to learn from these dreams and trances—
that she was crazy?

The only useful data Ria discovered were case histories
of people who could stop and re-direct their dreams at
will. The knowledge that such a thing could be done fired
her resolve to try it herself. Even if she couldn't wake up,
she might be able to alter the dream to something
pleasanter.

She fell asleep that night daring the frigid sea-dream to
come so she could change it. . . .

❋   ❋   ❋

It came. She could not change it.
The ladder was as cold and perilous as before.

❋   ❋   ❋

Frustration made Ria angrier, and in that anger lay a
new reservoir of strength. She flogged her weary mind
and body to new exertions all that week, with surprisingly
productive results in the professional sphere.

She designed a series of graphic displays to chart corre-
spondences between tectonic and historical events. Enough
were obvious to suggest that Professor Clyde's thesis had
some merit. How could such a blowhard be a creative
scholar?

Her resentment faded before the fascination of the ma-
terial itself. She ran through a condensed course in earth

science and conferred with geologists so that she could serve as a liaison between them and Clyde.

Office squabbles receded in scale like events viewed from some great height. Ria felt a curious, almost mystical attraction for her subject. She longed to be one with those titanic forces that moved continents, lifted mountains, spouted flame, and rent the rocks asunder—while civilizations rose and fell with the fortunes of the land that bore them.

She wanted her own share in those powers. A shred of prophecy came to her: "And in those days they will say to the mountains, 'Fall on us,' and to the hills, 'Cover us.'" But when that happened, Ria planned to be above the crashing peaks, not under them. Someday, the Ring of Fire would be her own arena of wonder.

The cautious part of her mind recoiled in abject horror from these fantasies: first paranoia, now megalomania. Surely it was time she voluntarily surrendered herself to PSI. She had no right to evade treatment. Any day now, she might go noncomp and slaughter her associates or wreck her workplace.

Ria's adventurous side, newly awakened after years of stern repression, was not about to be stilled. Each night she did battle with her agonizing dream. Memories of the fire that glowed at the Earth's core heated her body as she climbed the icy ladder. Although she couldn't quite will herself back into her own warm bed, the crow's nest at the top of the ladder was coming visibly closer.

Ria's furious determination upset her co-workers even though they were safely ignorant of the cause.

In the week following the librarians' trip to the Dream Center, Carey withdrew into himself to nurse some private humiliation. Hannah, on the other hand, kept smiling languidly to herself, as though to suggest that she'd been favored with some especially choice hallucinations.

Ali treated Ria with an almost embarrassing solicitude. Ostensibly, she was trying to make her feel as normal as possible. The results were just the opposite in practice.

Whenever the word *dream* came up in any context, Ali glared. Ria's disability was not to be hinted at, muchless discussed—which inevitably made it a matter of obsessive interest. Ria began to wonder if this weren't her supervisor's real intention.

Ria's suspicions were confirmed Saturday evening when she returned from a walk to find Ali waiting for her in the lobby.

"What a nice coincidence, Ria." The older woman's round face beamed. "I happened to be passing through and wondered if I'd run into you."

Ria doubted that it was a chance encounter but pretended to accept Ali's explanation. "Perhaps we could have a cup of coffee in the snack bar," she said. "It isn't busy this time of night." She did not want to invite Ali upstairs, lest she have trouble getting rid of her or somehow betray herself.

Ali stepped briskly to keep up with Ria's long legs. "The snack bar would be fine. I've been meaning to have a private talk with you outside of working hours."

They got coffee from the snack bar's vending machine. Ali also picked up a cream-filled cake.

"Just a little something to keep me going." She laughed too warmly as they sat down in a vacant booth.

"Now, Ria, I've always liked to think of myself as a mother to my group. And as a good mother, I must tell you I'm concerned. You just haven't been yourself since the accident. Are you sure it left no permanent damage?"

"So the doctors said." Ria drank her scalding coffee black.

"But you're looking downright ill. You didn't used to have such heavy dark circles under your eyes."

Ria started to interrupt but Ali went on talking.

"Oh yes, I can tell they're still there, under the makeup." She pointedly avoided asking why Ria had started wearing makeup in the first place. "And you're not just tense anymore, how shall I put it? You're *fierce*. If you want a special leave of absence to really lick whatever's bothering you, I'd be happy to make the necessary arrangements."

Her first bite of cake exposed the creamy core.

"That won't be necessary," Ria replied. "I can take care

of myself." She clenched her hands into fists under the table.

"Hospitals are full of people who thought they could take care of themselves. The myth of self-reliance has lots of victims. There's no shame in getting a little counseling or whatever's needed." Ali finished the cake in quick, neat bites.

"Are you offering me leave, or ordering me to take it?"

"Order? Who said anything about ordering you to do anything?" Ali's voice softened to a purr. "I'm just giving you friendly advice, as a responsible manager must."

"Has my work been unsatisfactory?" Ria kept her tone carefully level.

"No, you seem to be accomplishing a great deal on Clyde's project. But you mustn't let him drive you too hard. That man has no sense of feasibility whatsoever."

"But if my job performance is adequate, what's the complaint?"

"Frankly, you're upsetting the rest of us." Ali held up an admonishing hand. "Only yesterday, little Hannah came to me on the very verge of tears because you'd snapped at her. Such a sweet child, I don't understand why you can't get along with her. As for Carey, you seem to set him off, too. He was a fine team player until he began hanging around with you after working hours—yes, we know all about that, don't we?" She smirked. "I simply can't allow personal tensions to disturb my office."

"In other words, I might find myself looking for another job." Ria's nails dug deeper into her palms.

"Doctors do marvelous things these days, Ria, even about stubborn allergies. I knew you'd see things my way. Let me know which days you want off," she said, rising to leave.

Ria looked up with what she hoped was a docile expression. She remained seated until the other woman had gone. Her coffee was now too cold to finish.

Ria stayed calm until she was safely back in her apartment. She chewed on her pillow to muffle the sound of her weeping.

Threatening employment was the next thing to threatening one's life. Perhaps Ali was worried that a higher supervisor might drop by and be displeased with the atmosphere in their office—to Ali's discredit. Ria was certain her superior was more interested in protecting herself than helping a subordinate.

If Ria were banished from the University, she'd be lucky to find work as a data processor in the local corn oil plant. She couldn't bear to think of exile. The University meant everything to her, as it had to her parents before her.

This weekend was her last chance to regain control of her life. She had to stop the dreams at any cost.

Ria changed for bed and washed her face. Ali was right about one thing: there were hollows in her cheeks that hadn't been there before. She was definitely losing weight. If she could get her color back to normal, the new contours would really be an improvement. She smiled bitterly at the novelty of vain thoughts.

An inspiration struck just as she was getting into bed. If dreams could not be stopped or changed, perhaps they could be finished. She lay down to commence a new round of the duel. . . .

✼　　　✼　　　✼

She pushed her gear and helmet before her up the passage. Her lamp showed red clay stains along the gray walls. They made a tidy pattern like waves on the limestone. Her jeans and shirt were slimy with mud. Her boots picked up more of it every time she dug in her toes. Her right pad had twisted around, leaving her knee to be gouged with every move. She kept crawling, pulling herself along at a jerky pace. It was sweaty work despite the underground chill. She tried to wipe her face on her forearms and only made it muddy. There was an itch at the back of her head that she couldn't reach.

The passage narrowed. The bedding planes' sharp edges raked her body. She thought for a moment she was going to get stuck. Her heart raced. She felt an extra surge of adrenalin boosting her progress. Her caving skills were equal to the challenge. She had chosen to explore. She knew where she was going.

A cool draft led her forward. She suddenly found herself heading down instead of up. A cavern must lie ahead. She crawled faster, sensing the goal within reach. At last she slid out onto a mud bank, into the blinding light of torches held by unseen comrades.

✻ ✻ ✻

VII

Ria awoke about noon on Sunday enveloped in languorous warmth. She snuggled back under the covers, trying to hold onto contentment as long as possible. The need for food finally drove her up, but without the urgency of the day before.

This was no day for concentrates. She prepared lunch with a slow precision worthy of the Japanese tea ceremony, savoring her very hunger while she cooked. Putting cider instead of milk in the batter produced uncommonly delicious apple pancakes.

Perhaps she had never really bothered to taste apples before: sweetness, tartness, softness, crispness, blandness, tanginess, all resonating together. Cinnamon was a delight but apples were miracles. She picked up the last piece of fruit on the counter and caressed its glossy skin, red as any blood.

The tree whence it came must have been planted before she was born, budded and blossomed long months past, set fruit that swelled without her notice. Its seeds could sprout into trees that would outlive her. Whence had she grown and what fruit would she bear if she blossomed?

Satori from an apple?

Ria laughed at herself. She buffed the apple to a fine gleam and placed it atop her display screen.

She took a luxuriously long shower, enthralled by the caress of the water running over her skin. Toweling dry, she found she could stand to look at herself in a mirror now without cringing. Was this a body some man could take pleasure in?

Sexuality aside, there was something inherently fascinating about the human form. Why did her ego inhabit this particular kind of body rather than another? Why skin instead of feathers or scales or—

Her reverie was interrupted by her neighbor pounding on the door for admittance to their common bathroom. She swept up her gear and retreated to her own apartment.

Ria refused to feel guilty over her breach of House etiquette, preferring to concentrate on combing out her long hair. Few people bothered with long hair any more, but she was glad inertia had kept her from getting hers cut. Today, she'd let it flow free like a mane, instead of confining it to sensible braids.

Ria wanted to get drunk on beauty. She started with an old American vintage—Copland. She dropped her tapes of *A Lincoln Portrait* and the ballet suite from *Appalachian Spring* in the player. As the music unreeled, she opened an artbook on C.C. Wang that Carey had brought to her attention.

She contemplated the paintings without making any conscious effort at understanding them. She did not even bother to distinguish mountains from clouds or water, choosing instead to experience the images only as ensembles of light and darkness.

The whole universe seemed to lie before her in a single fuzzy drop of ink. The barrier between it and her was thinning. She could pierce it. She could see without seeing. Her essential self could emerge from the doorways of her eyes, could enter those hidden places on the other side of the painting—

The tape ended. There was no other sound in the room except her own soft breathing.

Ria laid the book aside. The afternoon light was fading, and with it her euphoria. She was left with a mild, sweet

ache of desire aroused and unfulfilled. It shocked her to
find herself wishing that she did not have to sleep alone
this night.

Later, as she finished her tea, Ria tried to set develop-
ments in perspective. A good night's sleep—novelty though
that was these days—could not of itself have produced
such joy. It couldn't explain her exuberant sense of accom-
plishment or her new confidence in achievements yet to
come. If the doorway had been too small this time, why
then, she'd enlarge it. It could not withstand her forever.

Seizing control of the cave dream had made all the
difference: she'd gone from patient to actor. Could she do
the same with the historical trances? Could she induce one
by choice? Light reflecting from shiny metal seemed to be
the trigger.

A spoon had worked once; it might again. Taking note of
the time, Ria lay down on her unmade bed and held the
spoon before her eyes. Sunset rays gathered in the bowl
like flames bursting over water. . . .

❋   ❋   ❋

The woman next to her plucked at her sari. She squeezed
aside to give the other more room. A hundred or more
people were gathered together this time in the chill
dusk.

Little tremors of expectancy flickered through the crowd.
Soon Gandhiji, their beloved Bapu, would appear to lead
them in evening prayers. Could they but raise sufficient
truth-force, surely Hindus and Moslems must cease slaugh-
tering one another. Bapu alone held the key to the peace
that all—at least all here present—craved.

Ah, at last, there he was, hobbling along the pergola, a
dear familiar wisp muffled in a white *khadi* shawl. His
attempt at briskness was pathetic, for she knew his recent
fast had left him weak. He had to lean on his two favorite
walking sticks—his young kinswomen Manubehn and
Abhabehn—for support.

People opened up a path as the girls helped him up the
garden stairs to address the crowd from the terrace. She
rose with the rest in his honor.

He returned their greeting, placing his palms together in a humble *namaskar*.

A man in European clothes lunged from the crowd. Manubehn raised her arm to bar his way. He shoved the girl aside, but in stumbling, she dragged him down with her.

After the gunshot came the screaming.

Was Gandhiji hit?

Men and women pushed forward, trampling each other in their anxiety to get a clearer view. She herself grabbed a faltering old woman and held her safely upright in the press. One man threw himself on the assassin. Then others dragged the unresisting fellow away, lest the crowd rend him.

The Mahatma alone remained calm. He squatted on the grass, quietly reciting the *Ramanama* while Manubehn bled to death in her weeping cousin's arms. . . .

❃ ❃ ❃

Ria snapped back to consciousness. Her hands now lay crossed on her breast still clutching the spoon. A glance at the clock showed that only 35 seconds had elapsed during the trance. Events in that Indian garden had taken longer— fifteen minutes at least.

Time did seem to run at a different pace within these imaginary worlds, just as legends said it should. A single night in the Hollow Hills equalled a century outside; an epoch passed on Earth for every instant of eternity.

Her knowledge of myth must be shaping these hallucinations as much as her knowledge of history did. She clung to the conviction that all the dreams, whether realistic or fantastic, were products of her own imagination and ultimately subject to her control. If she could act on that faith and cure herself, she could escape the notice of PSI.

This very night she would take command of her own mind. Rather than wait passively for whatever dream her subconscious might toss up, she'd design her own.

What should it be?

Something as far from that dank cave as possible.

Ria paced about the room thinking. Open air. Height. Man-made.

Why not the new Lincoln Avenue Residence Hall?

She stared out her window at the skeletal building, memorizing its structure, complete to the tiny cone of the topping-out tree on its roof.

That done, Ria was determined to put the matter completely aside for the rest of the evening. She was now too hungry for further speculations. For once, dinner in the cafeteria did not seem such a daunting prospect.

❋   ❋   ❋

The moon was her spotlight. She danced to the strains of half-heard music through bare, unfinished rooms. She pattered down dusty spiral corridors and bounded up raw concrete stairs. She posed in arabesques at unglazed windows.

Beyond one unwalled floor hung a steel girder that gleamed like polished bone in the moonlight. She leapt upon it and ran its length. However slowly or swiftly she moved, the beam held steady: it was as if she possessed no weight at all. Untroubled by fear of falling, she could spin and balance at will for the sheer pleasure of feeling her gown swirl.

She gestured skyward and the crane silently hauled her perch aloft.

The roof was her proper stage, a shining platform so vast its edge defined the horizon. The music came clearer. She circled ever closer to the living tree at its center. She was leaping higher and higher at every turn. She could clear the tree if she chose. She could jump all the way to Polaris on a whim. Nothing was beyond her reach.

For now it was enough to dance and watch the evergreen grow.

At last she recognized the music. It was the hymn-tune theme from *Appalachian Spring* that swelled around her:

> 'Tis the gift to be simple, 'tis the gift to be free,
> 'Tis the gift to come down where we ought to be,

And the fir tree soared up to the stars. . . .

❋   ❋   ❋

Ria's exaltation endured into the new work week. One especially welcome effect was her new confidence in dealings with Hannah.

Monday afternoon, Ria deliberately returned from lunch early to speak with her foe in private. Hannah never ate a real lunch. She claimed to subsist on an occasional millet seed or bean sprout.

The petite blonde was sorting papers, performing even this simple task with ostentatious grace, in case an audience should suddenly materialize. Hannah did not simply crumple unwanted printout sheets. She folded them into rigidly tidy packets, running her thumbnail along each crease to make it sharp.

"Back so soon, Ria?" she asked, not bothering to turn around. "I could tell it was you by your walk. Have you ever thought of taking dance lessons? It could restructure your whole pattern of movement."

"I'm content to leave the dancing to you." The corner of Ria's mouth twitched as she remembered last night's dream. "Actually, dancing's what I want to talk to you about. I saw a notice for your group recital on the House calendar this morning. I'd like to buy a ticket."

"You would?" Hannah spun around in her chair, staring up at Ria.

"Yes. Make that two tickets."

"Two?"

"One for me and one for Carey." Ria restrained a smirk, content to merely loom over her rival. How tiny the other woman was. On stage, she'd be just one small pale body among many.

"I didn't think you were interested in dance." Hannah ruffled her papers.

"Given a choice, I'd sooner watch traditional ballet, but elitist art's out of fashion."

"And quite properly so. All that unhealthy adulation of soloists. Today's choral dance, on the other hand—"

"You don't have to sell me your art, just the tickets."

"I'll bring them tomorrow. You had no cause to snap at me." She swept her remaining printouts into the wastebasket, slipping out from under Ria's gaze.

At that point Ali and Carey returned. They must have eaten lunch together. Carey nodded briefly at the other two women and retreated to his desk. The eczema on his neck looked raw.

"I saw Professor Clyde on the way, Ria," said Ali. "He's looking forward to your progress report Friday. How fares the project?"

"Well enough," answered Ria.

She left Ali wondering what that might mean and settled down to work.

Not only was Ria's research progressing, she was actually enjoying it—for all that she felt guilty about finding pleasure in a study of death and destruction. Even at a safe historical distance, human suffering appalled her, yet its patterns fascinated her nonetheless.

Disasters and Destiny ought to be a notable book. She regretted that she wouldn't be writing it herself. With luck, perhaps Professor Clyde might acknowledge her contribution. In any event, satisfactory completion of the assignment would mean extra work points. One couldn't have too many of those.

She began investigating the role of human error in these catastrophes. How had folly and misjudgment made them worse? Pompeii should've had few casualties—Vesuvius gave ample warning—yet many residents had perished because they were unwilling to flee. Up until the last moment, they kept hoping the deadly rain of ash would cease.

The Minoans, in contrast, had evacuated Thera in time. It wasn't the eruption that killed them, but the tidal wave and crop failures that followed—or so the theory ran. Ria wondered if memories of prudent flight were much comfort to those who starved to death later.

Not that there was any question of forethought saving lives. Modern building codes and emergency policies did make a difference. That had been proven from Pacifica to Pan-Asia. Until the Federation had imposed uniform safety regulations worldwide, too many people had kept rebuilding on the ashes of their forebears and died when their turn came.

Fraud used to make the cost of apathy worse. In the twentieth century, West Coast cities used to conceal the location of fault lines, lest fear inhibit urban growth. On the Caribbean island of Martinique, politicians had deliberately concealed a volcanic threat because they wanted their supporters kept home to vote on election day. The lying officials had been incinerated right along with Mount Pelée's thirty thousand other victims.

Perhaps it was best not to put too much blame on governments. A man in Clyde's position had to be politically sensitive. He wouldn't want anything controversial in his book, lest he offend the powers that made grants and assigned privileges.

Still, if the data were there, readers might draw their own conclusions. They might start wondering if the Pacific coast was really as secure against the coming of the oft-predicted Big Quake as the authorities claimed.

Matters continued on this favorable course for the next three days. Ria discovered that she could move Hannah about the office like a chess pawn simply by standing over her or invading her personal space too closely. The game was so easy that it soon bored her.

Ria knew it was unwise to back an enemy into a corner, but her new-found confidence was making her reckless. She walked taller and straighter, now that she no longer cringed. When Ali remarked on her brighter mood, Ria let her imagine it was the result of counseling.

The spell held until Thursday night's dream. . . .

    ❋   ❋   ❋

The captain and the pilot had chosen to bicker in English, their only common language. He could make out enough of it himself to follow their arguments—and to wish he could not. They had been at it ever since the pilot had boarded off Ponta Munduba.

To begin with, the Old Man had no sympathy for Latinos. Said they all had a *mañana* complex. (That should be an *amanha* complex in the case of *Senhora* Pilot, no?) And he didn't much care for women, either.

Now they were arguing about the speed of approach.

Everybody on the bridge could feel the tension. The captain was complaining that they'd miss their target time. He kept pointing to the digital clock. Did she have any notion of what it cost to transport liquefied natural gas? They were burning money by the minute. (Not to mention the captain's bonus.) Perhaps they would prefer to burn cargo? With bay traffic snarled by a recent wreck, *Kyushu Maru* would have to wait its turn.

The captain fretted. He refused to sit in either of his chairs, but kept pacing the length of the bridge.

The first officer had sailed with the esteemed *Capitán* long enough to be used to his moods. He tried to ignore the situation, standing ready at the pilot's side to relay her orders when they came.

But the rabbity *alemán* at the helm looked as if he'd rather be anywhere else at the moment. That pale body was visibly quivering. For his own part, he was glad to be tucked safely behind the lines with nothing more taxing to do than keep the log.

Vessel Traffic finally gave them the signal and they headed up towards Santos. The pilot was conscientious, you had to give her that. She watched the windows as well as the displays. But she gave so many course corrections that he had trouble logging them all.

The captain's running commentary was not helping anybody's concentration, especially when he pounced on an ambiguous order. He made her clarify that she meant "to 20 degrees" and not "220 degrees." This puffed his ego at the expense of breaking her cadence. The helmsman's face was turning gray.

No sooner had they gotten that squared away than the collision alarm sounded. Radar blips showed an oncoming freighter veering out of her channel to cut around the wrong side of the buoys marking the wreck. They blew five blasts at her.

What was the cowboy trying to do? Pass them starboard to starboard? Getting entirely too close. They ought to be turning by now. Why weren't they turning?

The captain was shouting.

Then he noticed why.

¡Dios mio! The helmsman was frozen in place.

The pilot whirled to confront him, repeating her order with horrible clarity. The first officer heeded and wrenched the wheel free.

They went hard starboard.

With his own hands, the captain pulled the hapless seaman out of the way and flung him in a corner. Then the captain stood at the windows, his hands balled into fists against the glass, in silence that was worse than cursing.

The freighter skimmed by them at the last moment. The gap between the two craft was so narrow, they could read the name *Nelson Beak* on her bow. She was barely starting to swing back safely into her own channel. . . .

❋　　❋　　❋

Ria awoke shuddering convulsively. The bad dreams had returned. She had only won a skirmish, not the war.

All too well she recognized the event she'd just dreamed. It wasn't much of a feat. Almost any adult now living could recite the bald facts.

In 1984, the liquefied natural gas carrier *Kyushu Maru* had collided with vessel or vessels unknown outside the industrial city of Santos in what was then Brazil. The cloud of escaping fuel had enveloped the harbor and exploded, thereby detonating the huge gas storage facilities ashore, which in turn obliterated tank farms, refineries, petrochemical plants, an airbase—

And every human being within a 20-kilometer radius. A million souls, more or less.

The *Incendio*, as it came to be called, had triggered anti-tech riots all over the globe. The Collapse followed. After a decade of depression, famine, and war, the Federation had emerged to impose a new world order, one that still reigned.

The causes of the *Incendio* had been investigated for 30 years without precise conclusions. *Kyushu Maru*'s role was obvious, since she had been the only LNGC present at the time. The identity of the other craft involved was unknown.

Until now.

Ria wasn't going to bother checking out the fate of the

freighter *Nelson Beak*. What she had seen was no figment of her imagination. It had really happened. She was now unshakably certain of that.

A belligerent captain, a nervous pilot, and a catatonic helmsman had brought down civilization.

The knowledge was more than she could bear. She huddled in a tight fetal ball. But the nightmare had to be true. The only alternative was to admit madness.

VIII

For a long time Ria lay huddled in bed, all her senses smothered by panic.

When she revived, there was a taste of blood in her mouth. She rolled over numbly to check the clock—she hadn't heard the alarm buzz—and discovered that she was already late for work.

She scrambled out of bed and called the office. Luckily, it was Carey who answered. He accepted her excuse more readily than the women would've. She made him promise to stay away until she let him know she felt better. After rescheduling her appointment with Professor Clyde, she made herself a huge breakfast.

Food had its usual tranquilizing effect. She could at least start confronting her problems again. Watching the *Incendio* begin had left her devastated. No one should—

Insight struck so fast, Ria knocked over her teacup. She didn't bother to blot the spill off her robe.

The disaster had *not* happened!

The two ships had scraped past safely in her dream—no collision, no million deaths.

That was the single factor common to her four latest dreams. Each had shown a disaster averted: no Time of Troubles for Russia, no Fourth Crusade in Constantinople, no peacemaker slain in India, no city leveled in Brazil.

She'd been getting too entangled in the historical details to grasp the recurring theme. Were these dreams mere wish fulfillments, yearnings for what might have been?

No delusions could be that realistic—or schematic. The

four dreams of disaster averted dovetailed too precisely with the earlier trio of waiting dreams to be the products of mere chance.

Ria scribbled summaries of all the dreams on paper. She attacked each as if it were a myth-text. Analyzing structures, she extracted the recurring motifs—fire, water, travel, ascent, birth, death, peril, victory. She reduced events to their simplest scenario—expectation, crisis, salvation. The patterns were so pronounced that they suggested a code.

Who could be sending her such messages? Nothing in the available scientific literature suggested that specific dream-plots could be induced. If PSI could beam particular images into her head wherever she was, day and night, then PSI could do anything. She might as well slash her wrists right now and have done with it.

Never! It would give her mother's ghost too much satisfaction.

Even if PSI's vaunted powers were finite, she might still be the subject of someone else's experiment. Ria could not shake the feeling of being cheered through a laboratory maze by joyful cries too faint to hear.

Joy was not a word one associated with PSI. Neither was *cheer*. Then who was conducting the experiment? The mysterious old woman and her giant otter were the only candidates left. Could phantoms design the illusions they appeared in?

Ria's glimpse of those two had been every bit as realistic as her other historical dreams. Talking otters did not exist and had never existed—

But could she prove that they could never exist in the future . . . in *a* future?

Allow one possibility and an army of others would rush through the breach. Ria was amazed at her own calmness. The precision of her logic overpowered its sheer insanity. So beings possessed of vast and arcane powers were tampering with her mind for inscrutable and transcendent purposes. Ah, psychosis were paradise enow.

Enough of the gallows humor. The beings in her dream—what were their names? Kara and Lute?—had seemed entirely earnest. They had claimed they were going to teach her something. . . .

But of what earthly use was the power to dream on cue? Did it perhaps have some *un*earthly use? She'd spun all the theories she could on her own and changed her opinions too many times. The only way to get real answers was to question her self-appointed instructors themselves.

Any form of communication had to work in both directions. If they were able to send messages, then they ought to be able to receive them equally well. Ria disdained to speak her request aloud. Let the others read it directly from her mind. Let them show her another instance of disaster averted. Only this time, let the example be drawn from her own research files—something with a volcano or an earthquake. Make that a volcano.

Were Kara and Lute listening?

Ria flopped on the unmade bed, folded her arms, and waited for results.

Nothing happened.

She had forgotten to trip the trigger. She needed the flash of a shining surface to begin a waking dream. She rose, grabbed a dirty teaspoon, and polished it clean on the sleeve of her robe.

No sooner had she resettled herself on the bed than the bowl of the spoon dissolved into dark, choppy waves. . . .

❋ ❋ ❋

He could scarcely see the crescent of beach through the constant pattering rain of ash. The pretty town beyond with its tile roofs and banana trees was completely hidden. Stifling dust had been falling for days. It fouled the ocean and lay in heaps on *Roraima*'s unswept decks. It sifted into the fabric of his uniform and clung to his sweaty skin. He wiped his face once again in silence, too dispirited to curse. His collar itched abominably. His nose and lungs alike protested the sulfurous reek in the air. The sky was filthy and empty of sea birds.

Babbling sounds in French drew his attention back to his duty. Another longboat crammed with excitable refugees was coming alongside—another pack of die-hards who'd insisted on staying too long. Not all of them would be spry enough to manage the Jacob's ladder. He must see that the crew got them safely bestowed by other means.

Blue lightning flickered in the clouds about Mount Pelée. . . .

✻   ✻   ✻

Ria wavered back to consciousness. Her phone was ringing. She half-expected to hear Kara's voice on the line but it was only Ali, calling during her lunch hour to check on Ria's illness.

"It took you so long to answer, I was getting concerned," said Ali.

"Sorry. I just got back into the apartment. I'd been out of it for a moment. You mustn't make so much out of a simple case of indigestion."

"Carey gave us the impression it was something more—because he tried so hard to make it seem trivial. Now Ria, it's my nature to be fussy—and my duty as well. With what all's been happening to you lately, I had to find out for myself how you were doing."

"A little bit better than when I first woke up. Please don't worry about me." Ria tried to sound properly meek and grateful.

"Now if this continues, you will go over to Health Service?"

"It won't come to that. Really. I'm sure I'll be back at my desk by Monday." She could stall that long before an examination became mandatory.

"No chance we'll see you at the Library Halloween party tomorrow night?" Ali was in no hurry to release her. "I hate to see you miss all that fun."

"You can have my share of the treats, Ali. Thanks for calling."

Ria hung up before her supervisor could prolong the conversation further. She'd forgotten about the departmental party, but judged it fun well missed. She'd be under even more scrutiny there than at House festivities. These days she felt safer out from under the shadow of Ali's wings.

Ria munched on an apple while rewinding her thoughts. Her order for a volcano dream had been filled briskly enough: she and her obliging instructors must've read the same sources. She recognized the scene as an evacuation

from the city of St. Pierre before the eruption of Mount
Pelée on 8 May, 1902. The disaster they called "The Day
the World Ended" wasn't going to happen there. Wherever *there* was.

But what of the fantasy dreams, the ones that had nothing to do with history or reality? What was she supposed
to learn from those horrid ordeals—climbing techniques?
That was the sole recurring element she could identify in
her struggles with the rope, the mast, the cave, and even
the lovely interlude on the rooftop. If Kara and Lute
wanted to cause distress, surely a nightmare about walking
stark naked down Neil Street would've served as well.
That had been one of her commonest—and presumably
spontaneous—nightmares during her years at University
High School.

Whatever their purpose, let them give her something of
her own choosing to climb now. How good were they at
improvisation? Ria closed her eyes and pulled a book off
the nearest shelf at random. Luckily, *Myths of Ancient
America* was illustrated.

She pitched her apple core in the direction of the sink
and paged through the book. The pyramid of Quetzalcoatl
at Teotihuacán would do as well as anything for the experiment. She fixed the image in her mind and slammed the
book closed with a crack.

She lay down again crying, "Once more into the spoon,
dear friends. . . ."

        *   *   *

The steps were treacherously narrow and steep. They
were never intended for feet as large as hers. She could
easily catch her heel on a chipped edge or cracked tread.
No proper balustrade, either. It was such a long way down
if she stumbled.

Why was she here? Would the view from the top be
worth it? The calves of her legs were beginning to quiver
already. She brushed vainly at gnats. The sun was making
her dizzy. It hadn't seemed so hot when she started. She
should have waited for a cooler day.

The carved stone heads of the feathered serpent flanking the stairs shimmered in the heat. They were melting

before her eyes, gaping jaws softening into a blunt muzzle, scales flowing into fur. The whole pyramid was stretching and flexing like a living thing.

The pitch of the steps rose ever steeper. She was crawling up them now on all fours, tearing fingernails as she clawed for purchase, yet the gap between her and the summit only widened.

A broad, bewhiskered head as big as a temple appeared on the platform above. The stairway was no longer stone but rippling hide. She lost her grip and skidded down into darkness. . . .

    ❋   ❋   ❋

Ria awoke more indignant than disappointed. The pyramid had shrugged her off as easily as a huge beast shaking off an insect. Was that all she was to them, a human fly who could be forced to scale impossible obstacles? Psychic sadists—that's what they were!

She'd get her freedom yet, no matter how many climbs it took.

She hurled her spoon down with such force, it bounced off the bed. Her apartment was too cramped to pace in properly. All her long strides accomplished was the bruising of her shin on a corner of the bed. Bending down to rub the scrape, she collided with the table, nearly knocking the flimsy thing over.

Oh, to be someplace where she could safely scream!

Ria stomped to the window and pounded her fists on the sill. An autumn storm was blowing up. Rain beat against the glass, mocking her fury. Wind shook the water-blinded panes. Sirens faintly blared above the howling but she could see nothing of the world outside.

How small a thing her anger was. She pressed her forehead against the chill glass. She willed the coolness of it into her mind, trying to breathe in rhythm with the pelting rain. She poured herself into the water that ranged so free.

The windowsill she leaned against became the leading edge of a chariot. She was a goddess driving the pale horses of the storm before her: Rain and Sleet, Fog and Snow. Down they sped from high heaven, wheels that rolled thunder, and hooves that flashed lightning. They galloped across an empty prairie that knew no bounds.

The rain slackened; her anger ebbed.

She could again see traffic moving on the street below. Its flow fairly hypnotized her, all those new-washed busses, trucks, and bikes. Reflections of their lights traced bright tracks on the wet, black pavement. Pedestrians streamed by, comfortably anonymous in their raingear, safe in the company of their shrouded fellows.

But she was alone, trapped in her cell of a room, wrestling her private and particular demons.

Hearty bean soup for dinner calmed Ria's shivers and cleared her mind to attack the mystery once more. It was easier to feel stubborn on a full stomach.

Perhaps she had been too arrogant in her choice of battlefield. Her mentors—tormentors, rather—wouldn't allow her to complete the climb in a hostile mood. So the pyramid had mischievously turned into a colossal animal. Not just any creature, an otter. A *smiling* otter. They were said to be a playful species.

If the naturalists only knew! She wished the being called Lute would find himself some other plaything.

Why couldn't they permit her some activity besides climbing for a change? What was so special about that? Ria knew that in myth, ascension was a well-nigh universal metaphor for spiritual progress: one had to struggle upward toward the Light.

A generalization that broad was little help. For specifics, she must tap data banks. Ria punched out a preliminary search program on ascent symbolism in world mythology, keyworded with motifs from all her dreams. She avoided reading the printouts until she had cleaned up the dishes.

This done, she hefted the stack of paper, fanned it through her fingers, pretending to estimate the amount of computer time this research was costing. She read the hard copy with skittish glances, afraid to linger too long on any one line. She tried hard not to see the emerging pattern, but truth trapped her before she'd finished. She'd known the answer from childhood without recognizing it, known it ever since she first rode a dream-horse with eight wooden legs.

Ria sat motionless for a long time. Desk and wall blurred out to her unblinking stare like backgrounds viewed through a close-focus lens. There was no place left to hide from self-knowledge.

She sighed her resignation and entered orders for the appropriate reference books. At least one of them was by Eliade, a familiar authority to guide her explorations. She needed all the briefing she could absorb before attempting any more dream journeys.

Tomorrow was soon enough to try again—assuming she'd be allowed to rest tonight. By now, she was too numb to be anything but humble in her plea for a respite from more visions.

Saturday morning found Ria no more eager for confrontation than the previous evening. Unexpectedly, her schedule gave her an excuse for delay: she was due to pick up her bi-weekly grocery order.

Ria groomed herself for this routine public appearance with almost ritualistic care. There was a cautious touch of self-assertion in the new way she twisted her hair into coils and tinted her skin. If she could face a throng of housemates now, perhaps she could face an old woman and an otter later.

The lines at the loading dock moved as slowly as usual. This time, however, instead of trying to shut out her tedious surroundings, Ria forced herself to observe the people around her as distinct individuals. Wearing a uniform didn't automatically make anyone a cipher, much less an enemy. Each person was still unique, could she but see it.

Ria tried tabulating the body language displayed by the buyers—even the typical resigned slump had multiple variations. Most waited as she did, in passive silence; others chattered nonstop, flaunting their sociability. The voices of two women behind her stood out in the general buzz.

"So when the results were posted yesterday, Barby, I wasn't all that surprised. I always win at the first New Orleans race meet."

"Jen, I know your luck holds at the Gulf tracks and

practically everywhere else, but the horses you tell me to bet on most times run in slow motion."

"Some of us have that certain instinct. Don't look so glum. I'll buy you a drink out of my winnings. On my quota, yet."

"Your quota?" A laugh. "You sure do know how to get round me." There were small giggles. "I'll return the favor if my lottery ticket—my Regional Game lottery ticket—comes up. When I think of all the slop work I did around the House to earn that particular piece of paper. . . ."

"But look at the payoff. Credit alone won't get you past the door of a Restricted Access shop."

"That's what keeps me playing year after year. I want that admission card and the chance to dress like a department head."

"How exactly *do* they dress on their own time?"

"You know, I'm not all that sure. But I want to find out. This time it's going to work. Mind you, I didn't grab the first ticket on the list. I picked the number by this special formula, very scientific. First, you take your birthdate. . . ."

Ria reached the counter and missed the precious details of Barby's scheme. By the time she'd taken delivery of all her supplies, she'd stood in line three more times and was bloated with other people's intimacies. She had ample opportunity to reflect that cooperative shopping was a triumph of ideology over common sense.

On her final haul, Ria had the satisfaction of saving the pumpkin that an old man had dropped down the stairs. She blocked it with her foot before it could roll all the way down and smash. The owner's gratitude more than compensated for her bruises. She regretted not ordering a pumpkin for herself. A cheerful jack-o'-lantern would have brightened the apartment this Halloween night.

Ria stowed all the food immediately instead of leaving it scattered about the kitchenette as she often did. She also washed the dishes promptly after lunch. Instinctively, she felt that her quarters ought to be in perfect order before she attempted further experiments. Cleanliness was an outward sign of inner discipline. However, there was some delay in achieving that state. Cleaning equipment was in heavy demand today, so she had to wait her turn at the ultrasweeper.

Later, while straightening stacks of tapes on the shelf over her window, she witnessed a street accident.

An Illibus rammed a slow-moving delivery van into a tree. The van driver crawled out of her airbags and beat at the sealed door of the bus. Ria could imagine what language punctuated those futile blows. Security Officers arrived and subdued her before she could reach the other driver. They'd call it another noncomp incident rather than recognize it for simple human frustration.

The damaged vehicle was soon removed. Ria had to admit she'd run out of ways to waste time. She meant to reach the old woman and the otter today, on this the night when the Door Between the Worlds swung open. She'd keep at it until she hammered down the barrier—or her mind shattered.

Brave intentions were one thing, figuring out the mechanics, another. Should she try to rig up some sort of costume? She decided that she was most typically herself clad in the University's livery. Also, she ought to redo her hair again. And she wanted a more dignified instrument for inducing the trance than a teaspoon.

Ria rummaged in the bathroom cabinet until she found a small steel travel mirror her grandmother had given her. She'd never had occasion to use it before.

Lastly, she needed a focal image. What was the noblest thing she could mentally climb? Only a mountain would do. Make that *mountains*—The Mountains of the Mind.

Ria lay down, on her belly this time, with the mirror cupped in her hands. She flashed afternoon sunbeams in her eyes and fixed her gaze on *Strange Peaks Above the Clouds*. She was blinding herself to see more perfectly. A watery shimmer glistened in the air between her and the door. . . .

❋   ❋   ❋

She had left the gray village behind. The road sloped gently at first, then lost itself in a barren maze of folds and fissures. She could not have retraced her steps if she had tried.

She chose the path that seemed the straightest, but it only led her along the mountain's flank to the edge of a wide crevasse.

The sole route past the gap was slashed by clefts she had to leap. The crumbling stone trembled beneath her weight. Every step sent more fragments tumbling noisily into the depths. Once across, a series of meandering switchbacks brought her to the first summit.

She gazed past a river of mist to the higher range beyond. Much as she dreaded the climb ahead, she had to reach those peaks or perish. Mist was too thin a barrier to bar her. It had no more substance than fear. A road she could not see would take her past the boundary. Blinded, drenched, and chilled, she trudged along the hidden way.

All the cracks led upward on the other side. She followed one fissure to the foot of weathered battlements ringing the highest peak. The storms of years had beaten like surf against this citadel of stone. Its eroded walls, rough as bark, offered natural footholds for her hands and feet. She climbed through thinning air that seared her lungs with cold. At this height, the wind blew without pause or pity.

Layer by layer, it scoured away her clothes, her skin, her very flesh. She was a shining skeleton toiling across a white mantle of eternal snow. Where this covering had blown away, ridges of pure crystal glittered, setting rainbows dancing on the frozen waste.

The final slope was as gentle as the first. At last she reached the ultimate pinnacle, a spur upraised against an inky sky.

Kara and Lute were waiting to welcome her there.

❋ ❋ ❋

IX

Kara and Lute leaned over the bed, looking exactly as they had before. Ria was back under the same blue and white coverlet, animating the same young male body as on her earlier visit.

"How dare you smile!" she screamed. "After what you've done to me!"

Ria tore back the covers and struggled to rise, but her borrowed limbs would not respond. Each movement sent pins and needles of pain stabbing through her. With a massive effort, she managed to pull her torso nearly upright.

Lute's furry arms barred further progress. She tried to squirm away from his touch.

"Let go of me," she cried.

"Rest easy, dear lady, rest easy now." Lute gently lifted her under the arms while Kara slipped pillows behind her back.

Neither of them seemed disturbed by Ria's anger. Why should they be? She was scarcely a threatening figure, lying pinned against the headboard, wearing only a night-shirt hiked over her knees. She clawed at the sheet in short, jerky strokes.

"When you decide to sit still, child, Lute will release you," said the old woman, picking up the staff and drum she'd laid on the bedcovers.

"Do I have a choice?" Ria glared at her.

"We can't allow you to move freely until you've learned to control young Julo's body," Kara explained.

"If you fall, Ria, he gets left with bruises."

Lute pulled the covers up to Ria's waist. He fetched a chair so Kara could sit near the head of the bed. Then he settled down beside her, resting on his haunches.

Ria sullenly counted the leaves woven into the coverlet rather than face Kara's serenity or Lute's huge, happy eyes. This wasn't the kind of confrontation she'd planned.

Lute broke the silence. "Ria, I'm glad you're back, so glad m'whiskers are tingling." The otter's speech trailed off into pleasant burbles and the bells on his harness jingled softly.

"Winning your way here is an achievement that stands," said Kara matter-of-factly, "whether you take joy in it or not."

"What was I supposed to enjoy?" Ria snarled. "The electrocution? The seizures? The endless nightmares? You must excuse my lack of gratitude."

"Were all your dreams nightmares?" Kara asked.

"Of course!" Ria turned to snap at her tormentor.

The white-clad old woman sat patient as stone.

"No, not quite," Ria admitted. "Dancing on that rooftop was glorious. I wanted that dream to last forever." Her voice fell to a whisper.

"Every ending is a beginning," said Kara. "The seed dies so that the tree can grow. For the moment, your ears are closed to what we are telling you."

"What I want you to tell me are some answers." Ria's tone sharpened again.

"So ask us a question. Come on, ask us anything."

Lute bobbed up and down, making his bells jangle again. Kara stilled him with a tap of her staff. She folded her hands over the hide drum on her lap.

Ria swallowed hard. "What I want to know . . . is . . ." She swallowed again. "You're shamans, both of you."

Kara bowed and touched her broad bosom: "*Solexa*," she said. She pointed to Lute: "*Solexam*." He kissed the tips of his stubby fingers at Ria.

Her pent-up tensions had burst like a boil, easing Ria's hostility.

"I finally figured it out last night. My mind must be a little slow—it had to be battered to the breaking point before it reacted. I should've guessed you were shamans right away, just from your gear."

"You mean Kara looks like some wisewoman's picture you've seen?"

"No. She looks like all of them." Ria took a deep breath before continuing. "Can't you get enough recruits wherever you are? What possessed you to try making a shaman out of *me*?" She twisted her hands together awkwardly.

"But Ria," protested the otter, "You agreed to take instruction in *solarti*. We forced nothing on you 'gainst your will."

"I didn't realize what I was getting into," said Ria.

Kara's silence rebuked the excuse.

Ria continued. "You promised to teach me marvelous things. You promised to show me the way over the mountains in my childhood Dream."

"Child, we are doing exactly as we promised," replied Kara. "Each journey begins with a single step. You must learn to climb ropes before mountain ranges. You did not think to ask the cost of the knowledge we offered."

"It hurts too much to learn your lore."

"How else could you win it, except through pain?" Kara's shrug expressed her opinion of Ria's pain threshold. "Would you argue with the hard-won wisdom of a hundred centuries?"

"Not to mention six centuries among the *perfur*?" Lute broke in. "More of us persons of fur have the soul-art than persons of skin."

Kara clasped her comrade's furry hand. "Neither we nor anyone else can teach you how to shamanize by rote," she said. "We can only place you in situations that allow you to discover the core of the art for yourself."

"In effect, you threw me in the water to make me learn to swim."

"Yes." Kara placed her right hand on Ria's shoulder. "To you, child, the initiation seemed a long and terrible ordeal. In reality, it was among the shortest I have witnessed in my long practice of *solarti*."

Lute rose and stood behind Kara.

"Listen and believe, Ria," he said, stretching out every word with uncharacteristic solemnity, "from sea to sea runs the fame of Kara ni Prizing. No greater *solex* has been born into our age."

"If you're so important, then why are you bothering with a nobody like me?" Ria began to cry.

Lute started to reach out to her but Kara waved him back.

"You are scarcely qualified to judge yourself, child. Your talent called to us out of a time not ours. By our oath to our art, we could not leave that call unanswered."

"If you had a young one with a gift for making music," said Lute, "would you cultivate it or let it wither?" His muzzle wrinkled. "M'sister used to twist my tail when I didn't practice my *gouar* enough. Not as some say—" he gave Kara a hurt look "— when I practiced it too much."

The byplay was lost on Ria. She demanded their full attention.

"Altruism always sounds fine in principle. What do you get out of this?" Ria glanced from one to the other.

Kara's blue eyes caught hers.

"I get the one thing life's denied me—a true daughter of my spirit."

Ria's face twisted in revulsion. She covered it with her hands to hide her tears.

"Dear lady," sighed Lute. "We know why you're crying. Mustn't be afraid of us. Hands down, please, and look at me."

Ria wiped her blubbery cheeks as best she could and turned towards the otter. Calm spread over her mind like a cool mist. Blotting her tears on a corner of the sheet, she realized she was now using the borrowed limbs as her own.

Kara continued: "I had no child of the flesh. My niece who is now the Wisewoman of Chamba in my stead is a good enough worker in my way, but not the kindred spirit I longed for. No apprentice—no *human* apprentice—" she winked at Lute, "has grown as tall as I'd have wished."

"And you think that I—oh no! I come from a world of science, not magic. I work with books and bytes of data," Ria protested frantically. "I can't talk with animals or summon spirits or sense weather or handle fire like a shaman is supposed to."

"Can't you?" Lute snuffled merrily and shook his bells. Kara could barely suppress her laughter.

"What's so funny?"

"You." The otter gasped between snorts. "You don't know yourself as well as we do."

"What Lute means," said Kara, punctuating her comments with taps on her drum, "is that you seem determined not to recognize your unique gifts." She touched Ria's arm lightly with her staff. "You mentioned the mastery of fire—a key *solarti* power. Consider: You survived an electric shock unburned. Both heat and cold affect you less than other people. In your tenth year, you kindled a grass fire with your unaided mind."

Ria's mind went blind with panic.

The old woman continued, "Ah yes, we saw you do that. Such a burst of talent drew us to you like a beacon."

"Deny your powers if you choose," Lute added, "but they're inborn, just like ours."

"Once we'd discovered you," Kara said, "we could not bear to lose you." She patted Ria's hand. "Lute tracked you back to your beginnings and implanted that Dream of riding over the mountains. You had already taught yourself how to enter trances while astride the rocking horse. He merely placed the proper scenery before you on your flights."

"Images came right out of your memory, they did. The art's all in the arrangement. Not a bad job, eh?" Lute's whiskers twitched. "Dream wore like hardwood over the years, didn't it?"

"Lute's asking you to compliment his handiwork, Ria. He's proud—perhaps too proud—of his skill as a dream-shaper. It wouldn't occur to him to wait until you knew more about the art before asking for praise." She raised a thick white eyebrow. "Now by your gracious leave, my dear *perfur*, I shall continue."

Lute pretended to ignore her remark. He sat meekly stroking his chin whiskers. It was Ria's turn to smile.

Kara went on. "Lute rekindled the mountain Dream within you throughout your youth—we had to keep you yearning for the heights. But once you were a grown woman, stronger measures were needed to drive you upward."

"For the present," said Ria, "I'll take it on faith that you did to me what you thought was necessary. I can accept you as the source of those weird climbing dreams. I can even understand the symbolism behind them." She brought the tips of her fingers together. "But how could you make me experience unfamiliar episodes from history, episodes that never occurred in my world? How could you alter events in the past that happened before you knew I existed?"

"The places we reach are real enough, but located in times branched off from ours." Lute pantomimed the growth of a tree.

"In theory," continued Kara, "all leaves on the Cosmic Tree are equally accessible at any moment. There are limits in practice. About fifteen hundred years backwards or forwards in time is all we can attain."

"Is all any known *solex* has reached." Lute interrupted the old woman. "Kara says I'm too proud, but she's too modest. She's given the ancient soul-art new twists that make our jumps a lot more precise."

Kara waved his compliments away. "But I did need mathematicians to turn my ideas into equations and it's still the territory that holds my interest, not the map."

"Mathematicians?" Ria sat bolt upright.

"Our university here in Chamba has several fine ones. Did you take us for barbarians, child?"

"More to civilization than plastic furniture, Ria." Lute's fur bristled. "Chamba's University is one of the best in the Republic."

"I meant no offense." Ria's shoulders sagged. "But I still can't make sense of what you're saying. Do you expect me to believe in the possibility of mental time-travel?"

"*Possibility?* All those soul-flights and you still can't believe? What does it take to convince a human?" Lute snorted in puzzlement.

"I'm trying as hard as I can to believe. While things are happening, I start to be convinced. Afterwards, doubt always creeps back on sly little paws—and I wonder if I'm going mad."

"Arguments create no faith." Kara shook her head. "You

must seek the truth within yourself. Once you learn to trust your own experiences, we can help you perfect your skill at soul-flight."

"Our help's yours for the asking, Ria."

"You're still talking in riddles. What is this 'soul-flight' business?" Ria was startled at her own shrillness.

"Exactly what the name says—travel in spirit." Lute's muzzle wrinkled in puzzlement.

Kara turned toward him. "She's not comfortable with the word *soul*. People in her world have forgotten that they have them."

Then she asked Ria: "Would you prefer *essence*? *Persona*? Or *the standing wave that is the sum of all one's living functions*? Whatever you chose to call it, this inmost self is what we who are blessed with the talent can project into the bodies of other persons, here or on other branches of the Cosmic Tree."

Ria responded in a halting voice. "The medieval schoolmen used to say: 'An angel is where he works.' "

"Quite right!" cried Lute.

Kara continued. "Angels aren't the only ones to fly unseen. Once inside a host, we can tap memory and use senses without being detected."

"Then what's my body doing while the 'essential I'—as you put it—is here?"

"Running like clockwork," said Lute. "You'll return to it in a few moments of your own time. With practice, you'll flash in and out in an eyeblink."

Ria shuddered. "It sounds like possession—a better pastime for devils than angels—if there were such a thing as possession, of course."

"Devils indeed!" The otter sprang to his feet, bells jingling madly. "Are you a devil? You're in Julo's body, looking out through his eyes, speaking with his mouth. And in what language, eh?"

Ria gabbled briefly in English, suddenly self-conscious about using the boy's memory. She could not talk and think of *how* she was talking at the same time. Her speech trailed off into gibberish.

"Easy, m'lady. You being there doesn't hurt Julo. He likes playing host, says it's the soundest sleep he ever gets. We're not making him do anything we haven't done ourselves, many times over—receiving and exchanging souls is part of *solarti*, too."

Kara motioned him to be seated again. "Julo is a special case. His persona slumbers while another is in residence. He's proud of his talent—it's the only one he has left since his brain was injured."

"Julo got kicked in the head by a horse," said Lute, tapping his own skull. "But he has enough wits left to be good help for us 'round the house."

"He wouldn't be alive, much less able to do anything, without *solarti*. I was visiting his parents' farm at the time of the mishap. I numbed his pain, controlled clotting, and reduced swelling until the doctor came. Lute still treats his bad headaches."

"You've lost me again." Ria had her syntax under control once more. "What does soul-flight as you've described it have to do with medicine? Shamanic healing was all suggestion and sleight-of-hand."

"Still, those suggestions sometimes cured, although the old shamans didn't know the real reason why," said Lute.

"Think, Ria." Kara waved her staff. "Surely you know that pain, fear, grief, madness, and so forth have a chemical basis. Disposition and attitude can affect recovery. Having access to a host's nervous system, a *solex* can alter brain chemistry and stimulate individual cells to foster a cure. When the subject is well known to the *solex*, this can be done without soul-flight, as when Lute calmed you a few moments ago."

"Healing of minds and bodies is the biggest part of a *solex*'s work." Lute preened at the usefulness of his gift. "Taking away hurt, giving peace, that's what I love to do." His huge dark eyes glowed.

"I've read that shamans can deliberately induce or stop seizures in themselves. Are you saying this is some kind of telekinesis on the molecular scale?"

"Down to the electronic scale." Kara corrected her. "That is how we can master fire—or electricity. For all that your world is scientific, I may have a more intimate acquaintance with the electron than you do."

"Kara." Lute tapped the old woman's arm. "I think

we're overloading her. We don't have to explain every-thing at once."

"Very well. We'll dismiss you in a moment, Ria."

Her weathered face turned solemn. She raised her staff in formal salute.

"One more test awaits you before the fullness of the art can be yours," Kara proclaimed. "We will summon you again later tonight. You must go where you are sent. Stay there no matter what happens. And eat well before you retire—*solarti* requires tremendous energy. If you had a God, I would suggest you pray, but since you have none—"

"We'll do the praying for you," Lute added.

Ria turned from one to the other. She fought the quaver in her voice. "I came here screaming for revenge but I might as well have tried to throw rocks at the sea: you've absorbed the force of my rage completely. I will try to do whatever you ask." She wept quietly.

Lute sprang up, rummaged in a bureau drawer, and brought her a cloth handkerchief.

"I keep asking you not the cry, m'lady," he said, bend-ing over her.

Ria blew her nose. Lute's fur smelled like summer.

"You're using Julo's arms well enough," said Kara, smil-ing again. "Try the legs also. Carefully slide them around and sit on the edge of the bed."

Ria obeyed. Kara gripped her right shoulder and Lute her left, steadying her. She took a last look around the sunny bedroom.

In one corner, the same forsythia branches were still blooming in their vase. Not one day had elapsed here since her first visit to Kara and Lute—weeks earlier by her reckoning. . . .

Ria shivered and bowed her head.

"Do what must be done."

✼ ✼ ✼

X

A dream of dawn came to Ria in darkness. . . .

＊　　　＊　　　＊

Early morning sunlight glittered on the water. He stared at it transfixed, wanting the brightness to hurt.

Its dark after-image hung before him like a tiny cloud as he stared aimlessly around the hospital garden. There was still dew on the grass and a giant spiderweb outlined in silvery drops spread across one camellia tree.

Patients sat in wheelchairs or walked along the brick pathways, renewing their strength from the freshness of spring. He could hear them laughing and chatting with staff members, some of whom he recognized.

These people would recover. He did not want to look at them.

He focussed on the lily pond before him instead. Red-gold carp lurked under the pads, slowly fanning their delicate fins. The haughty-looking creatures would dash to the surface quickly enough at the first sign of breadcrumbs. He used to enjoy feeding them every day after lunch.

He had no food for them today. He hated them for being at home in the water. Carp were ageless; Vicky was only twenty-seven. His jaw muscles knotted. How could the Lord be so unfair, to let fish live and Vicky . . .

A little black-haired girl dashed up to the pond.

"Fissie!" she squealed.

103

The fish scattered in panic as her chubby hands splashed in the water. He grabbed the back of her pinafore just as she was about to leap in. He swooped her up in his arms and returned her to her mother. The woman had been too deep in conversation with an elderly gentleman to notice the child's absence.

"Hold on to her tighter, ma'am. It only takes a moment to drown."

His voice strangled on the last word. He was gone before she could thank him.

He checked his timepiece. He could delay no longer. The issue would have to be faced. He stalked through the doors and down familiar hospital corridors, now grown alien overnight. He waited for an elevator to take him to Intensive Care.

Dot Schiele approached from the opposite direction. He blanched at the sight of her. She was as tall and darkly regal as Vicky—people kept mistaking them for one another. There was a time he used to confuse them himself.

"I heard when I came on duty, Paul." She gripped his hand tightly. "Of all the goddamned luck. I couldn't feel worse if Vicky were my own sister."

"I know they've done everything humanly possible. I'm trying to hang on to that last thought. Hard."

"The kids?"

"With my parents."

"If you feel like talking about it, Jay Dub and I could stop by this evening. That's only if you want company, *cher.*"

"Would appreciate it. Y'all give me a call first." His throat was tightening up again. The elevator door opened. Dot nudged him gently toward it.

"As I explained over the phone this morning, all the tracings have stayed flat another twenty-four hours. Lord knows, I wish the news were better, Paul."

Jake Russ had never learned professional detachment. He still died a little with every patient—and this was one of the Royal's own. His fleshy face sagged. Tiny broken capillaries flamed on his cheeks. Who would be consoling whom?

Jake continued. "Doctors Guidry and Paine examined her again this morning. I've got their opinions here for your inspection."

He forced himself to read the prognoses carefully. "So they concur that it's total brain death?"

Jake nodded.

"I can face the term, Jake." Clinical language was a safe way to think the unthinkable. "I'm not going to crumple up and stick you with another case."

"I didn't expect you would." Jake rubbed his balding head.

"Where are the papers for me to sign?" A bitter smile twisted his mouth. "Handy that I already know the routine. You won't even have to decipher the organ donor forms for me."

"You're taking it well, man." Jake's eyes asked if he weren't perhaps taking it too well. "Sometimes hospital people are the hardest to handle at times like this. Do you want to see Vicky, ah . . . again?"

"One more time."

They walked around to the Critical bay.

"Any change in Mrs. Tomasino's condition?"

"None, Doctor." The nurse stepped back.

He'd never thought to see the medical hardware he designed put to this particular use.

The wan figure lay entangled in tubes and sensors that proclaimed its lack of function on attached monitors. The figure's matted hair tumbled across the pillow. Vicky would've never let herself appear in public looking like that. There was nothing to be gained by postponing the inevitable. He made the Sign of the Cross on the body's forehead and walked out.

He couldn't remember how he got home afterwards.

He found himself sitting in his own kitchen drinking a small black. The coffee had no taste.

He ought to pick up the phone and call Mama. No, let Petey and Marianna play a while yet in peace. Not that you could explain much to children that young.

That was the worst of it—they'd grow up without knowing their mother. They'd put flowers on her grave on All

Saints' Day and forget her the rest of the year. Nothing he could do would keep her alive for them very long.

There were still the funeral arrangements to think of. Let Mama be in charge of those. She would whether he liked it or not.

For the moment, he didn't want to talk to anyone, however dear, not while doctors were cutting Vicky to pieces. How easy and noble to donate her organs, easy to think of her doing good after her death, easy to speak of her living on as part of other people's bodies.

Oh God! Why was it so hard to accept when it happened?

They'd have been prepping the operating room before he left the hospital. Calls would be going out to gather prospective recipients—he nearly said "customers." This triggered the grisly image of doctors walking up and down Prytania Street hawking baskets of fresh human organs, like old-time vendors in the Quarter.

He put his head down on his arms and cried.

When he had no tears left to shed, he resolved to work the horror through, step by step—catharsis by flow chart. He forced his mind to picture procedures he'd witnessed many times.

First, divert the blood through the heart-lung machine. Lead it cautiously through yards of tubing. Dictate respiration. Open the abdominal cavity to expose the dark liver and pink kidneys. Snip, snip, hoist on slings, perfuse, and chill. Watch their healthy color fade.

Saw the breastbone. Take the lungs, spleen, and heart—take particular care with that moist, glossy heart.

Less need for haste now. Strip the blood vessels, pluck the glands, harvest the corneas. Tidiness counts for more than speed.

Don't overlook the bones. Spongy, red cancellous bone is always in demand. Root it out.

Last, but scarcely least, peel off the skin. Try for long, continuous strips—they make the neatest rolls for storage.

In time, they'd find a use for everything but the squeal.

A thunder of velvet paws and a familiar stench roused him from his morbid reverie. The cat's scratch pan needed cleaning. Life in all its grubby details continued on schedule without Vicky.

He took care of the back porch chore and tried to coax Minet out of hiding. She stubbornly remained under the bed.

No use trying to take a nap, wrung out though he was. He knew he couldn't sleep. Vicky's scent was still on those sheets. When he washed them, he would lose one more bit of her presence.

And what of her clothes? They'd fit Dot Schiele, but she'd never accept such gifts. He'd have to call the St. Vincent de Paul people to take them away.

Rather than sit home brooding, he should do his daily stint of running. If he ran himself into the ground, he might be able to rest.

He changed clothes and opened the *armoire* to hang up his suit. As he swung the door out, the contents of an otterskin pouch suspended inside clinked sharply. It was a medicine bag Vicky's Red Indian grandmother had left her. He'd never peeked inside nor ever intended to. Although he had no idea of what it meant, he'd keep the thing for Marianna when she grew up.

It was a cruelly perfect day for running. The mild, rain-washed air was heavy with fragrance. The Garden District lived up to its name most fully in this season, when azalea vied with magnolia, wisteria with honeysuckle.

But he saw the flowers of spring only as pastel blurs as he sped along. The St. Charles Avenue route was so familiar that instinct sufficed to keep him on course down the middle of the old streetcar tracks.

He concentrated on the act of running. Grief receded. His world shrank to a path bounded by steel: he was a breathing machine that pumped its arms and legs in strict mechanical rhythm mile after mile.

A flash of golden letters caught his eye barely in time. He darted aside from a truck emblazoned "Centre Builders, Ltd."

A bit more absorption in his stride and the vehicle's wheels would've put a period to his sorrow. Crushing that cowardly thought before it took root, he proceeded with grudging alertness to Audubon Park.

He followed his daily path along a well-worn public

track. Its clay surface was still moist, spotted here and there by patches of slippery leaves blown down by the storm. It wound around the lagoon where swan boats and swans glided together across calm water.

He warmed down under the moss-draped branches of his favorite live oak. He could hear faint music from the direction of the merry-go-round where he used to ride the "flying horses" ages ago.

A raffish blackbird challenged his right to stand under its tree. He whistled back. The bird flew off straight into the midday sun. . . .

✳   ✳   ✳

Ria fought to break free of the blinding brightness, but could find no way out. She relaxed, sensing other presences restraining, then guiding her through a haze of light. . . .

✳   ✳   ✳

She was in a white-tiled room that reeked of chemicals. Before her lay a woman's naked corpse stretched out on a slab. With sinewy black hands that were not hers, she wrapped the flayed and sutured form. Then she bound up the jaw of the body that had once been her own. . . .

✳   ✳   ✳

XI

Kara and Lute still clasped Ria's host body. She'd returned to the same moment she'd left hours earlier.

Lute's greeting was an ear-shattering whoop, hugging her so hard that they both tumbled back onto Julo's bed.

"You passed! Dear lady Ria, you passed the last test!"

Ria thrashed feebly in the otter's embrace. He was as wild as a noncomp.

"A rowdy *perfur* will soon have my permission to celebrate out of doors." Kara's smile belied her rebuke. "Help our new colleague up, Lute, so she can savor her triumph."

Lute obeyed, chittering streaks of apology at Ria.

Kara stood up and raised her shaman's staff in salute.

"We are so very proud of you, child." She kissed Ria's forehead, then settled back in her chair.

"Please explain," asked Ria in a small voice.

"Already told you," answered Lute. "You're one of us now."

"He means that you've completed your initiation. You've become a *solexa*."

"All because I saw my own corpse?" Ria shuddered. "Because I was the woman who died in that dream?"

"No," said Lute, "you will *be* that woman about seven years from now—on another branch of time."

"Of course, that event is long past from our vantage point," Kara continued. "Victoria Legarde Tomasino died April 4, 2017 in the Royal Hospital at New Orleans."

Curiosity deflected Ria's fear. "What's a *Royal* Hospital doing in twenty-first century New Orleans?"

Lute snorted. "Being a great medical center, what else? No American Revolution on that time line. Most of our continent stayed British."

"There's a smaller hospital on the same site in your world," Kara added. "It's called Touro Infirmary."

"Back to my original question. Why did you force me to watch my alternate self die?"

"Your readings on *solarti* offer no clue?" asked Kara.

Ria's brows creased. She strained to remember the relevant details from Eliade's book. "Do you mean . . . that my dream was equivalent to the visions of death and dismemberment that novice shamans must undergo before they can obtain their powers?"

"Quite right!" said Lute. "I searched long and hard for the right incident—had to find that one tragic case among a flock of others."

"Then it wasn't a prediction of how I'm going to die?"

" 'Course not!" Lute snorted. Indignation set the bells on his harness jangling.

Kara said quietly, "You are afraid that your life's no longer your own."

Ria nodded.

"Does a twig lose its identity because similar twigs grow on the same branch?" Kara reached out to grip Ria's hand. "You are yourself and none other, no matter what happens in another part of the Cosmic Tree." She paused until Ria met her eyes. "Neither Lute nor I have spied on your particular future, to preserve freedom of action for all of us."

Ria relaxed slightly. Success hadn't been inevitable. They'd actually been willing to take a chance on her. Yet . . .

"Something more was involved besides death and transformation. Lute, why did you call my experience a test?"

"Can't you tell when you're being tempted?" He rubbed his chin whiskers in puzzlement.

"Review your feelings during the transfer, Ria." Kara was wholly mentor now. "How did you feel when you recognized Vicky as another self?"

"I wanted more than anything to make her live again. Her husband loved her so much. . . ." Ria's voice turned hoarse. "I felt a closer bond with him than with any other host. To feel his grief and be powerless to help him . . ."

"Empathy carries a price. Go on." Kara tapped her drum.

"Seeing her in that hospital bed, I wondered if I could jump from his body to hers, stage a miraculous recovery, and live happily ever after. I assumed I could reanimate Vicky's body the same way I'm operating Julo's."

"What stopped you, since you believed her life to be more favored and useful than your own?" Kara's drum sounded again.

"Believed? I could see that it was far better. She had everything that I lack—and people loved her." Ria swallowed hard. "When it came down to it, I couldn't bear to steal Vicky's happiness."

"Wouldn't you call that a moral test?" Kara struck her drum once more.

Ria hid her face in her hands. "It didn't necessarily prove my virtue. Maybe I was just too timid to cheat."

"Ria, Ria, when will you learn to think well of yourself? You only want to accept unpleasant truths." Kara shook her head. "Perhaps you assume that truth is always unpleasant? In the long run, the right thing will prove to be the best thing. Here, the wrong choice carried its own immediate punishment. If you'd tried to take over Vicky's body, you'd have trapped yourself in dead flesh you couldn't control—or leave. At best, you'd have produced a state of permanent coma, thereby prolonging the sorrows of her loved ones."

"It wouldn't have been like this?" Ria flexed her host body's arm.

"Julo's alive," explained Lute. "Even damaged, there's still lots of unused capacity in his brain. Vicky was really dead by the time you saw her—machines merely gave her the semblance of life. With her brain gone, you'd've had nothing to work with. You could've entered Vicky's cat with better results."

"So you see, tales about old shamans killing youngsters to take over their bodies are only ugly fables." Kara spread her empty hands.

"What about swapping souls to get a younger or better body?" asked Ria cautiously.

"Do you think you're in danger, child?" Kara chuckled.

"After so many years of struggle, I begin to long for the eternal rest. I can pass the Door without regret now that I've seen you made a *solexa*."

"I didn't mean to suggest . . ." Ria stammered. "But aren't shamans in your world ever dishonest?"

"Anybody who misuses *solarti* in one way, will misuse it in other ways, too."

"We'd detect 'em and destroy 'em," cried Lute.

Kara continued. "That happened sometimes in the past— evil *solexes* had to be purged from the community of the art. But I've never heard of body-stealing in my lifetime. Our testing does seem to screen out the unworthy candidates."

"You succeeded, dear lady. Accept it." Lute kissed Ria's fingers.

"Let's have some tea before proceeding further," said Kara. "Lute, find her a wrap and slippers." She left the room.

Lute retrieved a pair of woolly boots from under the bed. He searched a cabinet but was unable to find Julo's robe. He muffled Ria in the coverlet instead.

Supported by his arm, Ria stood up and took one shaky step. A few more tries taught her steadiness.

Lute led her through the bedroom door into a skylighted atrium that was full of the sweet, moist scents of spring. Vines fell in green torrents down the walls to mingle with rows of potted trees and flowering plants. Fat cushions were heaped around a pool in the center of the tiled floor.

Ria wanted to pause to sniff a bowl of pink hyacinths, but Lute steered her towards the kitchen.

Inside, Ria glanced about shyly. It was the largest private kitchen she had yet seen. Kara seemed less formidable here, surrounded by pots and pans and mellow oak furniture. She now wore a simple linen blouse over her skirt, as she stood slicing dark bread. The kettle was heating on an actual fire, fed by gas.

"Don't just hover, child. Look around." Kara laughed and swept a spiral in the air. "Our world holds more than Julo's bedroom."

"Come see the greenhouse," said Lute, nudging her to the right.

Turning, Ria noticed that the kitchen's back wall was glassed with small, bubbly panes. She and Lute passed though an adjacent door into a small greenhouse that occupied one corner of the building.

"It helps keeps the kitchen and Kara's bedroom warmer," Lute explained. " 'Course it grows things, too."

He showed her flats of tiny seedlings.

"When these're ready, Julo'll plant them out back, in the vegetable garden next to my pond." *My* had a strong proprietary ring.

Ria stared where he was pointing. She could make out the pond about fifty meters distant. Beside it grew a grove of huge, fan-shaped trees, faintly green with new leaves.

"What species is that?" asked Ria. "I thought I recognized all the common trees."

"They're elms."

"You have elms?" Ria yelped in amazement.

"Shouldn't we?"

"They've been extinct where I come from for half a century."

The notion of a land without elms set Lute's whiskers quivering. "What happened to them?" he asked.

"Disease. Spraying didn't save them." Ria cocked her head from side to side, trying to get the best view through the wavy glass. "Could I go look at your elms up close, on some other visit?"

"That'd please me no end, m'lady, to introduce you to these noble trees. It's fitting that I live among them: they're my own totem. My *harnama*, the formal name I took from my coming-of-age dream, is Sings Under the Elm Tree."

"Lute makes more of that coincidence than it merits—as if elms did not grow everywhere." Kara had joined them unnoticed.

"Sometimes, Kara, you're too hard-headed."

"One of us has to be." Kara hugged him lightly. "Our tea is ready."

Lute snorted and kept muttering about humans' lack of sympathy towards *perfur* while the others took seats at the kitchen table.

Before the otter joined them, he removed a plate of

peeled hardboiled eggs from the cold-box. He threw an egg up in the air, but sheepishly caught it with his hand, not his teeth. He set the plate beside the teapot, sat down on a padded stool, and curled his tail about his legs.

"How many dozen so far this week?" asked Kara. ·

"I haven't kept count," Lute replied between bites, reaching for another egg.

"Now, Ria, you see a prime weakness of the *perfur*: they're mad for a food their farms can't produce—chickens and chittering don't mix."

"Flighty birds drop dead at the least little noise." His whiskers drooped briefly until he consoled himself with yet another egg.

Ria stifled her giggles lest she choke drinking tea. It was an herbal brew, pale and pungent, with a taste she couldn't identify. She only nibbled at the bread, delicious though it was, because her host body wasn't hungry.

Ria was amazed at how easily she accepted the fantastic situation: she might have been talking to giant otters all her life.

Warmed by the tea—and even more by friendship—she dared to ask: "What year is this?"

"By your reckoning," Kara paused for a mental calculation, "This is 2691."

Ria drew a sharp breath. "When did your timeline split off from mine?"

Kara replied: "The final break came when your world went to war in 1914."

"They called it the War to End All Wars," said Lute, baring his fangs. "It wasn't."

Kara continued. "But our branch—like all new branches—had begun budding decades earlier, when the English queen Victoria abdicated in favor of her eldest son. As a result, the nations of Europe forged different alliances in our past than yours and avoided major conflict that—"

Lute broke in. "Nothing's sudden as it seems. Every moment grows out of those that went before. Every instant decisions're made one way or another."

He waved his hands in opposite directions. "Mostly, they cancel each other out and the bud's reabsorbed into the original branch."

"But," he brought his hands together and paired his stubby fingers, "let enough of them line up in the same direction—affect enough lives—and there's a new branch on the Great Tree."

"I almost understand." Ria nodded. "Almost."

He continued. "Give you a simpler example: you know that the Santos *Incendio* of 1984 made your world what it is."

"You forced me to witness the nexus point."

"Ah," said Kara, "The world you saw—where the ships *didn't* collide—was already budding away from yours, one of many branching off a larger break-point two generations earlier."

Ria frowned, casting back through her slight knowledge of that period.

Before she could frame a question, Lute asked: "When was World War II?"

Ria stared at him blankly. "That's not really my era. . . ."

"Forget the name. Was there a big war in Europe about mid-century?"

"Oh, you mean the one against the Nazis? That was fairly short—over by 1940, as I recall. The French and British beat the Germans and drove their leader—Hilter? Hitler?—from power."

Lute waved his teaspoon at her. "It was just a short European war on *your* branch. Elsewhere, it lasted til '45—or even longer. Fought all over the world. Terrible loss of life."

"You mean," said Ria, "that Nazi business got mixed up with Japan's struggles against the Chinese and Soviets? I don't know much about it, but I think that was the bloodiest fighting of my twentieth century. The Far East was just starting to recover when the *Incendio* triggered global anarchy."

"On timelines where World War II happened," said Kara, "scientific discoveries and political changes came faster, too, pushing those branches far from yours."

Lute smoothed his whiskers. "Not saying that war's any blessing, mind you."

A certain puzzle fell into place for Ria. "The dream you

sent me last month about an earthquake on the Pacific coast—did it come from one of those worlds?"

"Quite right! Getting so I know your history better'n my own." He snuffled. "Don't ask me what my Rolling Shore tribe was doing a hundred years ago—"

"You're wandering off the path, Lute," said Kara.

Lute stared meekly at his teacup. Leaf fragments floating in it seemed to require his utmost concentration.

Kara smiled wryly and continued. "As I started to explain, Ria, our branch was spared the horrors of global war. Scores of millions who otherwise would have died lived out their full lifespans, unshadowed by the cynicism and despair. Those extra minds and hands created works your world never knew. Progress came swifter and drew Earth's nations together peacefully."

She poured another round of tea.

"With the mastery of genetics and the conquest of space, mankind's ancient dreams of plenty seemed fulfilled. In those days, they shaped the stuff of life at will and built homes for themselves beyond the sky." Kara's voice turned wistful. "Our telescopes can still find their colonies in orbit—dry husks left after the whirlwind."

"What happened?" asked Ria.

"Their world was green and fair as any Eden—and just as lost to us."

A grayness settled on Kara's wrinkled face. She took a sip of tea and continued.

"Flushed with success designing microorganisms and modifying plants, the engineers of genetics turned their attention to larger creatures. Since law and custom barred them from tampering with human genes except to mend gross defects, they yearned to create useful new species of animals. Some even argued that mankind had a duty to compensate for those it had exterminated. And so, with every good intention, they bred macro-rats—the hated macrats that trouble us to this day."

"How large is 'macro'?" Visions of elephantine rodents trampled through Ria's mind.

"Macrats're big as large dogs." Lute measured the air for emphasis. "But it's their brains, not their size, that makes them so dangerous. They're bright as apes—or so the ancient records claim—we've no apes left for comparison."

"Are those ugly things around here?" Ria shivered. A shadow had crossed the sun. Perhaps this world wasn't the cozy refuge it seemed.

"Chamba is considered secure," said Kara, "thanks to the watchful zeal of our *perfur* friends."

Lute preened graciously. "Even so, meet a pack of macrats in the wild or in a ruined city and you'll most likely stay for dinner—as the main course."

"They eat people?" cried Ria.

"And even *perfur* when they can get them. Which is seldom."

"Like natural rats, their food is anything they can find," said Kara.

"No peril here, dear Ria, nothing we can't handle." He patted her shoulder.

"But just think, without the macrats as a trial, my people might not have come into existence."

Lute could find a positive interpretation to anything.

Kara explained: "The *perfur* or macotters were the next step, a choice suggested by the needs of sea-farmers. A radically improved otter was the goal, not merely a larger one. They blended and adapted traits from many species: the size of the Amazonian otter, the conformation of the Asian otter, the clawless hands of the Cape otter—"

Lute wriggled his opposable thumb.

"—this patchwork heritage shows in the way they act, as well as in how they look."

"Hybrid vigor. Yes. Yes!"

Lute jumped up and spun around, ringing his bells joyfully.

Admiring his grace, Ria finally understood that he wasn't simply a giant-sized otter. His cranium was higher, his muzzle blunter than an animal's and, although his carriage was stooped, his legs were longer and better adapted for walking upright.

"Hybrid vigor—with the emphasis on vigor." Kara beckoned him back to his seat and continued her story.

"The scientists wrought better than they knew. They brought forth an entirely new creature with a mind fully the equal of man's own—the fairy tales of talking beasts had at last come true.

"This discovery ripped the human sense of self to shreds. Only the arrival of beings from another star would've caused more frenzy." Kara shook her head sadly. "Some viewed the macotters as rivals to man."

"They feared we'd replace you, since we can speak your language, use your tools, walk your land." Lute bowed his head, covering his eyes for sadness.

Kara went on. "The worst fools hailed macotters as angels in fur who'd show mankind the way to perfection."

"As if we couldn't sin, too." Lute snorted, clenching his jaws.

"Treated you like the ultimate Noble Savages, did they?" Ria added bitterly.

"And look what became of the continent's original Noble Savages." Kara nodded at Ria. "As you, their descendant, know. The same fate might've overtaken the macotters, except that a group of fanatics decided to hand over the earth to the new 'persons of fur.' "

"They hated themselves because they weren't us," said Lute.

"What did they do?" asked Ria.

"They designed a lethal virus," replied Kara. "It spread like the common cold but was so slow to start killing that every human being on Earth—and off it—had been infected before the first symptoms of the deadly fever appeared. That was the Great Death." Kara shuddered. "One in a thousand survived."

Lute continued. "But a scientist on the macotter project got the colony into safe hiding before she died." He kissed his fingers, saying: "To the memory of Sarah Mischling, She Who Bled."

Kara found her voice again. "Once the Death passed, the macotters flourished. Soon hundreds of them—now called *perfur*—were living along the now-empty shores of Chesapeake Bay."

"Then a man who'd been a student of exotic cultures encountered them and joined his destiny to theirs. They shaped him as much as he shaped them—so much so that he is known to us only by his *perfur* name, Never Smiles."

"Although he'd no talent for it himself, this scholar recognized the first stirrings of *solarti* in *perfur* and human alike. He saw in it the seed of a new civilization."

"He was our first great comrade, our brother-in-skin," said Lute. "He made the compact between our two peoples that endures to this day." He stretched out furry hands to clasp Kara's and Ria's.

"May it be so forever," Kara sighed. "Much has been lost, but much has been regained. We've climbed a few mountains of our own, haven't we, my children? And many more await us." She leaned over to kiss Lute and then Ria.

Ria discovered that her borrowed body could blush.

To mask her embarrassment, she asked another question. "If that plague is a branch-point for you, then there must be other timelines—maybe a whole clump of them by now—where it never happened. Do your shamans—I ought to starting saying *solexes*—explore those worlds? Do they know what's happened on those branches since the time of the Great Death?"

"No one really cares to know," said Kara. "When I was young and proud I once glanced in that direction. I would never willingly return. Nor would any of my fellows. Cherubim with flaming swords couldn't guard those branches half so well as our regret for wonders lost. I've faults enough without adding despair."

"*My* world's hardly one you'd envy." Ria grimaced, clutching her empty teacup.

Lute shook his head. "There're worse ones, m'lady. Far worse. Wait till you've seen more branches before you judge. Point is to make yours the best it can be."

"Each thing in its season." Kara brightened. "Your talent is a newly opened flower. There's much more to be learned before you can bear fruit. Come to us like this daily and we'll teach you whatever we can."

"But how can I find the way to the right moment?" Ria was beginning to grasp the magnitude of what lay before her.

"We can't tell you in words—you've got to confront the Great Tree for yourself," said Lute. "For now, we'll guide you to the time we want you here. Pretty soon, you'd no more lose your way than a bird'd forget how to fly."

"Bear in mind, Ria, that what you are about to see is merely a symbol, a symbol cut to the scale of mortal minds."

Ria nodded. " 'Humankind cannot bear very much reality.' "

"Neither can *perfur*," said Lute.

"However, we can strive to bear as much of it as we can." Kara rose and led them back into the atrium.

Kara's *solexa* costume was lying on one of the cushions beside the fish pond. Kara donned it again and sat down, motioning Lute and Ria to join her.

"I don't—" Ria began.

Without speaking, Kara took a silver ring from her own finger and slipped it on her pupil's.

She raised her staff and drum of office skyward and intoned:

"By sunlight, starlight, firelight, reflections of the Light Eternal, forward we fare together."

Kara struck her drum with her staff—hard. The leather disk gave a sharp, dry crack like snapping wood. She beat a brisk, unvarying rhythm.

Ria's heart pounded in synchrony. She breathed in steady, counted measures.

Hearing was all. Her other senses guttered out like spent candles.

Sound became substance, silence void. Between them, they defined creation.

A sudden jangling overrode the drumbeat.

Ria's attention turned abruptly to Lute. He was running his hands over his harness, ringing brash cascades of bells.

He glided up from his cushion in one fluid motion and began dancing to the shifting tempos of his own music. His body flowed through rippling arcs along the narrow margin of the pond.

His tail brushed Ria's bare leg as he passed. He dipped so close, she could smell an exciting new muskiness on his fur.

She longed to shed her wrap and rise to partner him.

Instead, she watched his shadow flicker across sunlit water. Brightness and darkness meshed with sound and silence. She flashed Kara's ring before her eyes, bespelled by the liquid sheen of the silver. . . .

❋   ❋   ❋

Ria could see neither herself nor the others, yet the presences of Kara and Lute enfolded her as if with shining wings.

Furrowed ridges of exposed root loomed before her like gray mountains. She could have easily lost herself among the peaks and canyons of the bark, but the party kept moving upward in a rising clockwise gyre.

They circled the mighty trunk, seeking its smoother, higher reaches where curving branches defined a globular crown. They sped through networks of ever-finer branches out to the terminal twigs.

On each stem grew seven oval leaves arrayed pairwise with a singleton poised like a lancepoint on the tip. Some leaves were pale, translucent green; others shaded off to bronze, magenta, wine, and gold. Frizzy clusters of reddish flowers sprouted next to winged brown seeds. Bare twigs bore blunt dark buds and leaf scars notched like crescent moons. Supple fresh twigs and stiff rotten ones sprang from a common branch. Where whole limbs had broken off, new bark swelled to seal the wounds.

Budding, leafing, blooming, fading, the Eternal Now held every season.

The three *solexes* spun the cycle closed.

> To turn, turn will be our delight.
> 'Till by turning, turning we come round right.

❋   ❋   ❋

XII

A benediction of snow was falling when Ria awoke Sunday morning. The thick, soft flakes were coming straight down, scarcely drifting. Street lamps still glowed in the darkness, their light blurred and mellowed by the snow, yet the first glow of the rising sun was starting to show in the east.

Nothing moved within sight of her window. For a moment, Ria felt as if she owned the dawn.

Then a Security car sped by, leaving deep tracks behind it.

The freshness of snow was fleeting as a dream.

Ria remembered a poem she'd written during her first year of high school:

> *Now that I am grown,*
> *I cannot walk*
> *Upon new-fallen snow*
> *And let the snowflakes*
> *Gather in my hair*
> *Like bright new diamonds*
> *Scattered there . . . .*

What was stopping her now? If her soul could fly, surely her body could walk. This was no day to sit indoors counting the hours until she could return to Kara and Lute. She ought to celebrate her victory out where living trees grew.

After breakfast, she phoned Carey and persuaded him to go walking with her before the snowy wonder faded.

Dressing in her warm winter pants for the first time this season, Ria was surprised to see how loose they were. She'd lost more weight during her ordeal than she'd realized. Shamanizing must burn calories at a prodigious rate. She did not, however, see it becoming a government-approved weight control technique.

The snow was half a meter deep by the time Ria and Carey got out of the House. Footing was treacherous on the unplowed walks. Ria gripped her smaller companion's arm, lest he flounder.

"I could always pick you up and carry you," she said mischievously.

"Don't you dare!" Carey slogged forward with new determination. "I was crazy to come along. You were crazy—"

He stopped short, abashed at his tactlessness.

Ria laughed. "On the contrary. I'm perfectly sure I'm sane. Don't you recognize healthy joy when you see it?"

"So how often does one see it?"

"Not often enough. But happiness has to be shared and you're the only person I can share mine with." She pumped Carey's arm so vigorously that she nearly knocked him off balance.

"I'm flattered—I think. A little less heartiness next time, huh?"

They tramped on in silence for a while, stumbling and sliding while flakes continued to fall.

"Ria," he complained, "we'll never make it to Crystal Lake Park. Wouldn't Carle Park do as well? It's a lot closer."

"But so much smaller. Where's your trailblazing spirit, Carey? Look, the next section of Green Street's been plowed. If we walk along the curb, the going'll be easier. Security's not likely to bother ticketing us."

Carey saved his breath for walking until they reached their destination.

As Ria led him under the park's snow-decked trees, he compared their white branches to Venetian lace. This launched him into a pedantic lecture on the evolution of European lacemaking, punctuated by much handwaving.

Yet Carey had no energy and less enthusiasm for physical fun. He even refused to join Ria in making snow angels on the bank of Boneyard Creek.

"Carey," she said in exasperation, "I don't think you ever learned how to play."

"What do you mean?" He scowled. "I always got good marks in my playgroup."

"Did you now?" Ria stood up and dusted the snow off her clothes. "I couldn't say the same myself. Were you a model of cooperation like those children over there?"

Ria pointed to a band of preschoolers beside the nearby frozen lake. Their counselors had lined them up to throw snow balls at a target. None hit the mark, perhaps because each child was muffled so tightly against the cold. A little girl who'd been building a snow castle by herself was marched back to the group. When her turn to throw came, her snowball went astray like the others.

Ria applauded the performance, clapping with exaggerated vigor.

"Glory be to sociability!" she cried loudly enough for the children's counselors to hear. There was no danger of them recognizing sarcasm.

"Carey, your nose looks alarmingly red. Mine probably is, too."

"No, actually yours isn't," said Carey, rubbing his frost-nipped nose.

"Well, I'm feeling chilled inside. Let's go get something to eat along Main Street."

They left Crystal Lake Park at a quicker pace than they had entered it.

Ria was comfortably weary by the end of the day, glad to be tired from exertion, not anxiety.

After preparing for bed, she lay down holding her grandmother's steel mirror. It became a radiant pool she could stir with her own hand. . . .

❋   ❋   ❋

It was night when she awakened in Julo's bedroom.
Kara and Lute stood waiting as before, although neither
wore shamanic costume.

They welcomed Ria with kisses.

"How do you feel now, child?" asked Kara.

"Amazingly good—here *and* back home."

"That's as should be," said Lute, snuffling quietly.

"I expected the sight of the Cosmic Tree to leave me in
some delirious ecstasy. Instead, I'm calm but merry. Now
I know who I am, even if I don't know where I'm going
yet."

"That'll come in its own good time," said Kara. "Your
joy in the art is our joy. More training will deepen that
joy."

"To the kitchen for your next lesson." said Lute.

Rising from the bed, Ria stared at the nightshirt her
body was wearing.

"One small favor, please?"

"Anything, m'lady," said Lute.

"Could you arrange to have Julo fully dressed the next
time I'm due to occupy his body?"

"We can ask him," said Lute. "His hosting stints're
usually scheduled for times when he's asleep."

"Thanks. I feel silly walking around in night clothes."
She smoothed the rumpled gown.

"My people don't have to worry," Lute chirruped, running his fingers over his glossy pelt. "We're always correctly dressed in our sleek fur."

"Come along." Kara beckoned.

Ria was pleased to find that she needed no assistance
walking.

Lute punched a wall switch to turn off the lights and
followed them into the kitchen.

"On your previous visits," said Kara, "we had to bundle
you carefully for warmth. By now you should be able to
control your borrowed body's temperature."

"I'm comfortable, if that's what you're asking."

"Control of fire goes beyond questions of comfort. Sit
down, child, and roll up your sleeves."

Ria obeyed her.

Lute brought an enameled bowl filled with water and crushed ice out of the cold-box. He dipped a linen towel in the water, wrang it out, and wrapped it about Ria's right arm.

"Hey! That's freezing! Take it off!" She jerked away from Lute.

"Warm your flesh, *solexa*." Kara's blue eyes glinted.

"Do *what*?"

"You're s'posed to dry the cloth with body heat, Ria," Lute explained. "Feel your way through the flesh. Concentrate. Burn those calories quicker."

Ria fought the cold, drawing energy from sources she couldn't identify. She sensed vibrations quivering at a faster rate, felt mutual attractions broken and reformed.

The towel was no longer wet.

"That'd save me money at the House laundry," said Ria, giggling nervously.

Lute snorted. "Time was, naked shamans got wrapped in dripping sheets and put outdoors in the winter wind. Or they got ducked in frozen lakes. Mastered inner fire in one galloping hurry, they did."

"Our ways are gentler now," said Kara. "This simple exercise required you to alter metabolic reactions in one specific area. Feel your arm under the towel."

The band of skin was feverishly hot to Ria's touch.

"Now do the same with the left arm," Kara commanded.

Although the towel was wetter this time, Ria dried it even quicker.

"Both arms at once."

Lute produced a second towel and the experiment was repeated.

"What's next?" asked Ria. "Self-combustion? This lady's not for burning."

"You can heat more'n your body," said Lute. He poured most of the water out in the sink, then folded the dry towels into a pad and set it under the bowl.

"Bring it to a boil," he said, tapping the container's rim.

"How?"

"Apply the same techniques you used on your flesh," said Kara patiently. "Energize the water molecules to raise their temperature."

"We know you can do it," said Lute. "Trust us. Try."

Ria struggled to perform. At least she knew what a water molecule looked like, even though her description of "flapping hydrogen wings" had pained her primary school science teacher. It had to be a matter of making them flap faster.

She was sweating by the time the first tiny bubbles appeared.

Lute invited her to confirm the water's hotness. She held her hand above the lightly steaming surface, then abruptly plunged her fingers in.

The simmering water didn't scald her—the same power that could warm flesh could also cool it.

"Is this why I've never been badly burned?" Ria asked.

"You've been using your gift instinctively all your life, child. Now you can do so with fuller understanding." Kara beamed at her pupil's progress.

"Want some tea while you're thinking that over?" asked Lute.

"As long as I'm not expected to boil the kettle myself."

" 'Course not, Ria." Lute snorted. "We don't use *solarti* for everyday things. We'd wear ourselves out."

After tea had been served and the dishes cleared, Lute set a small tripod brazier on the table. It held bits of crumpled paper.

"You expect me to set that on fire." Ria's comment was a statement, not a question.

Lute nodded. "You can do it. Treat the tinder the way you did to start that grass fire when you were little."

Ria trembled. Sickening memories clutched at her— stifling rooms with locked windows, sun-rotted curtains gray with dust, dry weeds billowing in a brisk wind . . . a single milkweed pod exploding in flames.

A nervous tongue of fire licked the fuel in the brazier.

Other experiments followed. Under her mentors' direction, Ria induced static electricity, drew an electric spark across an open switch, and even induced a tiny motor to make a few revolutions.

"I assume you two are experts at all this," said Ria with studied casualness.

"Quite right!" Lute did no more than glance at the motor than its vanes began whirring too fast for the eye to follow.

"In fact, this is how you caused my accident at the library. No wonder Repair couldn't find anything wrong. My terminal didn't try to electrocute me—you did!" She glared at one and then the other.

Lute showed the tips of his fangs. "Don't you blame Kara! It was my idea and my doing."

Kara shrugged. "It didn't harm you, child. We caused you no more pain than necessary. You'll face worse suffering than that in your life as a *solexa*."

"Granted. But I still owe this dear *perfur* something for his trouble." Ria flicked a spark at Lute's muzzle that made his whiskers stand straight out.

He yipped and rubbed his injured nose. "Not nice!"

"That was unworthy of you, Ria," said Kara sharply.

Ria was aghast at yielding to a violent impulse. "I'm sorry," she said. "I remember grievances too long."

She stroked Lute's face gently. His stiff whiskers folded back as he tilted his cheek against her hand. She let it rest there for a long moment.

Ria framed her next question in a chastened voice: "What you're teaching me is dangerous. I could go around starting fires, blowing out equipment. Aren't you worried that I'll misuse these powers, misuse them a lot worse than I did just now?"

Kara replied: "We know your heart to its core. How could we not know it after all these years? But if you should ever give us cause to doubt your character, we could—and would—disarm you instantly."

Ria wondered exactly what was meant by *disarm*. "But you've never tried to initiate a subject on a different timeline before. Has anyone? Surely that's risky."

"The prize is worth the risk. There's some purpose at

work in you, child, that I feel but cannot clearly see. It will not let me rest."

Kara's last words were almost a groan. The old *solexa* closed her eyes and rubbed her forehead as if to smooth away the furrows of age.

She continued, "But is this Providence in action, or merely my own pride? Has my wisdom deluded me at the last? I was always so quick to see what needed to be done. Now I've done it all and still don't know what remains undone."

It came to Ria that initiation went on throughout one's life. Perfect mastery was never attained. She wanted to say something comforting to Kara, but no words came.

Lute jarred the table getting up. He paced back and forth nibbling at his fingers.

"Know the risks? Don't we just! You're reminding us of something we wish we'd never learned. Yours wasn't the only great talent we found exploring the past. Tell her, Kara, tell her about the self-made *solexam*."

Kara chose her words slowly. "This man—may his evil name perish unremembered—was born in China at the end of your eighteenth century. He came of an ancient and distinguished lineage and was amply equipped to pursue the life of the mind.

"Although as a righteous Confucian he despised both Buddhists and barbarians, he nevertheless mastered the mystical practices of Tibetan Buddhists and learned the ways of Mongol shamans. He became, as Lute said, a 'self-made *solexam*' with a notable flair for dream-shaping. In this alien art, he saw a means of destroying the alien Manchus who were then ruling China.

"Through *solarti*, he discovered a fitting instrument to realize his plans, a youth named Hung who'd been driven mad by repeated failures in the imperial civil service examinations. For forty days and nights, he smothered Hung with visions, until the lad believed himself to be the chosen Son of God and King of Heaven."

"All at a distance, understand." Lute broke in. "The scheming adept never met his disciple face to face nor explained what he was doing to him. *We* played fair with *you*, Ria."

Kara continued. "The cunning *solexam* died suddenly, before he could complete Hung's initiation and set his plans in motion.

"But who can halt a boulder once it starts rolling down the mountain? Hung proclaimed himself a prophet and messiah, blending misunderstood scraps of Christianity with his own delusions. His message won so huge and rabid a following that he dared lead a revolt to replace the hated Manchus with what he called his Great Kingdom of Heavenly Peace. By the time this T'ai P'ing Rebellion was put down—"

"Twenty, maybe forty, million people had died." Lute snapped his teeth together.

Ria's face twisted in horror. "You say you watched all this happen. Couldn't you do anything to stop it?"

"No, child, we couldn't. That tragedy lies in our past— and yours. Therefore, it's fixed and changeless from our standpoint. We can't lop off the branch whence we ourselves sprang."

"Yet you feel free to interfere in *my* life." Ria's trust in them was stretching dangerously thin.

"Don't make it sound like a game, m'lady." Lute stepped behind her and kneaded her shoulders.

Kara regarded her with weary patience. "Have you forgotten your previous lessons so quickly? We were free to affect you because you aren't part of *our* past—we occupy separate branches of time. And we've deliberately avoided looking into your future so that all possibilities remain open."

"Sounds like the old debates over Free Will versus Predestination." Ria tried another line of questioning. "What if my training backfires like that fellow Hung's did?"

"You're being trained right and your heart's right," said Lute. "Makes all the difference."

Kara added: "We'd have never touched your soul if we didn't believe that you'd use *solarti* wisely. We cannot undo the deeds of that *solexam* in old China. Yet maybe the debt incurred through one man's sin will be repaid somehow through one woman's virtue. Have faith in your future."

Ria slumped. "Forgive me. I've been afraid so long."

"You can stop being afraid of yourself right this minute." Lute slid his hands under Ria's arms and pulled her upright again.

Ria noticed an ugly pallor creeping over Kara's face.

"I'm tiring you," she said.

Kara sighed. "That you are. I begin to feel my years as the hour grows late. No need to try everything the first night—there's no lack of lessons yet to come."

Lute led Ria away.

❊   ❊   ❊

XIII

Kara and Lute continued to teach Ria new aspects of *solarti* every night that week. They put particular emphasis on the mastery of fire, which seemed to be Ria's special strength.

Ria continued learning on her own. After delivering her preliminary survey of earthquake and volcano disasters to Professor Clyde, she had more free time to pursue her own research.

Mastering fire was supposed to enable her to master biochemical processes, above all in her own body. Now that she knew how to make electrons dance to her tune, she should be able to alter the rates at which her heart beat, her lungs pumped, and her blood clotted, as well as subtler modifications. But these feats required more knowledge of the life sciences than she possessed.

Ria set about remedying her ignorance by ordering some computerized instruction and signing up for biofeedback lessons at her House. It was daunting to realize how many disciplines she would be called upon to master in her vocation as a *solexa*.

Over the course of that week, unseasonably warm weather melted the deep snow. Its once-lovely whiteness was reduced to mud, although icy heaps left by snowplows loomed like miniature glaciers along streets and walks.

The following Monday, Ria and Carey emerged from the east door of the Main Library at lunch time. The noon sun was so warm that they left their coats open, unlike the nude sculptures flanking the doorway, who remained chastely concealed by packed snow.

Ria grinned. "They look better covered up, don't you think?"

"Who?" Carey hadn't been paying attention.

"Laredo Taft's ladies—*I Haven't Got a Thing to Wear* and *I Can't Do a Thing with My Hair*." She pointed toward the statues, so named by generations of students because the one hugged her bare body and the other clutched her tangled locks.

Carey chuckled. "Possibly. But I've better things on my mind than stone females—the University's winter cinema series, for instance. Since you dragged me out into that awful blizzard last week, the least you can do is let me coax you into watching some films."

"Depends on what they are."

"Swashbucklers."

Ria stared blankly.

Carey explained: "Rare adventure classics from the last century—sea battles, sword fights, guys swinging from chandeliers." He thrust an imaginary rapier at her. "And no pretense at offering anything except entertainment."

"Mindless films full of violence?" asked Ria. "No social message? We'd better see them before they're suppressed. I wonder who let them out of the archives?"

"The daring bureaucrat probably went noncomp right afterwards. If we're going to catch *The Thief of Bagdad* tonight, we'll have to get—"

They almost collided with a crowd on the sidewalk before a scowling Security officer waved them all back.

The officer and her team barred access to a throng of smartly uniformed University dignitaries clustered around a copper-haired giant of a man. The visitor was doubly remarkable for wearing serviceable denim coveralls and stout boots.

"Can that be?" Carey's mouth twitched. "Yes it is. Ria, that's the Head of Agriculture—Ivan Mackenzie-Frazer. I read that he's in town for a high-level Ag conference at Allerton House. He likes to get out of Washington once in a while to inspect the hinterlands. He's from way up north in Wheatland himself, where they still make a big deal about direct communion with the Land."

"I've never seen anyone that important in person before," said Ria. The faces television showed belonged to things, not people. "Let's take a closer look."

"Not too close, or we'll make his escort nervous."

Ria pointed. "They're heading for the Morrow Plots."

The continent's oldest corn testing site was an obvious attraction to show the continent's agriculture chief.

Ria and Carey slipped farther to the front of the crowd but prudently remained on the sidewalk. Meanwhile, the dignitaries cut across the soggy lawn and into the soggier field. Ankle-deep in mud, they surged between rows of standing corn like so many foraging hogs, knocking over stalks as they jockeyed for position. One man fell on his face.

Mackenzie-Frazer soberly inspected the memorial plaque summarizing the history of the Plots and read the signs recording last year's yields. He even posed for the cameras, shucking a few dry ears from stalks that must have been left standing expressly for the purpose. He seemed noticeably more impressed with the corn than with his hosts.

Ria turned away, shaking her head. "If that's power, Carey, I don't want it."

"What makes you think you have any choice?"

✳   ✳   ✳

On her next visit to Kara and Lute, Ria awoke out-of-doors. The scent of bridal wreath hung in the late afternoon air. Blackbirds whistled overhead. She was lying in a hammock near Lute's pond. The macotter put aside a curious musical instrument to greet her.

"No, don't stop," said Ria. "What's that thing you're playing?"

"We call this a *gouar*."

He held it up to give her a better look. The instrument's neck was carved and painted to resemble a cock pheasant's head. The two globular sounding-chambers were gilded. It had more strings than Ria could count easily.

"A *perfur* instrument?"

"Our favorite—my favorite, anyhow. Some of us favor the boat harp or the chalice drum but nothing thrums like a *gouar*."

He struck a chord buzzing with complex resonances that raised the hairs on the back of Ria's neck.

"It's all in the sympathetic strings that run under the ones for melody. See them? Kara doesn't like thrumming. Makes me play outside."

"Perhaps the *gouar*, like the bagpipe, is best appreciated under the open sky."

Lute gave a good-natured snort and ran through a complete melodic line.

Ria spoke up quickly before he could favor her with an entire composition. "Do you mind if I take a look at your elms? They've leafed out nicely."

She swung out of the hammock and walked beside Lute among the handsome trees.

"It's an old grove," he said. "Older'n Kara, even."

The grove extended beyond the back fence and into surrounding yards. Ria admired the proud, high arch of the branches and traced the sawtooth edge of an elm leaf with her fingers.

"May I?" she asked and climbed up on a low-hanging limb.

Her perch gave her a better view of Kara's boxy-looking brick house. The atrium skylight rose like a shimmery bubble from the center of the steeply hipped roof. Glass panels for solar heating showed on the roof's south face. Outbuildings Ria hadn't noticed from indoors clustered on either side of the greenhouse corner.

All that room for just three people!

A wagon rumbled by on the gravel street fronting Kara's house.

Ria swung lightly down from the branch. "I couldn't have done that in my own body," she said, dusting her hands.

"Easier time moving now, eh? Everything comes in time. Want to help feed my carp?" Lute pointed to a pot of table scraps on the pond's banked edge. "But watch this first."

He sat down on his haunches, completely still except for

slight twitchings of his whiskers. Scores of fish rose to the surface, churning the water in a swirling frenzy of color—red, gold, black, bronze, and white. Their mouths gaped wide for food before any of it had been thrown.

"You called those fish with your mind?" Ria asked.

"Tickled the brains of a few and the rest followed. Now give 'em their reward."

Ria crumbled a stale roll and scattered it over the surface. Lute dumped the rest of the pot's contents into the seething water.

"Practically all our *solexes* can herd fish—in ponds or out—but humans seldom have that art. Guess they can't understand water creatures as well."

"Ever hear the medieval Italian legend of St. Anthony preaching to the fish?" asked Ria.

"Why'd he do that?" Lute rubbed his chin whiskers. "Fish haven't got souls that need saving. We *perfur* herd 'em to catch 'em."

Kara called to them from the kitchen door.

Lute whooped and chirruped, his whole body rocking and swaying.

"What is it?" cried Ria.

"Must admit," he replied, "must admit, I've been stalling you out here until our surprise arrived. Come meet her."

Kara waved them into the atrium where a female *perfur* stood waiting. Numerous black leather pouches and a skirt of thin gray fringe hung from her body harness.

"All hail," cried the newcomer.

She whistled at Lute. He threw his arms around her neck and kissed her nose. After repeated nuzzlings and snufflings, they separated.

Lute started to make introductions: "Julo is playing host today—"

"Could tell that right off. Walks different," the strange *perfur* muttered. Her choppy speech was hard to understand.

Lute continued as if he hadn't heard the interruption. "—to the soul of Ria Legarde, a new *solexa* that Kara and I are training."

"Honored," said the visitor, holding up her hands with the palms turned out. "What's your *harnama*?"

"I'm not . . . from here," answered Ria. "I don't have a mystic name."

The newcomer's nose wrinkled. She turned to Lute and asked: "This the one dreams 'bout the horse?"

He nodded.

Turning back to Ria, she said: "Rides in Air—that's who you are. I name things right. I'm Amris, Red Mountain at Sunrise. Lute's big sister."

Ria bristled but had the wit to raise her hands in *perfur* greeting.

Lute said ruefully, "My sister's used to giving orders. She's the Ranger Captain of the Wabash Valley."

Amris shrugged. "Easy work, compared to mindin' Lute as a cub."

Ria studied the visitor. Not only was Amris older than Lute, she was larger. Her ears were chewed to rags and a wide scar slashed across her nose. She reeked of roses.

"Just show m'calling token." Amris opened one of her belt pouches. "No sense givin' it, since only your soul's here."

She held out a stamped and dyed leather disk for Ria's inspection.

"My mark." Amris pointed to a stylized peak and rising sun, then flipped the disk over. "My Twin Stars clan mark."

Ria saw "a star of six points counterchanged," instinctively applying the language of medieval heraldry. She wondered if the *perfur* had a college of heralds to keep their emblems in order.

"Now you've met me proper and true." Amris stowed the token away.

"That pouch new?" asked Lute. "Like that silver clasp." He bent down to admire it.

Amris nodded. "Basala's work. Lined with tree-tiger fur, too."

She showed Ria and Kara how her disks fit in cunning rows of pockets. Rough Amris might be, but her taste was elegant.

"Basala made m'new scent bottle, too." Amris pointed to another accessory.

"Don't open it," cried Lute, covering his nose in mock horror.

Amris glared back. "Happen to like m'scent. Can't wear it on patrol."

Kara, who had been watching the byplay in amused silence, broke in: "Will you take some whiskey with us, Amris?"

"Pleased to, Lady Kara." Amris found a seat among the cushions on the atrium floor.

Ria's eyes widened at the sight of a sheathed knife hanging at the back of the ranger's neck. She stared at Amris's gear piled beside the atrium entrance. Could that long, leather-covered object be a gun?

Lute got glasses into their hands with a surprising minimum of fuss and also set out a plate of chocolate meringue puffs. He looked so smug and Amris so gleeful that Ria concluded these must be a rare treat. Seeing Kara decline the confections, she did the same. Within moments nothing was left of the meringues except a few sticky crumbs on the macotters' fur.

Kara glanced from empty plate to full glasses and said to Ria, "How dull if *perfur* tastes marched with human ones step for step." She offered a toast: "To our differences."

Ria took only the merest sip. Prohibitive taxes had effectively barred her from trying hard liquor at home and she was unsure of its effects on Julo's body. Having sipped, she wished she'd asked Lute to water her drink.

Lute noticed her hesitance. "Something wrong?"

Ria handed him her glass to finish.

Amris wrinkled her meringue-smeared muzzle. "Least she's not wasting Quail Cloud's best."

"Who could bear to waste a drop?" said Kara to Amris. "Your kindred on the Kankakee River are justly famed for their corn liquor." She took another swallow. "How fares your hunting?"

"Too well." Amris touched the fringe hanging from her belt.

Lute and Kara nodded gravely.

"Worry much more, I'll start shedding," continued the ranger. "Every circuit sees more rat-sign. Record. Report. Can't sweeten words enough for Fort Wayne to swallow.

What're they paying me for? Upriver and down, talk to sheriffs—those sons-of-cousins. One says his county's been clean twenty years. 'Nother says a rat drive's too dear. Railroads, canals, manufactories not too dear! What use, the day humans find crunched bones 'stead of their kin?"

"That's the day they'll listen. Not before," said Kara. "Until then, your very competence may be making humans feel weaker."

Lute refilled his sister's glass. "Where's the major buildup?"

"Mouth of the Wabash. Macrat're eatin' Posey County bare. Everything below Fort Vincennes is a-crawl. Lost a ranger there last spring."

"Who?" asked Lute sharply.

"At Burning Hills, nobody you'd know." Amris briefly kissed her fingers to her comrade's memory. "They've lost more'n one in Kentucky of late. Fort Louisville's talking grim. Word'll get north sooner or later. Humans heed humans better. Shouldn't complain so much long as bounty money's good."

Amris brushed again at her skirt of fringe, which Ria finally recognized as dried macrat tails. She was glad she'd eaten nothing.

"And what will you do with this wealth?" asked Kara.

To Ria, such a question was unacceptably personal, but *perfur* seemed to appreciate opportunities to boast.

"Invest in cross-cousin Rakam's pork-packing outfit," replied Amris.

"Is he still chittering about the perfect ham?" Lute snorted. "If he found it, he'd eat it all by himself."

"Eats his share, he does, but sells enough to line both our dens right well. Live to retire, I'll be one rich *femfur*."

"Careful somebody doesn't try to marry you for your money, dear sister."

"*Masfur* tries that, I tear his head off."

Ria pitied the male macotter who roused the ranger's temper. Indeed, she was anxious not to arouse it herself. Her clenched hands betrayed her nervousness to Lute. He bent over to give her a reassuring pat.

"She's never actually ripped the head off any person—of fur or of skin."

"Lute's still got his. Keeps it, 'less he spills m'drink."

Ria tried to explain herself. "Where I come from, violence is taboo. It's bad taste even to joke about it." She didn't want to admit that she found Amris unnerving.

"Then you'll have to learn to adapt, child," said Kara, "if you're to continue working with us. Violence is very much a part of our world."

"No macrats, how'd I earn m'living?" said Amris bluntly.

"You'll hear rougher talk than m'sister uses when we take you to the Midsummer Feast," said Lute. "*Perfur* aren't tame people."

"When you take me to *what*?" asked Ria.

"The gathering of the season," said Lute, "when we go home to our clans to celebrate summer." His whiskers quivered with excitement. "More food than you ever saw! Torchlight dances! Water races! Music contests!" He trilled.

Amris snorted. "Just like Lute: talk of food, 'stead of ritual."

Kara blocked his retort. "The treaty that Never Smiles made with the first band of *perfur* is also renewed at this time each year, in front of chosen human witnesses. I've been invited to serve in this role for Twin Stars. I can extend this honor to you, Ria, as my guest. Will you come with us?"

"You're kinder to me than I deserve," said Ria meekly.

She forced her hands to relax. If she could endure the trials of her initiation, surely she could survive the rigors of macotter merriment. But a whole village full of them. . . .

※　　　※　　　※

XIV

November wore on. Every spare moment Ria honed her new shamanic skills, but the manner of that sharpening was now hers to choose. Kara and Lute mostly confined themselves to evaluating her progress and suggesting new directions during her brief nightly visits.

Ria taught herself how to extend her mastery of fire to encompass electronic devices. Such equipment did not exist in her mentors' world, nor had Kara and Lute ever had occasion to investigate the apparatus of more technologically advanced timelines.

Ria spent an amusing afternoon running her tape player through its paces without touching the controls. Reveling in this small achievement, she felt like an undergraduate who'd published a scholarly paper.

She *could* make her own discoveries in *solarti*. She wouldn't have to remain under tutelage permanently.

Ria also gained enough confidence to practice medical procedures on her own body that Kara and Lute hadn't permitted her to try with Julo's. She designed simple experiments to accompany a programmed course in basic physiology that the University data bank offered.

Building on scientific knowledge, *solarti* let Ria experience the chemistry and physics of life with absolute immediacy. When enzyme embraced substrate, when helix begot helix, when antibody duelled with antigen, she was there. Her delight was to contemplate the energies of her own

being. Her challenge was to master each of these interior
fires.

Ria waged her first campaign against the heart. She
quickly learned to spur or slow its beating, pinch off
circulation or restore it.

Breath control came as easily. She was attaining the
powers of a yogi without formal yoga training.

The endocrine system presented more of a challenge,
but adjusting her appetite was also a more useful accom-
plishment. Ria could actually monitor *solarti*'s energy demands as they burned off her excess weight. Fine-tuning
her menstrual cycle had equal benefits—no more moody
spells. And by controlling adrenalin flow, she could drive
herself past normal limits of exhaustion or relax in the face
of provocation.

But too much manipulation of insulin levels gave her a
nasty episode of hypoglycemia. After that cheap warning,
she resolved not to meddle capriciously in her body processes.

Nevertheless, Ria's initially cautious exploration of the
immune system gave way to reckless pride. Once she'd
learned how to induce and eliminate allergies in herself,
she was able to heal Carey's chronic eczema without his
knowledge. Then as she preened at her secret benevolence, she realized that secret vengeance could be accomplished just as easily.

Alluring fancies invaded Ria's mind. She saw Hannah's
fine pale skin turned scaly and oozing, clawed raw by
frantic nails. She heard her foe wheeze in harsh asthmatic
gasps. She felt the quick spasms of anaphylaxis choking off
Hannah's life.

The slightest cellular nudge . . . the right cascade of
reactions . . . the fatal flow of histamine . . .

Ria wept for shame.

The old fear of misusing her powers came surging back.
She plunged through troubled waters of thought to consult
Kara and Lute. . . .

❋   ❋   ❋

A cold spring afternoon shed dismal light on the atrium.
The room smelled of fresh flowers and damp earth.

Kara waited alone on her cushions. A lap robe lay across her knees and a tufted wool rug was under her feet.

"Stop me, Kara!" cried Ria, kneeling before her. "Don't let me kill Hannah! I'm afraid—"

"I can see that." Kara interrupted her in a voice that held neither pity nor disgust. She sighed heavily and leaned forward to clasp Ria's shoulder.

"You're larger and stronger than your enemy," Kara continued. "You could slay her with your hands as readily as with your art. But you haven't done so."

"Certainly not!"

"So the ease of killing doesn't determine whether you murder her or not."

"No," said Ria softly.

"Then why are you so disturbed?" Kara frowned.

"I don't really intend to harm Hannah. It's just . . . I'm ashamed of myself for wanting to do so. Violence goes against everything I've been taught."

"Thoughts alone can't kill, not even the thoughts of a *solexa*."

"But my revenge fantasies were so ugly." Ria turned away, unable to confront Kara's gaze.

"Ah! There we have it. The *ugliness* of your desires offends you, not the malice they express." She forced Ria's head back so that their eyes met. "You're confessing one fault in order to conceal another."

Ria pulled free, burying her face in her hands.

Kara continued in a gentler tone. "People of your time imagine that they can scour hearts clean of every blemish. They labor in vain. Accept your weaknesses, child, and go on." Her voice roughened as she started coughing. "The more you struggle to deny unworthy thoughts, the more they'll bedevil you."

Ria timidly raised her eyes, forcing herself to notice the marks a lifetime's private battles had left on Kara.

The sound of china smashing broke the tension.

"I'll see what Lute's up to," said Ria and hurried off to the kitchen.

The hot tea Lute brought them—and Lute himself—lifted Ria's spirits. She couldn't stay depressed for long with the *perfur* beside her. She eased her tense body against the rippling warmth of him and restated her problem for his benefit while Kara listened.

"Try to understand, Lute," Ria concluded, "I've grown up in a strictly guarded world."

"That didn't protect you too well, m'lady." He snorted.

"It protects most of the people most of the time. But you two have thrust dangerous powers into my hands." Ria took a last sip of tea. "What if I kill someone with a medical procedure? What if I burn down the House by accident? I'm terrified that I'll abuse *solarti*, even without meaning to."

"Stay frightened and you're sure to slip." Lute chopped the air with his hand. "Our cubs aren't scared of knives or fire—they're just tools they need to stay alive. So they start using 'em early."

"They don't hurt themselves?"

"Not often," he answered with casual pride.

"Lute fails to mention that *perfur* elders instruct their young carefully before they arm them—" Kara coughed "—and watch them closely afterwards."

"Still . . ." Ria shifted uneasily in her chair.

"Self-control has to be learned sometime," said Lute.

"Cubs who don't learn it perish." Another fit of coughing racked Kara. "We thought you had more sense than a *perfur* cub, Ria. Perhaps we misjudged you. You will either deal with your fears yourself or you will forfeit our attention. At the moment you weary me. Please leave."

Ria left.

✳   ✳   ✳

She returned to her own body chastened. Kara and Lute were telling her "naught for your comfort and naught for your desire."

They were right, of course. She'd never gain self-confidence by refusing to explore.

On the other hand, it might be safer to concentrate for a while on positive uses of *solarti*.

Which ones? Healing looked innocent enough, yet it had its pitfalls. Since *solexes* could alter the rates of biochemical reactions, they could mend torn flesh faster than torn cloth. Too much satisfaction with this skill could lead to aberrations. Kara had mentioned mad *solexes* in past centuries who liked to cut their bodies to pieces and restore them for show. Ria's own world had legends of adepts tearing out their eyes or removing limbs at will.

Better stick with something safer . . . controlling pain, for instance.

So for the next week, when Ria stumbled on the sidewalk or crashed into furniture, she forbade her body to ache or even show bruises. From passive numbing she moved to active pleasuring. No laboratory could rival the subtle euphorics she coaxed her brain to make and send flooding through her nervous system.

Maintaining herself in a steady state of well-being smoothed out the peaks and valleys of daily living, but Ria found it surprisingly difficult to adjust to contentment. She kept testing her mood like a new dental filling: was she as happy now as she'd been a moment before, an hour before? She searched frantically for signs of old anxieties seeping through the calm—and searched all the harder when none were detected.

Ria's nightly visits to Kara and Lute lost their excitement. She began resenting her mentors' guidance: they asked questions and set goals. Their demands stirred pools she preferred left still.

On Thanksgiving, she didn't report to them at all. Instead, she lay cocooned in her blankets all that day and most of the next, too enraptured to move.

By Friday evening, Ria stirred. She stoked herself with sufficient biochemical cheer to face a House party.

She wanted to show off the shimmery white dress she'd bought to celebrate her new slimness. Counting the luxury tax, this garment had taken most of the money she'd saved for a bicycle. But the effect was worth it: the bodice rippled around her breasts and the flame-shaped hem swished against her knees like steady caresses.

Ria emerged from her apartment just as her bathmate was leaving his. She hadn't seen the gangling, thin-lipped man since their initial introduction eight months earlier. Her simulation of a neighborly smile went unnoticed.

He seemed no more sociable than herself and perhaps equally uneasy about it. She pitied him briefly before erasing her concern biochemically. Ria's long strides left him behind in his glumness as she swept down to the party alone.

The House lounge was painfully bright. Gape-mouthed plastic turkeys strutted on long tables laden with refreshments. Cafeteria leftovers from yesterday's feast returned as sandwiches and sweets. Residents munched greedily, thankful for anything free.

Ria threw herself into the spirit of the evening, trying to show that she could squeal and cheer as well as any other resident during the approved games. Whenever her glow threatened to fade during the frantic rolling of balls and passing of ribbons, a slight neurochemical adjustment brightened it.

No such stimulation was needed later when she asked men to dance with her, yet none attracted her enough to invite further attention.

Afterwards, Ria found Carey talking with Hannah beside the buffet table.

"But I like cranberry jelly, Hannah, honestly I do," he protested. "I hardly ever get to taste the stuff."

The petite blonde gazed reproachfully at his plate. "Eat it if you must," she sighed. "Sad enough that people desert sound nutrition for outmoded customs at Thanksgiving dinner, but to compound the error. . . ." She lowered her long pale lashes.

"Don't let her make you feel guilty, Carey," said Ria. "Fill your plate as high as you like. After all, it's our social duty to eat what's put before us without complaint." She took a mincemeat tart and bit the sticky little morsel in half.

"I understand perfectly why you'd break your diet, Ria, in the face of so much sweet temptation." Hannah gestured at the platters with her carrot stick. "But we dancers can't allow ourselves even one fattening meal."

"When did I say I was dieting?" Ria ate another tart.

"But you've lost weight," said Carey, looking as desperate as a civilian trapped on a battlefield. "You might perhaps consider wearing skirts more often. Becoming, highly becoming. I should've said so sooner."

"Some ladies have to wear pants all the time because

they can't afford sheer hose." Hannah's soft blue eyes focussed on nothing in particular.

"So you're as solicitous for my bank balance as my waistline. Try not to wring your hands too hard, Hannah. You might damage them."

Giggling at her enemy's outrage, Ria nearly missed the measuring look that briefly hardened the other's features.

"Are you ready to be rescued, Carey?" asked Ria.

"Uh . . . if you don't mind, I'd rather eat than dance just now. You don't . . . mind, do you, Ria?"

Ria scooped up a handful of spice cookies and left, still laughing.

Later, when she was about to retire, a note slid under Ria's door. Although it was unsigned, she recognized Carey's tight, round hand. She sat down on the bed to read it.

> *I'm writing instead of calling so we can't*
> *be overheard. Are you going noncomp,*
> *taunting her like that? She told me*
> *she thinks you're taking illegals. What*
> *if she reports you to PSI? Please watch out!*
> *I'm afraid for you.*

Ria shrugged sadly. Carey was entirely too nervous. He lacked her means of scaling her lofty plateau of calm. Perhaps she would do something for him. Or perhaps not. . . .

As she let the crumpled note fall, Ria's gaze flickered across a gleaming doorknob. A huge wave smote her down into roiling surf. . . .

❋   ❋   ❋

A floor loom dominated the cluttered, book-lined workroom. Ria found herself sitting bolt upright on a hard chair. Her hand was cranking a yarn-winding frame. Beside her, Kara was spinning wool on a wooden wheel. Lute hovered in front of them brandishing a pair of heavy shears.

"We are most especially pleased to welcome you this morning, Ria." Kara barely inclined her head in greeting. Her wheel spun steadily on.

"Why'd you do this?" Ria cried. "I thought you were through dragging me to and fro."

"We were," said Lute. "But you swim out of your depth, we'll haul you home every time."

"Explain that!" Ria sprang up to challenge Lute.

Despite his stooped posture, she had to look up to meet his eyes—his unsmiling eyes. Noting that prolonged sitting had left Julo's body stiff, Ria automatically began to erase the ache.

"Not so fast." Lute pushed her back down on her chair and stood over her, keeping his left hand on her shoulder. His shears were uncomfortably close to her chest.

"That hurts." Ria pouted.

"Meant to. You're not going to muffle every little twinge today. Or flit home till you've heard us out."

"We make no apology for our harshness," said Kara. "Your present danger requires rough measures."

"What do you mean? I'm feeling fine. I've never felt so fine in my life."

"In a few days your quest for fine feelings has come close to unraveling all the months and years of effort we've lavished on you." The spinning wheel slowed to a halt.

"You're addicting yourself to those painkillers your own brain brews," said Lute. "Cunning compounds, those neurotransmitters. Can't get enough of 'em now, can you?"

"What's wrong with stopping pain? I thought that was a major use of *solarti*." Ria tried to squirm out of Lute's grasp.

"Yes," said Kara. "We comfort those afflicted in mind and body. That's Lute's special work. But we don't try to shield ourselves or others from every pinprick life inflicts."

"Will you listen with a clear head?" Lute's voice softened.

"And if I won't?" Ria thrust out her jaw defiantly.

"Be warned, m'lady," he was grave again, "you're not meddling with one molecule in Julo's body while I'm standing here. I can follow you into your world and do the same there. Waking or sleeping, I'll stay with you till you come to your senses." His lips slid back from his fangs. "Otherwise, touch your brain here, touch it there and—"

"—I'll go no more a-roving. I understand." She clamped her mouth shut in a tight line.

"Some new *solexes* get drunk on their power over pain,"
said Kara. "Those like you, child, who passed through
bitter times in childhood, often fall into this trap. They get
so wrapped up in their own pleasures that they forget
whose well-being their art exists to serve. How can you
guard your people if all you watch is yourself?" Kara's
words rolled in steadily as the tide.

"Don't I deserve some pampering? If you're my friends,
why don't you want me to be happy?" Ria glanced from
one to the other until tears blurred out her sight of them.

Lute's hand slide across to stroke her neck.

"May all beings be happy," he said.

"May they also be strong enough to endure unhappiness
when they must," said Kara.

"Joy's not real 'less you earn it," Lute added.

"Do tell me about joy, Lute. It's built right into your
genes, isn't it?" Ria knocked his hand away. "Your precious *solarti* has brought me damned little joy to date.
Pain and pitfalls, that's all it is.

"So what if I can run up and down the Tree of Time like
some misbegotten monkey." Ria gestured at him. "I've got
books and pictures and data banks. Why must I go snooping into other people's minds for information?" she raged
on. "I've got as much conventional medical care as I
need—you don't but I do. So what's the use of self-healing
gimmicks? I wish you'd never found me!" Ria wept in
great, tearing sobs.

Lute tried to soothe her, but she batted him, cutting
her left hand on the shears he was still holding.

Kara came to her side. "That's quite enough, Ria. Stop
your bleeding before you stain the wool."

Directing her attention to healing the injury stopped
Ria's crying. Self-consciousness made the task go slower
than it would have at home, but the results seemed to pass
inspection.

She turned to Kara, expecting further encouragement,
only to reel back from words that battered her like pounding surf.

"Listen to what I say, daughter of my spirit. Hands are
sweeping round the clock and shadows lengthening even

as I speak. I thought I could die content once I had seen you made a *solexa*."

Kara's eyes narrowed to blue slits lost in wrinkles.

"I was wrong to think of contentment." She continued with a sigh. "Now I long and pray to at least see you standing on your own feet, outgrown my care, before I pass through the Last Door. Each foolish crisis of yours delays that satisfaction. My patience is wearing thin.

"Either take up the challenge of your calling without tears or cease pretending to be a *solexa*." Kara waved one hand, then the other. "Neither Lute nor I can live your life for you. We merely opened a path; you will walk it yourself—or not at all."

Lute slipped an arm around Ria's bent form. "Maybe you're struggling too hard with the art, m'lady. More to living than that. You think Kara and I practice *solarti* every waking minute?" He snorted.

"There are many other things we enjoy learning and doing," said Kara, smiling again.

"Let me show you," said Lute. "You haven't been in this part of the house before." He bobbed around like a spring with its tension suddenly released.

Ria obediently followed him to the bookshelves that covered one entire wall of the room. She groped for a response to Lute's obvious pride in the collection, feeling a twinge of nostalgia for the days when librarians dealt with actual books, not bytes of data.

"I couldn't fit a tenth of this in my apartment," she exclaimed. "Mostly, I have to depend on computer or microfilm."

"The University library's at hand but we like to have our own copies of the basics." Lute pointed to the labels identifying each section. "We've got a full range of arts and sciences—'most anything a *solex* needs." He gave Ria a confidential nudge. "Get my tail trod if the lot's not kept neat."

"*Perfur* need encouragement on matters of order." Kara chuckled. "As Lute's desk over there bears witness."

Ria scanned the titles, noticing Eliade's *Shamanism*, the same text she'd studied at home during her initiation. "I never expected to find Eliade here," she said, pointing to his book.

"Why not?" asked Kara. "It is said that books, like men, have their fates. Good work can outlive the time that bred it."

"But this copy looks fresh." Ria had pulled *Shamanism* from its shelf. "It can't be from before the Great Death."

"It isn't." Lute bit out his words. "Books do crumble after six centuries. We reprint 'em. Even publish new ones."

He returned the book to its place.

"Pleasure reading is commoner in our time than yours, Ria," said Kara. "One of the many thriving presses in our Republic is here in Chamba."

"M'lady, when you visit longer—as you will someday— you can read things that don't exist on your timeline."

"Such as?"

Lute chose volumes from the literature section and handed them to Ria. "Wonderful stories like *Sabbath Candles* by Anne Frank or *Ezana's Memoirs* by Mikael Yekuno. And here's Kara's favorite, *The Flowers of December* by Wilfred Owen."

"The poems of his deep age," Kara explained. "They take on fresh meanings for me as each year passes."

"What's your favorite, Lute?" asked Ria.

"My taste's more modern. Kara and I could argue till evening—but won't this time—no need to frown, m'lady. Can't be faulted for favoring m'own people's words. Take *Nightscents* by Manis Ghostclaw of Tidewater. Bought it at last year's Midsummer Feast."

He showed Ria a thick volume wrapped in a black suede covering that reminded Ria of a medieval book chemise.

"Nothing but the best for the song-poems of Manis," said Kara.

Lute untied the wrapping and riffled the pages of the volume inside. It was bound in blind-stamped black calf. Each page was both tinted and printed in different colors and bore a single lyric within an exuberantly interlaced border. The paper smelled of gardenias.

"Are the *perfur* trying to top William Morris?" murmured Ria under her breath. But before she could get a better look at *Nightscents,* Lute had closed, sealed, and reshelved it.

He chirruped on. "Lately we've been getting access to works that aren't part of our own past. Clever *solexa* out east—a 'word-huntress' she calls herself—reads the best books on other timelines and brings them back page by page in her memory. Bought one, didn't we, Kara? What's that author's name? Can't pronounce it."

"Alexander Solzhenitsyn."

"Grim going. Didn't understand it enough to finish it." Lute nibbled his fingers. "Must visit those time and places till I do understand."

Ria shuddered. "Spare yourself. Prison camps and firing squads aren't for your kind."

She handed the books she'd been holding to Lute. He crammed them back on the shelves in no particular order, but Kara didn't protest.

"Lute, show Ria the rug you're making."

He opened one door in a wall of cabinets and pulled out a roll of cloth and yarn. He unrolled the lot to show how a few tufts of wool had been tied onto a canvas backing marked with swooping curves.

"Kara's teasing me about being slow to get started on this one." He turned toward her, twitching his whiskers. "Made all the rugs in the atrium, didn't I?"

"I've every confidence that you'll finish—in your own good time, of course," said Kara. "Winter's still a long way off."

She explained to Ria: "I've tried to interest Lute in weaving, but it bores him. So he dreams designs for me. Look at these lovely patterns."

After showing Ria sketches on Lute's desk, she beckoned her to inspect the floor loom standing at the far end of the room.

Ria peered at it, keeping her hands clasped behind her back, afraid to touch anything lest she damage it.

As if sensing her nervousness, Kara invited her to take a closer look and put the loom through its paces to demonstrate how the parts worked.

"Dressing the loom and tying it up is far more tedious

than weaving the web," said Kara. "Once each warp thread's
secured in its proper place, the work goes quickly."

"What's this fabric going to be?" asked Ria. "It has the
same shades of red and blue as the rug Lute's making."

"It's to be a tapestry for my bedroom. See, this Tree of
Life design's reversible. I mean to finish it off in white
fringe."

Ria frowned. "But it's only June here. A little while ago
you . . ."

"Spoke as if I might die at any moment?" Kara smiled.
"In the event I happen to be mistaken, I don't want to face
cold weather with bare wall or floor. One does the task at
hand in the moment at hand."

Kara tightened the warp tension and pressed the trea-
dle. "Would you like to throw the shuttle once?"

Ria hesitated, but at Lute's urging, obeyed. The shuttle
flew between the warps.

Kara beat the new thread into place and relaxed the
tension.

"You did that correctly, child. If you hadn't, I'd have
pulled your thread out and bade you try again. One way or
the other, we'd have gotten it right."

She kissed Ria's forehead. "Go home now and think well
on what you've learned today."

※   ※   ※

Back in her own body, Ria lay stiff and sleepless. Her
mind flew back and forth like a busy shuttle, but what it
was weaving was hidden from her sight.

After the scolding Kara and Lute had given her, she was
afraid to induce sleep biochemically. She tried counting
warp threads, imagining an endless array of parallel fibers
stretched so tightly that they sang.

The singing turned to moaning.

Ria wasn't imagining these sounds. They were coming
from next door. Her bathmate seemed to be having a bad
night. Had the party gotten the better of him this early?

The moans grew louder, broken by short, gutteral outbursts that had to be curses.

Ria listened for noises in the corridor. Nothing—at the
moment.

But if her neighbor were still ranting when others were around to hear him, someone would surely report him to the authorities. He had to be wildly drunk to be carrying on that way.

Hearing him come into their common bathroom, she expected to hear sounds of retching. There were none.

Now his complaints came through with hideous clarity. Hiding her head under the covers didn't keep them out. No one should overhear such a litany of anguish. What was wrong with the crisis monitor? Was his mumbling too deeply pitched to trip it?

Ria stood up and timidly knocked on the bathroom door.

"Are you all right, citizen?"

"Go away!" he cried. "No help. Don't need no help!"

"If you say so."

Ria backed away and sat down on the bed again. The hysterical edge in the man's voice slashed at her. She shivered, remembering where she'd heard the like before. Her neighbor must not be allowed to go the way of her mother.

But if she called Suicide Prevention, he'd be sent to PSI for treatment. Their cure might be worse than his disease.

Could *solarti* save him? Could she wield her shaman's powers when they were really needed? Grabbing her steel mirror, she broached the swelling waves. . . .

✳   ✳   ✳

He gagged on the last swallow of amaretto.

"My God, Gin knows I hate the stuff. Why'd she give me a bottle? Throwing her money around. Why couldn't Gin have given me gin?"

He guffawed, flashing a death's head grin at the mirror.

"Last laugh is, I won't be here to feel the hangover."

He poured a spoonful of white powder into his empty glass. Who'd ever miss ten grams of cyanide from that teaching lab? Who'd ever miss him?

He filled the glass with water and swirled it to dissolve the poison.

He raised a toast to bid himself farewell.

The mirror exploded in sparkling darkness as he fell. . . .

❋　　❋　　❋

Ria lay on her bed quivering. She staggered up and put her ear to the bathroom door. She heard nothing except the sound of the tap running. The fainting spell had felled him like a tree, just as she'd intended. With luck, his glass had smashed in the sink and the water would wash its contents away. The ventilating fan ought to pull off the suspicious odor. Anything left would be attributed to the amaretto.

She need only alert the House staff to her neighbor's accident.

XV

Saturday afternoon, Ria's neighbor came calling. Her privacy reflexes flared briefly, but when she saw the trembling man's distress, she had to let him into her apartment.

"My name is Leigh Franz. From next door." He waved feebly in that direction.

"They told me you were the one who summoned help when I . . . last night . . . my fall." He tugged at his knobby fingers. "I want to thank you for getting the medics here." He stressed the word "medics."

"It seemed the right thing to do when I heard you hit the floor."

He reddened. "You can hear a lot through that door."

Ria kept her voice carefully light. "Not all that much. The fan's noise blurs most of it. I was about to fix some tea. Will you join me?"

She brewed and poured the tea.

While Franz sat waiting for his cup to cool, Ria delicately nudged the biosynthetic pathways in his brain. Her brief occupation of his body the previous night made adjustments easier. He'd attribute a brightening of his mood to the tea.

"You must've gotten quite a bump," said Ria.

"Don't remind me." He winced, touching his lank brown hair. "But no concussion or anything worse than a citation for drinking. Filling out the accident forms'll be more of a pain than the fall itself—not to mention working off my penalty."

159

"Anything you survive. . . ."

He nodded warily.

"But we can still talk sometimes. Would you like that?" asked Ria.

The ringing of his telephone jabbed through the wall. Ria let Franz out through her bathroom door.

He returned a few minutes later, his tight face loosened into a grin.

"That was my lab—I'm a biochem tech—I've got to get over there right now."

"On a Saturday?"

"You harvest your bugs when they're ready: they don't keep University hours. The new fermentation route *did* scale up. Yesterday, I was sure the batch was ruined."

The news meant nothing to Ria, but he seemed pleased. Franz didn't look as pathetic when he smiled.

He turned back on the threshold, suddenly grave. "Last night if . . . I'd've never learned that our experiment worked. When you need a favor, any favor at all. . . ."

He shook her hand hard and left.

Ria decided to visit Kara and Lute at once. She couldn't sit still through *Captain Blood* this evening with such news bubbling inside her.

Mirror in hand, she flashed through waters that glowed like molten steel. . . .

※   ※   ※

The warmth of her friends' greeting overwhelmed Ria. Lute hugged her so hard that they tumbled out of the atrium cushions and rolled across a shaggy rug together.

"And who lectures me about damaging Julo's body?" Ria gasped.

"What damage in a good romp?" Lute snorted with injured innocence.

Had she dared, Ria would've held his supple body against hers a moment longer.

Against Julo's body. *What a pity. . . .*

She straightened her cushions and sat down next to Kara. Lute sprawled at their feet.

Ria's account of her adventure with Leigh Franz brought warm hugs and cheers of approval.

Kara said, "Because you'd stopped looking at yourself, you were able to see your neighbor's need." Noontime sun shone down on her weathered face.

"Now forget your temptations," said Lute. "Don't fret over what's past. Without testing, you don't learn."

"So glib now, Lute?" Kara gave a wry smile. "After your fears that Ria might fail and forfeit her powers?"

Lute combed his twitching whiskers.

"Ah, but you *perfur* cannot stay gloomy long," Kara continued. "Joy's as much a part of you as your fur. Or as you say, 'Living is dancing.'"

"But we miss the dancing more when it stops," said Lute so softly that only Ria heard him.

He fetched glasses of whiskey and they toasted Ria's success.

Kara reminisced as she sipped, speaking as one professional to another. "Child, because your crisis has passed, I can tell you it was like one I myself faced when young.

"Unlike you, I was publicly marked out to be a *solexa* from my earliest years. Since my elders expected great feats from me, I drove myself mercilessly to perform. When I discovered how slight manipulations in brain chemistry brought blessed relaxation and then oblivion . . ." She stared past Ria, confronting the memory as if it were fresh.

"First the craving, then the loathing, until the craving for solace doubled and redoubled. But my master—" She kissed her fingers to the memory of a man decades dead. "—spied the danger quickly. When I denied I had a problem, he actually did to me what Lute threatened to do to you: he blocked my powers. He didn't permit me to use *solarti* again until I'd learned other means of easing tension and understood why I felt so tense in the first place.

"How it stung my pride to have my swift progress halted! In time, I could stand aside a bit from that pride and fix my sight on the art instead of what I, the great soul-artist, meant to accomplish."

"The secret I bequeath to you is one Lute knew without being taught: lose yourself to find yourself." Kara drained her glass. "Then the happiness you receive will outshine the pleasure you reject as the sun above does a tallow candle."

"I begin to see it, Kara," Ria said. "I saw it in my neighbor's living eyes."

Ria bent down to take Lute's hand. "Perhaps you can teach me other ways to help Leigh. But please," she added timidly, "May I take a break from medical experiments for awhile?"

"Don't have to ask our permission," said Lute. "You've learned most of the healing skills a *solexa* who isn't going into medicine needs to know."

Ria squared her shoulders and raised her head. "If I decide to halt my current line of study, what do you suggest that I put in its place?"

"You might practice placing yourself in time and space," replied Kara. "Blaze a trail along selected branches so you can climb the Great Tree alone with surefooted steps."

"But no climbing just now, dear lady. Stay a while, this day's so fair."

He rippled upright, staring hopefully at Kara.

"Before you start wheedling, Lute, I'll grant your wish. Just this once, to celebrate Ria's triumph, you may play your *gouar* for us inside the house."

Lute chirruped merrily.

❋   ❋   ❋

Ria approached her new assignment bristling with earnestness, determined to prove herself both cautious and humble. But as the week passed, absorption in the challenge banished her worries.

Feeling like a fledgling bird as she clumsily beat her way from branch to branch of the Tree, she found that she spun and crashed less when she returned to points that she'd visited previously. The congenial minds she'd entered during her initiation made attractive targets. Soon she could travel up and down these persons' lifespans, awkwardly at first, then with ease and precision.

Ria climbed one branch to see the nervous young journalist grown into an esteemed editor, old and mellow as a chess queen carved out of bone.

Up another branch, she found Major McCauley become

a white-bearded patriarch enthroned on a horsehair sofa, reading Kipling to a parlor full of round-eyed grandchildren.

Down a third branch, she beheld the aged Englishwoman as a young wife proud of her new matron's wimple, singing while she weighed gold for her husband to cast.

No instant Ria shared was ordinary. Every particle of every cell in the Great Tree was someone's personal universe, none inferior to any other. She could have spent a lifetime exploring each one.

Kara had guided her rightly: not the artist but the art—and the limitless reality it revealed.

Surely she would discover hard tasks awaiting her, tasks uniquely hers, yet she was equally sure of returning here to contemplate beauties ever ancient, ever new. The hand that stirred the water in the pool had cured her at last of the need to be useful.

One step nearer to mastery, she sped to Kara and Lute with strong, swift strokes.

✳   ✳   ✳

Evening shadows and soft humming filled the atrium. Lute was playing the *gouar* with unaccustomed delicacy.

Since Ria couldn't see his face clearly in the darkness, she touched his arm to signal her presence.

"Know you're here, Ria," he whispered, "been expecting you."

"Let me tell you what I've learned." She kept her own voice low. "Kara—"

"Kara's asleep."

The old woman lay back on her cushions breathing raggedly.

"This moment's for listening, m'lady."

Ria curbed her eagerness to talk. She stretched out beside him and closed her eyes.

The *gouar* thrummed like a chorus of insects. Anxiety ebbed away. The urgency to report her insights faded. Surely Lute could sense the new peace in her spirit without being told.

Ria savored the aromas of fish stew and fresh bread wafting in from the kitchen. They all must have eaten earlier. She could taste the stew on Julo's lips.

She sorted through the damp green smells of pond and plants. There had to be lilies somewhere in the room.

The fishy, flowery, musky scent of Lute himself beckoned her. She brushed his fur.

"Would you sing for me?" Ria asked softly.

"A song by Manis please you?" Lute bent toward her and sang in a thin, shivery keening:

> *The sickle moon*
> *Shears through thin clouds*
> *To harvest stars*
> *Like silver blooms.*

More Tidewater melodies unrolled beneath his fingers. Luminous waves rode the glowing sea, mingling as they crashed on dune-ringed shores, and falling back in drops of living flame.

Ria trembled on the threshold of his mind.

The doorbell jangled.

Lute sprang up, tripping over his *gouar*, and dashed off to answer the front door.

As he punched on the lights, Kara awoke in a fit of coughing. Ria helped her sit up straight.

Lute returned glaring and making flapping motions with his arms.

"Her?" Kara winced.

Lute nodded. "Her. The Buzzard Lady herself. Can't get rid of her."

"I will see her exactly one more time." Kara set her jaw.

Moments later, the caller swept in with a rasp of ruffled petticoats. She was dressed entirely in black and decked in heavy jewelry. Unnaturally black curls topped her wrinkle-netted face.

"I told the otter you would see me, Lady Kara. He actually tried to send me away."

"My colleague has a name, as well you know, Wilamine Hork."

Kara did not rise or offer a gesture of greeting. Ria remained kneeling at Kara's feet, trying to keep her expression blank.

"Luke, Lute, whatever you call him, was distinctly rude."

She adjusted her massive gold necklace. "A woman in my position isn't accustomed to such treatment. When my late husband was alive, he saw to it that I had respect. As a client I insist—"

"When were you ever a client of mine?" Kara chopped her off. "I refused to treat you while I was still the chief *solexa* in Chamba. I'll go on refusing you while life and breath are left to me."

"I can pay any fee you name. Besides, you have to accept me for treatment. It's your sworn duty." She dabbed at her eyes with a monogrammed handkerchief.

"My condition baffles everyone else. If your niece or that fellow Lerrow over in Lafayette were half as good as people claim, they'd have cured me long ago."

"No *solex*, however gifted, can cure an ailment that doesn't exist."

"I haven't spent a single day free of pain since my husband died. Not that I care to discuss my symptoms in front of your servants."

Ria struggled to look meek, but she noticed Lute's muzzle wrinkling to expose his fangs. A rank scent spread from him.

Hork was too intent on impressing Kara to notice.

"If healing were really your concern, and not the healer's name," said Kara, folding her arms across her broad bosom, "you'd be seeking Lute's aid instead of mine."

Hork shrieked. "Let one of *them* touch my soul?"

"Another such outburst, foolish woman, and more than your soul will be touched."

A fit of coughing seized Kara. Lute rushed to attend her.

When Kara found her voice again, it was as grim as her face. "Julo will show you to the door, Wilamine Hork. Never return."

"I can find my own way there without the half-wit's help."

Hork stalked out.

Ria did not need to be told to leave.

❋　　❋　　❋

Her dreams that night were troubled.

❋   ❋   ❋

An unhorsed knight, weaponless and lame, staggered across the bed of some vanished sea towards a mirage of cool mountains. Clouds of powdered salt raised by the wind seared his throat and burned his skin.

The shadow of a vulture swung lazily across his path. He saw gems glittering on the beak and claws that would soon be tearing his eyes out. A dainty golden bell hanging from the bird's bare neck tinkled softly as she spiraled down upon him.

❋   ❋   ❋

Ria awoke to a fresh snowfall. The view from her window was as sere and white as the desert in her dream.

Carey stopped by in the afternoon, burbling about the evening's film series entry, *The Four Feathers*.

Ria was in no mood for cinematic crises, much less an epic of the sun-baked Sudan. She introduced Carey to Leigh Franz and sent them off to the theater together.

Perhaps the two lonely men's needs would mesh, leaving her a bit more time and energy for her art.

Anxious to confer with Lute, she pierced the disk of brightness.

❋   ❋   ❋

Ria was sitting at the kitchen table, facing Lute's back. He was working with a fishbowl on the counter opposite her chair. His expected grace and unexpected concentration held her silent for a few moments before she felt obliged to announce her presence.

Rising quietly, she stepped up behind him and touched his neck.

"Heard you coming, Ria. Can't take a *perfur* by surprise."

The caress turned into a massage.

"Feels good," he said. "Keep it up."

Ria was delighted to give comfort for a change instead of always receiving it.

"Who was that dreadful woman—last night or whenever it was?" she asked.

Lute's body stiffened. He turned around. "Wilamine

Hork—she's the biggest lamprey in the lake—richest woman in Chamba. A whiskey-maker's widow. Keeps trying to force Kara to treat her. Can't understand why Kara won't. Gets nastier each time she's refused."

"Hork's illness isn't real?"

"Only to her." He snorted.

"Kara said you could cure her."

"Straightening bent minds is one of m'gifts, but that one wouldn't call for me on her deathbed. Nobody's making her suffer but her."

Lute cleared away his utensils. "Makes me want something stronger than tea," he said.

Fetching a dark bottle, he pointed to the label. "Quail Cloud's brand of whiskey, not Hork's."

Ria cut her drink with water, but Lute took his neat.

"Your people don't always love mine," he said, "not always."

Ria was embarrassed for her species. "Surely there aren't many like the Hork bitch?"

"And may the Most High keep them few." Lute took another swallow. "Kara keeps that kind at bay for me. But if she couldn't. . . ." He chewed his fingers.

"Kara's still resting from last night," he continued. "She's persuading her lungs to clear."

"May I see her?"

"No. Not till she's stronger."

Ria accepted his judgment. "I'm sorry Kara's not well but it's you I dreamt were in danger."

She described seeing a knight menaced by a vulture, wondering if she ought to apologize for envisioning him as a man.

"There's some basis to what you saw. Hork may try to harm me when I'm left alone—as I must be someday." His tone was detached. "But a dream only shows thoughts, not the real future. Must ask Kara what she's been dreaming of lately."

"And if she saw a vulture, too? I think I've shared dreams with others in the past."

"Quite right. So've I, with Amris, when I was small and she was still at home. Those were accidents. You and I ought to try it on purpose. An experiment. An experiment's the very thing."

Ria knew he was trying to avoid discussing Kara's health. Did he doubt her capacity to withstand bad news? But her doubts might be justified. . . .

"How can I share my dreams with you," Ria asked, "when you don't let me into your mind?"

"Matter of meeting, not entering. You see the difference?" He poured himself another glass. "We'll give each other cues before going to sleep, compare results afterwards. Never heard of it being done deliberately across timelines, but you and I . . ."

Their eyes met briefly before Ria looked away, flushing. "I don't think I could break into your mind or Kara's no matter how hard I tried."

"Not yet. Our skills're still greater. We can block you or pull you here at a particular moment but you can't do the same to us."

Lute sipped his whiskey. "Before you go wailing about weakness, let me tell you there're some humans—never met any myself, but records say they've existed—that *solarti* can't affect. Tempting to think they lack souls. No, not right, everybody's got a soul. Everybody."

The notion of soulless intelligence clearly distressed Lute.

Ria tried to turn him back on the track. "It hurts to be kept out of your mind—it says you don't trust me. Will you ever let me in?"

"Someday. Not now. Take it on faith, we've got reasons. Don't frown so, m'lady. I've been dreaming about you already, without needing to host your soul."

Ria brightened. "What did you dream?"

"I was climbing a spiral stair in a darkened lighthouse. A weary business—those metal treads weren't meant for *perfur* feet. Climbed for miles. Not a minute's rest." He rubbed his back, remembering the illusionary ache.

"Oh, the anguish of it all!" cried Ria in mock sympathy. "After some of the things you put *me* through in dreams. . . ." She tried to snarl like a *perfur*.

Lute twitched his whiskers. "When I got to the top, I couldn't get the light to turn on. Then you appeared and hit the switches with me. Beam clove the darkness like a shining sword."

Ria smiled shyly. "Maybe you were thinking of joint

projects? I wish you were. But I don't stay here long enough to pursue any."

"You'll get your chance during Midsummer Festival," promised Lute. "Two whole days at least."

"Is that enough time for anything worthwhile?" she asked.

Lute chuckled and offered to refill her glass. Ria declined.

"While you're with us, you've got the use of that silver ring that Kara gave you," said Lute, tapping her finger. "Should have one in your own world. Can't count on having bright metal around when you need it. Can work without a trigger if you have to, but it takes extra effort."

"I can't afford silver," Ria protested. "Certainly not right now, after I bought that expensive party dress."

"Steel then. Anything shiny." He shrugged.

"No taboo on cold iron?"

"What?" Lute snorted. "This isn't magic, Ria. Unless everything is."

He swept his arm around the kitchen. "Plants flower. Fish breed. Descendants of apes and otters think. Just as magical to be a poet as a *solex*." He planted a bourbon-scented kiss on her nose and waved her home.

✸   ✸   ✸

The next day, Ria put the question of a ring before Carey. Instead of offering advice on where to buy cheap jewelry, he offered to design and make the ornament himself. She happily let him take charge.

The following Saturday, Ria and Carey returned to her apartment after a pleasant evening viewing *Cartouche*.

Carey pressed a small box into Ria's hand, holding his breath while she opened it.

The handsome ring nestled inside surpassed all her expectations. Although it was merely a disk of stainless steel set in clear plastic, it achieved an austere elegance worthy of its purpose.

"It's magnificent!" cried Ria, slipping the ring on her bridal finger. "And it fits." Its massiveness rode well on her large hand. "Thank you, Carey, thank you so much."

She hugged him warmly.

"Glad you like it, Ria," he gasped.

"Now what do I owe you?"

"Owe? Ria, it cost next to nothing." He was more grateful for her gratitude than she was for the ring.

"All I did was sniff around the hobby room, talk to some people taking the plastic crafting course, and cobble it up from various kits. The resin came from an off batch one guy was about to throw out—perfectly durable, don't worry about that. It just sparkled too much to suit him."

"Surely our world needs more sparkle, not less?"

They laughed together.

After Carey left, Ria sat admiring her new possession. She had never owned a ring before. The mirror-bright metal within the shimmery bezel cried out for use.

She composed an image, flashed it in Lute's direction, and dived into liquid stillness. . . .

* * *

The mountain stood alone, rough and black as doom. In a riot of lightning and roiling ash, it split asunder. Lava streamed down its flanks to cool in streaks like clotted blood.

Its crater caught a century's rain until clear waters lapped a rim grown green with trees. The sky-hued lake within reflected clouds . . . and Lute's bewhiskered face.

* * *

XVI

Winter vacation brought Ria and the rest of the Library Research staff the welcome prospect of attending their annual, all-expense-paid, professional meeting. It was to be Ria's first outing as a University employee. She was eager to visit this year's destination, Chicago, a place that travel taxes ordinarily put beyond her means.

The week of their departure opened with a blizzard that heaped fresh drifts over the existing ice-encrusted snow. Then bone-deep cold set in.

As the bitter days passed, Ria sensed even worse weather coming. Her instincts were confirmed when an official Winter Storm Watch was posted on the morning they were to leave.

Yet despite potential hazards, Ria's group had no choice but to proceed. They were required to enjoy themselves on schedule.

Ria herself was reluctant to beg off the long-awaited expedition. The Health Service would have to verify any plea of illness. Could she fool the doctors well enough with self-induced symptoms? So she decided to gamble on taking the trip.

By the time Ria staggered into the central bus depot, the west wind was already rising. Its force convinced her anew that not a single tree grew between Chambana and the Rockies.

Carey spied her through the glass doors and offered clumsy assistance. They walked to their boarding gate together so they could sit next to each other. Now that

171

they no longer felt self-conscious about being an odd match, Ali and Hannah had given up smirking at them.

Carey gave his luggage to the baggage handler without paying the woman any particular notice, but the sight of her stunned Ria. The worker in the greasy uniform used to be her senior English teacher at University High School.

"Instructor Russell!" she cried. "What are you doing here?"

"Pu ah on nah bus," the blank-faced woman croaked back at her.

"Aren't you Marie Russell?"

"Pu ah on nah bus." The other repeated her gibberish, trying to wrestle Ria's suitcase away from her.

"I'm Ria Legarde. I was one of your pupils five years ago. Don't you remember me?"

Ria seized the woman's shoulder, struggling to make herself understood. The baggage handler jerked away, backing against the side of the bus and raising her hands to shield her face.

"On nah bus," she whimpered.

Carey tugged at Ria's sleeve. She bent down to hear his whisper.

"Let it go, Ria. Maybe she was your Marie Russell once. She isn't now." He mouthed a single ominous syllable: "PSI."

Ria lunged up the steps into the assigned bus.

Snow showers burst upon them before they were out of Chambana. The wind rose even higher in open country. Under its attack, the bus wobbled and shuddered like a living thing.

Ria stared grimly at the snow pelting her window, stared till the swirling gusts became rampaging stallions, death-white steeds with eyes like frozen stars.

She let their screams blot out the fresh memory of Marie Russell's tortured voice . . . and the older memory of that voice declaiming poetry in tones like ringing steel.

All visions failed as the bus skidded off the highway and rammed head-on into a huge snowbank.

Their tour guide was on her feet before the screaming stopped.

"Everybody okay?" she called, motioning their rumbles

of assent to silence. "Aren't we glad we were wearing our seat belts?"

She flashed a kilowatt smile that reassured no one. "We're going to have to sit tight for awhile," she said, pulling a route map down from the ceiling. "We're midway between the Buckley and Onarga exits." She indicated their location with a colored flashlight. "It's too far to walk in either direction. The nearest rescue squad is based at Paxton—here." A red beam marked the spot. "We'll just have to wait until they can get here."

The guide neglected to mention how long and frigid a wait that might be: Paxton was more than 20 kilometers distant. Nothing would be moving very fast in this blizzard.

She continued briskly. "Mustn't let the delay get us down. How about giving the person next to you a big, warm hug?"

"How about getting out and trying to free the bus ourselves?" yelled some man from the back row.

Ria and everyone else swiveled around to stare at the speaker. It was old Eli Blume from Rare Books.

The guide was too professional to waste breath answering him. She let the others shout him down, then proceeded to work her way up and down the aisle, soothing and jollying with relentless concern.

The travellers huddled together in quiet desperation, too well conditioned to complain.

Ria offered to draw Carey close to share warmth, but he turned rigid at her touch. Ali fussed over Hannah as if she were a tropical bird, even lending the younger woman her muffler for extra protection.

Ria withstood the temptation to blast Hannah's perfect cheeks with frostbite.

Instead, her thoughts turned back to a nastier winter emergency when she was twelve.

She'd been riding with her father in a University truck—a flagrant breach of work rules—when he lost control and flipped the vehicle in a ditch. With her father knocked unconscious and having no luck raising help on the truck's radio herself, she trudged five kilometers to the nearest farm station through searing, cracking cold.

She came through the ordeal unharmed, but her father's

face was badly frostbitten by contact with frigid metal. The accident also cost him his rank as chief campus arborist. He died the following year, crushed under a falling tree.

Unwilling to bore—or worse, alarm—her colleagues with the account, Ria settled deeper into her coat as if going to sleep. She turned her head toward the wall, cautiously sliding back her glove to expose her new ring. Turning the setting around to the back of her hand, she blinked rapidly to make its polished center flash.

Released at last, Ria plunged into the shining ripples of her own mind. . . .

※　　※　　※

Ria awoke to scents of macotters, water, and sunbaked wood. She was lying on cushions spread between Kara and Lute. He helped her sit up, playfully brushing a damp lock of hair from her forehead.

Ria found that they were riding amidships in a small motor launch operated by two *perfur* she didn't know. Despite an awning to shade them from the sun, her shirt and twill trousers were drenched with sweat and the glare off the river hurt her eyes.

Wooded banks sped by until their vessel approached a dock where an adult macotter and three cubs waited.

"All hail!" cried Lute, waving madly at the shore. "Look, it's Amris come to meet us."

Kara waved in a more restrained manner that Ria copied.

They docked and debarked. Kara thanked the boathandlers while Lute bounded ahead to greet his sister. The cubs broke away from Amris and swarmed over Lute, squealing so shrilly that Ria's ears protested.

Amris stepped in, restoring enough order to let Lute make introductions.

"First lil' scamp—"

"*Big* scamp, Lute, big!" The largest cub jumped up and down, protesting.

"This *big* scamp—who still goes by his cradle name, Dasher—is our cousin Rakam's oldest."

"Rakam the meat-packer?" asked Ria, scrambling for connections.

Amris nodded, rumpling Dasher's fur.

"His friends," Lute continued, "are Mossy and her baby brother Puff."

Mossy let the humans pet her stuffed toy duck, but Puff clung to Amris's leg.

Sitting down on her haunches, Amris gently dislodged Puff's tiny hands and held them up in the polite *perfur* greeting.

Kara knelt beside them, gravely returning the gesture. Puff squeaked with shy pleasure.

"Made your manners, off we go." Amris swept up Puff in her arms.

Dasher and Mossy scurried ahead, racing up the steps beside the dam that separated the Tippecanoe River from Evening Star Lake. Dasher reached the top first, a feat that seemed to matter more to him than to Mossy.

"Catch us, Amris!" Dasher cried as he and Mossy scuttled away.

Amris took off in pursuit, the rifle case on her back swinging as she ran.

Lute spoke quietly to Kara. "If the steps bother you," he said, "I'll—"

"You're fussing too much," she answered, waving him away.

"With reason." Lute gave Ria a stern look and left them.

At least Kara agreed to avoid the stairs, choosing to take an easier path to the village.

Ria stayed protectively close as they walked back past the dock where another boat was unloading. They picked up a gravel road that climbed eastward from the landing alongside a row of red clapboard buildings. Kara identified these as warehouses, pointing out similar structures across the river where workshops ran on power supplied by an adjacent water mill.

Since even a gentle pace had Kara panting, Ria halted at strategic spots along the way, as if taking in the sights. Between wheezes, Kara obligingly called her attention to gardens, fish ponds, and pastures farther south along the river's floodplain.

By easy winding stages, they reached the crest of the bluff where the village proper stood. This was a single interconnected complex of brightly painted wooden buildings surrounded by stretches of patchy grass. Ria could barely see the structures, much less make her questions heard, for the noisy throng of *perfur* swarming around them.

Scores of excited macotters rushed to and fro, yelling and chittering in happy chaos. They were carrying lengths of lumber, wads of bunting, armloads of evergreen boughs, hand tools, baskets of fish, and outlandish musical instruments. Some were setting up dealers' booths while other seemed equally busy impeding the workers.

If a plan guided their efforts, Ria was unable to discern it.

No sooner had Ria and Kara located Lute, Amris, and the cubs, than Dasher broke away from them to hurl himself at a thick-bodied *masfur* who was trying to mediate a standbuilders' dispute. The cub's squeals drowned out the adult macotters' angry humming. All three disputants glared at him.

"Asked you to keep him in hand, Amris," complained the *masfur* in charge.

"So y'did, Rakam," said Amris, ignoring his criticism. "Father's busy, Dasher," she called. "Let him work."

"Busy for days," the cub whined. "Him 'n mother both." He trudged back to Amris, rolling his eyes in a bid for pity from the others.

Rakam noticed the newcomers. "Oh, Lady Kara, an honor." He raised his hands in formal greeting. "Pay m'respects as soon as duty permits."

"I understand the demands of your position," said Kara.

"Wouldn't want to come between you and duty," said Lute.

Rakam was left to his executive labors.

"Pompous," muttered Lute.

"Cures a good ham," Amris countered.

"Comes of his closeness to th' pigs."

Ria tried not to smile, lest Lute be offended. She could afford to find Rakam amusing—he wasn't her cousin, this wasn't her world. On the other hand, how would Lute react to a Professor Clyde?

Making their way through crowds of Festival workers, Ria and her friends reached the village's biggest building.

"Our *koho*," said Lute proudly.

"This is the clan's community house," explained Kara, "where the feast will be served tomorrow."

The cubs snuffled eagerly at the mention of food.

Lute boasted, "It's the best *koho* in Rolling Shores territory—roomier than Quail Cloud's, finer than Burning Hills's—"

"We've been on our land longer," said Amris.

Lute snorted.

"Bet it uses the brightest colors," said Ria, playfully shading her eyes against the building's garish decor.

Each board of the siding and each shingle of the roof was painted a different hot color, arranged for maximum clash—scarlet next to lemon yellow, magenta beside burnt orange. Each post and pillar of the long porch was fashioned like the stalk of a different flower. Carved and painted vines twisted around the frames of small-paned windows.

With the cubs scampering ahead, they continued around the *koho*. Ria craned her neck, expecting to see gargoyles on the second storey, but the rainspouts and chimney pots were blossom-shaped.

At the west end, a ridgepole in the shape of a tree branch supported a weathered brass bell, so plainly made it must have come from humans. A pair of massive oak doors opened below it. Ria recognized the emblem on one door as the sign of the Twin Stars clan. She was told that the other stood for the Rolling Shores tribe to which all the clans of the region belonged.

Looking back toward the lake, Ria was surprised to see a man talking with a *masfur* and a *femfur* in the shade of a huge ash tree.

The trio welcomed Kara and Lute as old friends, but stared curiously at Ria.

The human, a comfortably shabby, bespectacled man in his fifties, spoke first: "That's your servant Julo's body, Kara. Whose soul does it host today?"

Kara answered, "Here is my pupil, Ria Legarde, a *solexa* of great promise."

"The one you told us of? The very one?" the *femfur* chirruped.

"Herself," said Lute, beaming.

The *femfur* and the man exchanged eager glances that the short, white-muzzled *masfur* noticed without sharing. Amris seemed on the point of asking a question, but kept silent.

Kara completed introductions, starting with the *masfur*. "Ria, meet Gemai, clan chief of Twin Stars; Ellesiya, the clan's prime *solexa*; and Doctor Wan Lerrow, prime *solexam* of Lafayette."

All three raised their hands in formal salute. The *perfur* also showed Ria leather disks bearing their personal marks, just as Amris had on first meeting.

Knowing less of rulers than shamans, Ria naively asked Gemai: "How were you appointed, sir? By the tribal elders?"

"By them? Way off on the Michigan dunes? We pick our own chief, Lady Ria. You must come from far, not knowin' that." Gemai stroked his long white whiskers.

"I'm not an actual mayor like Oren Henderlund of Lafayette—we're waitin' on him 'n his folk now," the clan chief continued. "*Perfur* are wary o' power. Rituals keep me busy but m'job's mostly stayin' calmer than m'clanmates so they'll let me lead 'em in a crisis."

"Gemai," said Ellesiya with a fluid wave of her arm, "your greatest gift's the way you make light of your gifts."

Ria half-expected the graceful *solexa* to pirouette. She seemed to be dancing while standing still.

"*Perfur* aren't famous for being meek," said Lute to Ria.

"You'd know, Lute," muttered Amris, drawing a hurt look from her brother.

Gemai affected a pose of abject humility that made everyone laugh. The cubs laughed hardest, to see their elders at play.

Ria was thoroughly confused: important persons in her world did not poke fun at themselves or mingle with such easy intimacy.

Kara got them moving again.

"Come along," she said. "Our friends have things to do. So do we." She called to Lerrow over her shoulder. "When you're free, Wan, please come to me at the guesthouse. We need to talk."

Lute and Amris led them to the quarters for human

visitors, which lay past sprawling flowerbeds on the north side of the *koho*. This cottage, like other outbuildings, was connected to the *koho* by covered walkways, reminding Ria of a medieval manor house.

Thick walls made the cottage pleasantly cool inside. It was arranged like Kara and Lute's home, with a square of rooms grouped around a skylighted atrium. Ria and Kara found their bags waiting for them in the chamber they were to occupy during their stay.

The whole party relaxed in the atrium while Amris handed out mugs of warm, dark beer that was far sweeter than the brew Ria was used to. But it shocked Ria to see the cubs served as well as the adults—even though the portions were tiny.

Mossy and Puff held their small mugs carefully in both hands. Dasher waved his about carelessly and spilled beer on himself.

While Lute was drying him off, he squeaked:

"Guess what, Lute, guess what? Amris let me watch her shoot her gun. Bang!" He sighted and fired an imaginary weapon. "Macrats, look out! An' I got to hold it, too. Bang!"

Ria blanched. "You actually let a little one handle a gun?" she cried. Firearms were strictly controlled in her world. She'd never actually seen—much less touched—one.

"What harm?" asked Amris. "Empty. Safety on. Got to start learnin' self-defense young. Where you come from, humans don't?"

"We're not allowed—we don't need to," Ria corrected herself. "No macrats there."

Amris wrinkled her muzzle in disbelief.

Before she could reply, Kara said: "Show Ria your rifle, Amris. She's suspicious of unfamiliar things."

The cubs chittered with excitement as Amris unslung her weapon and removed it from its fancy leather case. She held it out for Ria's inspection.

The rifle was not unlike pictures of old guns that Ria'd seen, but images hadn't conveyed the lethal efficency of the thing.

"A genuine Colson," said Amris proudly. "Don't see

many nowadays. Can throw an 11 millimeter slug 650 meters in a second." She stroked the brown-toned barrel.

"A family heirloom," Lute explained. "We've been rangers for generations."

"Stock's new, made to m'measure," said Amris.

It was burl walnut, carved with the *femfur*'s mountain-and-sunrise mark. Ria wished she dared touch the satiny wood, but her social conditioning held.

"I'll be a ranger, too," said Dasher. "Found the rifle sign last Yule." He pointed to a tiny silver charm hanging from a chain around his neck.

"Game doesn't always hold true, young 'un," said Amris. "Kept finding cradles every year I played."

Lute guffawed.

"What's your calling to be, Mossy?" asked Kara.

"Music-making," she replied. "Maybe." Mossy showed them her harp charm.

"And what of Puff?" Kara continued.

"Too little to play Find-Your-Life." The other two cubs giggled.

"Don't be so quick to claim pride of place because you're older," Kara warned them. "Perhaps Puff has the makings of a *solexam*. Perhaps he'll be the one to find the silver tree next Yule. But for now, allow me to find some rest while the rest of you find some food. I'll eat with Wan later."

They toasted Kara with the last of the beer as she left the room.

XVII

"Is this going to be a picnic?" asked Ria as she strolled through the woods with Lute, Amris, and the cubs.

"Eating out of doors? Yes," replied Lute. "But it's our brother Siote's cabin we're heading for, not some bare spot under a tree."

"Your people don't actually live in the village?"

"Not in warm seasons," said Amris. "Winter's when we den up together in the *koho*."

"This time of year, families scatter, throw up cabins all 'round the lake." Lute waved his arms in a double arc.

Dasher tugged at Ria's leg. "Not us. We live north o' the lakes. Live there all year."

"Got to stay by the hog barns," said Amris, scooping up Dasher to ride on her shoulder.

The cub squealed like a piglet.

"He's trying to say, we don't do everything the same," explained Lute. "Only part of our clan's here at any one time. Rest of us work for ourselves or for humans across the Wabash Valley."

The trees opened into a clearing where half a dozen or so *perfur* were milling about a thatched cabin made of upright logs. Waving greetings, they left their cooking fires to swarm over Ria's party, chittering and kissing noses.

As her hosts moved in, Ria felt a shiver of panic—those powerful furry limbs, those heavy fangs within the smiles.

The cacophony of scents they wore—cedar and mint, sassafras and honeysuckle, fennel and roses—mingled with the odors of mud, fish, and leather, without entirely masking the macotters' natural muskiness. She recalled with a shudder that the *perfur* were mustelines, thinking cousins of the mink and the wolverine—while she was merely human.

The introductions confused Ria. How could she tell *perfur* apart? She tried to note distinctions in size, coat color, or markings. Siote was shorter and darker than Lute. His wife Nirena—referred to as a "weather watcher," whatever that might be—was plumper than Amris and unscarred. Nirena's younger sister Manita and her husband Tahar showed their newlywed status in constant cuffs and scuffles that drew ribald jokes from the rest. Ria never caught the names of a neighbor couple and their half-grown daughter who joined the group.

All these *perfur* were talking at once in voices louder and shriller than Ria could bear. At first, they tried to speak slower for her sake, but soon jabbered on fast as before in their eagerness to tell Lute all the family news since spring.

Only the meal of fish steamed in grape leaves slowed the conversational pace.

When Dasher tried to prove that *perfur* could talk just as fast with their mouths full, he nearly choked on a fish bone. No sooner had Lute pulled it out and treated his scratched throat than the cub was chattering as madly as before.

How could a dozen *perfur* seem so many?

Walking back to the village afterwards with Lute gave Ria a few peaceful moments to savor. Sunlight filtering through the leaves dappled their path. Twigs cracked underfoot. Apart from Lute's soft, happy snuffles, the only other sounds came from birds and insects.

Ria wished they could linger on the path, but all too soon they were back in the storm of busyness.

More *perfur* had arrived in the village over the noon hour, raising the noise and confusion to ear-threatening levels. Would the Festival be the luncheon party writ large?

Lute was not immune to the general fever of excitement. From his darting eyes and quivering whiskers, Ria guessed that he now wanted to be with his clanmates, rather than her. As a passing work party hailed them, she waved him off to join them.

"Why don't you go help your friends?" said Ria. "I see Wan Lerrow coming out of the guesthouse. I can talk to him."

Lute chirruped his thanks and scampered away.

Ria watched him help hoist a plank onto a platform being built beside the lake. Turning around, she found Lerrow standing behind her.

"A lot wilder than what you're used to, yes?" he said.

"How do they get anything done?" Ria shook her head. "Obviously they do: these buildings didn't grow from acorns. But Lute and Kara didn't explain much."

"Your work's going to involve diagnosis, figuring things out for yourself." Lerrow made a tent of his fingers.

"Can't I have some hints?" Ria begged.

"This time, m'lady." Lerrow grinned, straightening his steel-rimmed glasses, which were held together with a bit of wire. "You'll have to take this on faith, but *perfur* festivals do come off nice as you please every year. Just the set-up's noisy. You know they can't so much as walk into a room without raising a ruckus."

Ria nodded emphatically.

"Main thing is," he continued, "*perfur* won't take orders from on high. They've got to see and smell whoever's in charge. Takes lots of tail-twisting to persuade them to act, but once they make up their minds, they work like hell's merry imps—until something distracts them and the persuading has to start all over. Let a rare butterfly flit by this minute and half the workers on those booths would rush off to chase it."

"With the other half chasing them?" Ria added. "Rakam wouldn't like that." Ria giggled, picturing the pudgy *masfur* huffing after the deserters.

"Daresay not. Next year, he'll be pounding nails while someone else's in charge. He'll resent it all the more since his wife Lekera's a dance dreamer and runs her part of the show herself every time."

They dodged a passing *perfur* who couldn't see them for the bundle of pine branches he was carrying.

"Come time for ritual, though," said Lerrow, "those *perfur*'ll get more solemn than a church full of humans. That's obeying the voice of tradition, you see, not any one individual."

"You seem to know them inside out."

"Might say that." He chuckled at some private joke. "It's part of my job, in fact, as you'll see tomorrow night."

"How many *perfur* will attend the ceremony?"

"Five hundred, maybe."

Ria shuddered.

"The good weather Nirena promised is bringing more in than usual," he continued, grinning. "That sounds like too many *perfur* in one place to you."

"I'd only met Lute and Amris before."

"And Amris takes some getting use to."

"Yes."

"I keep forgetting your world doesn't have *perfur*. Me, I can't picture doing without them."

"I think I could do with less of their galloping good cheer." She thrust her hands into her trouser pockets. "It depresses me."

"Let's go indoors, then, away from the worst of it and out of the sun." Lerrow took her arm. "We could go back to the guesthouse. Kara's resting there now. Or would the *koho* interest you more?"

"Let's not risk disturbing Kara," answered Ria.

They sidestepped a troupe of choristers—at least, Ria assumed that's what they were. Each was singing a slightly different version of the same trilling tune. Ria's ears protested.

Past the *koho*'s double doors, Ria felt as if she'd fallen into a page from *The Book of Kells*. Every bit of woodwork, from the hall pillars to the balcony railings to the roof beams, seethed with carved and painted patterns, swirls of interlacings as restless as the *perfur* themselves.

Bustling activity inside the community house matched the mood of the decorations. Trestle tables thudded and skidded on the brick floor as workers shoved them into place in two rows down the length of the wide hall. Shrieks interrupted grunts and chitters when feet or tails got in the way.

From the expanse of tables, Ria judged that tomorrow's feast would be a huge spread. It had to be, to satisfy *perfur* appetites. Five hundred hungry *perfur* appetites. . . .

Lerrow led Ria to a sprawl of cushions and tabourets clustered in front of the great hearth on the east wall.

Three elderly *femfurs* sat there tossing counters on a cloth-covered gambling board. They didn't bother looking up as the two humans approached.

Lerrow awakened an even older-looking *masfur* who was dozing beside racks of kegs and bottles. He ordered beer for himself and Ria. The sleepy bartender shrugged when they declined hard candy as an accompaniment and set the bowl beside the gamesters instead.

After they were served, Ria asked: "Why do the others call you *Doctor*? Is that a title of respect here?"

"Medicine's where I use my *solarti* gift. I'm both *solexam* and physician."

Ria raised her eyebrows.

"Yes, m'lady, we've got proper doctors—not as advanced as your world's, to be sure. But the art makes up for some of the equipment we lack."

"So the medical exercises Kara and Lute put me through have practical use?"

"Wouldn't've made you do them otherwise." Lerrow took a long swallow of beer. "You've met a young *femfur* named Manita? She was born with a septal defect—"

"A hole in her heart?"

He nodded. "The kind of heart surgery your folk could do to correct it is beyond our world's means. So I patched the defect, cell by stimulated cell, through *solarti*. Manita's a fine fit *perfur* today."

"Now wait," Ria said, raising her hand. "You speak of 'my world' and 'your world.' So you know my real origin, although Amris and Gemai don't."

"Kara's told me—and Ellesiya—all about you. You're unique, young lady." Lerrow toasted her with his mug.

"People keep saying so." Ria squirmed.

"But Kara wants to wait a while before publicizing the results."

"Until she sees if the experiment worked?" A touch of bitterness crept into Ria's voice.

"Partly," he admitted, refusing to argue. "But initiating a *solex* on another timeline isn't something we'd want everyone with a smattering of the art trying."

"Still, she told you."

"Kara's consulted *solexes* in foreign parts, too. I happen to be the nearest thing she's got to a peer in this corner of the land—not that any *solex* living's quite the peer of Kara ni Prizing."

Lerrow continued. "It was Lute who insisted Ellesiya be told. They grew up together, so he knew she could be trusted. If he'd stayed here instead of going off to study with Kara, he'd be the chief soul-artist here, not her—as well she knows. But someday, when she's the prime *solexa* of all Rolling Shores and he's still in private practice, who's to say which choice was best?" He shrugged.

"Didn't Lute want the post?" Ria couldn't comprehend indifference to status.

"He's too much the scholar. Day-to-day responsibility for the clan would hobble him," Lerrow explained.

"You look surprised, Lady Ria. Don't you realize yet what a powerful talent our friend Lute has? I can see that you don't." His brows knitted.

"Are you saying I've been entertained by an angel unawares?"

"Well put! Not an angel—the mischief he used to make! But a new piece in our world's game. I'll not live to see half the plays he'll make."

It was Ria's turn to frown. "You sound like Kara talking about me."

"What's wrong with her, Doc?" Ria found herself wringing her hands. "It seems serious, but Lute won't discuss it. Instead he says things like 'I should get her a kitten to boost her spirits.' Kara's faded noticeably, just in the few months I've known her."

"Truth is," Lerrow looked grave, "her heart's giving out—chronic congestive heart failure. Our drugs and treatments can ease but not cure it. Even if we mobilized a whole team of medically gifted *solexes*—which she'd never permit even if they could be found—the prognosis would still be poor because of her advanced age."

"Why would the operation take so many shamans?"

"Because each of us can only leave our bodies for a brief interval. Remember, I said I'd patched Manita's heart cell by cell? Damn slow work it was, too. Stimulating tissue growth in a newborn *perfur* cub's heart was a lot simpler problem than the massive intervention Kara needs."

"Could I make a difference?" Ria pulled at his sleeve. "I'm here in a host body. I can leave it for as long as I want."

"Maybe if you were a trained surgeon and could handle the whole operation yourself. *Maybe*." Lerrow stared out at the darkest corner of the room.

"Tell me what to study!" Ria cried. "Please, I want to help. Kara means so much to me." Ria couldn't bear to think of losing her mentor so soon after finding her.

"More beer," said Lerrow, with a nod toward the bartender. He looked at Ria again. "You're a generous lady," he said, "but Kara and Lute tell me your main talents don't lie in the medical area, even though you can do some basics now. That's why they haven't said anything. They don't want you wasting time you need to prepare for your proper specialty, the mastery of fire."

"Couldn't they let me choose for myself?" She drank to hide her agitation. "They're still not treating me as a—colleague."

"You almost said 'equal.' That's what I'm curious to learn, Lady Ria—exactly how equal you are."

Once again Ria felt like the pawn of forces beyond her control.

"A moment ago," she said stiffly, "you called Lute a gaming piece. Is that all we are, he and I, nothing more than gambling tokens like the ones those old *femfurs* are tossing?" She pointed at the gamesters by the hearth.

"Their game's played with peach stones." The eyes behind the spectacles grew enormously gentle. "A fruit stone is really a seed."

"I think I'm up to facing the *perfur* multitudes again. Alone, if you please."

Ria left her beer unfinished.

XVIII

Ria exited through the back door of the *koho*, which was connected to the separate kitchen by a covered passageway. Outside, five *perfur* were unloading baskets of eggs from a wagon.

Ignoring the workers and their cargo, Ria headed straight for their draft horses, four splendid animals that reminded her of black Belgians.

Horses close enough to touch!

Murmuring regrets that she had no apples to offer them, Ria shyly stroked the thick curves of the horses' necks and praised the red tassels braided into their manes. The team accepted her attentions as placidly as they did the noise their *perfur* masters made—shrieks over a dropped basket merely drew an extra flick of the ears.

Ria gave the horses a last pat and left them patiently brushing at flies.

She wandered north and west of the *koho*, towards the main concentration of traders' booths along the lake. Some merchants were already open for business; the customers drawn to these first offerings hampered efforts by other traders to lay out their wares. A book dealer and a seller of spiced fish paste were quarreling over the rights to a choice site. How could hagglers hear one another above the excited chitters and irate humming?

Ria let the crowd carry her along, peering as best she could through the shifting tangle of furry bodies.

She saw displays of body ornaments and marzipan fish, seed mosaics and packs of dye, gaming boards and gleaming knives, pine needle baskets and knotted string bags. She listened to a lutier play a peacock-shaped *gouar* while a drum-maker beat time. She fingered blankets woven from strips of rabbit fur, gaudy feather cloaks, and strands of freshwater pearls. She sampled honey that tasted like mustard and liqueur made from maple syrup.

After an hour or so, Ria shook herself free to spare her overloaded senses.

Beyond the booths, closer to the edge of the lake, Ria spied a crowd of *perfur* clustered around a red-striped tent. Drifting closer, she caught the final verse of the poem they were hearing chanted:

> *So every spring*
> *She counted time*
> *For kindred sped*
> *Beyond death's Door.*

The audience howled its approval. The performer, a *femfur* draped in strings of fish-scale sequins, thanked them. She accepted the contents of a bag passed among her listeners and retired into her tent.

Ria walked on, wondering what the poem meant.

She was getting close to the lake. Short flights of limestone stairs led down to the water, where latecomers were still unloading their boats.

Absorbed in these bustling processions, Ria nearly collided with two heavily laden *perfur*. After a flurry of apologies, she helped them gather up the bulky leather boxes they'd been carrying. Noticing that the *masfur* was bent with age and the *femfur* had a crippled foot, Ria insisted on hauling part of the load herself.

Getting all the goods to the booth had Ria sweating, despite the strength of Julo's body. The *perfur* weren't even winded.

While Ria paused to catch her breath, the two traders introduced themselves, welcoming her as a guest soul. The elderly *masfur* was Habale, a scent mixer, and the *femfur* was his daughter Basala, a leatherworker.

"Basala?" exclaimed Ria. "I've heard of you. And I've

seen the beautiful token pouch you made for the Ranger Captain Amris."

Basala snuffled happily. "Honor to serve the brave captain. Pleasure, too, with her sure taste."

"Could we serve you, Lady Ria?" asked Habale. "Want to watch us unpack? See our full stock? Won't last long. Not at all, not at all." He chirruped at the prospect of brisk sales, pointing to the prospective customers who'd already begun to notice them.

Ria couldn't refuse such an invitation.

She helped Basala hang canvas sunshades while Habale slowly and methodically set up measuring gear, gauze bags, racks of tiny stoppered bottles, and stout pottery jars. Only when his array was complete did Basala start bringing out her own wares.

The aroma of Basala's leathergoods delighted Ria almost as much as Habale's fragrances. Articles of genuine leather were expensive luxuries in Ria's world, but she hadn't seen any to match the quality of these. She ran appreciative fingers over belts and harnesses, boxes and pouches, that were tooled, dyed, woven—or splendidly plain. After Ria admired the available selection, Basala showed her a pattern book from which other items, such as curiously shaped saddles, could be ordered.

"Not meanin' to pry, Lady Ria," asked Basala, "but what's your *harnama*?"

"Ah . . ." Ria fumbled briefly for the special name Amris had given her. "Rides in Air. That's it. Took me a moment to remember," she apologized. "It's so new."

"Got your tokens yet?"

"No, I—"

"Like me to design your emblem?" Basala's whiskers quivered. She reached for her tools.

"I hadn't thought . . ." Ria hesitated, knowing how important personal emblems were in this society and aching to belong.

"If you have time . . ." she continued more briskly, "Yes. Please do."

After brief interruptions to serve other customers, Basala made several trial sketches on a wax tablet that she smoothed with a mere touch of her finger. The design Ria chose used a few fluid curves to suggest a horse and rider galloping above a cloudy mountaintop.

"Can you remember the look of it, Lady Ria?" asked Basala. "No use stampin' leather disks you can't carry home."

"Could you make a copy for me to leave with Kara? And what do I owe you?" Ria asked, reaching into her pocket for the spending money she'd been given.

Basala waved the coins away.

"Fair exchange for your help settin' up. Besides," she lowered her voice to a theatrical whisper, "favor to a visitin' *solexa*'s good for business, same as a favor for a ranger.

"Though any that fights macrats is m'friend," continued Basala, no longer joking. "Raiding party killed my mother. Workin' on me when Amris's uncle drove 'em off." She clamped her jaws shut with a crunch.

Ria couldn't help staring at the *femfur*'s body, confronting what courtesy had ignored earlier.

Most of Basala's right foot was gone. Both her legs were deeply scarred and her tail was missing its tip.

"No shudderin' now." Basala patted Ria's arm. "I'm proud o' surviving."

Before she could reply, Habale shuffled over to join them. He studied the design for Rides in Air, then turned to Ria with a searching gaze. His eyes were watery and a little sunken.

"Experiment," he murmured to himself. "Yes, yes. Fine experiment. Must try it."

"Try what, Father?" asked Basala.

"Mixing a scent with only the soul to work from," he replied. "Lady Ria's soul."

"Is that enough to go on?" Ria frowned.

"Come back tomorrow to find out." He rubbed his hands together. "Coriander'll be the base note. Give you the recipe so you can have it made up at home."

"Thank you," said Ria, clasping the old *masfur*'s hand. "But I must tell you, where I come from, nobody I know wears perfumes."

The two *perfur* were shocked into silence.

Ria left her new friends to their eager customers.

She continued alone along the curving lake shore, past

the now-completed ceremonial platform. Clamor faded as she moved away from the village. The huge red sun was sinking into billows of rose and gold.

Some *perfur* were calling fish into weirs to be held for tomorrow's feasting. Others left curving wakes behind them as they swam. Canoes gliding far out on the sunset waters were pared to silhouettes by the fading light.

At long last Ria found Lute sprawled on a jetty down at the lake's edge. They stretched out together awhile without speaking, simply letting their fingers trail in the water, idly watching leaves drift by.

"My own waters," said Lute. "I don't swim in them as often as I should."

Ria gazed out across the darkening lake and recited:

> *What color are the waters of evening,*
> *Lit by the evening star?*

"Lovely."

She laughed nervously. "My attempt to rewrite Ausonius."

"What's that?"

"*Who,* not what—a Roman poet. He sang of a quivering leaf afloat on a quiet river while the Empire was crashing around him."

"The Romans? I've heard of them." He nodded. "But the Fall of Rome's a lot farther back from us than from you. Too far for *solexes* to reach."

Lute's voice turned smug. "I once made it all the way back to the Middle Ages. Wasn't easy. Sat in a bowman's mind at some battle—what'd he call it? Poitiers." He sighed. "Didn't like to watch the killing. Never went back. Wonder what became of that serjeant named Jack?"

"You and Kara have taught me too well." Ria said. "I'm starting to take soul-flight for granted. I keep forgetting the time gap. Keep forgetting that in your here and now, I've been dust for six hundred years." She cupped her chin in her hands. "If I searched long enough in Chamba, would I find my grave?"

"I haven't seen it, m'lady," Lute answered softly.

"Have you looked?"

"Only your body's dead here, not *you*," he cried, turning toward her.

She snorted. "You believe that?"

"Don't need to believe. I know where eternity begins. Show you sometime." He fell silent for a moment, then brightened. "Till then, want you to feel comfortable whenever you are, in whatever body."

Ria tried to lighten the mood. "I'm uncomfortable enough in this body to want a cooling swim. Come with me?"

"This instant."

"Let me undress first."

As Lute pulled off her boots, Ria squinted at her reflection in the water. It rippled too much to show a clear image.

"What does Julo's face look like?" she asked. "You've never let me see it."

"We thought it'd be less awkward for you in the beginning," he explained. "Forgot afterwards. Could find you a mirror here, or wait till next time we're home."

Lute sat up. "It wouldn't show Julo as he normally is, only yourself looking out of his eyes. That's all I saw when I guested in his body."

"So I need another vantage point."

Ria stood up beside him and took off her shirt. She admired her muscular male chest with its flat little nipples and fair curly hair. She was unbuttoning her fly when a *perfur* cub's head bobbed up beside the jetty.

It was Dasher.

"Lute 'n Ria! Come to the *koho*. Tahar 'n Manita're goin' to Build the Bones."

Dasher clambered out of the water with Lute's help and promptly drenched them shaking himself dry.

Ria glared, but put her damp shirt and boots back on without comment. She hoped she'd get a chance to change clothes before the *perfur* swept her up in new activities.

Dasher chattered brightly all the way back to the community house.

"Tracked you down so quick, shows I'm meant to be a ranger. Gonna track macrats." He mimed a search and fired an imaginary gun. "I get places fast. Bet Mossy's still lookin'." He scuttled around Lute and Ria's feet, nearly tripping them.

They found Mossy sitting quietly with Puff near the main doors of the *koho*. Dasher resentfully joined them, boasting of his prowess and complaining about the exclusion of cubs from the ceremony.

With the huge doors open, there was just enough light inside for Ria to recognize Amris, Gemai, and some of the other *perfur* she'd met earlier. Dozens of them stood gathered in the wide aisle between the buffet tables, facing the great hearth.

They parted to let Ria and Lute reach Kara. She was seated in a chair at the front of the crowd with Doc Lerrow standing beside her.

Tahar, Manita, and Ellesiya crouched on a richly embroidered cloth in the open space beyond. The mates faced each other, flanking Ellesiya who confronted a tall wooden candelabrum in the shape of a tree.

Ria felt the press of strongly scented furry bodies. It wasn't the dampness of her clothes that made her shiver.

The ceremony began.

Ellesiya lifted her hands.

She and all the *perfur* present intoned:

> *By sunlight, starlight, firelight,*
> *Reflections of the Light Eternal.*

The candles burst into flame of themselves.
The *solexa* continued alone:

> *May the Most High bless this newly pledged pair.*
> *Make him bold as Rue,*
> *Her wise as Lis,*
> *First parents of our people.*
> *May they found a clan that lives*
> *Till every leaf be fallen*
> *And every bough be dead.*

The crowd responded:

> *Till all the seas shall fail*
> *And rivers no more run.*

Ellesiya handed the couple a beaded white bag and stretched out prone on the floor.

Manita and Tahar shook the bag three times, then scattered its contents like seed. Tiny colored flakes fluttered down upon the concentric rainbow circles stitched on the cloth.

The crowd sighed with one collective breath. Each *perfur* craned and squinted to get a look at the glittering pattern that formed. They did not seem to like what they saw.

Ellesiya rose up studied the array and gave her reading. Her tone was guarded.

"Nothing to be seen on time's nearest branch: Manita died young there; Tahar never was born. Remember, fish scales fall to tell us what may be, not what must be."

She pointed to specific circles. "Blue on the water ring, green on the woods ring—fertile country where they're settling."

"Not fertile us?" asked Manita. She touched a brown ring where no scales lay.

"Reds for danger, reds for rats," said Tahar. "Too many."

Ellesiya nodded slowly. "This oracle says two things at once: prosperity and peril. Now Build the Bones together, to show you can meet all fortunes well."

She untied a black pouch from her belt, loosened its strings, and set it before them.

Tahar and Manita took fish bones from the bag one by one and lay them in the center of the design. Layer by layer, the dainty stack grew, a skeletal tower that a breath might blow away.

The crowd prickled with tension, growing muskier by the minute. Hands spontaneously joined. Ria feared Lute would crush her fingers by gripping them so hard.

Surely so much striving must will a favorable sign into being. . . .

Screams tore the stillness. Tahar's hand twitched. The bones scattered.

Everyone ran to the doors at once, jamming against each other in their haste. Ria elbowed her way through.

Dasher lay bleeding but unmoving just outside the threshold.

Puff kept shrieking, "Hurts! Hurts!"

Mossy only whimpered.

Amris gathered them in her arms while Doc Lerrow examined Dasher.

"What happened?" asked Amris.

Mossy pointed to the ridgepole. Even in the dusk, a white cloth could be seen fluttering there. A cloth like a small winding sheet.

"Climbed up there." She sniffled. "Goin' to muffle the bell so it wouldn't ring tomorrow. Fell—"

Her wailing set Puff crying again. Amris muffled their sobs against her chest.

Kara joined Lerrow and Lute beside the injured cub.

"Will it be the Door?" she asked calmly.

Lute groaned before answering. "Better if it were. His neck's broken."

"Third cervical. Cord's severed," added Lerrow.

"He's not suffering now," said Lute, fighting for composure. "Doc stopped the bleeding and I'm holdin' the pain. Puff's feelin' it worse then Dasher. Give 'em here, Amris."

Puff went limply quiet in his arms.

"Dasher'll never move again." Lute's voice broke.

"Merciful God," whispered Kara.

Chaos erupted. As the news spread, score on score of *perfur* abandoned their tasks and rushed to the accident scene. They swarmed about the *koho* writhing, wailing, and gnashing their teeth.

Ria's teeth chattered along with them. She began shaking uncontrollably. Quadriplegia was tragic enough in a human, but for a *perfur* cub . . . It mustn't happen! She wouldn't let it happen!

Ria clapped her hands to get their attention.

"Are you just going to stand around snarling?" she yelled. "If *solarti*'s so wonderful, let's heal Dasher with it. There's got to be a way. There's too much talent on hand not to find a way." She made no move to wipe away her tears.

Kara turned slowly to face Ria. "There may be a way, daughter, if you can open it."

Raising her voice, Kara addressed the crowd. "Listen to me, friends of fur! Lady Ria, who now guests in the body of my servant Julo, hasn't simply exchanged souls with him as visiting *solexes* normally do. This powerful *solexa* hasn't come from a distant land. She's come from a separate branch of time!"

The crowd muttered uneasily.

Kara continued. "So Lady Ria is free to move from body to body without displacing the soul within, without costing her host effort. I propose that Lady Ria enter Dasher to repair his broken neck while all the rest of us who know the art support her efforts."

"I see it, Kara!" Lerrow slapped his thigh. "Four experienced *solexes*, maybe another hundred others with measurable talent, could be enough to pull it off. Get those nerve fibers rejoined straight, inhibit scarring—that cub'll swim again!"

Ellesiya didn't waste time commenting. She took command.

"Find a pallet for Dasher," she ordered. "Get torches. Rouse the whole village. Summon every pattern dreamer, art maker, beast tamer, weather watcher, every lighter of the family flame."

The crowd exploded in all directions to obey.

Ria watched in a daze, desperately hoping that her slight medical knowledge would prove equal to the task.

She heard Lute pleading with Kara in words that seemed to come from a great distance.

"You can't take the strain, Kara. It'll kill you."

"So? Isn't Dasher's life worth dying for?"

"Ellesiya, Doc Lerrow, and I can handle it. No one'd blame you for stayin' on shore."

"I would blame myself." The finality in her voice brooked no argument.

"But you're lying on a pallet to work. You'll listen to me that much." Lute hummed with annoyance as he stalked away.

Ria had no more time to ponder the burdens of power. She watched as Dasher was cautiously moved clear of the doors. Scores of *perfur* lay down on the grass between the *koho* and the mighty ash tree, forming petal-like rows with the four *solexes* closest to the patient.

But Ria didn't see the final preparations. Three half-grown cubs escorted her to the guesthouse where they were to keep Julo occupied during the treatment process.

The young *perfur* offered nervous encouragement as Ria lay down to begin her work.

She tried to imagine Dasher's face on the surface of her borrowed silver ring. Aiming herself, she dropped like a stone into unknown waters. . . .

✳   ✳   ✳

Ria hit her target.

She knew the place with the passionless immediacy of an angel. The being called Dasher was an array of cells, a concert of energies, each one subject to her ordering. Focusing her awareness on his spinal cord, she perceived the severed neural fibers as masses of unbleached yarn.

Time to re-dress the loom mischance had wrecked. Kara had shown her, was showing her, would go on showing her what to do until the task was done.

Sley the reeds, tie the harnesses, every warp thread in its rightful place, so the weaving could commence. So many threads . . . more threads than she could number . . . each one more fragile and elusive than the last.

She fastened them all.

Raise, lower, throw, beat, went the rhythm of the living loom.

Lute upheld her, Lute and a host of others who surrounded her like breaths of brightness.

Raise, lower, throw, beat. . . . Crews of weavers sped to and fro in time to Dasher's heartbeats, the pattern-makers themselves a pattern upon the glowing web.

Raise, lower, throw, beat. . . .

✳   ✳   ✳

XIX

Ria awoke in full daylight, astonished to feel so lively after last night's exertions. Then she remembered that Julo's body had played no part in her soul's work. She stretched languidly.

And went rigid with fear at the sight of Kara's empty bed. Its coverlet was still slightly rumpled from the old woman's nap the previous afternoon.

Ria sprang out of bed to search the guesthouse. She anxiously prowled the rooms, still in her nightshirt, until she found Lute's sister-in-law Nirena working in the kitchen.

"What's happened to Kara?" cried Ria.

"Worn out, that's all," said the *femfur* and went on slicing ham. "Kara's restin' in the sickhouse. Can see her 'n Dasher soon as you eat."

"How's the cub?" Ria had nearly forgotten him in her anxiety over Kara.

"Should recover, says Doc. Course, no dancin' for a while. Your doin', Lady Ria." Nirena gazed at her with a mother's happy eyes. "Best thanks is to feed you."

While Ria dressed, Nirena prepared a huge brunch of ham, scrambled eggs, cornbread, honey, and fresh blackberries.

"Have you know this ham's from cousin Rakam's private stock," explained Nirena as they sat down to est. "Sent it over this mornin' as a gift for you 'n Kara."

"It's delicious," said Ria. "I can see why Rakam would keep it for himself."

Nirena cut herself another piece of ham. "Rakam claims

he's changed his coat." Her whiskers twitched. "Enjoy it
while we can. Soon be his old stuffy self. Get you somethin'
else?"

"Thanks, no. There's more good food here than I can
finish."

"You aren't as hungry as the other *solexes*? Rest of 'em
came to limp as dead fish. Rest of us with th' art were
pretty wobbly, too. Now eat up: got to get that strength back
before tonight's feast." The *femfur* nudged the honey jar
closer to Ria.

Ria didn't quite follow the logic of eating to get strong
enough to eat more, but merely said: "Hope all my colleagues are eating this well. You're too kind, Nirena."

Ria bridled her impatience long enough to help Nirena
clean up before leaving the guesthouse.

Her patience was barely equal to the scene outside.

Throngs of noisy *perfur* loaded with food and serving
dishes swarmed around the *koho* and the adjacent commu-
nal kitchen, already busy preparing the feast.

Ria could neither dodge them nor detour past them for
the press of chittering well-wishers trying to thank her for
saving Dasher. More than one dish was dropped and tail
trodden before she reached the small building east of the
kitchen that served the clan's medical needs.

She found Lute and Doc Lerrow conferring outside the
door of the sickhouse.

"I wouldn't let her do it again to save my own grand-
child," said the doctor.

"Throw a block on her myself before—" Lute waved at
Ria.

"Is Kara all right?" asked Ria anxiously.

The caution in Doc's voice was itself an answer.

"She's resting peacefully. You can look in on her if you
like," he replied.

"That isn't quite what I asked."

"She's not in any immediate danger, but the prognosis. . ." He shook his head.

Doc and Lute took Ria inside. The hospital area was
surprisingly cozy, with curtains dividing it into small, den-
like compartments.

Ria could see for herself that Kara was indeed asleep

and breathing normally. A young *solexam*, one of Ellesiya's apprentices, was keeping a careful watch over her.

Ellesyia herself was in an adjacent section attending Dasher. With her were Amris and the cub's mother, a skinny *femfur* named Lekera.

Dasher looked pitifully small, lying there immobilized in a heavy body-cast. More shame than pain showed in his half-closed eyes.

"How're you feeling, Dasher?" asked Ria, a touch too heartily.

"Not Dasher any more," said Amris. "Gave'm a new name—Still There."

"Take a lot on yourself, Amris, changing m'son's name without askin' me. Long as it teaches'm to be quiet." Lekera's voice was as thin as her body.

"Don't hurt now, Lady Ria," squeaked the cub.

"Thank the *solexa*," said Lekera. "She saved your skin."

"There were scores of us," said Ria firmly. "Others in this room deserve equal thanks."

Which weren't likely to be forthcoming from Lekera. She and Rakam must make a fine pair.

"Didn't mean to cause trouble! Didn't!" The cub broke in. His eyes went so wide that their white rims showed. "Promised Mother no more jokes."

Lekera snorted.

Ellesiya sighed softly. "No jokes at all, Still There? Rest of us need that bit o'laughter. Even more need *you*."

She brushed his eyes closed and sent him to sleep.

The visitors took this as a sign of dismissal and left.

Back outside, Amris was the first to speak. "He'll be a ranger yet," she said, in a voice gruff enough to be a growl.

She shook herself, as if shedding water, and continued more normally: "Won't live to see it, less I get somethin' to eat."

"There's ham in the guesthouse kitchen," said Ria. "Rakam's very best. Help yourself."

Amris dashed off grinning. She threaded her way through crowds of busy clanmates with the ease of a hunter slipping through brush.

Ria, Lute, and Doc followed her at a slower pace, held

back by clusters of *perfur* clamoring to greet them. Ria was too happy to let the tumult annoy her this time, but her friends were fairly quaking with frustration by the time they reached the guesthouse door.

Inside, Lute and Doc trampled each other's words in their eagerness to talk.

"Know what last night's work means?" cried Lute, exploding into frantic chitters.

"We'll call it ni Prizing's Method," said Doc. His leathery face flushed with excitement. "Lute and I were fit to burst our skins waiting to tell you about it."

"Tell me about what?" asked Ria.

Doc gave a rueful chuckle. "Pardon. When I'm around *perfur*, I get to sounding like them." He waved Lute to silence.

"Lady Ria," he continued, "we've got us a whole new way of doing surgery by *solarti*. A *solex* like you from a different branch of time can work with a team here as long as needful. So we'll be able to try complicated operations otherwise beyond us."

Doc hugged her. "Think of the lives that'll be saved because that fool cub broke his neck!"

Ria shivered in his arms. "You won't expect me to sit in on every operation, will you?"

"'Course not, Ria," answered Lute. "Anyone strong in the art will do, long as they're from another timeline."

"Forgive me for being glad that I'm not the only fish in the sea." Ria wiped her brow in mock relief.

"God alone knows how many *solexes* there are on the whole Cosmic Tree," said the doctor. "But the more of them we reach, the more we can do without putting too much strain on any one individual."

Ria thought of service quotas, like House duties back home. But no, this world didn't impale persons on schedules.

Doc continued. "We've only found a couple of other branches close enough to ours that we can use for checking probabilities—to make weather predictions and such. But that may change." He looked closely at Ria. "You just might start some new twigs sprouting all by yourself, young lady."

Ria pretended she hadn't heard that last statement.

"Why so few branches?" she asked, frowning. "The Great Death must've been a major nexus point. Didn't it bring lots of new timelines into existence?"

"Made for some sharp bends, all right," said Lute. "But we *perfur* didn't survive on every branch. Or else didn't make friends with humans." His lips drew back from his fangs. "Could show you timelines where your people wear fur skinned from mine. Could, but won't."

Doc abruptly changed the subject. "These visiting *solexes* don't have to be physicians. You've proven that, Ria. They can even come from primitive cultures that don't know how *solarti* works."

"And," said Ria, her voice rising triumphantly, "your *solexes* can return the favor. You can help tribal shamans elsewhere cure their patients, too."

Ria glowed with healthy professional pride. Maybe she was actually starting to fulfill the potential her colleagues claimed to see in her.

"Let's get our thoughts in order while Kara's resting," said Doc. "There's plenty of time before the feasting starts. Then we'll have something on paper to show her when she wakes up."

The three of them sat down in the atrium to work. A pot of hot tea provided by Nirena fueled their labors.

Doc's enthusiasm didn't keep him from laying out his theories in orderly fashion, accompanied by esoteric diagrams and mathematical formulas. Although Ria couldn't follow most of the technical points he argued with Lute, she gained new respect for the caliber of their minds. The Professor Clydes of the cosmos didn't have a monopoly on brilliance.

They were able to work undisturbed for several hours until the arrival of Mayor Oren Henderlund and his party from Lafayette.

Henderlund was a trim, dapper man of perhaps forty, with the amiable face of a beagle. He shook Ria's hand as if campaigning for her vote and seemed indecently glad that ni Prizing's Method had been discovered in his own district. They had to restrain him from calling on Kara in her sickbed.

Ria, Lute, and Doc were obliged to join these visitors for the rest of the afternoon. Together they watched swimming and boating contests on the lake.

Although competition was alien to her, Ria applauded when Lute did, sharing his pleasure in his youngest nephew's canoe victory and his niece's performance in the water-dancing.

After the prizes were awarded, Doc and the Lafayette people withdrew to banquet with the clan leaders of Twin Stars while Ria and Lute went to eat with his family.

The feast itself surpassed all her expectations.

Hitherto, Ria had loathed fish as a bland but necessary protein source. She'd never imagined there were so many ways to prepare it. The *perfur* weren't content to merely broil, fry, smoke, pickle, bake, or steam fish. They glazed it with aspic, wrapped it in crust, poached it in liquor, doused it with yogurt, and sauced it with fruits, nut paste, or flowers. They nested sets of individually stuffed fish inside one another for layer on layer of contrasting tastes.

They were equally inventive with eggs, pork, duck, frogs, eels, snails, chicken, turtle, goose, and crayfish: Ria couldn't always identify ingredients. A vast array of tinted meringues, berries, puddings, torten, and achingly sweet egg candies plus beers, wines, and fruit punches filled out the menu.

The eclectic extravagance of it all reminded Ria of a medieval banquet. She half-expected to see a castle of pastry and gilt paper as the centerpiece. Such thoughts were perhaps better left unvoiced lest the *perfur* be inspired to act upon them.

Ria concentrated on filling her own tray.

She wanted to taste everything, even the anise-flavored eel. To hell with sane and sober food! This world held a richness she'd been hungry for all her life without knowing what she was missing.

The buffet line moved through the *koho* with loud good humor and reasonable dispatch. Doc was right: *perfur* could organize when they chose to.

Today, the mingled scents of furry bodies didn't bother Ria. They made a fitting counterpoint to the insistent aromas of the food. On some visit she ought to have

Habale make up that perfume formula he'd promised her. Then she'd be able to hold her own with the *perfur*.

By the time Ria had made her first pass through the buffet line, she realized that the meal was as much a cooking contest as a feast. Each elaborately garnished dish bore the name-marks of the family, work team, or social circle that'd made it. As her friends explained, good cooks earned prestige, a commodity no *perfur* ever had enough of.

The awesome logistics of these feasts also forced the clan to cooperate as well as compete. Ria wondered if their government did much besides coordinating the four seasonal festivals observed by all *perfur*. She'd heard that a new clan gained full recognition the first year it celebrated the complete cycle from its own resources.

How long would it take the foundation Manita and Tahar were planning to achieve that status? No name had been chosen for their clan yet. They were waiting for one to manifest itself, a development that might not occur until settlement was actually underway.

Perfur spilled out onto the village grounds to dine picnic-style with much chittering and merry chaos.

Ria and her friends occupied a shady spot, thoughtfully chosen in advance by Nirena. They sat on blankets spread on the ground and feasted heartily.

Repeated trips to the buffet line throughout the afternoon eventually satisfied bottomless *perfur* appetites and left Ria overstuffed. She was amazed at how much Julo's young male body could consume.

By the time everyone had cleaned up after themselves, the sun was low. Hanging lanterns were lit. The Midsummer ritual was about to begin.

The clan slowly gathered before the lakeside platform that Ria had seen under construction the previous day. Since then, busy crews of *perfur* had thoroughly soaked it with water and had heaped a man-sized mound of brush upstage. They were just now lighting a pair of huge, three-pronged flambeaux to provide light along the sides.

Kara was brought out in a chair and given the place of honor at the center front of the audience with Lute and Ria flanking her. Lute snuffled happily and kissed her hand, but the sight of Kara tightened Ria's throat so badly that she couldn't speak. Taking a deep breath, Ria knelt at the left of Kara's chair and lay her head in the old *solexa*'s lap.

Kara stroked Ria's hair. "No need for grieving, child, on my account or any other. It's the ceremony that deserves your attention tonight, not me." Her wrinkled face was unreadable in the dimness.

Lute cried: "Look who else is coming!"

Ria stood up for a better view.

Two *perfur*—Amris and a young apprentice *solexam*—were carrying Still There on a pallet. The cub was perfectly quiet. Ria touched his mind briefly, confirming that this was an induced slumber.

Amris and the apprentice set Still There's pallet down on Lute's right and sat down behind him. Rakam and Lekera took their place on the other side of their son.

Meanwhile, the rest of the assembly area had been filling up with *perfur*, uncommonly subdued out of respect for the occasion.

The ritual commenced with the ringing of the clan bell, the same bell the mischievous cub had tried to muffle. Torchbearers led a solemn procession from the great doors of the *koho*.

Ria scarcely recognized the marchers in their ceremonial costumes. Doc wore the same kind of iron cap and charm-laden white poncho that Kara had been wearing when Ria first saw her. He also carried a disk-shaped drum and an iron-tipped wooden staff like Kara's.

Beside Doc walked Ellesiya, wearing a metallic mesh vest covered with tiny silver bells and a matching silver headdress adorned with the Twin Stars clan crest.

Behind her came Gemaï, gloriously swathed in a cloak made of feathers. His partner Mayor Henderlund was almost as colorful in a rainbow-striped tunic and buckskin pants.

A band of *perfur* musicians—plus one human trumpeter—walked behind the four celebrants, carrying rather than playing their curious instruments. Four *perfur* couples in flower-trimmed harnesses brought up the rear.

To Ria's surprise, the spectators stayed perfectly quiet

during the entrance. Only the tinkle of Ellesiya's bells and
the crackle of torches broke the silence as the procession
approached the platform. All except the torchbearers and
musicians mounted it. The celebrants took up positions
towards the back of the platform with the *perfur* couples
ranged in front of them.

The trumpeter stepped forward and blew a fanfare.

A flicker of motion on her left drew Ria's eye. She
turned and spied the Lafayette party getting to their feet.

On her right, Kara stirred and struggled to stand, using
Ria's shoulder to lever herself up.

"Get up, child," she whispered. "We humans rise for
the anthem of the Republic."

Ria scrambled to obey, taking care to wrap a protective
arm around Kara.

The trumpet solo had a blood-stirring majesty that was
ever so slightly familiar. But Ria couldn't recall where she
might have heard it before.

Kara and the other humans began to sing, their voices
few and small against the starry sky:

> *Mine eyes have seen the glory*
> *Of the coming of the Lord.* . . .

Ria joined them for the later choruses in a baritone so
strong and true it startled her.

> *Glory, glory hallelujah.* . . .

The refrain kept ringing in Ria's ears after the music
ceased. She stood rapt for a moment, until Kara's sinking
back into her chair nearly threw her off balance. Ria
resumed her own seat while the *perfur* musicians readied
their strings and drums.

Now the persons of fur stood for their own song. A river
of melody rose shimmering and rippling from five hundred
throats:

> *Brightwater children:*
> *Sunray and moonbeam*
> *On sleek fur gleaming.*

> *Seed-time to leaf-fall,*
> *Starlight to fireglow,*
> *Living is dancing.*

The singing ended. The *perfur* sat down.

The music flowed on to accompany the dancing of the four young couples up on the platform. They swirled and glided like converging currents. They swept up Doc and Ellesyia, set them at the eddy's heart, and spun away.

The two *solexes* confronted each other, the quick, lithe body of the *femfur* opposing the slow, thick body of the man.

Her bells spoke to his drum.

Their hands touched.

Their bodies entwined in a formal embrace.

They turned halfway round their common axis and parted.

Now the man moved with fluid sureness while the *femfur* lagged.

No one had to tell Ria that the two *solexes* had exchanged souls.

Together they intoned the renewal of the ancient friendship oath between their peoples.

> *By sunlight, starlight, firelight,*
> *Reflections of the Light Eternal.*

Ellesiya spoke through Doc's lips:

> *We persons of fur,*

He answered through hers:

> *We persons of skin,*

They spoke jointly:

> *Are children of the same Earth.*
> *We pledge ourselves comrades:*
> *No hate or harm between us,*
> *Only fellowship and faithfulness.*

She said:

> *As it was in the days of Rue and Lis,*

He said:

> *As it has in the days of Never Smiles and Sees Inside,*

They said:

> *So may it ever be,*
> *Till every tree is ashes*
> *And raindrops turn to dust.*

Again the embrace and the half-turn.
The *solexes* were themselves again.
They led the dancers down the stairs.
Then Gemai and Henderlund stepped forward and touched the palms of their hands together. They crossed to opposite sides of the platform and cautiously lifted the huge flambeaux from their holders.

The torches' triple flames reminded Ria of the tridents that medieval men used to hunt otters. *Given enough time*, she thought, *maybe every cruelty could be redeemed.*

The *perfur* musicians and the trumpeter struck a fanfare together.

Gemai and Henderlund cried:

> *Out of multitude,*
> *Oneness!*

They plunged their torches into the cone of brush at the rear of the platform.

A pillar of fire erupted to the cheers of the crowd. The flames reflected far out on the lake, a spear of light to challenge the darkness.

Lute was beside Ria, pulling her up and spinning her around like a leaf in a whirlpool.

Through the exploding tumult she heard the cub Still There squeaking: "It's bright! Oh, it's bright!"

❋   ❋   ❋

Ria was back in her own body curled up on the seat of the stranded bus. Her coworkers were still huddled in shivering heaps exactly as they'd been a moment before. She could smell the stink of their fear.

Nothing had changed and everything had changed.

XX

Thanks to her mastery of fire, Ria endured the frigid hours of waiting for rescue from the marooned bus in tolerable comfort. With the energy boost from a food-concentrate bar found in her purse, she was able to keep her body warm.

Even though she felt scant sympathy for the other passengers, Ria tried to touch and calm the most distraught minds among them. But she lacked Lute's gift for easing pain. Perhaps she flattered herself to think that she was helping anyone.

She reproached herself—although not too severely—for failing to comfort Hannah. She had yet to scale the heights of heroic altruism.

She heartily joined the cheering when the headlights of the Highway Department vehicles finally appeared.

Their rescuers arrived in a snowplow followed by a heavy truck fitted with its own plow blade. The technicians off-loaded two snowmobiles from the truck to make room for the bus passengers. Then they rigged a chute of fabric between the tailgate and the emergency exit at the rear of the bus. With harsh efficiency, they hustled half the passengers into the covered truck, cramming them onto benches.

After the truck was disengaged, it followed the snow-plow back to Buckley.

Ali had insisted that Hannah leave on the first round of evacuation—and went along to watch over the younger woman. Ria didn't begrudge the privilege since it got the simpering creature and her protector out of Ria's sight.

Ria adjusted her seat to a more comfortable position and dozed while she waited for the second pass.

More than two hours later, the vehicles returned for the remaining passengers. This time, the snowmobiles accompanied the rescue team through the howling whiteness, flanking their retreat to safety.

Ria heard the stallions of the snowstorm trumpeting behind them, hammering ice-rimed hooves on metal, relentlessly herding them homeward.

Eventually, the whole party was settled in the Buckley community center and fed reconstituted rations that were somewhat past their prime.

The meal seemed even more wretched than it was after the feast Ria had shared with her *perfur* friends. *But that was in another country, and besides, the calories don't count.* . . .

It was all fuel for the inner fires, wasn't it?

After eating, Ria took a longer look at their refuge, the center's gymnasium. Its glazed tile walls were the color of processed cheese, bare except for tattered posters preaching tornado safety. The curtain across the stage at one end bore the logo of the local farm cooperative. A tinsel banner hanging from the ceiling proclaimed "WELCOME 2010."

Ria resolved not to let the dismal place depress her. Pulling out a copy of *The Prose Edda* that she'd brought along to read on the trip, she settled down to lose herself fighting Frost Giants.

But the Ginnungagap had scarcely gaped before their ever-helpful tour guide decided that the stranded travellers needed to play party games to keep their spirits high.

Ria was forced to put aside her book and join her fellows in hours of counterfeit fun.

There was no opportunity to read after the evening meal because flickering lights signaled the need to conserve power. An early bedtime was decreed for all.

As she obediently wrapped her quilted paper emergency blanket around her, Ria decided to cope with this latest strain on her patience by designing a dream for the sheer pleasure of it. It was the one way she could shape her world nearer heart's desire.

Ria fled her present darkness seeking waves of wonder. . . .

＊　　　＊　　　＊

She delighted to be with him, silent in the stillness, contemplating a void whose when and where had yet to be.

His hand stirred the pregnant emptiness.
Time began.
Seven ever-lengthening ages ran their alloted course. Currents of energy spread and matter foamed into place.
Sparkling galaxies spun from drifts of spume.
Novas burst like bubbles; bubbles swelled anew.

He called her to him, plunging through roiling clouds of nascent stars as if through surf, letting newborn suns splash off his fur like drops of water splitting light.
Their paths joined.
Sounding, broaching, whirling, drifting, parting, pairing, side by side they swam the dark depths and rode the bright billows of ethereal waves without a shore.

All the sky was sea and all the sea was sky. . . .

＊　　　＊　　　＊

Late the following day, Ria and the others were returned to Chambana by the same bus on which they had left. Some passengers grumbled about the delay, but considering the savagery of the weather, highways crews had done a speedy job of freeing the trapped vehicle and getting the road plowed for traffic.

Blue shadows were spreading over the deep, new drifts by the time Ria reached her apartment.

She entered, turned on the lights, and stared at her quarters with something approaching affection. After her ordeal in that reeking bus and musty shelter, she appreciated living in a clean, warm place of her own. A potpourri might make it even pleasanter. What had Habale the scent mixer suggested? Coriander?

Ria ate quickly, then unpacked at leisure.

After her adventures among the *perfur*, she didn't regret missing the junket to Chicago. But Carey seemed to be taking the disappointment hard: he'd barely spoken to her since the bus hit the snowbank.

Ria started to punch Carey's phone number, but hung up without finishing the sequence. Her constant solicitude wasn't good for him, any more than Ali's was for Hannah. Let him ask sympathy if he needed it.

Ria checked her computer notice board for announcements and messages. Headlines, schedules, and blizzard safety directives scrolled on. She saw a description of a new learning program on neurochemistry and placed an order for it.

Without warning, the machine began buzzing like an angry hornet.

Ria froze as a summons from PSI flashed on her screen: Psychiatric Services Integrated was ordering her to report for examination.

Once activated, PSI's dreaded white symbol locked her terminal against all other use. She couldn't even turn the unit off to escape the horrid buzzing. Receipt of the message had to be acknowledged before the local PSI office would encode a release signal.

If she ignored the order for more than twenty-four hours, she would face immediate arrest—and public disgrace. There was no place to hide from the pitiless scrutiny of PSI.

Ria had the wit to rage quietly. The system might be operating in two-way mode, transmitting the sights and sounds before it. Critical statements or gestures could be held against her.

Her wrath turned incandescent. She was ablaze to consume every traitorous circuit with avenging fire, all the way to PSI's world headquarters in Sydney.

And as for the informant who betrayed her . . . that had to be Hannah. Why, she could cook that skinny bitch's carcass from the inside out.

Ria spun around abruptly, strode to the window, and mentally hurled her anger from her. Let the blind drifts hide it until it sputtered out to sodden ash. Not fire but ice must serve her now.

She called for her appointment in a semblance of calm.

On a Friday afternoon of the following week, Ria sat in PSI's waiting room preparing to be judged. From her childhood experience with a different department of PSI, she had some idea of what to expect . . . and how to set a few defenses. Lute had promised to be with her during the interview, but she couldn't feel his dear presence yet.

Defiant—and pedantic—to the last, Ria silently chanted as much of the *Dies Irae* as she could remember, breathing in time to its iron-shod meter.

> *Dies irae, dies illa,*
> *Solvet saeclum in favilla,*
> *Teste David cum Sibylla. . . .*

But no harsh blast of a *tuba mirum* summoned Ria, just her I.D. number flashing on a wall screen.

She went to the office indicated.

The female therapist sitting inside didn't bother to rise when the new subject entered. She stared briefly through Ria as if through grimy glass before deigning to acknowledge her.

"You are Victoria Mariette Legarde?"

Ria nodded nervously.

"I am Vonh Blanca," the therapist said in a yogurt-smooth voice.

Her features were mannish and her hair an indefinite shade of brown. Although small, her body seemed abnormally dense, as though her bones were too massive for her size.

Blanca made an elaborate show of checking Ria's identity card against the display screen inset in her desk before permitting her to be seated.

The delay allowed Ria time to redouble her inner fortifications. The assault looked to be worse than she had anticipated.

Since poise would invite suspicion, Ria took care to project an air of innocent confusion. As directed, she meekly positioned her wrist on the sensors in the cradle-like arm of the examination chair. There was no strap—questioning under restraint was done elsewhere—so that the subject was forced to give continuous consent to the monitoring.

Ria took care to generate signals that were normal, but not *excessively* normal.

"Relax," purred the therapist. "What's there to be afraid of? You and I are simply here for a chat about certain *problems*"—she made the last word a euphemism—"that you appear to be having."

Ria smiled weakly.

Blanca continued. "We'll want a record of what we say, just in case it's necessary for us to meet again. This button starts the taping," she indicated the control, "and this board enters my notes."

Ria obediently stared where the therapist was pointing.

"Of course you can't read the symbols." Smugness crept into her tone. "They're in a special professional code."

Blanca's hand stroked the keys like a noiseless, patient spider. The painted fingernails on that hand looked too perfect to be real. Was the therapist a nailbiter?

Who's guarding the guardians?

Blanca began the interrogation by taking Ria's case history, with particular attention to childhood events.

"Now, how many weeks did you spend in fifth grade before you were advanced?"

"Not long, about a month," answered Ria.

" 'About a month.' Is that three weeks or four—or perhaps five?" She kept belaboring trivial points, trying to provoke unguarded words.

"I can't remember," said Ria, holding her temper in check. "Don't you have that information on file in front of you?"

"Yes, but I prefer to hear it from you." Blanca's hand poised over the keyboard.

"I've already told you that I can't remember exactly."

Blanca scrutinized the display screen and purred again: "But why can't you? Your test scores indicate that you have a remarkable memory. Overall, your mind appears to be exceptionally keen. Otherwise, you wouldn't have been chosen for accelerated placement, would you?"

The Eurasian tilt to Blanca's blue eyes fostered her claim to sagacity. Ria didn't try to meet their probing stare. She meekly lowered her gaze to the other woman's cheek, which bore the marks of botched dermabrasion.

The tedious quiz continued.

Blanca climbed Ria's family tree seeking diseased limbs. She forced Ria to relive the ugly details of her parents' deaths: the sleet-encrusted branch crushing her father, her mother leaping from a residence hall roof.

Ria tried to answer with enough sobs and awkward pauses.

Mere facts did not suffice. Blanca pressed for interpretations and reactions. Why had her mother's mother *really* defected from the Soviet Union while studying at the University? Surely it had to be something more than romantic infatuation with a local man?

Ria could safely plead ignorance on those points since the principals had died years before she was born. She likewise denied knowledge of her father's mother's involvement in the Native American movement of the previous century. Her Ojibwa paternal grandmother had been too wise to burden her with subversive information.

Round and round the thread of query went as Blanca spun her meandering web.

At length she reached the crucial pass.

"Aren't you curious why you were summoned here?" asked the therapist.

"Yes," replied Ria. "I want to see if the reason confirms my assumptions." At this point, candor might confuse Blanca.

But no surprise marred the therapist's creamy voice. "Would you care to share these theories with me?"

Ria groped for just the right touch of self-depreciation. "It was a rocky autumn for me. Nearly got electrocuted in September. Didn't feel quite right afterwards. The doctors said I was healthy, so I didn't want to bother them with trifling problems. Kept putting off making an appointment for follow-up. You know how it is." She flicked a nervous laugh.

"And what were these ah, 'trifling problems?' "

"Moodiness, trouble sleeping, lapses in concentration, outbursts of temperament. It's over now. I feel fit and stable, but I'd be the first to admit that I wasn't myself a while back."

Ria paused and looked straight at Blanca. "I suppose some overzealous observer must've thought I was about to . . . go noncomp and turned in my name. Isn't that what happened?"

"We discourage the use of the term *noncomp* here." Blanca smiled without showing her teeth.

"However," she continued, "the complaint lodged does fit the pattern of aberrations you describe. Aren't you glad that a fellow-citizen acted responsibly?" Her concern dripped in clots.

Ria agreed. "One can't be too careful these days, can one?"

"When we give you an official clearance—as I have every confidence we will—you can rest assured that you're a healthy unit of society."

"That certainly will put my mind at ease," murmured Ria.

"You almost said 'at ease *again*,' didn't you?" Blanca pounced. "The way you handle yourself suggests that you've seen PSI before."

"I had the mandatory counselling sessions after my mother died. Isn't that on my record?"

"Of course. But what about the previous episode?"

"A full trauma report must be on file." Ria shuddered involuntarily.

"Your faith in our omniscience is touching." Blanca favored Ria with a Buddha-like smile. "To be sure, the facts are before me, but I'd rather have it in your own words."

"You refer to my kidnapping," said Ria, swallowing. "I was ten years old at the time, which was early October, I believe."

"October fifth."

"Thank you. A noncomp—sorry—a deranged middle-aged woman snatched me off the playground after school. She held me captive in a condemned house for a couple of days."

Blanca studied her screen intently. "Witnesses said that the kidnapper kept crying: 'This one, I've got to have this one' as she dragged you into a stolen van. Why do you think she said that?"

"I've no idea. None." Ria made a particular effort to keep her response bland. She'd agonized over that very question for a decade, yet was no nearer to an answer. The kidnapper's choice of her remained a mysterious form of election that marked her off from other people.

"So she took you to a condemned house," Blanca continued.

"It was one of those Victorian mansions that'd been chopped up into student apartments fifty years ago. It had a turret sticking up in the middle, I remember that." Ria also remembered—but chose not to mention—the stench of the place or the sound of its scuttling cockroaches. "The whole neighborhood was going to be leveled for a new housing project. Nobody heard me when I screamed."

"How did she keep you in?" Blanca wanted all the details.

"She watched me every waking minute and tied me up at night." Ria had been forced to lie down bound hand and foot to her captor like a puppet on strings.

Blanca kept on probing. "Would you care to speculate about the woman's motives for taking you?"

Ria shrugged. "She was insane. Isn't that enough explanation? She also drank a lot. She said she wanted me to be her sweet little girl and live happily ever after with her in her beautiful home—she saw that boarded-up wreck as it used to be, with lacy curtains and crystal chandeliers. When she got really stinking drunk, she talked about 'sampling my charms.' "

"What do you suppose she meant by that?"

"I'd rather not know."

"Not know?" Blanca raised an eyebrow. "Surely everyone benefits when light is shed on dark corners. I must caution you that your earlier remark might be construed as homophobic."

Blanca pretended to step outside her professional role to exchange a confidence. "I've always been more male than female myself—and feel perfectly comfortable that way. Do you think I shouldn't?"

"We're taught not to be judgmental," replied Ria coolly.

Blanca studied her display screen again and smiled. "I sense a certain tension in you about sex. Perhaps it's your inexperience. Not many women your age are still virgins."

"I haven't had the occasion to change that status." Ria couldn't avoid a certain note of defensiveness.

"No? There are licensed partners available here in Chambana, the same as in other cities."

"I can't afford such services." Ria grew increasingly wary.

"A course of therapy prescribed by PSI would be free. In fact, that's my own clinical specialty when I'm not doing evaluations. Do keep that in mind when you decide that you want help." Blanca was downright avid to be of assistance.

Ria forbade her flesh to crawl and jumped back to the original line of discussion. "Too bad nobody helped the kidnapper when she lost her little daughter. I think that's what drove her mad."

"No one must've bothered to report her to the proper authorities." Blanca frowned at the irresponsibility of it all.

Ria went on. "I don't know how it would've ended— with me dead, I suppose—except that it was a dry October and a grass fire happened to break out in the yard behind the house. I smashed the glass in an upstairs window, crawled out on the roof, and yelled for the firefighters to save me. So I got away with nothing worse than a bad cut on my thumb. See the scar?" She held up her right hand.

"You must keep your arm on the sensors at all times," Blanca warned her. "Were there adverse social effects after the experience?"

"After I came home, people treated me as . . . tainted, as if I'd asked to be kidnapped. Other children wouldn't play with me."

Ria stared away briefly. "So counsellors recommended a transfer to the University's laboratory school. I'd been eligible for it all along, but my parents had refused to enroll me—I guess my intelligence bothered them. I was glad that PSI persuaded them otherwise." Her gratitude on that point was sincere. "With accelerated placement, I finished my education two years early. But I had little time for anything besides studying."

"So much for the reactions of others." Blanca circled her prey again. "What about your own feelings afterwards?" Her note-taking hand was poised to strike.

Ria chose a datum with maximum therapeutic appeal. "I guess the nightmare was the worst of it. I had the same one over and over from the first night I was held captive. This ghastly song the woman kept singing had put it into my mind. I couldn't get rid of it for weeks afterward."

"What was the song like?"

"Easier to sing than explain."

"You still remember the tune?"

"How could I forget? Besides, as you yourself pointed out earlier, I've got an excellent memory."

Ria wished she had the use of Julo's voice now to do the macabre waltz justice. But she could still perform it better than its creator, whose contralto had wandered almost as much as her mind. Taking a deep breath first, she sang:

> *A carousel laden*
> *With corpses of children*
> *Spins round in the night.*
> Libera me,
> Domine,

Libera me.
The muzak reels onward,
The steeds never falter,
Their burden's so light.

"That's what I kept dreaming about," explained Ria, "a black merry-go-round hung with crepe streamers—an unmerry-go-round if you will. The animals the dead children were riding were alive. All of them were monsters." Ria permitted herself an honest shudder.

"An impressionable child would find that disturbing, especially on the heels of the other experience." Blanca's sympathy dripped like poisonous honey.

Ria accepted it without flinching. Impressionability was a seeming flaw that Blanca would try to exploit. So let the therapist feel secure in the arrogance of her trade. Ria wanted her strength discounted so that her enemy would be content to fashion a weaker web than otherwise.

Ria widened her eyes a calculated trifle. "As I said, I stayed terrified even after the rescue. The repeated nightmares wore out what little patience my mother had with me. My father thought that an outing might help. So I was taken to Indianapolis to see their famous Children's Museum.

"I was really enjoying myself there—I can still recall gawking at their mastodon skeleton—until we reached the top floor. Nobody'd warned me that the prime attraction there was a beautifully restored antique carousel. One look at it whirling around and I ran shrieking down four flights of ramps and out the door to the parking lot before my parents caught me. They were so mortified, I think they wished that I'd kept running right out into the street and under the wheels of some convenient truck."

"Then subsequent professional care dispelled your nightmare," said Blanca smugly.

"It stopped."

Ria doubted that PSI's child psychiatrist had brought her relief. The dream had vanished like a video tape being switched off on the night that the imprisoned kidnapper hanged herself. But it still lingered like an after-image in Ria's memory.

"Now tell me how you interpret—" a buzzer signaled that the appointment was up.

"We seem to have run out of time before we've even begun to address your present difficulties," said Blanca. "I see that we'll require a series of interviews to resolve the issue."

"I want a chance to prove I'm healthy now." Ria laughed with mock bravado.

Blanca smiled back, languid and confident. "We're making appointments now." She punched a command. The printer in her desk disgorged a hard copy which she gave Ria. "Your schedule. I'm looking forward to our next meeting. You should, too."

Ria bobbed her head, pretending agreement.

She rose, and for a fleeting moment, stood straight and tall in front of the therapist's desk. Ria was fixing Blanca's smallness in her mind.

Ria turned and walked out of the PSI Center with carefully measured steps. She didn't begin to relax until she was out on the sidewalk, safely insulated by indifferent crowds.

XXI

Thick gray clouds scudded across the sky. The weather had turned grim and blustery while Ria was at the PSI Center.

At least it was too late in the afternoon to bother returning to work. Ria wasn't up to facing anyone she knew just now. But the long walk home should ease the tension. It was good to move her arms and legs again, good to brush against human beings instead of sensors.

Vile memories poured out of her like sweat.

Ria remembered far more of the madwoman than she had dared admit to the PSI therapist. How could she forget that gaunt giantess with huge bony hands that clutched and petted, wasted flesh that reeked of liquor and mildew, dark eyes that were never still.

The captor who was ignoring her captive's fright had nevertheless wept hysterically over a dead bird.

The poor cardinal—he must've flown in through a broken window and starved before he could find his way out again. The madwoman had picked up the dead creature and tried to speak to him in his own chirping language. Failing to revive him, she'd plucked his wings and stuck the flame-red feathers in her graying frizz.

The odor of onions frying in a campustown restaurant reminded Ria how hungry she was.

She'd been hungry during her captivity, too; but the food the kidnapper had offered her was rancid. After she spied rat droppings in the sunflower seeds, no amount of coaxing or threatening could convince Ria to eat anything.

Ria turned the corner onto Green Street. The force of the wind funnelling down the thoroughfare had tempted her to take an Illibus the rest of the way. But it blew at her back now. She'd get home under her own power—and sneer at Alma Mater's statue en route.

Ria's account of the charnel carousel was meant to appease Blanca: psytechs were fond of analyzing dreams. With luck, the bizarreness of it might distract the therapist from aspects of Ria's behavior that couldn't bear close examination.

She'd resisted the impulse to describe the nightmare to its last morbid detail. Why dwell on the way the children's corpses grinned or enumerate each monstrous steed? From mirror-pelted manticores to lamias with bloodstone eyes, the named and nameless horrors out of myth were there, coursing in waltz time, rising and falling, world without end.

And most unwise to mention the carousel's master, the skeleton of ice who plied the controls. Ria knew it for a *windigo* the devouring demon her Ojibwa ancestors had feared above all else. Only the most powerful of shamans could defeat this fleshless foe.

Cunning though Blanca was, she'd never unravel the nightmare's true meaning, or at least the meaning the kidnapper had claimed for her song. The madwoman had expounded her exegesis to Ria at tedious length: having a captive audience seemed to have loosed her tongue.

According to her, the carousel—the unmerry-go-round—was their world. The chill breath of Federation rule had killed the children who were humanity's future. In this frigid environment, only preening monsters could survive.

Ria did not care to repeat such treasonous sentiments to PSI—especially now that she was coming to share them. Her initiation as a *solexa* had opened her eyes to the profound wrongness of her society. More wrongness struck her each time she returned from Lute and Kara's world.

But when would she move from observer to actor? Ria was terrified by her friends' high expectations for her. Was she destined to be the only shaman available to challenge the *windigo*—whoever or whatever that was?

Well, it wasn't likely to happen any time soon. How

could she get the children off the unmerry-go-round when she didn't know how to free herself from one low-grade psytech's web? Hunger pangs hit Ria harder. She'd have to eat supper before seeking counsel from Kara and Lute.

Why hadn't Lute kept his word to help her during the interrogation? Were his promises written on the rushing waves?

❊   ❊   ❊

Summer sun filtered through gaps in the shades drawn across the atrium skylight, tracing paths of brightness on the shadowed floor.

Ria was kneeling on a pad beside the fish pond, up to her elbows in water and on the point of removing a slimy rock from the arrangement around the rim.

Julo's face stared blurrily back at her. It seemed an unremarkable young face—flatter, narrower, and fairer than her own. Yet it moved and responded in perfect obedience to her will.

The sense of being a transient guest in someone else's body overwhelmed her. The burden of responsibility was almost too much to bear. She didn't dare make a move. Kara and Lute had been wise—

Ria remembered why she'd come uninvited. Leaving the rock where it lay, she sprang up. In her haste, she nearly tripped over a pan filled with aquatic plants. She shook the water off her arms and wiped them dry on her pantlegs.

"Where is everybody?" she yelled.

Lute emerged from Kara's room. He was carrying a tray of covered dishes.

"Here already, Ria? Should've been watching for you, but Julo wanted to start cleaning the pond today." His voice was edgy.

"What kind of a greeting is that?"

Ria followed him into the kitchen.

"You act as if you're sorry to see me."

"You're puttin' thoughts into m'head, Ria."

He set the tray down on the counter and began scraping the dishes. The meal they'd held had scarcely been touched.

"You've got worries. So've I."

Lute was clearly not himself. Even his whiskers drooped.

"Well, my worries happen to be critical," said Ria angrily. "I come here for help and you're too distracted to give it. Some friend! Where were you during that interview? Don't you understand, Lute?" she shrieked, "that bitch could have me raped or brain-scoured or killed with one tap of a fake fingernail!"

"Woman," his voice rose in a humming snarl, "shut your brother-lovin' mouth! Or at least talk quieter." The humming ebbed. "Noise bothers Kara. Tryin' to make her comfortable, but she's weaker every day."

Ria blushed. "I didn't think. . . ."

"Start thinkin'. Stop divin' to conclusions. Said I'd be with you and I was. Every minute, except for a few in that PSI woman's mind—squalid!" He shook imaginary filth off his fur. "No wonder your world's so sick, with your healing arts in hands like hers."

"But I didn't feel your presence," Ria complained.

"Didn't mean you to. You were handlin' the current perfectly well without me." He patted her shoulder reassuringly.

"Didn't want to spoil your concentration," he continued. "Or risk messin' up your control. More sensors on you than you thought, like the camera focused on your eyes to record changes in pupil size. Didn't know 'bout that one, did you?"

"I'm sorry, Lute." Ria touched his cheek. "I'm just so scared."

"I'm scared, and sorry, too. Let's talk it out with Kara. But mind how you put your questions."

They found Kara sitting in bed, propped up by lace-trimmed pillows. Her face was nearly as white as the gown she wore and the flesh hung loose on her broad frame. She was knotting fringe on the hem of her Tree of Life tapestry while a half-grown calico cat attacked her ball of thread.

Ria hesitated in the doorway, reluctant to disturb her mentor. Kara's fragileness made her too precious to approach.

"Are you here to stare or speak, child?" said the old woman. "Come in and sit beside me."

"She's not staying long," said Lute firmly.

Kara chuckled. "You'd keep me wrapped in cotton batting if you could, Lute. We both know the end is coming soon. Are you worried that I'll drop dead while your back is turned and cheat you out of your chance to practice your art on me?"

"What surgeon likes to treat a loved one, Kara?" asked Ria, beginning to appreciate Lute's pain.

"Would it be any easier for my niece Dorel to do it, if she were here now and not away in Springfield addressing the Senate?" She shrugged. "You young folk are a gloomy lot. Whose deathbed is this, yours or mine?"

Kara paused to stroke her cat. "Open the window, Lute. We need fresh air."

He obeyed. The warm west wind bore the scents of roses and newly cut grass.

As she took her chair, Ria noticed more roses in a vase on Kara's tall chiffonnier. The breeze stirred them, scattering petals like drops of blood.

"See your strategy, Kara." Lute snorted. "You're acting nonchalant so we'll think you're a saint."

"Perhaps I am." Kara's blue eyes twinkled. "On the other hand, perhaps my soul is riddled with wickedness like so much dry rot. You'll know which is the case soon enough."

Kara measured thread along her arm before continuing, "The suspense is getting the better of you, my dear *perfur*. Next thing, you'll start shedding."

Ria listened bewildered. Their banter seemed better suited to a maternity ward than a hospice.

"I don't understand," she stammered. "You act as if you're waiting for a birth instead of . . ."

"Quite right," said Lute, a trifle too vigorously.

Kara explained gently: "It *is* a kind of birth. I'm waiting to give birth to my completed self. Only by dying are we born into eternal life. I've no regrets about passing—nor should you."

"Hasn't happened yet, Kara." Lute broke in. "Could be reading the signs wrong. Don't be in such a thrashin' hurry to leave us. Ria's problem needs lookin' at."

"Lute's told me of your plight, child. The threat is grave. Nevertheless, it can be mastered."

"How?" cried Ria. "No one ever gets away from PSI. I'm trying to be brave and unbending like you, but I'm afraid that I'll break if they push me too hard. See?" she sobbed. "I can't even keep my body from shaking!"

"Nonsense!" said Kara, sharply enough to make the cat jump. "You had enough self-mastery to keep the interrogator at bay."

"Once. Next time or the time after that, she'll get through. I can't hold off PSI forever." Ria's sobs dwindled to ragged sighs.

"You're brooding too much on resistance. Storms fell stiff trees, but those that bend survive."

"Stop being afraid of being afraid," said Lute. "There's more'n one model of courage. Rigid's not my people's style."

His supple body curled around Ria's chair.

This made Ria smile against her will, imagining rows of *perfur* stiff as fence posts. She ran her hand down Lute's curved back.

Kara said, "Once aroused, suspicions are difficult to quell. Don't try to feign health. Let them discover some defect or illness, then meekly let them cure you of it."

"Illness? Physical defect?" Ria thought for a moment. "Some sort of brain damage might account for my symptoms." Her confidence surged back. "What about epilepsy?" In a few cultures, the shamans were epileptics who'd learned to control their seizures.

"Might work, might work," chirruped Lute. "Make them think that's what's wrong with you."

"They'll be hard to convince," objected Ria, cautious again. "How can I do the necessary research in secret?"

But once formless worry had begun to assume a recognizable shape, her researcher's instincts rose to battle it.

Ria gazed ruefully at Kara and Lute. "And the demonstration is left as an exercise for the student."

"You're equal to this task, child—and to far greater ones yet to come," said Kara in a voice turned slow and soft. "Not every *solex* born can stand the climb. Some fall to their dooms never knowing that they had a special vocation. Such a one was the pitiful woman who kidnapped you."

"What?" cried Ria.

"She could've easily been you, Ria," said Lute. "From the bit we saw of her, she'd've made a great *solexa*. Had the gift but not the trainin'. Or puttin' it another way, you could've easily been her."

Ria squirmed with disgust, unwilling to accept the comparison. Yet there was no escaping the implications of Lute's statement. Twist and turn as she might, it confronted her like her own reflection in hall of mirrors.

The words choked out of her: "You saved me from turning into *that*? Are you saying that she snatched me instead of some other child because she saw herself in me?" Merely thinking of such kinship left Ria feeling unclean.

"Yet see what came of your ordeal," said Kara. "Fear, sleeplessness, and hunger stirred your latent powers. In fact, the rough *solarti* that you used to kindle that grass fire led us to you. Or as my old master used to say, 'By winding roads we reach the mountain's peak.'"

Ria continued. "If the kidnapper was a potential *solexa*, then I must've been picking up the nightmare directly from her mind. That's why it stopped as soon as she killed herself."

"Wasn't just a private horror, either," Lute observed.

"Lute and I think that the madwoman's talent shaped her dream. That carousel filled with dead children, spinning at a demon's bidding, is more than a ghastly image. It points to something real in your world's future."

"We can't guess what that something is—yet," said Lute. "Been lookin' at the question closer since Festival. All I know is, that merry-go-round's got to be stopped."

"By me?"

Ria sat transfixed, terrified of assuming the burden they were about to lay upon her. Her eyes pleaded for pity, or at least delay. Her glance wobbled aimlessly about the room vainly searching for someplace to hide. In her desperation, she'd have gladly changed places with Kara's sleeping cat.

She shuddered, but did not speak. There was no arguing with destiny.

Kara said with the full solemnity of her office: "This is

the task for which you were made, my daughter. I am certain of it now, for I am seeing all things more clearly in the twilight of my life."

Kara eased herself forward from the pillows to sit proudly erect. She rolled her needlework to one side. The gesture disturbed her cat so that it jumped off the bed.

She stretched out her right hand to Ria, who clasped it without being told. The wrinkled skin felt abnormally cool.

Lute stood behind Ria keening a wordless *perfur* melody that soared beyond the range of human ears.

"You must find the *windigo* and destroy it," Kara commanded. Her words fell like drumbeats. "Yours is the fire that will conquer its ice."

"But what is the *windigo*? Where do I seek it?" Ria matched her mentor's tempo.

"The frozen mountains of your earliest childhood dream, the mountains you could never spur your steed to climb, were blasted by its touch. You alone—"

Kara gasped in agony and fell forward.

Lute sprang to her bedside. He pressed comforting hands against her breast and laid her back against her pillows.

"Heart!" he cried. "Can't hold her on this side 'o the Door for long!"

Ria gasped: "What can I—"

"Nothing!" He snarled.

Lute's mind slammed Ria into a world of gray, distorted forms glimpsed from a corner.

The Old One was hurting. The Furry One and the Young One made sounds. The Old One opened her eyes and made sounds. She and the Young One touched faces. They all smelled sad.

Another splash of power and color vision returned. Ria was no longer crouched on the floor bristling and mewing. . . .

The spasm passed. Ria had hands again instead of spotted paws. She realized that she had watched Kara and Julo say farewell through the eyes of a panicked cat.

"Sorry," whispered Lute. "Had to get you out of Julo's way a minute."

"Understood," Ria whispered back.

She knelt beside the bed opposite Lute, unsure of what to do next.

Kara must have sensed her confusion. She spoke in a faint voice that was almost matter-of-fact. "You've never seen anyone die before. Lute knows how to smooth the passage. Give me a kiss for the journey, beloved daughter."

Ria clung to Kara briefly, dragging out a sob that should've been "Mother" from a throat too tight to speak. She released her and slid back to her place to watch through quiet tears.

Lute took Kara's hands in his for a dialogue without words. Joy softened the old woman's face.

He intoned:

> *The Shadow of the Door*
> *Now falls across your path.*
> *Kara ni Prizing,*
> *Do you chose to pass?*

She answered firmly: "I do."
And it was done.

> *Sunlight, starlight, firelight fade.*
> *Enter into Light Eternal,*
> *Brightness never failing.*

Lute closed the unseeing eyes.

> *Who created us all in the beginning,*
> *Receive us all at the end.*

XXII

The brightness hurt Ria's eyes. Its pitiless glare bounced from one slick plastic surface to the next, a dazzle that left no deep shadows to mourn in.

She blinked back welling tears, then flung herself on her bed and wept, heedless for once of the noise her grief was making.

How few hours out of her life had she spent with Kara. How priceless each of them now seemed.

Despite repeated hints, despite the warning signs she'd seen herself, she hadn't actually believed that Kara would die soon: "She seemed a thing that could not feel the touch of earthly years."

Now earth would lie upon her, as it would sometime on Ria herself.

And what of Lute? His loss was far greater than her own. Seeing him struck down by grief was the first after-shock of Kara's death. Ria had expected boundless good cheer and unfailing strength from Lute—as if he were some angel in fur and not a mortal creature.

But he'd collapsed as soon as Kara died, exhausted from the strain of leading her through the final Door. Ria had held him in her arms, warming his musk-reeking body with her own until he revived. She'd fed him honey and raw eggs to stop his trembling and summoned local friends to help him.

So Lute had his comforters—where were hers?

Craving the embraces she couldn't have, Ria hugged herself, squeezing her lonely flesh hard enough to hurt.

She had no one to confide in, not even Carey. She couldn't very well explain that she was in mourning for a woman who wouldn't be born for another five centuries or so.

Ria laughed hollowly, imagining what PSI would make of *that* situation.

Yes, whatever Lute was suffering, he was luckier than she.

And he had his primitive faith in immortality, didn't he? Wasn't that a handy anodyne? Right or wrong, it had to be better than the feeble simpers Ria's world made in the face of mystery.

Time to attempt some symbolic gestures.

Ria lurched up. She reeled over to the shelves and ransacked her store of tapes for suitable music. *Death and Transfiguration* was the only appropriate piece she found.

She dropped it in the tape player while she refueled her body with food she could barely taste.

Although Ria let the tape repeat, Strauss failed to pierce her apathetic gloom. Where were the transcendent insights it was supposed to ignite? The prairie wind could wail a finer dirge for Kara.

There was always literature. With a simple command, she could summon the texts of all the great poems on death ever written, from Gilgamesh's lament for Enkindu onward. She could smother herself in a blizzard of printouts if she chose.

Or would it help to contemplate art? Ria paged fitfully through a few books. What did she hope to find, models for a projected *Apotheosis of Kara ni Prizing?*

Try as she might, Ria couldn't picture the *solexa* poised on the snowy clouds of any traditional heaven.

Memory dredged up one set of images that might possibly solace her. Perhaps she needed to return to *The Mountains of the Mind.*

Ria called Carey to borrow his precious book on C.C. Wang, but his number didn't answer.

She managed a faint shrug. What did one more disappointment matter? She was too benumbed to care.

There were still other alternatives. She had all the necessary resources within herself—literally. Slight neurochemical adjustments could restore energy or induce euphoria.

Yet Ria hesitated, recalling her brush with addiction. Masking pain solved nothing.

On the other hand, neither did bleak endurance. Surely it was folly to reject relief for fear of abusing it?

Whooping and cheering erupted under Ria's window.

She looked down to see the sidewalk packed with people. It took Ria a moment to remember why they were there. Of course! They were lined up for admittance to the winter carnival that was being held on the House grounds this weekend.

The queue had just begun moving. For the rest of the night the complex would be swarming with noisy revellers indoors and out. She'd never get to sleep without resorting to *solarti*.

But the sleep that came seethed with troubling dreams. . . .

❋　　❋　　❋

The pathway curved between high banks of thorny hedge whose leafless boughs were pale as weathered bone. Foggy drizzle drenched the scene like tears.

However swiftly she ran, her footfalls made no sound on the pavement of crushed shell, nor could she hear even her own labored breathing. The hand she held before her face melted into mist.

Gone was the guiding skein of homespun thread she used to have. Devious turnings of the maze mocked her tearful desperation.

Never finding, never found, she fled alone down spiral ways that had no end.

❋　　❋　　❋

Ria awoke shivering. She warmed and calmed herself with care, running her fingers over her body, reassuring herself that she still wore living flesh.

It was the hour before dawn. The dimness oppressed her.

She turned on a small lamp above her bed, just enough light to make the steel in her ring sparkle.

With a grateful sigh, she slipped into deep, familiar waters. . . .

❋   ❋   ❋

She dipped her scrub brush in the bucket again, then dropped it with a splash.

Julo had been washing the atrium floor. Furnishings and rugs were piled haphazardly to one side of the room. Ria hoped he wouldn't mind a short interruption in his work.

"Lute, where are you?" she cried.

There was no answer.

She called again without reply.

The kitchen proved empty. Perhaps he was outside?

Ria lifted one shade, but she couldn't spy Lute from the kitchen window.

Stifling July heat slapped Ria in the face when she ventured out the rear exit. There was no sign of Lute.

Why wasn't he home? He had to be here, he had to be here whenever she wanted him.

She ran back into the house screaming his name.

Ria stopped short in the atrium at the sight of Kara's door.

On it hung the dead *solexa*'s shattered drum and broken staff, tied up with bows of white ribbon.

Ria backed away as if she had encountered Kara's corpse, nearly skidding on a patch of wet tile.

Giving the decorated door a wide berth, she opened the adjoining one. Behind it lay a bathroom equipped with quaint fixtures, including a huge, half-sunken tub.

Next door to the bath was the workroom, now in a state of wild disorder. Kara's loom was empty, her spinning wheel still.

Ria hesitated to enter what must be Lute's chamber, then took a quick, guilty peek. With the curtains drawn, it was too dim to see much, but she could make out fuzzy rugs covering the walls as well the floor. His bed—on which she scarcely let her eyes rest—was a nest of curving cushions.

The last bedroom in the square was Julo's. Here in this

bright, tidy room she'd first met Kara and Lute. Was it only a season ago?

Ria leaned her forehead against the cool door frame and closed her eyes.

After a while, she walked back to the spot where Julo had been working when she arrived. She knelt down beside the bucket and left him to his chore.

✸   ✸   ✸

Ria tried to rest after returning, but shame kept her wakeful.

Why hadn't she switched to another moment of time once she'd realized that Lute was absent? Had she dared, she'd have probably tried on Lute's bed for size, craving the scent of his fur.

All in all, a sorry performance from one who clung fiercely to every scrap of privacy her society let her have.

It was natural to crave Lute's company more now that Kara was gone, but she mustn't let obsession cloud her mind. She needed all her wits about her to save herself from PSI.

At length, hunger stifled self-criticism and Ria got up to eat.

She found her larder sadly bare. It was embarrassing to keep underestimating the size of a *solexa*'s appetite. Eating breakfast in the House cafeteria would count as penance for her sins.

Ria stared balefully at the food. The cholesterol-free scrambled eggs and the soy patties masquerading as sausage were fine opportunities for mortification. Both preparations were served in squares precisely sized to fit compartments in the plastic eating tray. No doubt the dimensions were standard continent-wide.

Ria's stomach protested from the first bite. She ate in cold blood, wondering what the *perfur* served at their other seasonal festivals.

Between bites, Ria surveyed the sparsely filled tables. The cafeteria drew little trade this early on a Saturday morning. There'd be even fewer diners without that contingent of weary merrymakers who looked as if they hadn't bothered to sleep the previous night.

But every face, fresh or haggard, strove to simulate contentment. One never knew what monitor devices might be watching.

After all, there were credible rumors of transmitters implanted in body tissues without the carrier's knowledge. Anyone and everyone might be a spy.

Or so the authorities wanted citizens to think: random, undetectable observation curbed behavior as effectively as total surveillance—and at much lower cost.

Carey walked past Ria on his way out, only one aisle over from her table. He didn't return her waved greeting, for he was intently scratching his neck. What new stress had raised his eczema again?

Later, Ria phoned Carey for an explanation.

"Pity we missed each other in the cafeteria this morning," she said. "Didn't you see me?"

"No, Ria, no I didn't. You're seldom there: people only see what they expect to see. Especially when they're as busy as I am."

She could hear him scratching over the phone.

"Will you be too busy for tonight's film?" she asked cautiously.

"Oh, not at all. Be there at the regular time." He cut her off without a chance for further questions.

She refused to satisfy her curiosity by invading his mind.

Ria spent the rest of the morning—and entirely too much money—buying groceries at a private market.

After lunch, Ria resumed her search for Lute. She was prepared to dive as many times as necessary to reach him. . . .

❋   ❋   ❋

Ria found Lute sitting in the workroom tying fringe on a tapestry, the same one Kara had been working on when she died. The room was dark except for the circle of lamplight surrounding him. A bottle of whiskey and a half-filled glass stood on a tabouret beside his chair.

Ria dropped the kaleidoscope that Julo had been playing with, walked around behind Lute, and placed her hands on his shoulders.

He quivered a little, recognizing her touch.

"Vexed her to leave this half-done, Ria," he said. "She liked to see everything through. Not a splashabout mind, not like a . . . *perfur.*" The word came out like a curse.

He clutched the edge of the fabric. "Goin' to finish it for her, show her I can do something right."

"What do you think you did wrong, Lute?" Ria probed gently, trying to sound calmer than she felt.

"Lost count of all the people I've led through the Door— guiding's a big part of m'work. Proud of myself for doin' it." He took a sip of whiskey. "Then why'd I fail Kara?"

His remorse clawed at Ria's heart. She drew his bowed head against her body, forgetting that she now lacked woman's breasts for him to nestle against.

"Fail her? How did you fail her?" asked Ria.

Lute rambled on, as if he hadn't heard her. "Rite depends on total nearness—*solex* and patient're closer'n partners in any dance, closer'n lovers."

Ria jumped to conclusions, frowning. "Do you mean that you were disillusioned?"

She was uncertain how to proceed. Presumably, *solexes* kept professional confidences secret.

"I can't believe that you uncovered any shameful secrets in Kara."

"Nothing like that!" Lute showed a spark of his old spirit. "We've been inside each other time and time again these seven years. But this last time . . . she held parts of herself back from me—from *me!*" His voice rose to a wail. "Didn't she really trust me?"

Ria had no answer. She clasped him tighter in her arms.

Perfur lived at extremes. Let their usual buoyant optimism falter, and they plunged into despair deeper than the average human ever reached. She'd thought Lute an exception to that pattern. Clearly, he wasn't.

"But Kara did die well," Ria protested. "She died free of pain and full of peace, thanks to you."

"Thanks for what?" he snarled. "She didn't need me."

"I still need you, Lute," she said softly. "I need you so

much, I came by yesterday when you weren't expecting me, just to see you." Her words sank to a whisper. "I flew into a panic when I couldn't find you here."

He turned aside, pulling away from her. "Had to make arrangements for buryin' Kara."

"May I come to the funeral?"

"Not in Julo's body." He turned back to glare at her. "He's got a right to be there as himself to mourn her."

Ria blushed at her selfishness. She'd already deprived Julo of his chance for a proper farewell at Kara's deathbed.

"I need to mourn her as much as he does," she pleaded.

"Didn't say you couldn't come. Doc's agreed to host you. But you're to ride strictly passive 'less you work it out with him."

"Why can't I watch through your eyes?"

"No!"

The rejection stung like a slap. "You come into my mind as freely as you please—so why can't I enter you this one time?"

"Not yet!"

"But we've already shared dreams." Ria wheedled. "You promised to let me into your mind someday."

"Day of *my* choosing. Hasn't come yet." He chewed dismally on his fingers. "Too haunted by Kara to deal with you now."

"Can't I be of comfort to you?" She brushed his drooping whiskers with her fingertips.

Lute burst into irate humming and batted her hand away. Throwing tapestry, thread, and scissors aside, he jumped up to confront her.

"Ria, for once, for once, keep your brotherlovin' hands to yourself!"

She cowered as he circled her. His fangs looked enormous.

"Think I'm a man in a fur suit? Swear sometimes you do." He ground his massive jaws together. "Let me swim alone a while."

Ria stood up slowly, her arms hanging limp at her sides.

"If that's what you prefer, I won't offer help—or ask for it—until you're willing."

She gave him a long, sad look and left.

✱   ✱   ✱

Ria lay on her bed like a heap of sodden flotsam cast up by a storm.

She shook herself alert. Her stubborn core still held. She already had to manage without Kara. If need be, she'd do without Lute as well. She'd find a way to escape PSI all by herself.

Such resolves did nothing to ease the pain of Lute's rebuff. Snarl at her, would he? Ria pounded her fists on her pillow, angry at herself for not snarling back. He could hardly have upset her more if he'd bitten her. Ria shuddered, thinking how easy it would be for a *perfur* to rip out a human throat.

Perhaps he'd be under less strain once the funeral was over. She wondered what the ritual would be like. More impressive, surely, than the hasty dispatchings her parents received. Could the ceremony cauterize the mourners' wounds and start them healing?

Ria earnestly hoped so. Her life had become so entwined with Lute's, any estrangement from him was anguish.

She noticed a smudge on the center of her *solexa*'s ring. Breathing on it, she polished the steel back to brightness with the edge of the sheet.

A strangely silent Carey met her at the theater that evening. Ria was surprised that he didn't favor her with one of his customary lectures on the finer points of cinematic art. Her questions drew only grouchy mumbles in response. So she let him alone, pointedly ignoring his impatient scratches and twitches. The wait for their tickets seemed to bother him excessively, although the delay was no longer than usual.

Wondering what was amiss with Carey, on top of her other anxieties, didn't dispose Ria to enjoy the swordplay and silly romance of *Scaramouche*.

But just as the foolish hero found the man who taught the man who taught his first fencing master, Carey pressed a tiny wad of paper into her hand. It could only be a note.

Ria held it for a few minutes, then carefully slipped it into her tunic pocket and sealed the flap.

She considered leaving her seat to examine the smuggled note in the rest room, but that area was likely to be heavily monitored. Reining in her curiosity, she forced herself to pay attention to the film.

The hero was getting clever; he'd become a performer of mime to hide his identity.

And there were more ways to communicate than Security could scrutinize. Ria slowly traced letters on the palm of Carey's hand:

W-H-A-T W-A-S T-H-A-T?

He flinched, then replied in the same fashion:

W-A-R-N-I-N-G

O-F W-H-A-T?

D-A-N-G-E-R T-H-E-Y A-R-E W-A-T-C-H-I-N-G U-S

L-E-T U-S T-A-L-K T-O-M-O-R-R-O-W A-T T-H-E P-A-R-T-Y

N-O-T S-A-F-E

I W-I-L-L M-A-K-E I-T S-A-F-E

H-O-W?

T-R-U-S-T M-E

Ria patted Carey's hand for reassurance, although she didn't really expect him to have much faith in her.

They sat very still while the climactic duel flashed on the screen.

Ria didn't have to feign attention. From the first swing of the chandelier, the fight was a technical marvel, shot as one continuous sequence.

How Lute would relish shows like this. She'd invite him to come along when things were—her thoughts braked. She was assuming a happy ending to her own adventures. The novelty of optimism quite stunned her.

The hero triumphed. The film ended. The audience clapped heartily as the lights came on.

Despite Ria's flush of positive feelings, the walk home with Carey was tense. He was still broody and wouldn't talk.

She had time to become afraid that they might commit some infraction of traffic rules, draw a Security officer's attention, and be caught with what must be compromising information.

Back in her apartment after bidding Carey goodnight,

Ria made a clumsy production of undressing and stowing her clothes. She contrived to read the note while appearing to rummage through dirty laundry.

Carey's message read:

> I know that PSI pulled you in for questioning and it's all my fault. That time I let you use my terminal and I.D., my place was under surveillance. They spot-check people with high government connections and I'm an extra risk because I was under PSI's care a few years back. I think they may have had an implant put in me during minor surgery. Assume they've turned the transmitters on and can hear everything I say. Assume our phones and apartments are bugged, too. I've got to watch every step. Can't risk any more black marks after this reprimand. One dose of PSI was enough. I wish I could help you but can't see how. At least I've warned you.

Poor Carey was blaming himself needlessly for her summons. Ria knew where the real fault must lie. But she decided to check his suspicions of an implant before attempting further contact.

A mere glide past the shining barrier brought her soul to Carey's sleeping body.

She sensed cold metal within warm flesh. A spy device *did* lair behind a small scar under his jaw. Disarranging a few atoms destroyed the microcircuitry. Any subsequent examination would suggest that a manufacturing flaw had made it fail.

As a further favor, she also touched the effector cells of Carey's immune system that governed allergenic cascades. Eczema should trouble him no more.

Having struck two puny blows for decency in the time it took to draw a deep breath, Ria felt ready to try another foray into Lute's world.

Doc Lerrow's mind awaited her there past radiant, beckoning waters. . . .

※   ※   ※

A real blazer of a sunset. Kara deserved that. Would set the stage for a Light Watch to remember.

He vowed to stay the full course until dawn, make a merry night of it for her sake. God send them all so good a death. There'd be a hard reckoning if he had to stoke his carcass with stimulants, but it was the least he could do to show respect.

Until then, a soft seat under a shady tree felt good to his creaky bones.

And it gave him a prime vantage point to watch other guests mill about eating green cakes and working up a sweat in their best white funeral clothes.

The way folks were swarming boded well for the festivities to come. There were carriages and saddle horses tethered all up and down the street. The paper lanterns were already up in the trees and Julo was hammering in the last of the flambeau holders. His loose young face scowled in concentration.

The sight of so many visiting *perfur* would set Chamba tongues flapping for weeks. Gemai had done Kara's family a kindness by persuading his clanmates to stay home and hold their own Light Watch. If all Kara's friends from Twin Stars had come, who could've fed them?

So Gemai and Ellesiya stood in for everybody else— except Amris, of course. She insisted on attending in person, and, like in most things, the ranger got her way.

But Amris had come in straight off the trail, mad as hell at herself for nearly falling into a macrat ambush. He'd have to check those dressings on her ears again.

At least her being here ought to steady Lute some. That one was taking his loss harder than he ought.

It was proof of Kara's fame that Rolling Shores clans more distant than Twin Stars sent official mourners, too. The Quail Cloud *solexam*—what was his name? getting harder all the time to remember everybody—had brought a keg of prime bourbon as a gift. Not quite sure if that was largesse or boosterism.

Well, he'd toast Kara in it cheerfully just the same. He could do with a cold glass of something right now, but he was too lazy to get up and fetch one.

Look at Kara's old comrade Birka, who used to be *solexa*

of Burning Hills. She hobbled along through the crowd
with her canes, moving slowly only because there were so
many people she wanted to greet. Might be a while before
they held her Light Watch. She was good for years to
come, bent as she was.

Birka was sounder of sense, surely, than Keramon, that
bumptious wondercub from Blossom Rain. If he didn't
stop trying to flirt with Ellesiya, he might get some cuffs
that weren't courting blows.

He chuckled. It was all part of the cycle. Life-wheel
turned the same whether you were *perfur* or human.

Dorel's two grandchildren scampered by, squealing like
perfur cubs. They were dragging a length of yarn for
Kara's cat to chase.

Dorel herself had a string of local officials in tow. She was a
right fine sight in her full regalia as presiding *solex*. The hair
under her iron cap was still mostly black, though it'd been a
while since she and he were Kara's apprentices together. The
Chamba title of Wise Woman had a proud ring that fit her.

But he was glad that the Lafayette *solex* wasn't called
"Wise." A plain fellow like him couldn't carry off the part.

A bell tolled.

Ah, the sun was officially down. Time to get moving.

Dorel led the party inside.

All those bodies pressing together made the twilit atrium
stuffy, but the mingled odors of potted plants, fish pond,
and the sharp-toned mourning scents the *perfur* wore
helped keep it bearable.

The guests were ranging themselves in bands like tree
rings facing Kara's bedroom door where the broken emblems of her office hung. A great thick beeswax candle
stood on a tall stand in front of the decorated door. He
found a place next to Lute in the front ranks.

Dorel signalled for quiet and the company joined hands.
She intoned the invocation:

> *By sunlight, starlight, firelight,*
> *Reflections of the Light Eternal.*
> *Let memory be kindled!*

The candle burst into flame.

"We have come together," proclaimed Dorel, "to celebrate the memory of Kara ni Prizing, Keeper of Roots."

The watchers raised the tribute hymn to a tune that was more than a thousand years old:

> *Her toil is over, labor done;*
> *To Light Eternal she has won;*
> *Now let our songs of praise be sung.*
> *Alleluia!*

Chanting spread outward through the circles, like ripples on a pool. One by one, Kara's friends acclaimed her. Sweet, rough, shrill, deep, their voices lapped like waves.

"Highest climber," Dorel sang.

"Beacon in darkness," Gemai sang.

"Far flyer," Ellesiya sang.

"Good lady," Julo sang.

"She hunted wisdom," Amris sang.

"Healer of all things broken," he sang.

He yielded his body briefly to Ria's control. His lips formed her words: "Mother of my spirit."

XXIII

Ria awoke Sunday morning intent on the struggle ahead. Determination burned in her like a steady flame, as if she'd carried back something of the Memory Candle's glow.

And being able to call Kara *Mother* seemed to have melted icy barriers within her heart, leaving her freer to respond to the threat posed by PSI.

Had the ritual lightened Lute's dark mood? Ria hoped so, but she decided not to contact the *perfur* until he gave some sign that he wanted her company.

After glancing at University announcements, Ria flipped on the news channel while she showered and dressed.

She paused in the middle of braiding her hair to watch coverage of a news conference featuring North American Science Bureau head Jon Detmold. Detmold's hairless face was instantly recognizable—and hard to ignore. Ria kept expecting to see a reptilian tongue dart out of his thin mouth. Ah, where was Rikki-tikki-tavi when one needed him?

This time, Detmold was defending his controversial proposal for earthquake prevention, something about nuclear explosions to relieve tectonic stress. Her research for Professor Clyde had left Ria with just enough knowledge to appreciate the problem but not nearly enough to evaluate it.

As if her evaluation counted. . . .

Ria shrugged and changed to the music channel.

The eerie trills and thumps of Katsusai's *Earth Spider Concerto* were uncongenial to orderly thought, but music about a monster fitted PSI so well that Ria left it on.

Convincing PSI that she was epileptic rather than insane required far greater familiarity with the condition than she had—or could get. Ria dared not use her own terminal or anyone else's to remedy her ignorance. The public Medivise was not to be considered. Buying medical texts was out of the question. She couldn't even risk searching in the Library stacks, because Security cameras would record whatever volumes she inspected.

Perhaps a less direct approach? It might be a trifle obvious to order Dostoevski novels, but what would seem suspicious about obtaining a biography of King Louis XI of France? Louis was the most prominent medieval epileptic that Ria could recall. She knew too little about more recent eras to think of other examples.

Ria turned to her well-thumbed copy of Eliade's *Shamanism*, mainstay of her theoretical studies in the art. Kara and Lute had confined themselves to oral instruction, saying Ria lacked the technical background for understanding treatises on *solarti* written in their world.

Eliade's discussion of epilepsy among tribal shamans carried ample footnotes. There might be enough medical data in his references to get her started. In any event, titles like *Primitive Religion* were unlikely to trigger suspicion.

But the roundabout route would consume lots of computer time. She might overrun her monthly quota.

Ria sighed. If she failed to convince PSI, debt would be the least of her worries. If she succeeded, she'd solve the money problem when it came up.

Ria tried not to think of another possibility: studying epilepsy on Lute's timeline. No. She wouldn't beg him for favors. She'd stitch up her own patchwork solution first. It was vital that she win this victory herself.

Ria entered her search commands and read output for hours until her eyes throbbed and her neck hurt.

Trying to clear her head, she paid a brief visit to the winter carnival outside.

The crisp air did refresh her. A sky blue as Limoges enamel set off the snowy grounds to perfection. Ria wandered through the crowd, sipping bargain-priced hot chocolate and even essaying an occasional smile. She got far enough away from her own problems to honestly admire the entries in the snow creature contest. Did that bold sculpture of Pegasus have a chance at the Grand Prize?

But a glimpse of Hannah, attired in sugary blue, skating on an improvised ice rink annulled all the benefits of the afternoon.

Ria's mood was not improved late when she realized that the anthropology references were proving only marginally useful. The last of that vein was mined out by nightfall.

She had to find a way of supplementing the meager returns from her research, through personal contacts if necessary. Tonight's House dance marking the end of the winter carnival might offer useful camouflage for such efforts. Even if it didn't, a small pretense at normalcy could help appearances.

Ria put on her white party dress like a knight donning armor for battle.

The House gym had been turned into a dance floor and given a seasonal sparkle. Counterfeit aurora borealis flickered on plastic snowflakes and foil ice. Hidden fans rustled the branches of artificial evergreens, wafting pine scent throughout the crowded room. What the scene lacked in authenticity, it more than made up for in noise.

After some searching, Ria found Carey huddled in the shadow of a cardboard sleigh. When he resisted her invitation, she simply dragged him onto the dance floor over his whimpered protests: the mouse cannot resist the hawk.

Neither Ria nor Carey were familiar with the figure being danced; they stumbled through an approximation of the proper movements as the rows formed and crossed. Her superior height made it impractical for her to whisper in his ear during their paired turnings so she spoke normally, hoping the music and other people's chatter would mask their conversation. PSI wouldn't have bother mobilizing the most sophisticated listening devices against them—yet.

"Quit the surly and silent act," Ria told Carey as they met to clap hands. "Say whatever you like."

The suggestion froze him in place.

"I told you why I can't," he mumbled.

She yanked him out of another dancer's path.

"You're worried about nothing."

"How do you know?" His eyes showed white rims.

"I have ways of finding out."

He frowned instead of answering. The pattern carried them to opposite ends of their lines.

Ria framed another approach as they worked their way back together: Carey might think an irrelevant question safe enough to answer.

"By the way," she asked in passing, "does anyone you know have epilepsy?"

"If they do, they're keeping it mighty quiet."

"No suspicions?"

"None."

"Think harder."

They swung around in a star formation.

"Wait," said Carey, "that time I took Leigh Franz to the Saturday film instead of you, he said something or other about epilepsy in his family."

"Really?" She tried not to look too eager.

"I don't remember exactly what he said."

The dance ended.

Ria lingered in the crowd, reluctant to surrender its cover. She kept a firm hand on Carey's elbow.

"Could you talk to Leigh for me, find out who has the condition?"

"I will not," he snapped. "That's too personal."

"Of course it is. I'm being perfectly outrageous."

"Then ask him yourself. He's *your* bathmate, after all."

"No, I'm asking you to do it for me, Carey." She spun him around to face her. "Please, as a favor."

"You ask the damndest things." He shuffled his feet and glanced around furtively. "Besides, Leigh's not here. Or at least I haven't seen him around this evening."

"Would you be so good as to call and check whether he's in his apartment?" asked Ria. "If he is, invite him down."

"All right," Carey agreed sullenly. "But you're awfully pushy tonight."

"Pushy, am I?" Ria drew herself up to her full height and placed her palms against her chest.

"Why," she said, "I could push you into the Grope Room right now. Who knows what I might force you to do in there?"

Carey backed away as if scorched. "Enough already! I'll make your call."

"Only joking." Ria grinned. "I do appreciate your help."

Her smile was not returned.

Ria stood beside Carey as he placed the call from a public telephone. Leigh was indeed at home but uninterested in the dance. Carey's tepid invitation did nothing to change his mind.

Ria thanked Carey and let him go his way. She hesitated to phone Leigh herself in case his quarters were bugged. *Solarti* might offer a more subtle means of persuasion, but she didn't feel like walking all the way up to her apartment to practice it.

Instead, Ria strode purposefully towards the Grope Room, a place that, despite her threat to Carey, she'd never investigated before.

The Grope Room offered none of the amenities to be found in commercial pleasure centers, only darkness and mattresses. With so much other activity to watch, the monitors weren't likely to notice her entering a trance.

Near the entrance, Ria nearly collided with Hannah.

"I didn't know orgies were your style, Ria." The little blonde smirked. "So. . .unaesthetic."

"Oh, do you find the Prospect Avenue establishments more to your liking?" snapped Ria.

Implying that she had to pay for sex threw Hannah into a fury. She stomped away, for once neglecting to be graceful.

Ria scolded herself—but not too harshly—for stooping to cattiness. Hannah couldn't possibly afford the rates charged on Prospect Avenue. It was demeaning to take revenge in such small bites. Kara might have said that it was demeaning to take revenge at all.

Ria sighed remorsefully and opened the door.

She nearly gagged on the stench of human rut. Subsonics

throbbed beneath the moans and giggles. Dim red lights on writhing bodies made it a scene out of Dante.

Turning to flee, she hesitated a moment too long. Several pairs of hands pulled her down and started mauling her. She kicked her assailants and scrambled free.

Screams chased her out the door.

In any other place, that much noise would've attracted precisely the attention she was trying to avoid. Misled by an excess of innocence, she'd been guilty of *hubris* again.

And mighty damn lucky to have escaped with nothing worse than a scare.

Ria straightened her dress and humbly climbed the stairs back to her apartment.

She invaded Leigh's mind from the security of her own bed. But hasty probes of his memory failed to reveal the data she sought. A thorough search would take more time and skill than she possessed and she wasn't about to beg Lute for help. She'd have to question him in person, but she preferred to do it amidst the safe clamor downstairs.

Could mental stimuli persuade him to attend the dance? When delicate flickers of suggestion drew no response, she attempted to conjure up the prospect of a desirable woman waiting downstairs for him.

Unfortunately, Leigh's mind assembled her signals into an image of the ex-lover he was anxious to avoid.

Patiently, Ria tickled am even lower appetite—an irresistible thirst for hot, spiced punch. She set the remembered pungency of cloves and cinnamon aglow within him and caused a slight, persistent chill that had him shivering for a warm drink. The dance was the only place he could satisfy this craving immediately.

Ria returned to herself and listened for sounds of hasty grooming in their common bathroom. She waited a few minutes after Leigh departed, then followed him downstairs.

She permitted herself a small, victorious smile when she found Leigh sipping punch near the refreshment table. She let him finish his cup before approaching him.

Steering him into the crowd at the edge of the dance floor, Ria began her inquiry.

"A while back, Leigh, you offered me a favor."

He nodded uneasily.

"I'm going to claim it by asking you a personal question that I hope you'll be willing to answer."

Even in the dim light, she could see him shudder.

"Do you know any epileptics?" Ria asked.

Relief flooded his face. "Yes. Yes, I do. It so happens, my mother's had epilepsy for years. But it's under control now."

He moved closer to Ria and lowered his voice. "I've been worried about going the same way myself."

"Why so?"

"I got a concussion in that . . . fall last month—still have headaches from it," Leigh explained. "A tendency to epilepsy may run in my family, which means we can develop it after head injuries other people might shrug off. At least, that's the way it was with my mom."

"What happened to her?" asked Ria.

"She had an accident, about ten years ago while I was in college: an elevator she was riding in fell. The seizures started after her skull fracture healed."

"That's too bad," said Ria. "Does the problem interfere with her working?"

"No, indeed," replied Leigh. "Mom's the administrator in charge of Kickapoo Park and has her own house in Danville, a nice house. I should get over and see her more often than I do."

Ria drew him out at some length about his mother, an easy task since he was proud of her achievements in the Park Service. These might be somewhat overstated— Kickapoo was only a minor facility. But one had to claim what status one could.

Ria and Leigh stood up for a few dances together, a surprisingly enjoyable activity because he was a skillful partner.

Leigh seemed pleased with his snap decision to attend the dance. Perhaps he was more sociable by nature than he'd first appeared.

This relieved Ria's misgivings over the tactics she'd employed to coax him down—and was about to employ again.

Ria maneuvered Leigh into the cozy seating area behind the cardboard sleigh where Carey'd hidden earlier. Sliding her left arm around him, Ria carefully tilted her ring to catch the shimmer of fake Northern Lights.

"You've been so kind, let me show my gratitude," she murmured, clasping him in a light embrace while her soul made a final inspection of his mind.

As she intended, he mistook her softness for ardor and pulled away embarrassed. Ria pretended to look sheepish, apologized, and withdrew to her apartment.

Sorting out what she'd accomplished, Ria bemoaned her clumsiness: the operation wouldn't have met her mentors' standards. How curious that she felt guiltier about peeping into Lute's room than intruding into two men's minds.

But physical proximity may have enhanced the quality of the data she'd gathered, data she needed to arm herself against PSI. Between her questions and the unspoken thoughts those questions had brought to the surface of Leigh's mind, she now had a sufficiently detailed portrait—and a thread of affinity—to locate Sheila Franz by *solarti*. One couldn't have too many cues.

Ria commenced the search at once. She had only four more days to mount a defense: her next appointment with the therapist was Thursday.

XXIV

Ria's first plunge found her quarry at home, sitting at a
well-equipped desk, wearily evaluating performance reports on subordinates.

Between breaths, Ria returned again and again, making
repeated forays to refine her image of Sheila Franz. Accu-
racy was essential. She had to get beyond Leigh's ideal-
ized picture of his mother to see the shadows as well as
the highlights in this busy woman's life.

Ria also needed an awareness of Sheila as a living organ-
ism. To develop this, Ria explored the chemical pathways
of her subject's brain. She touched the spot where frac-
tured bone had knit and sensed the blood-borne drug that
now prevented seizures.

Basic data in hand, Ria withdrew to seek an alternate
version of Sheila whom she could observe at length, free
of the limits to soul-flight on one's own branch of time.

Another plunge scarcely different from the first brought
Ria to her goal on the first try. This Sheila sat behind a
desk of different design, reading a microfilmed journal for
managers. Her calendar clock recorded today's date, just
as the other's had—17 January 2010.

The ease of finding what she sought amazed Ria. This
second branch was so perfectly parallel, it must be barely
budded out from hers. Unless some momentous event
altered many lives, this new growth on the Cosmic Tree
would soon wither and snap off into nothingness. Then

bark would creep over the stump, covering the spot where the stillborn twig had been.

Ria wondered why such a branch had come into existence and what must happen for it to continue existing. Finding the original nexus point would make a fascinating research project for study with Lute. *Assuming she survived and Lute allowed her to study with him again. . . .*

Scholarship would have to wait for that glorious sequel. Ria put her speculations aside and set to work.

But when she skipped back a decade seeking the moment of Sheila's accident, she arrived nowhere. The budding branch must still lie so close to her at that point that soul-flight there would, in effect, be travel into her own actual past. Ria beat her wings in vain against the walls of paradox.

She prudently retreated forward in time, back to the alternate present from which her search had begun. Then, using the scar on Sheila's skull as a marker, Ria hopped back in time: year by year, month by month, and finally week by week, trying to get as close as possible to the time of the accident without violating the laws of *solarti*.

Her patient efforts did get her to a point that was near enough for her purpose, when the regrown bone was still fresh and Sheila had yet to suffer her first epileptic fit.

Ria settled in to watch the progress of Sheila's affliction. She could still meet her deadline, even though she took as long as she needed to study the problem. Given her capacity for making careful observations and her excellent memory for recording them, she was confident that she would be able to simulate epilepsy well enough to fool PSI. Ria was proud of herself for getting this far alone.

Ria watched her subject confront unfamiliar technologies, finding herself surprisingly intrigued by the electro-encephalograms and brain scans that intimidated Sheila. She listened attentively with Sheila's ears as doctors explained the diagnosis; she read through Sheila's eyes as the patient educated herself about her condition. Ria thought of her host as a teaching machine that happened to be alive.

But as Ria discovered to her horror, she'd grossly underestimated the amount of data she needed to learn—especially when she had no control over the learning process.

Since Sheila was indifferent to charts, Ria never got a close enough look at eeg tracings to understand them, much less memorize them. Text descriptions of "six per second rounded waves" and "flat-topped four per second waves" didn't provide enough raw materal for mimicry.

Ria had originally planned to simply manipulate PSI's recorders, using *solarti* to imitate a tell-tale eeg tracing. But what if she misplaced waves and spikes, confusing the characteristics of *grand mal* and psychomotor epilepsy or creating some other anomaly? PSI's interest in her would be sealed—fatally.

Was she cramming for an exam that she was already doomed to fail?

Ria slept poorly and dreamlessly Sunday night. In her desperation, she'd have welcomed a nightmare just for the stimulus of new imagery.

She walked through her work Monday like a robot and returned to her apartment no more inspired than before.

Finally, Ria abandoned the treadmill of worry to fix dinner. This evening she cooked with ceremonious care, making the meal a disciplined act of defiance against all that was false and regimented around her. She boned her chicken like a surgeon and carved her potatoes like a sculptor.

January's alcohol allowance permitted her a bottle of adequate white burgundy. Ria used part of it for simmering the chicken with herbs and drank the rest. The food turned out surprisingly well—even Lute might've enjoyed it.

Relaxed by the meal, Ria was able to rethink her predicament. Clearly, she'd taken the wrong route by trying to be machinelike. She and her host were persons, not linked computers. Yet this inefficient, inconvenient humanness could be the key to victory. It wasn't enough to merely study Sheila's seizures; she would have to share them.

Ria turned from wine to waters deep as thought. . . .

＊　　＊　　＊

Something terrible was going to happen. She knew it deep in her bones.

But what could hurt her here in her own park?

It was that heavy lunch. Hadn't set quite right. And maybe one of her headaches was coming on. She gingerly touched the hair combed across the fracture site.

A walk around the Visitors' Center might do her some good. Too nice a day to be fretting.

The burning bush planted outside the main door had gone full scarlet overnight, and the woods showed the first touches of frost under a hard blue sky. A sugar maple at the swamp's edge waved one bright orange bough like a torch while the rest of its leaves remained green. Fallen acorns crunched under her feet and squirrels chattered overhead.

Three huge, raucous crows flapped by. Their wings cast shadows across her path.

What was that stink? Some camper's garbage on fire? She have the careless bastard brought in—after her walk.

A fine day for walking. Yes, indeed. Lake Vermillion looked so glittery beyond the trees.

Too glittery.

Everything was so bright.

Where was she? She'd never seen this place before—

Sheila fell forward with a cry. The gravel cut her face. Her body turned rigid as a fallen tree. Her limbs jerked spasmodically for a few moments, then grew still. A wet stain spread under her body.

✳   ✳   ✳

Pity as well as shame overwhelmed Ria.

It was one thing to read a textbook account of clonic shocks, another to inhabit a human body tormented by convulsions.

Ria resolved to help Sheila. Although she couldn't eliminate seizures that had already occurred, she might be able to free the other woman from dependence on medication by healing her inoperable epileptogenic cortex. The cure would seem like spontaneous remission.

And if she enlisted Doc Lerrow's aid, he could also treat the Sheila who lived on this timeline.

Ria badly wanted to make amends for exploiting the misfortune of others.

She devoted Tuesday evening to locating each seizure episode that Sheila had experienced before the right drug and dosage had been found to prevent them.

Then Ria leaped from one moment to the next, sharing these attacks. Neurons sparked in wild discharge. Metabolites peaked and troughed. Aberrant rhythms made flesh quake. It was as if she stood unsheltered on a headland above a storm-wracked sea and let the lightning crash about her.

Would Lute praise her boldness if he were here?

Ria's next step was to apply her firsthand knowledge and induce the same neurochemical reactions in herself. She needed at least one dress rehearsal before the command performance.

But what if she damaged her brain in the process? What if she had latent epileptic tendencies waiting to manifest themselves? Sheila's symptoms bore a worrisome resemblance to those Ria had displayed during her initiation ordeal. No wonder epilepsy and shamanism had been entwined throughout history.

Ria cringed at the risks she was taking. The odds against her were far longer than she'd let herself admit. She trembled so hard that she began laughing at herself, giving hoarse barks of gallows humor. If she didn't take control, her fear alone would precipitate the tragedy she feared.

But Ria decided to postpone the experiment until the next evening when she hoped to be better rested. And of course her performance would be pointless without a properly appreciative audience.

Ria waited until she heard Leigh return to his apartment Wednesday night. Her first knock on the bathroom door was answered.

Leigh must've been working late, since he still wore his lab coveralls and the cheesy odor of fermentation clung to him.

"What can I do for you, Ria?" he asked.

"I don't quite know," she mumbled. "I need. . . something. I'm looking for . . . something. I can't seem to find it. So I keep walking around and around the room trying to remember what it is." She gripped the door frame to keep from falling. "Oh please come talk to me. I'm horribly confused."

Ria gave a weak sigh, then groaned as a wave of nausea hit her.

Leigh frowned with concern. "Are you sick? You're so pale, you look like you're ready to keel over."

He followed her into her apartment.

She stumbled around squinting and blinking. "Why's the place so dark? Didn't I turn on the lights?"

"Ria, come sit down before you faint," he cried.

She obeyed.

Leigh perched like a stork beside her on the sofa bed.

Ria clenched her fists and willed a violent surge of voltage through the left temporal lobe of her brain. . . .

She tumbled into a dream where silent thunderbolts struck a frozen sea.

Ria nodded awake and stared drowsily at Leigh. His arm was around her shoulder.

"I don't know how to put this, Ria . . ." His words were nervously gentle, "but it seems to me that you've just had a fit—an epileptic fit. At least it was like what I remember my mom having. You'd better get over to Health Service."

"As it happens, I have an appointment with . . . a health professional tomorrow." Ria pulled herself up.

"You think it might be epilepsy? I'll tell you," she licked her lips, "I've been worrying about that possibility for months, ever since I nearly electrocuted myself at work—you did hear about that, didn't you? I've been too afraid to see a doctor since and find out for sure."

"So that's why you were asking those questions the other night. You and I have been worrying about the same thing." Irony wrinkled his shaggy brows, then he burbled: "This isn't the end of the world, Ria. They've got good medicines now to control seizures. My mom does just fine."

"That's good to know. Thanks for being here, Leigh. I needed you. More than you can know. Now let me get some proper sleep. I'm exhausted."

She waved him out.

"Sure you'll be all right? If not, you call me, hear?"

"Don't worry. Goodnight."

Ria grinned broadly as soon as the door closed behind him. Her performance must've looked convincing.

But could she fool trained eyes—and sensors? Tomorrow's review was the only one that mattered.

Ria stayed home from work Thursday to save all her energies for battling PSI. The timing of today's appointment might work to her advantage. By late afternoon, the staff would be restless to finish up and start their long Solidarity Day weekend. Would that leave gaps in their vigilance?

She began inducing epileptic auras in the waiting room. By the time the call board summoned her, Ria was sweating profusely. Dizziness hindered her trek to Blanca's office.

Once there, Ria observed that the therapist was as languidly watchful as ever. She mustn't be the sort to respond to holidays.

"And how are you feeling today?" Blanca purred.

"Not well. My stomach's in an uproar." Ria kneaded her abdomen.

"But fortunately not sick enough to cancel your appointment. It's dutiful of you to come despite this . . . indisposition." The merest quirk in her smile spoke disbelief.

"Pardon me," asked Ria, "is something . . . Is something on fire? Don't you smell it?"

"No. Do you?" Blanca sniffed and glanced around to humor her. "There's no alarm on, either."

"I know I'm being paranoid," Ria said with a self-deprecating chuckle, "but could you check in the hall? Please? Just to put my mind at ease."

Blanca gave her an indulgent stare. She rose, went to the door, felt it, and peeked out.

"There's nothing there," Blanca said.

"What?" cried Ria. "I can't quite hear you. The chimes—" Brightness blazed behind her eyes.

When Ria regained consciousness, she was sprawled

halfway out of her chair. Blanca was leaning over her, dismayed as a spider who'd leaped and missed her fly.

In her crispest professional voice, Blanca said: "According to the sensors, you appear to have had some species of seizure. Don't move until the Emergency team gets here."

"I wouldn't think of moving an eyelash," answered Ria dreamily.

"The snare is broken. The prey flies free." Lute's triumphant voice rang in Ria's mind.

XXV

The eagle soared sunward. Golden light shone through her outstretched wings, setting her dark feathers aglow. Beating her way in smooth, rhythmic strokes, higher and higher she rose, leaving the murky lowlands behind, seeking the cloudless edge of the sky.

A patch of grayish haze barred her path. The faint stain of it billowed out like a curtain of dirty lace, spreading faster than she could fly.

The barrier resolved into ragged mesh that touched her pinions—and clung.

She tumbled helpless through the air, caught in the sticky netting. Its smothering folds entangled her wings, binding her fast to await the hungry spider's bite.

❋   ❋   ❋

Ria awoke trembling. She fought free of the blanket cocoon that confined her and batted clumsily at her alarm clock. Her flailing hand found the right button just before it buzzed.

Still trembling, she rolled up to face the first day of February.

Mondays were bad enough without a prelude of nightmare . . . a recurring nightmare. Ria had dreamt of the eagle caught in the web three times now in the ten days since she'd fooled Vonh Blanca and won free of PSI.

Only she wasn't really free. No one was in this world.

Not her, not Blanca, not even the Federation's supreme
Head, Devi Vatsyayan in Sydney. Everyone moved warily
past walls of deadly cobweb.

And those walls were sure to close in on her if she
stayed in Chambana much longer. No matter how careful
she was, the suspicions already aroused would never entirely fade. But how could she afford to leave?

Ria showered away the worst of her gloom and flipped
on the morning's House announcements while dressing.

One feature of the upcoming Valentine's Day party caught
her eye—the "Weather for Lovers" contest. The resident
who guessed the maximum temperature, wind velocity, and
barometric pressure for the twenty-four hour period beginning at 1800 hours on 13 February would win 100 soft
credits, with lesser amounts paid to the next-best estimates.

Ria stored the contest rules for later inspection, noting
that entries were due by 2400 hours this evening.

A week's wages was a tempting reward for risking a
small entry fee. Could *solarti* help her win the prize?
Perfur weatherwatchers used it to make accurate predictions; she ought to be able to do the same.

Having planned her strategy over breakfast, Ria paused
to make a quick experiment before leaving for work. She
jumped to the same alternate timeline she had used while
researching epilepsy, again seeking the mind of Sheila
Franz.

This time, Ria watched Sheila checking weather reports,
a normal part of her morning routine. Ria gathered daily
figures for the last week of January, then returned to her
own world and compared these with published data.

The weather on both timelines was identical.

Lastly, Ria jumped ahead one day on Sheila's calendar,
read the report for 1 February, then came back and recorded it for future reference.

Ria's work day couldn't pass fast enough to suit her. She
spent the glacially slow hours wishing her office had a
window so she could watch the changing skies.

Later, the evening weather summary confirmed that
conditions had again been exactly the same in Sheila's
world and her own.

Ria all but squealed for joy. She couldn't lose! The prize

money—or at least a share of it—was within her grasp. Let her repeat this victory on a grander scale and she could flee Chambana.

Giddy with confidence, Ria jumped ahead two weeks, seeking Sheila's mind on 15 February.

But that morning did not find Sheila behind her desk at Kickapoo State Park. Instead, she was strolling across a hotel plaza in Orlando, attending a conference for park officials. The balmy breezes of Palmetto had banished all thought of Prairie weather.

Ria withdrew. Chewing her lips in frustration, she tried another route.

As far as Ria could tell, the alternate timeline paralleled hers in almost every detail. Very well then. Rather than hunt for weather reports, she would simply read the contest results from her own House signboard.

Reluctant to enter another version of herself, Ria sought Leigh's mind instead.

No Leigh existed in that world.

Shock sent Ria diving through choppy waters sullen as tarnished silver. . . .

＊　　＊　　＊

He wasn't going to win. He never won anything. Why'd he bother entering? What did it matter what Hannah thought of contests? If she didn't mock him about this, she'd mock him about something else.

He scratched roughly at his neck and breathed a curse on finding blood under his fingernails. Taking another sip of fruit juice, he pressed the metal can against his eczema, hoping the cold would numb his itching skin.

Minutes ticked by. Party-goers in pink foil hats surged towards the tote board, pushing him with them. An animated design of hearts and arrows flashed on. Winning estimates scrolled by to mingled groans and cheers.

None of the numbers quite matched. No one earned the top prize. . . .

＊　　＊　　＊

Ria scribbled down the precious data—2.77 degrees C, 51.6 kph, 774.2 mm—before she dared sigh with relief.

Her hands were still shaking as she punched in her entry
and sent it to the House computer.

Only then did Ria pause to speculate on why her Carey's clean-shaven counterpart might still be suffering from
a chronic rash.

For the next two weeks, Ria controlled her impatience
by taking special pains to do her job well. She meant to
finish her association with the Library on a strong note.

After a breezy night marked the advent of a high pressure system, Valentine's Day dawned unseasonably warm
and clear, just as Ria's prediction required.

Checking the evening weather report, Ria confirmed
that the figures on her contest entry were correct before
she went down to watch the announcement of winners at
the House Valentine party.

Warmed by this knowledge, Ria turned a mild eye on
the festivities, unperturbed for once by the silly games
and forced laughter. Decorations differed from those she'd
seen on the alternate timeline—the party hats here were
made of paper lace—but curiosity rose to a similar pitch as
the flashing signboard signalled the moment of revelation.

Ria drifted towards the sign with the rest and gleefully
watched her name and numbers come up in lights, matching the official data of 2.77 degrees C, 51.6 kph, and 774.2
mm.

Would a great fortune from these few credits grow? Ab
*asse crevit. . . . At least she was starting with more of a
stake than that Roman magnate's cheap bronze coin.*

Ria took her bow and broke away from Carey and Leigh
as soon as she decently could, anxious to share her victory
with Lute.

She sought her beloved *perfur* through waters tinged
rosy by sunrise. . . .

* * * ✱   ✱   ✱

It was a fine, soft morning. The sun had not yet burned
away all the dew. Droplets outlined spiderwebs among the
shrubbery. Scents of wet grass and cut privet leaves hung
pleasantly in the air.

Ria was trimming the hedge in front of Kara's house.

She kept clipping, unwilling to disturb Lute's roadside conversation with a man and woman who seemed to be his patients.

Only after the couple had driven off in their carriage did Ria signal her presence—to Lute's delight.

"Won your prize, did you?" he asked.

She nodded vigorously.

"Happy for you, m'lady."

"That makes two of us." Ria beamed. "Now I'd like to talk about my plans for those hundred credits."

Lute waved her into the house with a courtly flourish.

Over tea and blackberry muffins, Ria asked: "Is a parallel timeline good for predicting other things besides weather?"

"Depends," he said with a mouthful of muffin. "Natural things like weather run the same, long as people aren't doin' anything to interfere: conditions change when trees're gone and so forth."

"What about the actions of people—or *perfur*?" Ria's forefinger traced the rim of her cup.

"Likely to be the same—if the branches'are close enough." He smoothed his whiskers. "That's been studied a time or two. No use to our *solexes*: not another branch like ours on the Tree."

"No other Lute and Ria sitting somewhere drinking tea?" She shook her head wistfully. "But if a close parallel exists, like the alternate timeline I've been using, how far can I trust events on one to duplicate events on the other?"

"You'd have to figure the odds yourself."

"The same woman was the runner-up in both weather contests." Ria's brows creased. "But I didn't notice if her numbers were exactly the same on each timeline."

Lute helped himself to another muffin.

"What're you trying to predict?" he asked.

"Horseraces." Ria grinned, refilling her cup. "I want to use my prize money to play the horses. It'd be an easy way to win a fortune."

Lute frowned. "That much betting in your world? We've got racing—flat 'n harness both—at fairs, but nobody'd get rich on the wagers."

"Gambling's a big thing for us: racing, casinos, raffles, lotteries—you name it. Luck's one thing the government doesn't control."

Ria spun her teaspoon on the table. It came to rest with the bowl pointing toward her.

"Anyway," she continued, taking a bit of muffin for her reward, "the local betting stations never close, so you can call in wagers at any hour, on contests all over the globe."

"You don't have to go to the track?" Lute smoothed his whiskers. "No fun in that."

"But lots of money." Ria's eyes narrowed briefly. "And I need lots of money to get out of Chambana, out into the world where I might be able to do some good."

"Don't be so quick to decide your destiny, m'lady. Bloom where you're planted first."

Lute rose to clear the empty cups and plates.

"And don't think *solarti* solves everything. Still need luck to go with your art," he said over his shoulder. "I'll help you check race results if you like, but you seem to be makin' this climb just fine by yourself."

Ria hugged him and left.

❋　　　❋　　　❋

Lute was not the only person to whom Ria announced her plans. She told friends, coworkers, even the House news service, of her intention to bet her windfall on the horses. Invoking her past experience as a stablehand, she made this seem a natural enough way to spend found money.

Ria also made a conspicuous show of studying racing and wagering.

Universal off-track betting, complete with computerized handicap charts, made action available to all. Selling information earned the Federation's Gaming Bureau almost as much profit as taking bets. But with all bettors using the same accurate data base, successful horseplaying was more a matter of blind luck than in earlier generations. Contemporary preference for the so-called "exotic wagers" that specified exact orders of finish or picked winners in multiple sets of races reflected this: horseracing had become a kind of animal roulette.

Ria shared her findings with all who would listen, making a calculated nuisance of herself so that her eventual triumph would seem the outcome of single-minded zeal. She'd have felt guiltier about annoying Carey if he hadn't lectured her about calligraphy at such tedious length earlier. Describing how to wheel a trifecta was merely fit recompense for past discourses on the beauties of Insular pointed minuscule.

Ria selected Santa Anita for her experiment since its race meet was currently in progress. The Santa Anita Handicap, the richest purse on the continent, might be just the sort of contest to test a novice bettor's luck—or so she hoped her choice would look to prying eyes afterwards.

She groped through pools swirling with uncertainties. . . .

＊　　＊　　＊

Another day, another six million credits. The handle ought to be at least that high, the way the grandstand was filling up.

His view from the steward's stand was the best at the track—hell, it'd better be. He savored the rugged sweep of the Sierra Madre, airbrushed green this time of year. It matched the fresher green of the turf course that curled like a comma down to the flowery infield.

My compliments to the Set Designer.

Not to mention the groundskeepers—that artificial loam looked fast. A great day for running the Handicap.

He walked over to the urn and drew coffee into a real china cup, careful not to splash his blazer.

Damn uniform! That aqua, pink, and white against brown skin made him feel like a walking ice cream sundae.

Well, sweets for the sweet. . . . After stirring in seven lumps of sugar, he took a sip of coffee.

He loosened his tie a discreet fraction, adjusted his hat to a cocky angle, and sat down in front of his video display. It took a bit of wriggling to find a comfortable position, since he liked his trousers tight as paint. But it put the world on notice that his ass was still his own. . . .

＊　　＊　　＊

Over the next three weeks, Ria got to know the mind of

Track Steward Neal Davies, right down to his hatred of socks and fondness for grape jelly and pickle relish sandwiches on toast.

Through his eyes, she watched horses run nine times a day, the winners sealed by his board's approval. He and the other two stewards rarely disagreed, thanks to the cameras and electronic gear at their disposal. Their eyrie offered a unique observation post for Ria's purposes.

Repeated sampling demonstrated that race results in Neal's world matched those in Ria's almost exactly. The few discrepancies—caused by bad weather, spills, and fouls—reminded Ria that her scheme was no sure thing. She could bet the other world's winners and still lose. She could even lose by winning too well.

The evening before the Santa Anita Handicap was to be run, Ria's nerves cried out for Lute's soothing touch. Wearily, she let warm current bear her away. . . .

* * * * * *

It was night. Ria lay sprawled on the atrium floor, playing with Kara's cat. Lute was curled up in the cushions, tuning his *gouar*. Gentle rain pattered on the skylight glass, a steady accompaniment to the twangs and thrums from Lute's instrument.

Ria ruffled the calico's fur one more time and tossed its ball in a corner. The cat bounded away; Ria spun around and greeted Lute.

"Welcome as always, m'lady," he replied.

"Don't make me too welcome," she said, "I won't want to leave."

Ria propped herself on her elbows, gazing up at Lute.

"I'm nervous about placing those bets," she continued. "And I'm mad at myself for worrying. I can't lose more than my stake, in which case I'd start all over again." She chewed her lips.

"Who likes losing?" said Lute. "Think I do?" he snorted. "Or Amris?" He snorted louder. "Tell me what you'll do if you win, 'sides gettin' out of town." He strummed his *gouar* softly.

Ria sat up. "Well," she answered uncertainly, "all this jumping back and forth between parallel timelines has given me an idea. Since I can predict the future *here* based on what happens *there*, I could set myself up as a kind of prophetess, give oracles and read hearts."

"The very thing!" Lute slapped the strings hard. "Sibyl's role'd suit you, m'lady—if those fish-blooded folk in your world would let you play it."

"I think they might." Ria warmed to her subject. "As long as I didn't charge for my services, I wouldn't be breaking the law. And I'd have a legal job of course." Ria paused. "Even the old Soviet Union tolerated seers and psychics at the same time that it was punishing rational critics." She waved her hands for emphasis. "Given the right promotion, I think our government classes'll come to me for counsel just like the *apparatchiki*'s children flocked to fortunetellers."

Ria was on her feet now, looming over him. "At least I could open some minds to mystery while I'm waiting for that destiny you say I have."

"Easy now, Ria," said Lute. "Symbols're powerful things. Use the right ones, no tellin' what you might unleash."

"So give me a symbol to stand on and I'll move the world." She made levering motions.

"Maybe you're movin' it already." Lute put his *gouar* aside and motioned her to sit beside him. "Don't you see what makes that parallel world you're usin' different from yours?"

Ria shook her head, frowning.

"You, m'lady, you."

Ria cringed in horror.

Lute continued. "You died on that branch when you were ten. You didn't use *solarti* to save yourself from the kidnapper." He slipped an arm around her. "That's makin' enough difference to start a new branch on the Tree. Me, I want to know why."

Ria clung to him sobbing. "We'll never find out unless I win those bets tomorrow. Please be with me during the races. And let me know you're there this time."

Lute kissed her nose. "At your service, dear lady. Now go home and get some sleep. I'll send you a dream."

Ria returned his kiss and left. . . .

❋   ❋   ❋

They nestled against rough, gray roots that were wrinkled and twisted like chains of mountains. Her white dress shimmered against his dark fur. Their bodies were curled together like fellow cubs in a den.

Hidden by the leaves, things were chewing the branches above them, letting fall a continual spatter of bitten twigs. Another thing scrabbled and chittered up and down the trunk, while something else rasped within it.

These angry sounds faded with the light.

Stars peeped through the boughs.

The sleepers wakened.

He brought his *gouar* out of the shadows and sang while he played to her:

> *Living is dancing and you are the dancer,*
> *Within you the answer if only you dare.*
> *Tame lightning lancing, soar over you mountains,*
> *Drink at wisdom's fountain now, Rider-In-Air!*

The melody of his strings gave way to the music of flowing water.

They found a spring welling out of the earth.

He gave her to drink from his cupped hands. The drops that fell from his fingers sparkled like the stars. . . .

❋   ❋   ❋

Ria awoke Sunday morning calm and purposeful. She ate a sensible brunch and dressed with ritual care.

Since the Santa Anita racetrack wouldn't open until 1500 hours her time, Ria spent the early afternoon reading a classic collection of fairy tales entitled *There Was a Horse*.

If orphans prospered and peasant kids won kingdoms as often as they did in stories . . . she'd find her fortune yet—this day or some other.

Ria signed on with the computer at the nearest Off-Track Betting parlor and punched the codes for today's Santa Anita action. The daily double was available on the first and second races.

1:1.2 KILOMETERS. CLAIMING. purse cr. 8,000 fillies.
2-year-olds. . . .
2: 1.5 KILOMETERS. ALLOWANCE. purse cr. 20,000.
3-year-olds. . . .

Ria coupled Fuji Maid at 11-1 in the first race with Topping Out at 5-1 in the second and entered her bet of cr. 100.

Within half an hour, she had won cr. 8,750.

It was too good to be true! Race results on the two timelines did match! Now she had more money than she could earn in a year working at the Library.

Ria fixed herself a cup of tea to calm down. If she cashed in the winnings in hand, she could still play another time. . . .

"Why stop halfway up the mountain, m'lady? Can't stand the climb?"

Lute was right. She had to try. Take advantage of one lucky day when conditions were good.

Ria scrolled ahead to the eighth race.

8: 2 KILOMETERS. 71st. running of the Santa Anita Handicap. cr. 1,500,000 added. 3-year-olds and upward. . . .

Since the winner on her list was one of the favorites, there was little to be gained by betting him across the board. Instead, Ria bet an exacta of Incuse Square at 2-1 to win and Pandion's Crag at 10-1 to place. If either horse finished in a different position, she'd lose everything.

Ria stared at the screen for a long time before placing her bet.

Two hours passed. All betting on the Handicap closed.

By post time Ria was at the point of fainting. RACE IN PROGRESS flashed on her screen.

For two minutes she could barely breathe.

RESULTS registered: Incuse Square first, Pandion's Crag second, Ultima Thule third.

The OBJECTION sign flashed.

Ria whimpered as an explanation appeared. The jockey on Ultima Thule, the odds-on favorite, had lodged a claim of interference against Pandion's Crag. The stewards were studying tapes to decide the merits of his case.

Ria's moans turned to hysterical giggles. Her fate—maybe

the fate of the whole world—was in the hands of a man whose pants were entirely too tight.

Lute flooded her mind with calm.

OBJECTION winked out.

FINAL winked on. With Lute's cheers ringing her like a bell, Ria staggered up from her chair 258,125 credits richer.

XXVI

Spring came early that year. Amorous birds swooped and twittered in the boughs of budding trees weeks ahead of schedule. The first blades of new grass began sprouting before the last lumps of packed ice had entirely melted. Damp breezes carried hints of farm chemicals and freshly plowed fields.

On a Sunday afternoon in mid-March, Ria, Carey, and Leigh strolled among the greening graves in Mount Hope cemetery. They read the old tombstones and paused to admire a single white crocus that bloomed beneath a weathered memorial star.

Carey opened his jacket half-way, welcoming the sun.

"Ria, I can't thank you enough for that dinner last night," he said. "Haven't eaten that well since I left home."

"Fabulous." Leigh nodded emphatically, his bony face bobbing up and down.

"What's the use of having money if you don't spend it?" Ria hugged herself with glee. "I'm going to savor, relish, utterly wallow in being rich." She stretched like a playful cat, arching her back against the trunk of a battered oak tree. "It's fun doing things for people that I couldn't afford to do before, such as taking my friends to dinner at the Evergreen."

Leigh still seemed embarrassed by her generosity. "And the view was even better than the food—all that glass."

"Amazing how beautiful Chambana looks at night," added Carey.

Ria chuckled. "If you're up high enough, anything looks good."

From the right vantage point, even their drab university town could sparkle. Could the same be true of their world?

Carey scraped mud off his shoe on a tree stump. "The bit I can't get over is you sending your entree back to the kitchen. I wouldn't have had the nerve to complain."

"They tried to pass off mutton as lamb." Ria snorted. "Maybe they were saving the spring lamb for more important customers—they found some fast enough when I yelled."

"You dared to yell. That's the point," said Leigh. "Just like you dared to bet on one horse after another, pressing your luck, instead of cashing in your first winnings like any—"

"Like any sensible person?" Ria laughed and tapped Leigh's cheek. "I wasn't risking as much as you think. I had a foolproof system."

"Lots of people claim that," said Carey. "Yours worked."

Ria said nothing—there was nothing she could safely say. She gazed off into the distance, as if expecting the Assembly Hall to finally slip its moorings and zoom away like the flying saucer it resembled.

Carey shyly picked up the thread of the conversation. "You're not just bolder than we are, Ria, you're bolder than you used to be. Happier, too."

"Why shouldn't I be? I'm no longer worried about losing my mind."

Leigh shuffled his feet and looked away.

"And I hate to say it," she continued, "it's become almost a social advantage to have a handicap. People feel obliged to be nice to me—Ali's been absurdly considerate, especially since my promotion came through."

"Do you think that pity influenced her recommendation?" asked Leigh.

"No. That promotion had been in the works for some while—I don't have to tell you how slow the University is. My work on Professor Clyde's disaster book did the trick. I didn't get preferential treatment."

"I didn't mean to imply. . ." Leigh flushed. "But I agree with Carey. Something has changed about you besides your health and your work grade."

"You seem to have a new sense of purpose," added Carey. "Any special reason why?"

"Oh, you might say I've read a fiery gospel writ in burnished disks of steel." Ria waved her hand to make her ring flash in the sun.

Carey wrinkled his brows, as if he almost remembered what she was quoting. He ran his fingers nervously through his hair and asked in a small voice: "Any chance you could show me—show us—" he gestured to include Leigh—"how to read it too?"

Ria clasped the hands of both men, drawing them closer. "That's a message you have to read for yourself, friends." Her voice grew still gentler. "But the first step is learning who you are—not who society tells you to be. Since I nearly died in that accident last fall, I've been learning to trust myself." She caught their eyes—first Leigh, then Carey. "And trust my dreams. Could you try that much?"

"Sure," said Leigh bitterly. "If we had any dreams left."

"Then maybe I'd better work to bring dreams to the dreamless."

Carey snorted. "How much difference can one person make?"

Ria squared her shoulders. "It only takes one neutron to start a chain reaction—one neutron in the right place."

"Which is?" asked Leigh.

"Washington, of course," answered Ria. "I'm going to move to Columbia, that's where they keep the power on this continent."

"You can't be serious!" Both men yelled together.

"Serious enough to give notice at the Library," said Ria, with a hint of archness. "I'm leaving next Sunday."

"Aren't you forgetting something?" asked Carey. "Money can't buy you a residence permit in Columbia Region, muchless Washington itself. They're incredibly fussy about whom they let live there."

"That's been taken into account. I plan to find employment —a permanent job with residence rights—before my tourist visa expires."

"You? An unknown without connections?" Carey shook his head in disbelief. "That's a rarer feat than picking a whole day's winners at the racetrack."

"Speaking of horses . . ." Ria changed the subject with a shrug. "Let's go by the barns on our way home. The horses are sure to be out today."

The three of them walked out of the cemetery arm in arm.

The breeze gusted. A cardinal alighted in the oak tree and began singing to claim his territory.

Ria's last week of work sped by swiftly. She was too busy being happy to bait Hannah or evade Ali.

Come Sunday, she'd be rid of them for good.

Come Sunday, she'd be taking her first steps to becoming a sibyl—the Columbian Sibyl.

Move over, Cumaea, Delphica, Tiburtina, all you prophetic ladies. You're about to get a thirteenth sister. . . .

By Friday night, Ria could scarcely sleep for the excitement.

Her eagerness to start a new life made her eager to finish off a certain bit of her old one. She wanted to try crossing the forbidden mountains of her childhood Dream.

Ria hadn't dreamt of those mountains since the accident because Lute had stopped sending the images. But now she could induce it for herself. How she longed to pit her skill in *solarti* against that old frustration!

Kara had spoken of Ria's Dream just before she died. Did those words predict eventual success—or was she just hearing the message she wanted to hear? There was one sure way to test the prophecy.

Ria set her course and lay down to dream. . . .

❀　　　❀　　　❀

High above plowed fields and greening prairie, she rode a dappled golden stallion, sleek as polished wood.

The mountain rampart reared up as before.

And as before, the barrier grew to bar their way however high they flew. The road of air was closed, nor could mere wishing win them through.

She reined her steed to seek a trail on solid earth.

They lit upon the barren flank of the highest peak, where glaciers dripped like frozen tears.

Dismounted now, she led her horse along an avenue of

looted tombs whose sagging doors gaped wide to show gnawed bones.

Wind moaned in the grave shafts, whistled and wailed in rubble-strewn chambers, and raced roaring out of a hundred charnel mouths. It swept up shards of ice and flakes of grit to buffet, then blind, and lastly rasp off screaming flesh.

Storm-borne shreds of horse and rider fell in bits as bloody snow . . .

******

Ria's terror did not vanish on waking. She could still feel the assault of the flaying wind—and the wintry malice behind it.

Lines from an ancient ballad unreeled in a closed loop through her mind:

> O'er his white banes when they are bare,
> The wind sall blaw for evermair.

Would someone soon be mocking her bare bones the way the raven in that ballad mocked the remains of the slaughtered knight?

Ria was frightened, but not paralyzed, by the dream. She did not intend to change her course on its account. If her move to Columbia should prove fatal—well, better to die trying. . . .

Yet feelings of dread persisted even after Ria had eaten and dressed Saturday morning.

Perhaps the dismal weather was to blame. Dirty gray clouds had gathered overnight to spoil Chambana's taste of spring. Ria could sense a cold front moving down on them from the north. It was classic tornado weather. . . .

Turning on the weather announcements while she packed, Ria heard:

—POSSIBILITY OF THUNDERSTORMS THIS AFTERNOON WITH LOCALLY DAMAGING WINDS—

The forecast was threatening, but not alarming. Ria usually enjoyed watching storms: seeing energy unleashed exhilarated her.

Still, no previous nightmare had left such a residue of depression behind, depression with this peculiar. . . *flavor*. Was her dream a premonition of some specific disaster?

Lute would know.

And now she felt secure enough in her art—and in her feelings about him—to ask for advice without resentment. Their minds were learning how to partner each other.

Ria sought the remedy of soothing waters. . . .

❋   ❋   ❋

Ria's hand was full of fish guts. Lute stood beside her cheerfully boning carp. The kitchen sink was stacked with other fish awaiting attention. She reeled at the smell.

"Glad you're here, Ria." Lute chirruped and kissed her nose. "Must stay till evenin' and see Amris. Takes a lot to feed m'sister." He waved his knife at the pile of fish. "And I got her a watermelon, too, chilling in the cold box."

"Sounds delicious." Ria dropped the offal in the slop bucket and washed her hands. "Mind if I just watch? I don't know how to clean fish."

"And tomorrow. . . tomorrow, know what?" Lute chittered. "She'n I are going to visit Manita and Tahar. They're scouting Lake Vermillion this week as a possible aquaculture site. Then—"

"Lute!" Ria cried, tapping his shoulder. "I hate to interrupt you, but I didn't come to socialize."

"Why then?" He blinked.

"I had a nightmare last night that terrified me. Can you help me learn what it means?"

Apologetically, Lute offered her a chair and sat down with her at the table to hear her account.

By the time Ria finished, Lute was stroking his whiskers thoughtfully.

"Your instinct's right, m'lady. That nightmare could be a warning. *Solexes* can't see the true future, but events on other timelines can seep into our dreams uninvited."

"As if nearby branches were casting shadows on mine?"

"Quite right! But the shadows flicker so much, you don't know what's castin' them."

"How do I find out?" asked Ria, frowning.

"For a start, I'd scan that branch that's the twin of yours, the way you did to get the racing results," he replied. "Closest place usually gives the most crossover. Shouldn't need me to tell you that."

Ria blushed for overlooking the obvious. "But I knew what I was looking for that time. Am I supposed to jump blindly?"

"If some disaster's pending, the bloodshed'll draw you. Multiple deaths bend branches."

Ria nodded gravely. "I'll try it. But don't let me keep you from your work. Those fish shouldn't stand longer than necessary."

Lute bounded up. "Keep talkin' while I cut. This'll take a while. Make yourself some tea if you like. There's egg candy on that covered plate."

Ria declined, politely hiding her shudder.

Lute went on processing his catch.

"Tonight's a double celebration, Ria. Besides Amris coming, I got the better of Wilamine Hork today." He snuffled happily.

"Who? Oh, the Buzzard Lady, the one who hates *perfur*."

"Her." Lute nodded, chopping the head off a fat carp. "She's been circling me like a waitin' vulture ever since Kara died." He kissed his fingers to the memory of the departed. "Trying to stir up trouble over Kara's will, she was. Y'see, Kara left me this house and half her estate. So Hork went to Dorel with whispers of undue influence, even—" he snarled, "—hints of foul play."

"That rotten bitch!" cried Ria.

"What do you expect of a woman who'd marry her own first cousin?" He snorted, twitching his whiskers. "Never occurred to Hork that Dorel was on m'side, knew about the will since it was drawn up, and wasn't looking to break it."

"Such creatures assume that everybody else thinks like them." Ria's nose wrinkled.

"The mourning month's up today and Dorel's made it known she's lettin' me keep the stub of the Memory Candle. Shows the town she thinks well of me."

"That's a lovely gesture" said Ria, "but will it stop Hork from trying something else? I bet she won't give up that easily."

"I'll out-swim her next time, too." He laughed. "Not to worry, m'lady."

Lute went on happily cleaning fish.

Ria brooded on dead knights and carrion birds.
She got up and made them both a pot of tea.

The delightful evening with Lute and Amris that followed washed away Ria's anxieties for a while. But as soon
as she returned to her own world, where it was still
Saturday morning, her fears surged back stronger than
before.

There was no ignoring the problem: she had to find such
horror's source.

Ria decided to begin her search by checking today's
happenings on the adjacent timeline and working forward
hour by hour.

Wan waters roiled about her. . . .

※   ※   ※

Another ambulance yowled by.

For once, he was glad to be a rookie. Better to be stuck
on traffic detail than be up there mucking around for
bodies. Without thinking, he moved a few steps backwards as if to put a bit more distance between him and the
sodden ruins.

He shivered despite the warm sunshine.

His long shadow raked shattered display windows. A
solar panel from the building behind him had blown into
the dress shop opposite. Curly strips of roofing draped
across racks of clothes. Flying debris had pockmarked
plastic storefronts. Signboards were plastered with soggy
wrapping paper and smashed Easter eggs. A big plush
bunny, shapeless from the rain, dangled from a bent lamp
post. A mannequin's head lay in a lavatory sink on the
sidewalk. Filthy torrents raced in the gutters, puddling
around choked storm drains.

Seeing the red smear that had once been a bird raised a
taste of vomit in his throat. It looked too much like other
sights along Neil Street—bigger smears that hadn't started
out as birds. . . .

And if he tossed it before the day was over, well, he'd
just seen a veteran Emergency worker drop a body bag to
puke her guts out. He almost wished a few sonofabitching
gawkers would get through the Security cordon. Would

serve them right to see what splintered glass did to human flesh. . . .

＊   ＊   ＊

Ria fought down nausea of her own to make repeated plunges into minds at the disaster scene. She made herself look at the glass sleet and the bloody rain clotted together on familiar streets. She pieced the story together out of scraps drawn from many witnesses' minds:

During a thunderstorm, a funnel cloud had materialized without warning above Athletic Park and plowed a short but grisly furrow across downtown Chambana. Casualties ran into three figures, with major casualties in and around the Evergreen restaurant. Most of the victims had been attending an official Federation Day luncheon at the luxurious top-floor dining room when the tornado had shattered the glass walls around them.

Ria had less than three hours to prevent an identical tragedy from occurring on her own branch of time.

Even now, some two hundred leading citizens of Chambana would be preparing for their own version of that holiday banquet. Unless she found a way to intervene, most of them would die at 1305 this afternoon.

Ria gulped a second breakfast to refuel her mind.

Why hadn't the tornado sirens sounded an alert? Weather Service was generally reliable. People were well drilled to obey announced Watches and Warnings—one could be fined for ignoring the signal to take cover.

Using her computer, Ria hastily surveyed Weather Service operating procedures in the Prairie Region. She had to hope that she was reading the blur of data correctly.

Warnings of dangerous weather conditions originated at the North American Severe Storm Forecast Center in Kansas City. These were relayed to Chambana by the Federation Weather Service Office in Springfield, which also had the responsibility for issuing specific local storm warnings.

What had broken this normal chain of command?

Ria could find out by searching the parallel branch again at a time prior to the storm. She armed herself with all the biographical detail she could find on Ellie Corto, the meteorologist in charge of the Springfield Office.

Ria groped through murky waters. . . .

*   *   *

If I get one more funnel cloud report from District 10, I am going to go noncomp myself. I may garrote Samuels with his very own telephone cord. Sighted near Ivesdale this time, was it? No independent confirmations.

How very convenient.

Maybe there's a whole nest of pranksters out there inventing tornadoes every time a Cumulonimbus system rolls in.

How do I know those calls are really coming from Pesotum? Maybe some noncomp's found a way to access the system. All the more suspicious when the Marseilles radar's down, thanks to noncomp sabotage. It's not your random craziness like they claim, it's a goddamn conspiracy.

If Samuels makes one more whimper about "hunches," I really will strangle him. You can't send people scurrying for shelter on a whim.

We'll go by the book or not at all.

*   *   *

So that was it; at last Ria knew. Without the Marseilles radar, tornado tracks couldn't be plotted. Perhaps the Ivesdale funnel had dissipated before other witnesses could corroborate its existence. Apparently, the killer tornado had dropped out of the clouds without warning, directly over the heart of Chambana.

Ria checked the latest local forecast. While she'd been occupied with *solarti*, "possibility of severe thunderstorms" had been upgraded to an official Severe Thunderstorm Watch. The Marseilles problem didn't affect that announcement, since it originated at the main weather center in Kansas City.

A glance outside verified the danger.

The sky was darker than before. A wall of black clouds reared across the horizon and gusty winds whipped trees. Ria saw a flash of far-off lightning.

Could she impel her own world's Ellie Corto to issue a tornado warning before human lives blew away?

Again and again, Ria battered at the meteorologist's paranoid mind without avail. This woman was every bit as rigid as her counterpart on the other timeline. Bending a bureaucrat's will was a task that would baffle even Lute.

Ria's further attempts to work through the assistant meteorologist Langley Samuels only provoked a quarrel between him and Corto that left Corto even less receptive than before.

Ria shuddered, then tented her hands and drew a deep breath. All right, she could attack the local warning system itself via *solarti*.

Her computer gave the address of Chambana's Emergency Operating Center on Elm Street as well as the names of those who worked there. Details of the siren activation mechanisms were classified for security reasons. However, Ria was able to pluck them out of an employee's mind: her memory scanning technique was improving with practice.

The hardest thing of all was the waiting. Time that had earlier flown so fast now crept. She must sound the alarm early enough to give people adequate notice, but not so early that they would be tempted to leave shelter prematurely.

Ria ate while she waited, as much to relieve anxiety as to replenish energy.

Wind rose and thunder rolled.

Ria fretted.

On the click of 1245, she sprang. Her fury raged at the siren controls. Her ardor seethed along the open switch.

Nothing happened.

Ria cursed her inexperience, then regrouped.

It must require far more concentrated effort to melt a copper contact than to ignite a dry milkweed pod. At several kilometers' distance, the deed was beyond her present ability. But if she moved in closer, using a host, and called on Lute for help, she might yet prevail.

Like Dasher's broken neck, it was a case for ni Prizing's Method: Ria was limited in the amount of time she could spend in another person's body; Lute was less familiar with technology. They'd do it together—or not at all.

Lute burst through restless waves to join her fight. . . .

While lightning crackled outside, Ria and Lute found the mind of an Emergency Center clerk who was napping away his lunch hour at his desk near the control panel.

With this man as a vantage point, Ria and Lute willed warmth into the target. They sensed it gradually envelop the minuet of energies that was the metal. Temperature rose and with it, tempo. Atoms danced a mad gavotte, faster, ever faster. Contact closed. Electrons flowed.

The steady blare of sirens sounded their joint triumph.

Footsteps clattered in the corridor outside as Ria's fellow residents scampered for the basement.

Defying regulations, Ria made no move to follow. She refused to go huddle below with the rest. This day's work demanded some dramatic gesture of release, something befitting the energies that raged in her.

Ria opened her door, and finding the hallway empty, ran—for the roof.

Upstairs, Ria stayed inside the enclosure covering the exit to the roof. Protected by reinforced glass, she could watch the storm as pure spectacle. With her own eyes, she wanted to see the killer's blow fall harmlessly. And she wanted Lute to see it through her eyes.

He came to her as quickly as before.

Ria felt his dear touch in her mind, but they held their silence while the tempest raved. Two selves behind a single pair of eyes, they gazed westward into chaos.

The wind drove churning clouds before another lightning-riven squall line. The sky was one vast bruise, purple above, livid below. Layers of different darkness slipped past each other and twisted back upon themselves to form a vortex within the lowest ragged band of cloud.

Invisibly, the tornado struck.

Bursts of debris rose from the Chambana skyline. The top of the tallest tower erupted into gouts of shattering glass and wood. Outlined by dust, the snaky shape wavered another moment, then faded back into the clouds as quickly as it had appeared.

The rest of the storm passed over them, lashing at them

with rain so hard that their refuge might have been a diving bell at the bottom of a lake. They watched until the last thunder died and the sky was bright once more.

Ria stepped out on the wet roof and splashed through a few pirouettes among the solar panels. Only then did Lute speak:

"*Magnificent!*" he called within her mind.

"*It does make a splendid show—provided it doesn't hurt anyone,*" she replied, in the same silent fashion.

"*Why didn't those people you saw killed take cover? Danger couldn't be plainer.*"

"*They depended more on official warnings than on their own common sense. At least complacency didn't cost any lives—this time.*"

"*Your doing, m'lady. Kara'd be as proud of you as I am.*"

Ria might have wept, but Lute's masterful delight wouldn't let her. "*It's to your credit—and to hers—for teaching me.*"

"*Teaching's another sort of learning, climbing, growing. We do what we're put here for, what's there to fear?*"

For an enchanted instant, Ria felt that the two of them were utterly alone, invincible and content, on the summit of a very high mountain.

Joy caroled in her: "*Then shall we see 'no enemy but winter and rough weather?' *"

Ria whirled about one last time and skipped downstairs.

XXVII

Returning to her apartment, Ria met Hannah and Ali in the stairwell leading to her floor. The younger woman looked even paler than usual and clung to the older one's arm.

Ria greeted them with a nod and gave a hearty sigh. "Aren't you glad to hear that 'All Clear' sound?"

Ali only stared at her, eyes narrowing. "Why are you walking *downstairs* now, Ria, instead of up? Why didn't I see you in the basement?"

"Your clothes are wet," sneered Hannah. "You didn't take shelter in time like we did."

"No," said Ria boldly. "I didn't. I've just been up on the roof surveying the damage and splashing around in the rain puddles for fun." She brushed her soggy pantlegs for emphasis. "Go ahead and report me. The fine won't put much of a dent in my new fortune, now will it?"

Ria laughed bitterly, advancing on Hannah. "Go ahead and report me like you did the last time."

Hannah cringed behind Ali, trying to use her companion's bulk as a shield. "I don't know what you're talking about," she whimpered. "You can't talk to me like that. Tell her she can't, Ali."

Lute's voice spoke in Ria's mind: *"Hannah didn't tattle on you. Ali did. Saw that in the therapist's memory."*

Ria stopped in mid-stride. Her world had turned upside down. She retreated a step, taking a hard look at the two women. For the first time, she saw who the real victim here was—not herself but Hannah.

Clearing her throat, Ria stammered. "I seem to have misjudged you, Hannah. I do apologize. I was convinced that you were the informant who denounced me to PSI because I didn't think I had any other enemies."

Her voice steadied. "But I was wrong. There was one other, wasn't there, Ali?"

"Enemy?" Ali protested. "How could I be your enemy?" She touched her broad breast. "I had your best interests at heart. I'd do what I did for any person with . . . problems."

"And if they didn't have problems, you'd contrive some, eh, Ali?" Ria turned icily correct. "I'm not about to make a scene. You aren't worth the effort. In case you've forgotten, your authority over me ended yesterday with my job." She smiled grimly. "It's great to be getting away from you, Ali, from you and all you stand for."

Ria started to turn away, but paused to deliver a parting shot. "Someday, Hannah, you might consider making the same move. It's amazing how well one can stand on one's own feet."

Opening the firedoor to her floor, Ria left the two women speechless behind her.

Once she was back in her own quarters, Lute spoke again: *"Glad you did that, m'lady. Hate's uncreative. Here's somethin' pleasanter to think of instead: let me host you when Amris'n I visit Manita and Tahar at the lake."*

"You really mean that?" Ria was ecstatic. *"You're going to let me into your mind?"*

"Better'n that. Giving you control of my body for part of the trip so you can see what it's like to be a perfur."

"Oh Lute, what a wonderful holiday we'll have! How I wish you were here in the fur so I could hug you!"

✳   ✳   ✳

Ria couldn't stop petting her beautiful fur. Stubby *perfur* fingers were as sensitive as human ones and the sleekness of Lute's pelt proved irresistible. Fortunately, he seemed more amused than outraged by the liberties she was taking with his body.

But if fur was extravagantly sensuous, a tail was merely

comical. It interfered with sitting on chairs and never seemed to be quite where she expected it to be.

Adjusting to the radically different—and superbly fluid—body language of a *perfur* was more difficult than Ria had anticipated. This forward-sloping, head-bobbing gait of theirs still felt unnatural to her, despite practice at Lute's home prior to departure.

Ria had also wanted to try swimming as a *perfur* but Lute persuaded her to wait until they reached Lake Vermillion.

Getting used to her new eyes, Ria noticed that cool colors were muted and the visible spectrum was shifted to longer wavelengths. While roses in Lute's garden showed flamingly red, the irises and clematis vines growing near his house looked black.

Other senses were heightened. Ria found that she could detect a giddy profusion of scents and hear higher notes in bird songs than before. *Perfur* vocal chords allowed her to sing a whole octave higher than she could with her human throat.

She loved playing with her whiskers but startled herself the first time she snuffled.

Ria loved the train ride to Danville. The gaudily painted steam locomotive, the wood paneled cars with their lace curtains and antimacassars had the quaintness of another time. How unlike the swift but dull diesel-powered train that had taken her to Indianapolis as a child over approximately the same route.

The conductor obligingly adjusted their seats to accommodate *perfur* anatomy, but one sour-faced man made a point of changing his place in the car when she and Amris sat down near him.

The tracks ran due east from Chamba past tidy farms whose buildings were inevitably paired or clustered with those of neighbors.

Amris explained that this arrangement had been adopted centuries earlier as a defense against macrats—not to mention marauding men. People on adjacent homesteads often owned heavy equipment in common or marketed their harvests together.

Ria saw a horse-drawn mower haying. Horses and other

farm animals were much in evidence, but there were no beasts packed closely on feedlots. As in her world, corn was still the main crop, but the fields here were smaller and more wheat and sorghum were grown along with the corn.

Amris had arranged for them to be met at the depot by a friendly farmer named Webber Riksun. He was to drive them part way to their destination north of town.

Riksun, a fuzzy-haired bear of a man who looked strong enough to carry Lute under one arm and Amris under the other, greeted the two *perfur* heartily. He helped them clamber into the back of his wagon where they hunched down on sacks of flour and bolts of cloth.

Ria kept quiet, concentrating on keeping her seat during the jolting ten-kilometer ride; Amris chatted with her friend.

"Keeping your rat-watch keen?" Amris asked Riksun.

"Keen enough. You won't catch me letting shrubbery grow around my house like some careless folks. My fences're stout and I check my property for rat-sign regularly."

"More humans did the same, m'job'd be easier." Amris sighed. "Any sightings lately?"

"I heard tell someone south of town lost a lamb. A tree-tiger—or even two of 'em—couldn't do that. And poachers would've been neater about it."

Amris bared her fangs. "Not good. Rats're getting bad on the lower Wabash. Be raidin' up here before you know it. Talk to your sheriff after I've seen m'kin."

"Say, what's that young *perfur* couple up to at the lake?" asked Riksun, glad to be off the subject of macrats.

"Looking for land to settle. Twin Stars is about to bud off a new clan. The founders've got to scout the country themselves."

Riksun frowned. "That lake's too small to support a whole village. The Vermillion system's just a bunch of big creeks."

"Wabash Valley south of here's too deep," she answered. "Flood plain's too broad to suit us. Tryin' somethin' new: a clan of scattered settlements matched to human ones where we can earn cash money. This works, be a big thing for us."

Riksun grunted. "If you say so. Wouldn't mind hiring some stock handlers. Your kind's naturally good with beasts."

Ria's bones thought the trip would never end. How could Amris endure this jouncing with such good cheer? There she sat, talking nonchalantly about the current drought and the possibility that today's overcast would yield rain. Ria pretended to doze so she wouldn't be expected to participate.

Finally, Riksun let them off at the waist of the five-kilometer-long oval lake, at the spot where the dirt road passed closest to the water. Now the two *perfur* would circle north to Manita and Tahar's camp on the opposite shore.

Since she was still a bit uneasy in the presence of firearms, Ria offered to take charge of their pack while Amris carried all the weapons and ammunition.

So Amris added Lute's bowie knife and light shotgun to her Colson rifle. But before moving out, the ranger unpacked a wide band of accordion-pleated leather out of her pack. She laced it around her neck as a gorget, taking care to leave the throwing knife that hung between her shoulder blades free.

"What's that for?" asked Ria.

"Trail armor. Gives rat teeth something to bite on 'sides m'skin."

"Are you expecting trouble?" Ria's whiskers quivered.

"No more'n any other time." Amris closed her jaws with an audible snap.

The sound of Riksun's team and wagon dwindled away, leaving them utterly alone in the cut-over woods.

Ria refrained from speaking while they walked because Amris was so intent on studying their surroundings. A mild breeze helped make the heat of the August day bearable on her fur.

Amris signaled a halt after they'd travelled about a kilometer along the lake shore.

She whispered hoarsely in Ria's ear. "Total quiet from here on. Mind where you step. Been watching buzzards lighting ahead of us. Want to see what's dead."

Amris unlimbered her rifle and carried it loaded in the crook of her arm. She headed toward the spot where vultures were spiraling down, occasionally stopping to sniff the wind and listen.

Although unable to match the woods-wise ranger's gliding movements, Ria followed her quietly as she could.

In a blackberry thicket north of the lake, they found the kill.

It was Tahar.

He lay like some empty, ruined seed pod. His belly was a gory hollow, the viscera devoured by macrats. The bones of his upper arms and legs showed in gashes where flesh had been stripped away. His throat was bitten through and his tail was chewed to shreds. Vultures had already gotten his eyes and were reluctant to abandon the rest.

Amris drove off the last buzzard with her rifle butt.

Tahar's shotgun still hung from his strap, unfired. He'd managed to kill one attacker with his teeth. A second dog-sized gray form lay at some distance from the dead *perfur,* possibly killed by its fellows. The greedy rats had even finished the blackberries Tahar had been picking when ambushed. Crushed berries stained his empty collecting bag black.

Ria sat on her haunches squeezing her eyes closed against the horror, too paralyzed to retch. But she couldn't shut out the stench of rat urine and rotting meat . . . or the buzzing of the deerflies. . . or the delicate tickle of those flies' feet landing on her eyelids.

Why did this one death grieve her more than a hundred had in Chambana?

"Lute, get back here!" Amris growled.

He seized control of his body from Ria and tried to thrust her out.

"Go home!" he screamed silently.

"I'm staying with you, come what may."

Their wills grappled; she held fast. The stubbornness that surprised Ria angered Lute.

"Passive then," he said. *"Don't want to know you're there."*

"Agreed."

The scent of rat-filth fed his frenzy. He hummed and snarled and clashed his massive jaws.

Amris loomed over him, tall in the power of her office.

"Under orders!" she cried. "Save rage for killin' rats. Warn Manita! Warn Riksun!"

Obedience owed to a ranger curbed instinct. Lute sought Manita's mind.

The brain he touched was close to death.

His frenzy flared anew.

Amris cuffed him. "Too late for her? Warn Riksun! Humans have to know, 'case we die. Protect first. Then avenge."

Lute hummed in anger but obeyed.

Hard to find that human's mind. Hard to fit inside. Hard to care when kindred had been killed.

During his brief trance, Amris buckled on her ammunition belt. She handed Lute the bowie knife, shotgun, and pouch of shells.

Abandoning their pack, they raced to find Manita.

Rat-sign and *perfur*-scent marked the path clearly. They followed Tahar's footsteps along the lake to reach his dying wife.

The rats had ripped Manita's belly open and torn living flesh out of her haunches, only to vomit up the half-chewed gobbets beside her body.

She was not entirely dead.

"Done for spite," snarled Amris. "She'd gotten two of them."

She pointed at the slain rats lying between Manita and the water.

Lute lay down beside the dying *femfur* and joined his soul to hers. He drew her aside from the Door she was scratching to enter.

Holding her being against his own, he made the twisting straight and the roughness smooth. Ambition, giddiness, and pride faded out like mildew bleaching in the sun.

Lute took Manita's consent and led her into brightness, whispering:

> Who created us all in the beginning.
> Receive us all at the end.

Amris pried him away from the corpse.

Manita's blood ran in sticky rivulets down his fur. He sat dumbly, watching it drip.

Amris forced trail ration into his mouth, swearing at him to eat it.

She ought to know that he hated the stuff. It stuck to his teeth.

Would that bother macrats? Could they pick their teeth easier after eating *perfur*?

Amris was shaking him.

"Hurry up, get your strength back," she cried. "Need you lively. Wind's carrying them our scent. They'll scatter."

Amris showed him Manita's shotgun, gnawed and gouged by angry rats. The rats had also torn down the *perfur* couple's bough shelter and fouled their belongings.

Lute ate the gluey cake Amris offered, washed himself off in the lake, and within minutes was ready to follow her in the chase.

Rage welling back within him lent Lute stamina for the ten-kilometer run. He trotted after his sister tirelessly through crackling-dry woods and meadows towards a tree-lined river. The wind was behind him; the killers were before him. All else was a blur.

He almost missed Amris' signal to halt.

They squatted gasping as she scratched a map in the dirt.

Amris said: "This fork of the Vermillion's got swampy banks. Rats hit the river, they'll spread out. Can't circle behind us 'cause then we'd be downwind and would smell 'em."

She tapped the mark that stood for the river bank. "Want you to set fires on this side, north and south, closer'n closer together each time. Drive 'em against the water they hate. They'll charge rather'n swim and we'll pick 'em off. Tonight's rain'll douse the fire."

Amris gave him bearings for his *solarti* attack. He let his hatred of rats blaze up to kindle grass.

Parallel bands of smoke rose in response.

Lute let it burn awhile, then struck again and again until the fires nearly met.

Lute and Amris advanced cautiously towards the un-burnt stretch of riverbank. At last they spied their quarry from a rise overlooking scrubby land that flooded in other years.

Amris climbed the low crotch of an oak while Lute braced himself against the trunk below her. She was to have the first volley when the last fires drove the rats to charge. There might be as many as a dozen of them.

Lute struck two more sparks with his mind.

Vengeful flames leapt up.

Half a score of squealing rats erupted from the brush.

"Steady!" cried the ranger.

She felled four and wounded another.

"Now, Lute!"

He blasted the nearest rat. The rest of the pack was almost upon him.

"Release trigger," yelled Amris. "Squeeze again."

Lute shot another rat in the chest as the others closed. He heard Amris fire once more and jump.

Grasping his gun barrel in his left hand, he clubbed a rat aside while drawing the knife. The blade nearly took one animal's head off, but another ran under his guard to attack his throat. He stabbed clumsily at the rat's back. It held on, raking his chest with its claws.

Ria hurled her mind like a flaming spear into the rat's body. She had a fleeting glimpse of Lute's blood-soaked fur through its eyes before her wrath roasted its spinal cord.

Lute sliced the suddenly limp rat under the foreleg as it died.

The rat stunned earlier revived and began scrabbling at his legs.

Falling on it, Lute bit out the back of the rat's head and gorged himself on its warm, salty brains.

Afterwards, Lute sprawled on a sandbar in the river, coaxing his wounds to stop bleeding and hurting. The gashes kept threatening to open up each time the smoky wind made him cough.

Amris had only a few scratches. She'd knifed the last rats while Lute was struggling for his life—a life he now owed to Ria.

"Glad you stayed, m'lady," was all he could say.

"I'm stubborn, dear heart, stubborn." Ria fell silent to ease the awkwardness.

Amris appeared carrying a handful of rat tails.

"Twelve," she said, shaking them.

She tied them up with a thong and hung the bundle from her belt.

"Too bad no spare gorget, little brother."

"I'll mend."

"Won't have to spend the night in the open. Riksun and his folk should be riding in soon."

"They were by the lake, the last time I looked." He shifted uncomfortably. "Maybe humans'll start worryin' again about macrats on their doorstep."

Amris shrugged. "Worry more when their kind gets killed."

"One way or another, our kind'll come back. Be a new clan here yet."

"And still call Manita and Tahar founders." She kissed her fingers to the dead. "I'll have time counted for them here next spring. Tail-bounty'll pay a *solex* for the ceremony."

"Who'd ask payment?" Lute's flank twitched, as if bitten by an unseen fly.

Amris didn't seem to hear him. She stared across the river. A shudder of wind ruffled its surface. Rain was on the way.

Beyond the line of trees, the late afternoon clouds glowed red.

"New clan's got a name now," she said.

"What?"

"Bloodwater."

EPILOGUE

Wind damage at the Chambana airport delayed Ria's departure for Washington by one day.

She spent Sunday talking a final walk around campus, finishing up at the corner of Wright and Green. As she waited for an Illibus back to the House, she gazed about this familiar scene for the last time.

Twigs and other debris littered the sidewalk, but the magnolia trees that nestled against the dark stones of Altgeld Hall were unharmed. A pinkish tinge on their buds said they'd bloom within the week.

Alma Mater was splattered with wads of paper. A basketful of trash must've blown against the statue during the storm and dried in place.

Ria smirked at the mess. Why had she ever feared that silly lump of bronze?

She flicked a mental spark at a scrap clinging to the Mater's foot. The paper caught fire as her bus arrived.

Carey and Leigh looked almost tearful when Ria left for the airport early Monday morning. They insisted that they'd miss her. She found it harder to say goodbye to them than she'd expected.

Ria shed no tears over leaving. The redness in her eyes came from a night of weeping over the dead *perfur*.

She was still brooding over the tragedy as she rode to the airport. At least she'd had the satisfaction of killing a macrat.

What a shocking deed to boast of! If PSI only knew. . . .

But now she understood, contrary to what she'd been taught, that violence as well as calm had its place. There really was

> *a time to love and a time to hate;*
> *a time for war and a time for peace.*

In Lute's world, they knew which was which and were saner for the distinctions.

The weekend's events had left Ria bone-weary, but she was determined to enjoy her first plane trip. She even endured the tedious check-in procedures with uncommon good grace.

It was worth it.

Ria trembled with excitement as the ground fell away and the monotonous checkerboard fields of Prairie vanished beneath puffy clouds.

Already spring must be creeping up the Appalachians. There would be flowers waiting for her beyond the mountains in Columbia. She sang the old Shaker hymn softly under her breath. . .

And when we find ourselves in the place just right—

Lute came into her mind.

"*It's your happy day, m'lady.*"

"One I never thought to see. But how are you feeling now?"

"*The bites healed all right. Took nearly as long to mend my mood as m'skin. Had to talk it out with Ellesiya.*"

"The way your people died was hideous."

"*Hope I never attend an uglier death than Manita's. But that's my gift; I can deal with it. But I couldn't deal with the fighting. I'm a solexam, not a fighter. Done my share of hunting, but never fought anything like that, hand to hand. Never felt the killing frenzy before.*"

"That makes two of us."

"*Now, because of that raid, there'll be a big macrat drive in the fall,* perfur *and humans together. Going to sweep clear down to the Ohio.*"

"Then maybe Manita and Tahar didn't die in vain. But why couldn't they have lived lives as full as Kara's?"

There was a long pause.

"Not for me to say, m'lady. But I will say, Kara's passin' doesn't trouble me nearly as much as it did. Found a letter from her explaining everything. She held me off at the end to keep me out of her memory."

"Why?"

"To guard secrets for you. She risked goin' into eternity flawed so I couldn't know everything in her mind—and maybe passing something on to you."

"I don't understand."

"Kara didn't want me to learn what'll pass between you two in the future."

"In the future? What are you talking about?"

"Kara saw that you'd need help fulfilling your destiny as the Columbian Sibyl. She left blocks of private time for you to return and consult her. Each visit will 'always' have been, even though none's happened yet from your spot in time."

"In other words, we're making a clever detour around a time paradox. I've only begun to see the ways one can climb the Cosmic Tree."

"But remember, the number of hours is limited. They've got to last a lifetime. Don't go running to Kara every time you feel lonely."

"You can help me decide, can't you? Oh Lute, I watched you preside over Kara's death. I was with you when you opened the Door for Manita. Now I appreciate what your gift is. Will it be 'you who lean over me on my last day'? Say that it will."

"If I can, m'lady, if I can. Enough talk of dying. I'll leave you with a lucky image that'll bring fair dreams."

Ria closed her eyes.

She was still seeing the same outside view her airplane window gave. With a difference. . . .

❋   ❋   ❋

A bank of cloud became a mighty banner that bore in black the imprint of strange letters and the outline of a horse. Its saddle and bridle were splendid. On its back there rode a flaming jewel.

The stallion neighed and reared. It sprang forth from the cloth alive to gallop lightly on the air.

Leaping past thunderheads that towered mountain-high, the Wind Horse of Victorious Fortune raced across the sky.

And demons fled before its flashing hooves. . . .

Paksenarrion, a simple sheepfarmer's daughter, yearns for a life of adventure and glory, such as the heroes in songs and story. At age seventeen she runs away from home to join a mercenary company, and begins her epic life . . .

ELIZABETH MOON

THE DEED OF PAKSENARRION

"This is the first work of high heroic fantasy I've seen, that has taken the work of Tolkien, assimilated it totally and deeply and absolutely, and produced something altogether new and yet incontestably based on the master. . . . This is the real thing. Worldbuilding in the grand tradition, background thought out to the last detail, by someone who knows absolutely whereof she speaks. . . . Her military knowledge is impressive, her picture of life in a mercenary company most convincing."—**Judith Tarr**

About the author: Elizabeth Moon joined the U.S. Marine Corps in 1968 and completed both Officers Candidate School and Basic School, reaching the rank of 1st Lieutenant during active duty. Her background in military training and discipline imbue The Deed of Paksenarrion with a gritty realism that is all too rare in most current fantasy.

"I thoroughly enjoyed *Deed of Paksenarrion*. A most engrossing, highly readable work."
—**Anne McCaffrey**

"For once the promises are borne out. *Sheepfarmer's Daughter* is an advance in realism. . . . I can only say that I eagerly await whatever Elizabeth Moon chooses to write next."
—Taras Wolansky, *Lan's Lantern*

*   *   *   *   *

Volume One: Sheepfarmer's Daughter—Paks is trained as a mercenary, blooded, and introduced to the life of a soldier . . . and to the followers of Gird, the soldier's god.

Volume Two: Divided Allegiance—Paks leaves the Duke's company to follow the path of Gird alone—and on her lonely quests encounters the other sentient races of her world.

Volume Three: Oath of Gold—Paks the warrior must learn to live with Paks the human. She undertakes a holy quest for a lost eleven prince that brings the gods' wrath down on her and tests her very limits.

*   *   *   *   *

These books are available at your local bookstore, or you can fill out the coupon and return it to Baen Books, at the address below.

All three books of The Deed of Paksenarrion ____
SHEEPFARMER'S
  DAUGHTER   65416-0 • 506 pages • $3.95 ____
DIVIDED
  ALLEGIANCE   69786-2 • 528 pages • $3.95 ____
OATH OF GOLD 69798-6 • 528 pages • $3.95 ____

Please send the cover price to: Baen Books, Dept. B, 260 Fifth Avenue, New York, NY 10001.
Name_____
Address_____
City_____ State_____ Zip_____

THE MANY WORLDS OF
MELISSA SCOTT

*Winner of the John W. Campbell Award
for Best New Writer, 1986*

THE KINDLY ONES: "An ambitious novel of the world Orestes. This large, inhabited moon is governed by five Kinships whose society operates on a code of honor so strict that transgressors are declared legally 'dead' and are prevented from having any contact with the 'living.' . . . Scott is a writer to watch."—*Publishers Weekly*. A Main Selection of the Science Fiction Book Club.

65351-2 • 384 pp. • $2.95

The "Silence Leigh" Trilogy

FIVE-TWELFTHS OF HEAVEN (Book I): "Melissa Scott postulates a universe where technology interferes with magic. . . . The whole plot is one of space ships, space wars, and alien planets—not a unicorn or a dragon to be seen anywhere. Scott's space drive and description of space piloting alone would mark her as an expert in the melding of the [SF and fantasy] genres; this is the stuff of which 'sense of wonder' is made."—*Locus*

55952-4 • 352 pp. • $2.95

SILENCE IN SOLITUDE (Book II): "[Scott is] a voice you should seek out and read at every opportunity." —*OtherRealms*.

65699-7 • 324 pp. • $2.95

THE EMPRESS OF EARTH (Book III):

65364-4 • 352 pp. • $3.50

DAVID DRAKE
AND HIS FRIENDS

Let the bestselling author David Drake be your guide to excitement in strange new worlds of the distant future and mythic past. Meet some of the bravest, oddest, and most dangerous folk you can imagine.

Remember, with friends like these . . .

LACEY AND HIS FRIENDS

Jed Lacey is a 21st-century cop who plays by the rules. His rules. The United States of Lacey's day has imposed law and order with cameras that scan every citizen, waking or sleeping, and computers that watch the images for any hint of crime. Then it's Lacey's turn. He knows what mercy is, and pity. But he doesn't have either. Not for criminals. Not for victims. Not even for himself.

65593-0 • $3.50 _____

VETTIUS AND HIS FRIENDS

For centuries, Rome has ruled the civilized world, bringing peace and stability to a troubled age. But now, sorcerous powers gather, rousing the barbarians to battle, aiming to turn the Roman Pax into never ending chaos. Few men stand against the forces of Darkness. One is Vettius, an honorable soldier, but one as ruthless as the age demands. One other is Dama, a merchant whose favorite weapons aren't blade and shield, but wit and wealth. Two wildly dissimilar men, Vettius and Dama, bound only by their friendship, alike only in their determination that Rome— and civilization—shall not fail.

69802-8 • $3.95 _____